PENGUIN BOOKS
SUNLIGHT ON A BROKEN COLUMN

Attia Hosain was born in Lucknow in 1913. She was educated at La Martiniere and Isabella Thoburn College, Lucknow, blending an English liberal education with that of a traditional Muslim household where she was taught Persian, Urdu and Arabic. She was the first woman to graduate from amongst the feudal "Taluqdari" families into which she was born.

Influenced, in the 1930s, by the nationalist movement and the Progressive Writers' Group in India, she became a journalist, broadcaster and writer of short stories.

In 1947 she went to England with her husband and two children. Presenting her own woman's programme on the BBC Eastern service, amongst others, for many years, she also appeared on television and the West End stage. In addition she lectured on the confluence of Indian and Western culture and wrote *Phoenix Fled* (1953), a collection of short stories, and *Sunlight on a Broken Column* (1961), a novel.
She now divides her time between London and India.

PENGUIN BOOKS

SUNLIGHT ON A BROKEN COLUMN

Attia Hosain was born in Lucknow in 1913. She was educated at La Martiniere and Isabella Thoburn College, Lucknow, blending an English liberal education with that of a traditional Muslim household where she was taught Persian, Urdu and Arabic. She was the first woman to graduate from amongst the feudal 'Taluqdar' families into which she was born.

Influenced, in the 1930s, by the nationalist movement and the Progressive Writers' Group in India, she became a journalist, broadcaster and writer of short stories.

In 1947 she went to England with her husband and two children. Presenting her own woman's programme on the BBC Eastern service, amongst others, for many years, she also appeared on television and the West End stage. In addition she lectured on the confluence of Indian and Western culture and wrote *Phoenix Fled* (1953), a collection of short stories, and *Sunlight on a Broken Column* (1961), a novel.

She now divides her time between London and India.

Attia Hosain

SUNLIGHT ON A BROKEN COLUMN

WITH A NEW INTRODUCTION BY

ANITA DESAI

PENGUIN BOOKS

Penguin Books India (P) Ltd, 11 Community Centre, Panchsheel Park, New Delhi-110017, India
Penguin Books Ltd., 27 Wrights Lane, London W8 5TZ, UK
Penguin Books USA Inc., 375 Hudson Street, New York, NY 10014, USA
Penguin Books Australia Ltd., Ringwood, Victoria, Australia
Penguin Books Canada Ltd., 10 Alcorn Avenue, Suite 300, Toronto, Ontario M4V 3B2, Canada
Penguin Books (NZ) Ltd., 182-190 Wairau Road, Auckland 10, New Zealand

First published in Great Britain by Chatto & Windus 1961
Published with a new introduction by Virago Press 1988
Published in Penguin Books India (P) Ltd. 1992

1 0 9 8 7 6 5 4 3

INTRODUCTION

In India, the past never disappears. It does not even become transformed into a ghost. Concrete, physical, palpable—it is present everywhere. Ruins, monuments, litter the streets, hold up the traffic, create strange islands in the modernity of the cities. No one fears or avoids them—goats and cows graze around them, the poor string up ropes and rags and turn them into dwellings, election campaigners and cinema distributors plaster them with pamphlets—and so they remain a part of the here and now, of today.

In other ways, too, the past clings. As sticky as glue, or syrup. Traditions. Customs. "Why do you paint a tika on your baby's forehead?" "Why do you fall at your father's feet and touch your forehead to the ground?" "Why does a woman fast on this particular day?" "Why bathe in the river during an eclipse?" "Why does the bridegroom arrive on a horse, bearing a sword?" It is the custom, the tradition. No further explanation is required than this—it has always been so, it must continue to be so.

If there is a break in that tradition, then—"What will happen?" Things too terrible to be named. The downfall of the family, of society, of religion, of the motherland, India herself.

So a woman will paint a tika on her baby's forehead, a young man touch an elder's feet, a marriage need to be approved not only by parents but an astrologer as well . . . and so life is lived according to its rules, rules prescribed by time, centuries of time.

Of course time moves in other directions as well—TV and radio sets invade homes, the sari is given up for jeans, the old astrologer laughed at and the priest avoided, the past scorned. But it remains. Like the colour of one's skin, and eyes, it remains. It does not leave.

Attia Hosain's novel and collection of short stories are

monuments to that past: the history of north India, before Partition. A monument suggests a gravestone—grey, cold and immutable. Her books are not they are delicate and tender, like new grass, and they stir with life and the play of sunlight and rain. To read them is as if one had parted a curtain, or opened a door, and strayed into the past.

That is their charm and significance. To read them is like wrapping oneself up in one's mother's wedding sari, lifting the family jewels out of a faded box and admiring their glitter, inhaling the musky perfume of old silks in a camphor chest. Almost forgotten colours and scents; one wonders if one can endure them in the light of what has come to pass. But guiltily, with a laugh, the reader can't but confess "Really? Is that how it was? It must have been—" Glamorous? Fascinating? Outrageous? Impossible?

What are the precise ingredients of that now difficult to visualise past? For Attia Hosain it was an undivided India in which Muslims and Hindus celebrated the same festivals and often worshipped at the same shrines.

> Not only did he observe the rituals of his own religion, but in the month of Moharrum, he kept a "tazia" in a specially prepared shed. On the tenth day of the month, the elaborate man-high tomb made of bright-coloured paper and tinsel was carried to its burial in a procession. The Muslim servants recited dirges in memory of the martyred family of the Prophet, while he and his sons followed in barefooted, bareheaded respect. (Shiv Prasad, "White Leopard", *Phoenix Fled*)

Society was not then in flux, it was static, and it was a feudal society. To know what feudalism meant, one has to read *Sunlight on a Broken Column* or *Phoenix Fled* and learn how it was made—how the land belonged to the wealthy *taluqdars*, how the peasants worked upon it, what was exacted from them and what was, in return, done to or for them. How women lived in a secluded part of the house, jealously protected by their menfolk, and what powers were theirs, or not. How deference had always to be shown to the ancestors, to the aristocracy, to the priests, who could choose either to exploit or harrass their dependents or, if they had any nobility of spirit, protect and nurture them. How the one unforgiveable sin was to rock this hierarchy, its stability. How no one could offend religion or the family or society by going against it and only those who lived according to its rules could survive.

Born in 1913, Attia Hosain came from a background and a family that equipped her with all the knowledge she needed to write these books. Her father was a *taluqdar* of Oudh, a state in north India that the British knew as the United Provinces, the home of nawabs who dazzled even the wealthy colonists by the splendour of their courts. She belongs to the clan of Kidwais that has produced many distinguished and prominent men of this century. Her father studied at Christ College, Cambridge, and the Middle Temple, and like other young men in his circle of contemporaries, became well known in the political and national movements of his time. A great friend of his was Motilal Nehru, the father of Jawaharlal Nehru. Attia Hosain's mother came from the family that had distinguished itself in another world—the intellectual one—and had been educated in the old Persian and Urdu tradition. When her father died, Attia Hosain was only eleven years old. They were a family of five children, the youngest born two months after the father's death, yet the mother took over all responsibility for them, and for the estate—an unusual step for a woman at that time—and brought up her children very strictly, according to tradition. Attia Hosain says "I learnt from her how strong women can be when faced with tragedy and pressure." Although she had English governesses and studied at the La Martiniere School for Girls, she had lessons in Urdu and Arabic when she returned home, and read the Quran, kept close to the roots of her own culture by her mother and, before her, by her father who made sure they never lost touch with their ancestral village. During his lifetime their house had been filled with the political leaders and great figures of the society of the time and "We seemed to live with the cultures of the East and the West in a way that was not dissimilar from that of many Indian families," but the daughters of the house had a traditional upbringing nevertheless, and lived sheltered, rather secluded lives. Their religious education was liberal and they did not wear *burqas* but the car had silk curtains at the windows!

Attia Hosain read "any books I could lay my hands on" and as her father owned an extensive library, she grew up—"unsupervised"—on the English classics. She went to the Isabella Thoburn College in Lucknow, then the foremost college for women in India, and won scholarships. She persuaded her mother she should not be kept at home with her sisters and was the first woman from a *taluqdar*'s family to graduate—in 1933—from the University of Lucknow. In spite of this not inconsiderable triumph, she resented the distinction made between sons and daughters in the family and the fact that she was not sent to Cambridge as her brother had been. Her rebellion took the form of a marriage to her cousin, against her mother's wishes. He had been educated at Clifton and at Cambridge. Her father-in-law was also a *taluqdar* and, like her father, played a prominent role in the political, civic and social life of the UP; he was Vice-Chancellor of the University of Lucknow.

The family tradition of weaving together the political and the intellectual strands influenced Attia Hosain's life and thought. She claims

> I was greatly influenced in the 30s by the young friends and relations who came back from English schools and universities as left wing activists, Communists and Congress socialists. I was at the first Progressive Writers' Conference and could be called a "fellow traveller" at the time. I did not actively enter politics as I was (and may always have been?) tied and restricted in many ways by traditional bonds of duty to the family.

Her mother-in-law was right wing and represented the Muslim League in the UP Assembly but maintained her independent view that Muslim leaders should remain in India, not go to Pakistan, and look after the interests of Muslims in India. Attia Hosain confesses that her own ideal of womanhood was embodied in Sarojini Naidu, the poet/politician who made her "overcome my shyness and go the All India Womens' Conference in Calcutta in 1933".

As a well-educated, thoughtful young woman at the heart of the storm in an India on the brink of Independence and Partition, she wrote for *The Pioneer,* then edited by Desmond Young, and for *The Statesman,* the leading English language newspaper in Calcutta. She also wrote short stories—"some published, some unpublished"—but "never believed in myself as a writer!" In spite of her ideals and those of many other Muslims in India, Partition proved inevitable at Independence and, rather than go to Pakistan, the Muslim ideal in which she did not believe, she chose to take her children to England, a country she had come to know when her husband was posted to the Indian High Commission, and earned her living by broadcasting and presenting her own women's programme on the Eastern Service of the BBC.

> Events during and after Partition are to this day very painful to me. And now, in my old age, the strength of my roots is strong; it also causes pain, because it makes one a "stranger" everywhere in the deeper area of one's mind and spirit *except where one was born and brought up*.

To read her novel and short stories is to become aware of the many and varied threads that go to make up a rich and interesting life as well as the many doubts and struggles and contradictions it contained. They reflect her pride in ancestry and heredity as well as sorrow at the frequency with which they are tarnished by some heedless, unjust or selfish action. They present her ardent love for all that was gracious and splendid in the aristocracy she knew as well as her awareness of the dark obverse side experienced by hapless dependents. They show her keen sense of the two ruling concepts of Indian behaviour—*Izzat*/honour, and *Sharam*/dishonour—passionately adhering to the former and reworking in her mind the many forms taken by the latter, not always the traditional ones. They show her appreciation of the warmth, supportiveness, laughter and emotional richness to be found in the joint family as well as an acknowledgement of how often the joint family could become a prison and a punishment. She displays an enormous pride and belief in womanhood but creates many, widely differing representatives of it, some worthy of respect, others of pity, still others of shame. The pleasures she takes in privilege and all its accoutrement are never divorced from a sense of the responsibility of possessing them, an almost queenly sense of *noblesse oblige*.

The many-coloured threads that go to weave the matter of the two books on which Attia Hosain's reputation is based also give a distinctive quality to her prose. It is as rich and ornate as a piece of brocade, or embroidery, resembling the sari she describes in the short story "Time Is Unredeemable". "deep-red Benares net with large gold flowers scattered all over it and formalised in two rows along the edge as a border". Not for her the stripped and bare simplicity of modern prose—that would not be in keeping with the period—which might make it difficult for the modern reader not as at home as she with the older literary style, but it is in harmony with the material. It is also important to remember that Attia Hosain is actually reproducing, whether consciously or not, the Persian literary style and mannerisms she was taught when young, and reading her prose brings one as close as it is possible, in the English language, to the Urdu origins and the Persian inspiration. Urdu is a language that lends itself to the flamboyant and the poetic and so it is a suitable medium through which to describe the Muslim society of Lucknow and the Persian influence in north India, although married to the local Hindi of the Hindu population and modified by a Western education in the English language.

And the literary and the stylised are balanced by a certain delicacy and freshness as well as lightened by flashes of wit and humour. Her greatest strength lies in her ability to draw a rich, full portrait of her society—ignoring none of its many faults and cruelties, and capable of including not only men and women of immense power and privilege but, to an *equal* extent, the poor who laboured as their servants. Perhaps the most attractive aspect of her writing is the tenderness she shows for those who served her family, an empathy for a class not her own.

Attia Hosain's only novel, *Sunlight on a Broken Column*, first published in 1961, presents these themes within the framework of a family living in old Lucknow, a city loved by the nawabs and celebrated by the poets of its heydey, now long past. Faced by a daunting list of characters that prefaces it, and an even more bewildering one of the various forms of address used in speech, readers may doubt their ability to master the intricacies of such a world, certainly not today's. One has to remember that in India the nuclear family is considered unnatural and freakish, the joint family the only proper one for man, woman and child. Also that Attia Hosain has attempted not merely a portrait of a character or a family but of the feudal society as it existed then, ruled by traditional concepts, sometimes struggling to break or to change them and so presenting us with many aspects of this particular kaleidoscope.

One realises that she could have found no better way to describe feudalism than to bring to life its many representatives. The older ones are entirely ruled by the concepts of *Izzat*/honour and *Sharam*/dishonour. "You must never forget the traditions of your family . . . never forget the family into which you were born" is the echo that sounds throughout the book, coming from all directions, both high and low. The highest-born are Baba Jan, old and ill when the novel opens but still a commanding and formidable figure whose every cough brings the whole household to attention, and his circle of friends that includes Thakur Balbir Singh, "a fierce and generous Rajput," and Raja Hasan Ahmed of Amirpur, "a poet and builder of palaces". Of them it is said "They loved the city to which they belonged, and they lived and behaved as if the city belonged to them," and that they "in varying degrees had been helped by birth, privilege and wealth to assume such a position, but without some intrinsic quality they could not have maintained it".

What is the intrinsic quality? The abounding love of the land they own and dominate, yes, and ideally the sense of duty and responsibility that could justify such a power, but the younger men in the family, and some of the young women, begin to question it, stirred as they are by their liberal Western education as well as the ideas of freedom and independence that they have imbibed through their reading and heated discussions at school and college. The confrontation between generations is at its height during the election when sides have to be taken. Uncle Hamid, not in himself an impressive or forceful figure, feels confident enough to say

> "I am a part of feudalism and proud to be. I shall fight for it. It is my heritage and yours. Let me remind you of that. And that you enjoy its reactionary advantages. You talk very glibly of its destruction but you live by its existence . . . not according to your beliefs. Be prepared for sacrifices. Have the courage of your convictions and stop living on reaction."

The younger men are quick to notice a significant slip of the tongue made in an address of welcome to the visiting Viceroy by one of the representatives of the aristocracy they have come to question: "'We, the *taluqdars* of Oudh, are a special class with special privileges . . . we are aware that the property—er, prosperity of our tenants is our proper—prosperity.'" They laugh when, on hearing her son proclaim "'I am no Lenin and can establish no Soviets,'" the mother queries "'Linen serviettes? I do not know what you are talking about.'"

In spite of occasional laughter, the struggle is serious, and it is not only the wealthy and titled who live for *Izzat* and die for *Sharam*. The same primal passions possess those who live in the lowly servants' quarters of the compound. The washerman Jumman speaks in those terms of his daughter Nandi who he feels has disgraced his name when she is found in the garage with the cleaner. "'My honour was besmirched, and I felt possessed by a thousand devils,'" he says after beating her severely. But Nandi belongs to the younger generation and when the debauchee, Uncle Mohsin, comes along to prod her "with his silver-topped cane" contemptuously, saying "'This slut of a girl is a liar and a wanton'" she looks up at "that cruelly silent, staring ring of trappers" and cries out "'A slut? A wanton? And who are you to say it who would have made me one had I let you?'" Of course she is thrashed again for her impertinence, even though the young Laila flies to her rescue only to be told "'How could you have interfered? Aren't you ashamed?'" "'Yes, I am, I'm ashamed to call him uncle.'"

It is Laila, a troubled, thoughtful child, who questions her family's rules and society's customs and is often chastised for reading too much (education is seen as synonymous with "Westernisation" in its destructive effects).

"Child, put away that book. Those insect letters will eat away your eyes."

"But, Bua," I said, hugging her, "these books will be garlands of gold round my neck."

Others do not share her faith in education, or science. When the washerman Jumman's wife falls ill after a still birth—of gangrene, not possession by the devils as others imagine—she is infuriated to hear the women say "Go to hospital and have a baby with men standing looking on? Be shameless and be seen by all those doctors and half-doctors? Better to die at home." Laila tries to save her life by sending her to the hospital, but fails.

Her questing mind gives her loving aunt Abida much pain. "'Do not disappoint me,'" she begs the girl. "'I would have you strong and dutiful.'" Laila replies "'Dutiful to whom? To what? To what I believe is true? Or those I am asked to obey?'" She is told "'Your elders are your well-wishers and guides. You must honour and obey them.'"

Aunt Abida is the embodiment of duty and in fact sacrifices

her entire life by spending the first half in blind devotion to her father and the second to her husband. She tries to inculcate in Laila a love for Persian and Arabic as great as her pleasure in the English classics. "I thought you would learn one cannot live fully out of what is borrowed. You must not lose your own heritage and culture." Laila feels a deep love and regard for her self-sacrificing aunt but is hurt when her own choice of a husband drives a wedge between them and feels horrified by the family into which her aunt obediently marries.

The jealousies and frustrations in that household of women were intangible like invisible webs spun by monstrous, unseen spiders. And yet without each other they had no existence. Physically and mentally their lives crushed each other.

There are other women in the novel—the pleasure-loving Aunt Saira, the frivolous Zahra, the aged courtesan Mushtari-bai who is so respected and loved that she is even allowed to visit the zenana . . . Attia Hosain has painted a gallery full of portraits, varied and rich and interesting, lit by occasional flashes of humour like flakes of mica or mirror-work.

"Summer will soon be here. I hate the thought but at least it will prepare me for hell when we die."
"You will not find me there, but I'll think of you in heaven."
"When you are amusing the old, bearded *moulvis* (priests)."

There is besides the colour of the Lucknow streets and bazaars, the festivals—Hindu and Muslim—celebrated with such abandon, the lawns and gardens and fountains of the city, the muslin *dopattas* dyed in rainbow colours and spread on the earth to dry, the loved, lined, greying faces in the family.

Walking amongst the family graves, Laila muses

I wondered about the dead whose graves we had come to visit, whose stream of life flowed in us and through us. They had been kept alive by generations that respected their tradition. Did our alien thoughts and alien way of living push them into oblivion? Or was it final release for them and freedom for the living? Everything in those days of my years ended with a question mark.

It is because of her love, tempered by her doubts and questions, that Attia Hosain has earned the right to say, through the young Saleem: "O brave old world!"

Anita Desai, Massachusetts, 1988

Eyes I dare not meet in dreams
In death's dream kingdom
These do not appear:
There, the eyes are
Sunlight on a broken column
There, is a tree swinging
And voices are
In the wind's singing
More distant and more solemn
Than a fading star.

T. S. ELIOT, *The Hollow Men*

Principal Characters in the Novel

Laila	
Baba Jan (Syed Mohammed Hasan)	Laila's grandfather
Majida	his elder daughter
Abida	his younger daughter
Hamid	his eldest son
Ahmed	his younger son (deceased) Laila's father
Mohsin	his kinsman
Saira	Hamid's wife
Zahra	daughter of Majida
Kemal	Hamid's elder son
Saleem	Hamid's younger son
Asad	A distant cousin to Laila
Zahid	his younger brother
Raja of Amirpur	a friend of the family
Raza Ali	his son
Ameer Husain	his kinsman—married Laila
Ranjit Singh	Laila's friend
Nadira Wa heed	Laila's friend, married Saleem
Harish Prasad Agarwal	businessman, friend of Hamid
Sita	his daughter
Nita Chatterjee	Laila's friend
Hakiman Bua	Laila's nurse
Nandi Saliman	Maidservants

PRINCIPAL CHARACTERS IN THE NOVEL

Mrs. Martin	Laila's ex-governess
Waliuddin	Hamid's friend
Ejaz Ali	Abida's husband

It is disrespectful to address elders by name, hence various forms of address are used, such as:

Baba Jan, Mian, Bua, Bibi, etc.

Dadi	Grandmother
Mamoon	Mother's brother or cousin (female—Mumani)
Chacha	Father's brother or cousin (female—Chachi)
Bhai	Brother or cousin
Bahen	Sister or cousin
Ammi	Mother
Abba	Father
Apa	Sister
Betay or Beta	Son
Bitia or Beti	Daughter
Dadi	Paternal grandmother

Dopatta	Head-covering
Takht	Wooden divan
Angréz	Englishman
Piaray	Darling
Achkan	Long coat
Angarkha	Old-fashioned long coat fastened with loops
Lota	Vessel for water
Tazias	Replicas of the tombs of the Prophet's grandsons

PRINCIPAL CHARACTERS IN THE NOVEL

Burqa	Robe and veil for purdah
Khaddar	Hand-spun cloth
Dholak	Long two-sided drum
Charpoy	String bed
Ghazals	Love poems
Ji	Yes
Nikah	Wedding ceremony
Lathi	Long staff for protection
Khuda Hafiz	A term of farewell (God protect you)
Gharara	Wide pyjamas

Part One

Chapter One

THE day my aunt Abida moved from the zenana into the guest-room off the corridor that led to the men's wing of the house, within call of her father's room, we knew Baba Jan had not much longer to live.

Baba Jan, my grandfather, had been ill for three months and the sick air, seeping and spreading through the straggling house, weighed each day more oppressively on those who lived in it.

Aunt Abida withdrew into a tight cocoon of anxious silence, while Aunt Majida dissolved into tearful prayers. The quarrels of the maid-servants were desultory and less shrill; the men-servants' voices did not now carry over the high wall; the sweeper, the gardeners and the washerman drank less and sang no more to the rhythm of the drum. Visitors spoke as if someone was asleep next door, and Zahra and I felt our girlhood a heavy burden. Our minds had no defences against anxiety; we were uncertain and afraid.

I began reading even more than I normally did, with no censor to guard Baba Jan's library now, until Hakiman Bua, who had fed and nursed me, changed from her admiring, "My little bookworm finds no time for mischief" to remonstrating, "Your books will eat you. They will dim the light of your lovely eyes, my moon princess, and then who will marry you, owl-eyed, peering through glasses? Why are you not like Zahra, your father's—God rest his soul—own sister's child, yet so different from you? Pull your head out of your books and look at the world, my child. Read the Holy Book, remember Allah and his Prophet, then women will fight to choose you for their sons."

Zahra said her prayers five times a day, read the Quran for an hour every morning, sewed and knitted and wrote the accounts; but now all these things which she had always done merely interrupted her aimless wandering through the corridors and courtyards, returning always to sit by me though we had nothing in common but our kinship and our fears.

Her attempts at conversation wheeled round a constant pivot.

"What do you think will happen after he dies?"

"I don't know."

And then variations on a theme.

"Do you think Hamid Mamoon will retire and come to live here?"

"How should I know?"

"Do you think he will let us live here?"

"Why not?"

"He has such English ideas."

"Don't be silly."

"Do you think you'll go to College?"

"Why not?"

"How do you know what will happen after Baba Jan dies?"

"Do you? Does anyone?"

Chapter Two

IT was my fifteenth birthday. Not that it mattered to anyone else. My birthday was remembered only by me, and while at school, by the teachers when forms had to be filled up. Or by Sita, the only companion of my choice, whom I missed today because she had gone away on a holiday, and whom I envied always because she had a father, a mother, a brother . . .

At home if I mentioned it, my aunt Abida, who had brought me up, would say, "Your birthday? How old are you? Really? How quickly the years pass! Why, you are no longer a child." And Hakiman Bua would say, "Now let me see, light of my eyes, when were you born? The year you fell, Abida Bitia, and broke your arm; the year of the floods when the rivers came up to the fields across the road, and Ahmed Mian, her father, God rest his soul, went to the courts by boat, and was happy not knowing the future. Yes it was the year of the floods."

Fifteen; and the years were endless corridors stretching before and after. Fifteen; and how thin and shapeless, and not yet taller than last year's mark on the tall mirror's frame . . .

Inside the glass the light shivered, and the door opened. I turned quickly in embarrassment towards Zahra, but she had not noticed me looking at myself. She was too full of some personal excitement which shone in her eyes and quickened her movements. Her eyes were large, slanting and protruded slightly, and she emphasised them with the line of *kajal* drawn outwards, dark and long at the corners. She used them to ask favours and to attract sympathy. They drew attention away from her commonplace nose, her greedy mouth. I thought they squinted inwards slightly, and no wonder because she saw everything through herself.

"Ammi sent for Baba Mian this morning, and he is with

them now, and Mohsin Mamoon too," she said
tones of excitement in her voice.

"What is peculiar about that? Mohsin Chacha
wandering in and out; and if Baba Mian was sent for, is that strange considering he is so busy saving his soul he forgets his brother is dying?"

"God forbid!" said Zahra automatically, then added in her earlier tone, "It is about me they want to talk. And they will be sending for us soon."

"How do you know?"

"I was just going in to ask Ammi something," she said slyly, sharing a pleasant secret, "when I heard what they were saying. Then I heard Ammi ask Hakiman Bua to call us and I ran away. Hakiman Bua is so slow." She giggled.

Zahra found amusing ugliness in that dark bulk which to me embodied the abundance of comforting love.

"Laila Bitia! Zahra Bitia!" Hakiman Bua's voice came high and urgent from the corridor.

"There, you see," whispered Zahra as she sat down on her bed. "Now, remember, I have been with you a long time." Then she called out, "What is it, Hakiman Bua? We're here."

Hakiman Bua came in slowly, heavily, grumbling, "The miles one has to walk in this house! My legs are weighted with lead, and every joint has needles stuck into it." And without pausing she changed to her tender scolding, "Child, put away that book. Those insect letters will eat away your eyes. Now then, hurry! Abida Bitia is calling both of you."

"Bua, Bua," I said, hugging her. "These books will be garlands of gold round my neck."

I followed Zahra out of the room but walked slowly, not wishing to leave Hakiman Bua too far behind. She shuffled along, holding up her wide, trailing pyjamas. Her heavy, silver anklets looked incongruous worn over my discarded black school stockings.

When we came to the drawing-room that united the two

wings of the house, I drew nearer to Zahra. Into this vast room the coloured panes of the arched doors let in not light but shadows that moved in the mirrors on the walls and mantelpiece, that slithered under chairs, tables and divans, hid behind marble statues, lurked in giant porcelain vases, and nestled in the carpets. Footsteps sounded sharp on the marble floor and chased whispered echoes from the high, gilded roof. In this, the oldest portion of the house, I heard notes of strange music not distinctly separate but diffused in the silence of some quiet night as perfume in the air. I heard too the jingling of anklet bells.

But no one knew any of this.

In the corridor beyond there was light. It broke into the patterns of the fretted stone that screened this last link between the walled zenana, self-contained with its lawns, courtyards and veranda'd rooms, and the outer portion of the house.

Through the curtained door of the guest-room came the sound of voices in argument; the old, tremulous voice of Baba Mian, my great uncle Musa, crushed by the swaggering voice of Uncle Mohsin, whose degree of relationship, much to his annoyance, I found it hard to remember. He was the son of my grandfather's father's sister's daughter. He used to taunt me that if I could not remember such close relationships I would surely achieve my nirvana and become so English that my aunts and cousins would be strangers to me.

Silence fell as we came in, and as I lifted my hand to say "*Adab*" in salutation I moved out of reach of Uncle Mohsin's outstretched arm, and went over to Baba Mian, who kissed me lightly on the brow, saying, "Live long in the protection of Allah, my child."

Then he leaned back against the huge, white bolster, his restless fingers counting the amber beads of his *tasbih*, his eyes closed. Even when he spoke he kept them closed for the most part, and he swayed gently as he talked, his brow perplexed. Sometimes, even when no sound came, his lips moved in the crumpled face, framed by the white hair cropped round his ears, and by the gently straggling beard that flowed in thin wisps towards his chest. He wore a thick, quilted, black cotton waistcoat over his warm grey shirt, and his tight flannel pyjamas were crumpled at the knees, through sitting with bent knees in long hours of prayer.

I went and sat near Aunt Abida on her bed. She sat with one knee drawn up to her chin, her hands crossed over it so that the knuckles were white. The shadows of her pale yellow *dopatta* accentuated the pallor of her drawn face. Her eyes were wide and restless.

Zahra responded to Uncle Mohsin's invitation. He drew her near, rubbed his chin on her cheek and she squealed, "You haven't shaved properly."

He had a laugh that coiled out of fat-globuled honeyed depths, and bold eyes, red flecked. He sat on a chair facing the others, his legs stretched out and crossed, their strong muscles moulded by the fine white cotton pyjamas, tightly drawn over the calves, loosely gathered at the ankles, finely hand-stitched at the seams. He had a habit of rapidly shaking one foot as he spoke, almost slipping off the black velvet, gold-stitched shoe.

Aunt Majida, a large, loose bundle wrapped in a grey shawl, was cutting betel nuts nervously, her nose a little red, her eyes washed with recent tears. She had a calm, broad forehead, but her mouth was frightened and tremulous, and her cheeks sagged with depressing, downward lines.

Zahra sat by her mother and played with one of the carved, wooden cones placed at each corner of the *takht* to weight the white sheet stretched across it.

"And now that your absurd wish is granted, Abida," said Uncle Moshin, "now that the girls are here, have we your permission to continue our conversation?" His voice had echoes like the reflection of a complacent man smiling at himself in a mirror.

"In the presence of my elders," Aunt Abida replied

coldly, "I am not the one to be asked for permission; but your definition of absurdity, and mine, might permit of a great degree of difference, Mohsin Bhai."

"No doubt, no doubt. How can I understand the workings of the mind of a scholar of Persian poetry and Arabic theology infected with modern ideas?" said Uncle Mohsin with heavy sarcasm; and I heard Aunt Abida draw in a sharp breath.

Though Uncle Mohsin was the most frequent visitor amongst the male relatives allowed into the zenana, I noticed with acid pleasure how casually Aunt Abida treated him when she was not actually inimical. Zahra, characteristically, had discovered that he had wanted to marry Aunt Abida when young.

"Mohsin Bhai," pleaded Aunt Majida, "nothing will be gained by losing your temper. My poor head aches, so that to think is an added pain."

Aunt Majida's head ached perpetually and thinking was never without pain.

"Ya Allah! Ya Rahman! Ya Rahim!" breathed Baba Mian, and with eyes still closed said gently, "I have seen many things in my long life, and who knows the definition of anything but the Almighty? He draws us into error to prostrate our pride, and from error to savour His salvation. Only Death is a certainty."

There was a moment of cold silence in the room. Baba Mian was so old; death must have tired of his companionship and moved over to Baba Jan whose forceful old age was a challenge.

I looked at Zahra to share my bewilderment but she was looking demurely down, calm with secret knowledge.

Uncle Mohsin twirled the fine points of his moustaches, and prodded the carpet with his silver-topped stick.

"I consider all those things absurd that are purposeless," he said, just as if Baba Mian had not spoken. "Is the girl to pass judgement on her elders? Doubt their capability to choose? Question their decision? Choose her own husband?"

Aunt Abida's pale lips trembled as she spoke. "No, Mohsin Bhai, none of these things, I have neither the power, nor the wish, because I am not of these times. But I am living in them. The walls of this house are high enough, but they do not enclose a cemetery. The girl cannot choose her own husband, she has neither the upbringing nor the opportunity——"

"Would you have it otherwise?" he interrupted.

"But," she ignored him, "she can be present while we make the choice, hear our arguments, know our reasons, so that later on she will not doubt our capabilities and question our decisions. That is the least I can do," she added bitterly.

"We would not be scheming behind her back if she were not here. Our elders did not think our presence necessary, and we believed in their wisdom. It was a good enough system for them and for us," he said angrily.

"Was it?" Aunt Abida's anger matched his own.

Uncle Mohsin's eyes flamed and flickered.

In that moment of hesitation was concentrated the smudged failure of his life. Even we, the young ones, knew stories about him and the dancing girls of the city. The eldest of his four children was our age, sullenly obedient to a father she seldom saw and hated for her mother's sake. The mother, a negative, ailing woman, her tattered beauty a mendicant for love, knew her husband only to conceive a child after each infrequent visit home. He lived in the city with friends or relations, had a wide and influential circle of friends, dressed well, composed poetry, was an authority on classical music and dancing, and never did any work.

I disliked him.

His eyes searched for reactions, but Baba Mian was telling his beads and Aunt Majida was cutting betel nut and sniffing.

"Look, Abida," he said aggressively, but with less self-assertion, "I have not come here to argue with you. I came here with a proposal which you can refuse or accept; but I want an answer either way, and soon. Baba Jan's condition is well known to all of you. We have to make plans for the future of these girls, keeping in mind what is to happen to them, God forbid, after his death."

"What will happen to them? What will happen to us?" wailed Aunt Majida. "Look at me, a widow, and this child of mine, a girl without a father. Where will we go? And Abida, look at her, still unmarried! Abba found no one good enough for her; and refused one good proposal after another. And now what is to become of her when he leaves her so cruelly alone? What is to become of us:" she sobbed, and Zahra clung to her, also crying.

Aunt Abida's hands were trembling as she drew her *dopatta* over her head and turned towards her sister. "Do not raise your voice," she said wearily, "Abba is asleep."

I felt cold deep down inside me.

Aunt Majida wiped her eyes and nose with a corner of her shawl and moaned, "Oh what a miserable, ill-fated woman am I!"

"Ya, Rahman, Ya, Rahim!," said Baba Mian softly.

Uncle Mohsin cleared his throat impatiently, twisted his silver-knobbed stick, and said, "You must think now of the future. Zahra is seventeen and ready for marriage. I have brought you a proposal and you must come to some kind of decision. Whom else would you like to consult? Your father is ill. Your brother is not here, Baba Mian and I——"

"Hamid Mian will be coming home very soon," Aunt Majida interrupted.

"Will that make any difference? He is more a Sahib than the English. He will not take the responsibility."

"But he must be consulted; it is not right that he should not be," she said obstinately.

"Of course he will be, so as not to hurt his precious pride. But the decision can be made first. It is not easy to find suitable young men, and if you let this chance slip, how long will you have Zahra on your hands with your own future uncertain?"

Her sister's moans were cut short by Aunt Abida's sharp retort:

"You talk as if we were choosing a new horse for the carriage."

"Horses, my dear Abida, are chosen with more care than husbands these days. It is fashionable to decry the pedigree of men and to pay fortunes for the pedigrees of horses and dogs. Soon you will have to apologise for your birth and breeding, and not be proud of them. And now let me have an answer one way or another. Though you have insisted on staging this discussion as a ridiculous scene, with the girls as an audience, I am sure Zahra will do as her elders decide. She has not had the benefit of a mem-sahib's education; though I am glad to see certain abhorrent signs of it have been removed, and your young mem-sahib has given up walking around dressed like a native Christian."

The cold stone inside me was now burning lead. Aunt Abida put her hand on mine, and her voice was sharp like slivers of ice.

"What Laila wears or does is not under discussion."

Aunt Majida said reproachfully, "Mohsin Bhai, Laila was educated as her father would have wished. Abida carried out a beloved brother's wishes as not even the child's own mother could have done had she been spared to see her grow up. Even Abba respected his son's beliefs and set aside his own, so, God knows, you have no right to criticise."

Uncle Mohsin blustered, "I have every right to say what I believe is correct. I do not talk behind people's backs. That is my trouble, I am too honest. I say what I do because of my love and concern for the family. I do not want my nieces put in the way of temptation. After all, Zahra was brought up differently, correctly, sensibly."

Aunt Abida's voice cracked with anger, "I have told you I am not prepared to discuss this matter with you, Mohsin Bhai."

And Aunt Majida added, with a look of pride cast towards

the modest Zahra, "This is no time for quarrelling, Mohsin Bhai. True I have done the best I could for Zahra, in the light of my own little knowledge. She has read the Quran, she knows her religious duties; she can sew and cook, and at the Muslim School she learned a little English, which is what young men want now. I did what I could, and you know in my unhappy circumstances I could do no more, even had I wished otherwise."

At this point tears welled up in her eyes again. They flowed so easily that they had lost their significance, and were distantly related to a tale of sorrow which had lost its content through constant repetition.

It was fifteen years since Aunt Majida's husband had left her to serve the saints to whose tombs and charities he had sacrificed the fortune which had added to his virtues when Baba Jan had chosen him as a son-in-law. It was six years since he had died, a gentle madman, possessed with his love of God. In those six years Zahra had transformed him into a saint himself; it made the chill, deserted years of her mother's life a sacrificial offering to God.

"Curse the Devil!" shouted Uncle Mohsin and spat thick, red betel juice spitefully into the tall, brass spittoon standing by his chair. "Will you get back to the point and stop dragging me into arguments?"

"How old did you say the boy was?" Aunt Abida asked coldly, as if detaching herself from her anger.

"Thirty, but he looks younger. He is handsome—well, as handsome as a man should be. Light complexioned, quite fair, in fact."

"Was he married into some family of your aquaintance?"

"Yes, before he went to England for his training. He was a good husband. His wife died four years ago in childbirth. Fortunately the child died too, so our little Zahra will not be a step-mother; she will start her own family." He chuckled.

"God will she flower and bear fruit!" chanted her mother.

"And his parents?" continued Aunt Abida, her voice unchanged.

"They live in the family village. Mind you, they haven't much land, but does that matter when he is in Government service and his future is assured?"

"Yes, his future is assured; therefore, his past need not concern us, nor the fact that his breeding is not equal to ours. What does it matter? After all he is an official——"

Uncle Mohsin rapped his stick on the edge of the *takht* as he raised his voice to interrupt Aunt Abida. "I have seen rajas and maharajas, respected friends of your father's, laying their caps at the feet of officials. Only because they were white sahibs! The only man before whom Baba Jan bowed his head was the 'Lat Sahib', the Governor. And his daughter sits unmarried because no husband could be found equal in breeding."

"Mohsin Bhai," wailed Aunt Majida, "why must you talk in this manner? Why cast shadows of bitterness and anger over the future of my child? Let us wait until our brother comes, and decide with cool hearts and clear minds."

Before she could be answered, while Baba Mian breathed the names of Allah with greater fervour, Zahra sat in demure stillness, and I achingly watched the tight white face of Aunt Abida, angry voices sounded in the corridor, and Hakiman Bua shuffled to the door, calling urgently:

"Abida Bitia, come quickly."

Aunt Abida started, instinctively looking towards the door leading to her father's room. Then she turned angrily and said, "Stop that noise out there! Abba is sleeping."

Baba Jan was asleep in his room, but he was everywhere as always; and the long threat of dying added to his power.

I followed Aunt Abida out of the room because it was crowded with the presence and thoughts of Uncle Mohsin. Zahra was already in the corridor; her curiosity gave her mobility. It had the same quality that had crowded into the corridor several maid-servants, the orphan boy who helped the cook and the wives of the gardeners and watchmen.

They were all staring at a smaller group in the foreground. Jumman, the washerman, stood murderously over his daughter Nandi who cowered at his feet, shielding her head from the blow that lingered in his eyes, while his wife shaking with anguish leaned against the wall, her sari pulled over her head and hiding her face.

"Bitia! I appeal to you!" he called, the words forced out of his trembling lips.

"Silence," Aunt Abida said angrily. "Have you taken leave of your senses, coming here shouting and screaming?" She moved through them like a blade. "Follow me outside."

The silent procession shuffled behind her through the rooms to the courtyard. A soft breeze rustled the leaves of the palms in their giant red pots. On the steps to the lawn the parrot sunned himself in his silvered cage and chanted as he swung, "*Piaray* Mithoo. Mithoo *Betay*. Allah il-Allah." He parodied Hakiman Bua's voice.

"Jumman, whatever possessed you to burst into the house and bring down the skies outside the very doors of Abba Jan's room?"

The exaggeration of her words did not rob her voice of authority. But then all emotions seemed distended in this circumscribed household.

"Bitia," said Jumman, "I would willingly have killed her, but this woman, her mother, said I should come to you for judgement. Forgive me, *huzoor*. My honour was besmirched, and I felt possessed by a thousand devils. I leave her now to you to do with as you will." And he pushed Nandi roughly forward.

Jumman in anger seemed a stranger. His dark face, with its thick moustache in contrast to his cropped head, was made gentle by large dark eyes that held no challenge. He wore a thick silver bangle on each wide wrist, and a gold ring in one ear. His loin-cloth, white and spotless, was drawn high above his bony knees, because he stood long hours in the tank washing clothes, beating them against the tilted, corrugated board with a steady strong rhythm of breath and movement.

But now his eyes were squinting, and his voice was harsh. And he prodded Nandi with his foot as she huddled on the ground, hiding the face that Hakiman Bua used to say would be a scourge to her parents because it was not the face of a girl of the lower castes.

When I was younger Nandi was my favourite playmate, carelessly happy, fearless and free, graceful as a gazelle. When I was disrespectful Hakiman Bua said it was because I played with servant girls. I used to slip away to find Nandi in her steaming little room in the servants' quarters piled with damp clothes, hot with the coals kept ready to feed heavy, black, fire-bellied irons.

Nandi's favourite game used to be to act the bride, concealed in the thick hedge by the fountain so that no one would see this shamelessness. I used to perform the ceremony of showing the bride's face for the first time to assembled guests, removing her hands from her face with its tight-shut eyes, tilting up her chin, saying "*Masha Allah*! The bride is beautiful" and pressing imaginary gifts into her limp palms.

But now when Nandi's hands covered her face it was no game she was playing. Those were not the copied conventional tears of a bride that seeped through her fingers.

"What mischief has she been up to now?" Aunt Abida asked sharply.

Not long ago, Nandi had thrown an accurate and sharp stone at the groom of the English family next door, because he had peeped over the wall while she bathed in the enclosure where there was a tap for the women. A few days later she had bitten the postman, saying he had attempted to molest her.

"The wretch was found by the driver with the cleaner in the garage," said Jumman, hoarse with shame and anger.

"I went to give him a shirt that he had forgotten," whined Nandi.

"Be quiet, shameless hussy," thundered Jumman, "I have forbidden her to visit the men's quarters alone, Bitia. I had to suffer the indignity of seeing her dragged home by Driver Ji, and to hear his accusations. I cannot now live in the same compound as those two."

From Noor Khan, the driver who had been in the household only three years, my aunts observed purdah. Jumman and Jumman's father before him had worked with the family since boyhood, and they came from our village.

Aunt Abida turned wearily to Uncle Mohsin and said, "You had better ask Noor Khan what happened. This is a matter for a man to deal with." Uncle Mohsin prodded Nandi with his silver-topped stick contemptuously. "This slut of a girl is a liar, a wanton."

Nandi looked up with fear-crazed eyes, looked round at that cruelly silent, staring ring of trappers and cried out: "A slut? A wanton? And who are you to say it who would have made me one had I let you?"

Uncle Mohsin's face was distorted as he raised his stick and hit her across the shoulders. She fell forward, and as I ran towards her the next blow glanced across my arm and I screamed, "I hate you, I hate you", and ran blinded by tears to my room.

Chapter Three

WHEN Zahra came to tell me that Aunt Abida had sent for me and was in Baba Jan's room I hid my tears with sullenness.

I had turned away even Hakiman Bua when, anxious and pained, she had followed me asking, "My child, my treasure, are you hurt?"

"No, no, just leave me alone."

Why had Aunt Abida made no sign of recognition?

Zahra was full of information, "The cleaner is to be dismissed and Nandi will get the beating she deserves from Jumman, I am sure. Such wickedness, when she is so young! Immoral people cannot be allowed inside the house."

"That will be awkward for certain people."

Zahra ignored my remark. "The insolence of these menials that she should have dared to talk to our uncle in such a manner, and in front of everyone, of all those servants! Laila, how could you have interfered? Aren't you ashamed?"

"Yes I am. I'm ashamed to call him uncle. I'm ashamed that you have no pity because Nandi is a servant girl. Besides, I don't care what anyone thinks. I don't care."

"Do you know what is wrong with you, Laila? All those books you read. You just talk like a book now, with no sense of reality. The only cure for Nandi is to get her married quickly."

"The cure for a good girl is to get her married quickly; the cure for a bad girl is to get her married quickly. Do you think of anything but getting married quickly?"

"I suppose you think you will never get married?"

"I won't be paired off like an animal. How could you sit there listening to them talking as if you were a bit of furniture to be sold to the highest bidder? How can you bear the idea of just any man?"

"I suppose you're going to find a husband for yourself? Maybe you'll marry someone for love like Englishwomen do, who change husbands like their slippers. Your head is stuffed with funny ideas. But why do you want to fight with me? What have I done to harm you?"

Her eyes filled with ready tears of self-pity, and as always I felt a mean bully, but she had left the room dramatically before words could form in the haze of my anger.

In Baba Jan's room the light was blended with shadows weighted with silence. Aunt Abida bent over the foot of his wide bed, pressing his feet. Often she had cramps in her stomach from remaining in this position for a long time. Aunt Majida stood at the head of the bed, half-hidden by the headboard, holding up the folds of her long wide pyjamas with one hand, and a silver-handled fly-whisk in the other.

Chuttan, the young man who performed the duty of keeping a watchful eye on flies all day, always left the room when my aunts came in, but Karam Ali was allowed to stay because he was as old as Baba Jan, and had seen their babyhood. Zahra and I went to the side of the bed, bowed and said: "*Adab.*"

Baba Jan's eyelids flickered acknowledgement.

His head and back were propped against a bolster. His beard seemed whiter now and his face was darkly grey. We stood silent, with covered heads. The very silence of the room imposed immobility. So, too, did my fears.

In the corner, by the tall cupboard that spilled medicines from its shelves to the near-by table, Karam Ali squatted with his knees drawn up. His beard was thin and could barely hide the outline of his toothless mouth, which was open now as he dozed. He did not wear a uniform like the other servants, but always wore a white cap over his long hair which he combed neatly behind his ears; a striped shirt with silver buttons on a chain; a large red and black checked handkerchief over his shoulder, dark pyjamas that sagged at the knees—the mark of th who prayed five times a day—and were tight above h ankles.

He had fascinated our childhood with folk-lore and stories from the *Arabian Nights*, but now when he told them, puffing and drawing at his *hookah*, his voice would drone into sleep, his chin would sag, and his mouth open wide and hollow. That was the signal for his listeners to cough, and he would indignantly open his little eyes, draw a gurgling puff from the long *hookah* pipe and scold,

"If you fall asleep and do not say 'Hmmm-Hanh' to show me you are paying attention, I shall not waste my time and yours."

Aunt Abida sneezed. Baba Jan opened his eyes and closed them. Karam Ali started and said, "Bismillah." Then he dozed again.

I wondered if it was because she was angry that she did not look at me, but Aunt Abida's face had no angry tightness. And hope burst through my fear, telling me that she inwardly approved of what I had done.

We waited silently for a sign of dismissal; each second stretching taut to its limit and seemingly beyond.

Surely he could not die, this powerful man who lived the lives of so many people for them, reducing them to fearing automatons. But I knew he was afraid of dying, because he fought so hard to live. Those bottles of medicine, that paraphernalia of weapons against death heaped round the room, the procession of doctors, an army under the generalship of the Civil Surgeon, constantly changing its personnel and tactics—all these were not so powerful as he himself.

I wondered that I could think like this about his death. Was Zahra right when she said I was heartless and selfish? And yet I cried when reading stories and poems! What was wrong with me inside? What was 'wrong' in itself, and what was 'right'? Who was to tell me?

Baba Jan stirred and said, "What is the time, Abida?" His deep voice had been robbed of its power, but not of its authority.

"Six o'clock, Abba," said Aunt Abida softly.

"Is it not time for my medicine?"

"Yes, Abba."

"Well, give it to me then. Why must I remind you?"

"You were sleeping, Abba. I did not wish to disturb you."

"I was not sleeping. You will do more than disturb me if you neglect me."

"Forgive me, Abba."

"Where is that rascal Karam Ali?"

"I am here, Huzoor."

"Where is my medicine?"

"Here, Huzoor. It is one minute to six, Huzoor. The clock has not struck the hour."

"The devil strike you!"

"Yes, Huzoor."

On either side of the mirrored, heavy chest of drawers in the far corner, photographs in wooden frames hung on the wall. Baba Jan, his brothers and cousins, black-bearded, dressed in embroidered *achkans* and caps, with jewelled swords held in their hands, sitting stiffly in high carved chairs, with uniformed retainers holding steel-tipped spears standing behind them. Baba Jan alone, beardless, with a thick moustache curled up to piercing points, dressed in a suit, with shining pointed boots and spats. Baba Jan with a group of strained pompous Englishmen standing behind Englishwomen in long, laced, ruffled dresses with boned, laced collars that held up heavy heads of piled-up hair under wide hats.

Baba Jan had been young once, had probably smiled at those women. Could he have been tender and gay, and doubted and wondered? Was there ever a time when in his presence anyone could talk and laugh without restraint?

Karam Ali took away the silver basin and water-jug when Baba Jan had finished rinsing his mouth after drinking his medicine. Aunt Abida removed her supporting arm from under his head, smoothed his pillows, and wiped his mouth with the towel Karam Ali handed to her.

He lay quietly for a few moments. Then, with eyes still closed, he said, "You may go."

We bowed in turn in salutation, and the ritual of the audience was over.

Karam Ali began arranging the armchairs for the friends who came every evening after the doctor had made his last call. There was Thakur Balbir Singh, fierce and generous Rajput, each of whose embroidered cotton *Angarkhas* and delicate caps cost the sight of many workmen and more than the dowry of their wives and daughters, whose fighting cocks were unbeatable, whose pigeons outflew all others in the city, whose generosity and courage were a legend, who hunted bandits and tigers with equal unconcern, and whom we called *Hunstey Dada*, laughing grandfather.

And the portly Raja Hasan Ahmed of Amirpur, a poet and a builder of palaces who had his zenana guarded by negro eunuchs. When he had succeeded his parsimonious father he had lived riotously, emulating the legendary excesses of the late kings. It was said he had made naked women roll the length of the throne-room in a race for a bag of gold sovereigns; that he, copying kings, had played chess in the courtyard with nude girls and youths as pieces. But after the death of his first wife, to whom he was married at the age of twelve, he had married the present Rani, and curbed his sensual extravagances—or rather she had made him do so.

We called him *Motey Dada*, fat grandfather.

He was known now by the schools, hospitals and orphanages he had endowed, by his palaces, his elephants and his patronage of poets and musicians. Behind the scenes he was politically powerful, able to influence the elections of councillors and the decisions of ministers.

Finally there was Mr Freemantle, a skinny, square-bearded lawyer, a scholar of Sanksrit, Persian and Arabic, who wore Indian clothes when he visited the houses of dancing girls, and prim Victorian clothes at other times. He held frequent *Mushairas*, soirées where poets recited their verse in Urdu and Persian. He scorned motor cars and drove in his landau drawn by a perfectly matched pair of greys. The English community was suspicious of him but his wealth, influence and scholarliness forced recognition. He was *Gorey Dada,* white grandfather.

My aunts did not observe purdah from him, but they were careful that their voices, even the rustling of their clothes, were not heard by the others.

Baba Jan had ostensibly little in common with his three friends, considering his dour austerity. Yet they had in common a strange arrogance and a will to exercise power—always to be in a position which forced men to reach up to them; and if they ever stepped down themselves, it was an act of grace. In varying degrees they had been helped by birth, privilege and wealth to assume such a position; but without some intrinsic quality they could not have maintained it.

Thakur Sahib's sense of humour and his enjoyment of life and people made him lovable and human. Raja Sahib's pattern of thinking was on such a large scale that it saved his vices from pettiness, his virtues from priggishness, and lent him a grandeur that had become legendary. Mr Freemantle's scholarship and his brilliance as a lawyer were the measures of his worth, and not his uniqueness among his fellow-countrymen, which in itself would have reduced him to being a tiresome eccentric.

And Baba Jan's integrity gained him authority and recognition. It tempered the unchallenged tyranny which he exercised over his family—from his immediate household outwards to the family's tribal ramifications, and it earned him respect from those who came in contact with him—from the most ordinary citizen to the highest government official. His word carried more weight in the city than that of other *Taluqdars* with larger estates, and men with more money.

The four men loved the city to which they belonged, and they lived and behaved as if the city belonged to them.

Chapter Four

SINCE Aunt Abida had moved from the zenana we had had our meals in her room. Ramzano and Saliman, our personal maid-servants, carried the dishes on large wooden trays covered with gay cloths, from the main kitchen to the pantry of the English kitchen near the guest-room. There the meals were kept warm in the large 'hot case' until we were seated round the tablecloth spread on the *takht*.

All that had happened during the day weighted our minds and hearts to silence. Strange and unreal also was the fact that we ate alone—just the members of the household, and, because there were no men present, Ustaniji, who had taught my aunts Urdu, Persian and Arabic and had tried to teach us until old age made her deaf and nearly blind.

She was born in Lucknow in the very heart of the city like the many generations of her family who had served the royal family and taught in the homes of their courtiers. She spoke the sweet tongue of the true Lucknavi—delicate, flexible, rich in imagery, pointed with wit, polished with courtesy. Our rougher manner of speaking had always pained her, but she no longer had the strength to correct us.

Also present was Hajjan Bibi, whose husband had been a companion of Baba Jan's. He had spent his last impoverished years with us after losing all his money through speculation at the end of the war. Also Asad, eighteen, and Zahid, sixteen, who were orphaned sons of poor relatives. Their father, a deeply religious man, never very strong, had sacrificed his life and money in the cause of the *Khilafat* movement, fighting the British. From childhood they had been made to wear coarse hand-spun cloth and to hate all things foreign.

They were pale, sad-eyed, silent; Asad, shy, Zahid, sullen. Asad was our contact with the outside world, running errands for Zahra and me, buying those things with which we did not trust the servants. He wrote poetry, sad and questioning.

When Zahra smiled at him, Asad's pale lips twitched, and his eyes were like his poems.

Baba Mian's food was served in his room because he did not wish to interrupt his evening's meditation.

We ate in silence, and Ustaniji's heavy breathing sounded painfully loud. Sometimes it seemed that her asthma would choke her, but infirm years had not lessened her tenacious hold on life. Hajjan Bibi's head and hands shook so with age that it was hard for her bony fingers to bring the food to her toothless mouth. But she had a good appetite and liked rich food, though she groaned with indigestion and ate numerous black pills for which she had the recipe from her father, who had been one of the physicians at the court of the last king.

Even Hakiman Bua, who had supervised the cooking and serving of meals, did not complain tonight about the insolence of the cook, nor the laziness of the maid-servants, nor did she mutter her usual prayers to save us from the Evil Eye which she was sure Hajjan Bibi possessed. And she made no comment on our appetites such as, "Children, if you eat like birds you will grow up like stringy hens."

I felt the barriers between each one of us that forced me not to look at Aunt Abida. But when we had washed our hands in the large copper basin Ramzano held out to us, and rinsed our mouths with warm water poured from a chased silver *lota* by Saliman, and Hakiman Bua had gone to distribute food to the servants, and the two old women had shuffled off after commending us to the care of Allah, and Zahra had followed her mother, who said she was tired and wished to offer her prayers early—only after this heavy length of drawn-out time did Aunt Abida speak to me.

"Laila, come here."

I approached her bed. "Yes, Phuphi Jan," I said, but I could do no more than glance at her pale face on account of the anxiety of her large eyes.

"Laila, do you remember the day you did not answer when the sweeper woman said 'Salaam' to you?"

Resentful memory silenced me.

"I made you apologise to her. You were ten then. How old are you now?"

"I was fifteen today."

"Today?" She sighed, "God grant you a long life." Then her voice changed, "You have grown out of childhood. Remember, good manners are the truest sign of good breeding. Tomorrow when he comes you will apologise to your uncle."

"But what wrong have I done?" I burst out.

"To respect your elders is your duty. Surely I do not have to teach you elementary lessons of behaviour?"

"He was cruel," I cried, and the thought that there was no understanding made me sullen.

"My child, there are certain rules of conduct that must be observed in this world without question. You have a great responsibility. You must never forget the traditions of your family no matter to what outside influences you may be exposed. I have been responsible for you since the day God willed you to be without a father and mother. I do not wish anyone to point a finger at you, because it will be a sign of my failure. Never forget the family into which you were born. That is all I wanted to say to you. Now go and say your prayers."

I hated the absent Uncle Mohsin that she should be speaking to him through me. I wanted to reach out to the troubled tenderness locked within her, to the mirrored pride that kept me silent and set a frown instead of tears on my face. I wanted to say, "Why did you not bring me up like Zahra? Why did you send me among those other girls who are not torn apart?"

I did not go to my room to pray, but to Hakiman Bua in

search of the recognition I needed. The air outside was clear, and the dark lawn felt soft under my feet as I crossed it.

"Never forget the family into which you were born."

When we were small Ustaniji made us recite the names of our ancestors. Zahra remembered many more than I ever did who found it difficult to name even my great-grandfather. But since that time five hundred years ago when the first of them had fought his way across the northern mountains through the Khyber Pass to the refuge of green valleys many marches south, their ghosts had stood sentries over all action, speech and thought.

Hakiman Bua was sitting on her string bed which nearly filled the tiny room crowded with her meagre possessions. The light from the lantern on the ledge of the small barred window made shadows move and sway round the tin trunks in the corner, pots and pans on the shelf, and clothes hanging on a line stretched across a wall.

The room was cosy with love.

"What is troubling you, my daughter? Come and sit down." She moved the metal plate and bowl from which she had just finished her meal, unrolled a thin striped carpet over the bare strings of her bed, and said again, "Come and sit down."

I sat on the wooden edge with my back to the open door through which burst a hard yellow beam from the electric light on the courtyard wall. Above the splashing of water from the tap where the maid-servants used to wash and bathe and now cleaned their pots and pans, came the subdued murmur of Ramzano and Saliman's voices, chiselled by the clear cool night.

"Bua, what were they like, my mother and my father?"

I was not curious. I wanted assurance. No matter how often I went to Hakiman Bua, she gave it to me through her answers to my backward-searching questions, and through her simplicity that asked no questions itself.

"Your mother? How can I describe her? In yourself you

can see her as the moon is seen in a clear pool, like enough, but still a reflection."

"And my father?"

"A prince among men. If he had worn rags they would have seemed the robes of a king, and he had a heart that could have folded the world into it."

"And did they love me very much?"

"So much that it was perhaps the angels in their jealousy who deprived you of their love so soon."

Her sighs caught my throat.

"Bua, this house was different when they lived in it, wasn't it?"

"It was bright and light. It was a house of feasts and music and laughter and plenty."

From that little room of swaying shadows, on the light warm waves of her words I went back in search of light and love, each moment a festival.

Shubrat and a basket of magic fire, bursting in rockets of coloured stars, hissing in fiery snakes, slithering under the jumping feet of shrieking children, eyes shut to the banging of crackers, spiralling delicate starlets whirling at the end of twisted silvery wire held in eager hands.

Diwali, and the cool softness of glowing oil-dipped cotton wicks in tiny clay saucers outlining the curves of arches and the straight line of walls and roofs. Lights, lamps, more lights.

A hurrying and a scurrying in the courtyards, on the lawn, on the roof.

Eid. "Can you see it, there, by the branch of that tree, the moon of *Eid*?" "Hold me higher, Abba, higher. Oh I can see it, the moon of *Eid*, stuck on the church steeple, hiding in the branches. It is smiling."

Eid. The ceremonial bath, new clothes, silk, rustling, shining, gold-embroidered, gleaming, scented. Everyone gleaming, everyone scented, everyone laughing. Prayers, fairs, embraces, showers of money and kisses, *Eid Mubarik!* "God bless you!" Visiting friends and relations, relations and friends visiting us. Silver rupees to be clutched in eager hands until put away in safety. Bowls of *Sivain*, rich golden threads of honey sweetness decorated with silver beaten into paper light as whispers, flecking one's lips, and jugs of steaming milk, and thick many-layered cream waiting for visitors, visitors who gave gifts of money and happy embraces.

And the other *Eid*, *Bakreid*, not so shining, and filmed with blood. Sheep and lambs collected in the stables, bleating near the sacrificial pits. "Must it be killed too, the littlest one?" "Learn to be brave, little daughter, learn to give to God what is dearest to you, like Abraham who sacrificed his son. No tears for the sacrifice to God."

The butchers by the swaying, naked carcasses, digging down with their fists, tearing apart the shaggy skins from the flesh. All forgotten in the joy of new clothes and feasting. Roasted, crisped, spiced, enormous legs of mutton for days and nights and nights and days. Wondering curiosity as maid-servants filed past carrying huge round platters, meat-heaped, covered with bright cloths, while Ammi, my mother, and Bua sat on little stools in the courtyard, counting and checking the names of those who sent them. Then the counting and the sorting out of the meat, the checking of those to whom it had to be sent. Round and round the meat went to friends and relations, to mosques and orphanages, to the servants and to the poor. The little sacrificed lamb forgotten; only the excitement and the feasting remembered.

Holi. The sounds of the drums, of drunken singing in the men-servants' quarters, and on the streets. And Bua's admonitions not to go near the gates because those mud-splashed, colour-sprinkled hooligans made no distinction between believers and non-believers. In the afternoon friends came to 'battle' on the lawn until the pails of coloured water were empty, and weary hands could not pump the sprays.

"Child, child!" Bua said, turning my face to the light of

the lantern. "You are falling asleep. Come, I will take you to your room to sleep in the comfort of your bed."

"No, Bua, do not trouble yourself. You must be tired. I'll go alone." And as I put my arms around her I felt the soft breath of her sighs.

I turned to go; she reached out to me and held my face between her hands. Then, drawing them over my head, she cracked her knuckles against her temples, so taking upon herself my misfortunes as she whispered, "God protect you from all evil."

I walked as though compelled across the shadowed courtyard, through the long bare room where Ustaniji and Hajjan Bibi wheezed and grunted in their sleep, wrapped like mummies on their string beds; across the wide dark passage where the echoes of my footsteps on its stone floor slanted off undisturbed bookshelves and blind portraits, through the creaking door and into a silent, patiently waiting room.

I switched on the light and the darkness released its pressure on my throat.

The tidy, empty bed, the space-holding armchairs, the blank mirrors of the dressing-table all waited; I would find the other rooms the same if I passed through the motionless curtains into their silence. No trace now of those transient visitors who were permitted to stay a while in these rooms after the passing years had softened the shock of their sudden emptiness.

In my desperation of longing I tried to fill them again so as to make their stillness breathe. It only needed intensity of faith, concentration of desire. If the mind and spirit were emptied of all else they could receive the burning message. One night, holding me in her arms, under a starlit sky, my mother had told me of a man who had so cleared his mind of all but faith in God that God had heard his prayers and the Prophet had appeared and spoken to him in a dream.

And now if my need were pure and strong enough I could

make them return from the cruel depths of the river which had taken them from me.

But as the curtains stirred I felt the hidden fear in my heart flaming in the desire to escape through the imprisoning doors and out to the moonlit veranda, to the courtyard, to my room among those who were untouched by the transformation of dark death.

It was the greater fear of the next morning's questioning and impossible answers that made me switch off the lights before I ran away.

Chapter Five

AFTER his morning visit, when the doctor told Aunt Abida that Baba Jan's condition showed a remarkable improvement, it seemed that cramping weights had been removed from the seconds of the day and each one of us felt the lightening of a burden. Zahra and I caught ourselves once or twice in peals of laughter.

After lunch Aunt Abida said she wished to help Hakiman Bua prepare some Halva, sweets and biscuits as her stock of delicacies was running low through neglect during the past anxious days. She had a temporary brick stove built up in the maid-servants' courtyard near the store-room, and low stools were placed around it.

I liked cracking the delicate shells of eggs, throwing them in a shining heap, holding the golden yokes in my hands before sliding them in the big china bowl, and watching the whiteness of milk being poured from dark earthenware jugs.

In one corner Ramzano and the gardener's wife were grinding the wheat that had come on the previous day from the village together with the monthly store of fuel, grain and *ghee*. They sat, one leg folded under, one stretched out by the grindstone; and holding its thick upright wooden handle, they turned the top stone with a swaying, steady rhythm of their bodies' movement, while with one hand Ramzano fed the golden wheat into a hole in the stone.

Outside their room, on a small string bed that could be dragged out easily, Ustaniji and Hajjan Bibi sat wrapped in their white *dopattas*. They sunned their age-corroded cold bones, mouthed soundless prayers, turned the beads of their *tasbihs*, and stared at the movement in the courtyard from the distance of their years.

Aunt Majida said Zahra and I were more a hindrance than a help and we decided to dye our *dopattas* that had no man as consent

been lying white and unworn for many days. We carried enamelled bowls and water and packets of dyes towards the far end of the courtyard, so as not to disturb the others.

We dyed some green, the colour to be worn in the coming month of Muharram, and others orange, dyed in colour crushed from special flowers. Our favourites were in rainbow stripes, carefully dipped in seven bowls of delicate colours.

Zahra and I carried them to the lawn and spread them carefully on the grass.

"If Nandi had been here she would have helped us."

"She is safer in the village."

"Poor Nandi!"

"Nonsense, don't waste your pity on her."

We held the fine muslin outstretched in our hands and swung it gently in the sunshine, a rainbow rippling over the green grass.

At the far end the sweeper woman was sweeping dead leaves from the path. Behind her trailed two of her children, naked, thin-limbed, big-bellied, with dirty noses and large black eyes. She came nearer, bent over her broom of thin sticks.

"You blind fool," shouted Zahra, "do you want to bury us in dust? Can't you see the *dopattas* are lying there, still wet? Is this the time to be sweeping here?"

"Bitia, forgive me, but there is so much work inside the house. This is the only time I have for sweeping here."

I felt a guilty wonder at her resigned lack of resentment.

"Zahra, you need not have shouted in that offensive manner."

Zahra shrugged. "Offensive manner? She's used to it."

If I gave her a chance now, Zahra would mockingly reduce to mere printed hieroglyphics those books which had taught me to think of human dignity.

"You just raise them an inch off the ground and they'll be making a footstool of your head," warned Zahra.

"Who said that? Your precious uncle Mohsin?"

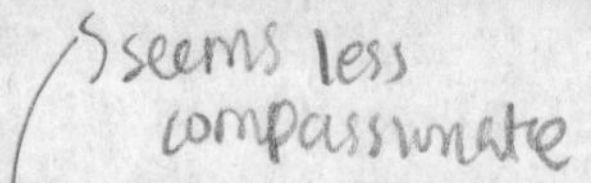

"Oh, no!" Zahra mocked. "Your grandfather, our Baba Jan, when the peasants said they wouldn't pay their rents."

"Many of them couldn't."

"That fat Bania's son could whose father squeezed money from the whole village like juice pressed from sugar-cane. Where would your fine talk and all this be if they didn't pay?" said Zahra, as she waved her end of the rainbow muslin towards the marble fountain, the green grass, the arched, carved, latticed, pillared sprawling house and then stopped, staring at Mrs Martin who was standing on the steps.

As she gushed towards us in her flowered dress and feathered hat, her voice smothered in refined cotton wool, we giggled our surprised greetings, then politely and seriously wished her "Good afternoon".

"Ah! my pretty ones, what a lovely picture you make!" she breathed through sugared butter-balls. "But, dear oh dear, how you've grown! Time flies! Time flies!" She laughed her high, coy laugh.

We giggled again for lack of words.

Over Mrs Martin's high wide bosom cascaded a string of amber beads. She walked with small unhurried steps, a squat battleship in festive bunting.

Her eyes were blue and lashless, her hair soft as butter-milk, her lips thin and blue-tinged; and many Eastern years had dried and dulled her skin and netted it with little veins.

"And where are my Begums, dear Abida and dear Majida?" she said, shortening the first vowel and lengthening the last one grotesquely.

"Cooking in the maids' courtyard, Mrs Martin," I told her.

"I'll take you there, mem-sahib," said Zahra eagerly as she folded the dried *dopatta*.

"Thank you, dear child. Are you coming, Lily dear?"

I felt my cheeks burn, hearing the alien name she had given me.

"In a moment, Mrs Martin. I have to put away these *dopattas* or the sun will spoil them."

"Ah yes, we mustn't allow these lovely, lovely colours to fade, must we? Such pretty clothes, so much more becoming to Indian girls than dresses. I am glad you wear them now, Lily dear, though I do remember the little frocks I had made for you, but you look so much prettier now. Come along, Zahra, take me to your aunt, dear child."

When I went back to the courtyard, Mrs Martin was sitting in an armchair, the centre of curiosity, stared at by the women as they ground the wheat, by the maid-servants as they fetched and carried, by the sweeper woman and her children sitting in a distant corner, and by Ustaniji and Hajjan Bibi as they mumbled and prayed. She sat with her hands resting on the arms of the chair. Her frock, stretched across her knees, showed her thick ankles. When summer covers, shrunk in the wash, were put over armchairs with thick wooden legs, they looked just as Mrs Martin did at this moment.

Mrs Martin welcomed me with affection.

"Dear Lily! Hasn't she grown? Who would think this is my little girl whom I taught her first words of English? Do you remember, Abida, when she recited her first poem to her dear parents? In a white frock and a blue sash, with a blue ribbon in her hair. I had kept it a secret from them, and they were so surprised and delighted. Her dear mother took off this gold brooch and gave it to me. I always wear it. Here it is."

Hidden under her chin and the lace at her neck was a tiny golden bird, holding a pearl in its beak. It seemed to darken the day's brightness with its memories.

"I shall always wear it and remember them. Ah! how cruel life can be! God rest their souls!" Mrs Martin sighed, Aunt Majida sighed too; Aunt Abida's lips tightened.

Mrs Martin passed over the moment unheeding. "But, dear Abida, the child has grown just as I would have wished stayed on. And I hear she has done very well at ol?"

Yes, mem-sahib."

"I'm not surprised. Most of my children do. Lay the foundations well, and the buildings will be strong, that is what I always say. I have brought up the Kishanpur boys as I did Lily. The Raja insists I should stay on as companion to the Rani after the boys go to school, but dear Abida, you know Kishanpur is so remote and primitive, no Europeans to talk to, and the Raja and Rani are so old-fashioned in their ways. Now here it was different; my own people at the Club; and as for dear Lily's father, well, he was just like one of us."

I burned with the intensity of denial, but Mrs Martin had not stopped talking.

"You know, dear, I'm not difficult to please, not a difficult person at all. I've lived with Indian families—the best Indian families—ever since my dear husband died, and I was forced to work. Poor dear! How unhappy he would have been; he did not let me lift my little finger."

Mr Freemantle, my grandfather's friend—of whom Mrs Martin disapproved because of his 'non-European' ways—once said, "This Mrs Martin actually exists—strange as it may seem, but who was Mr Martin? He must be a myth; no human being could have married that woman."

Mrs Martin simpered. "One does not grow younger, my dears. I must take my old bones Home." Mrs Martin always referred to England as Home though she had been there only once for a few months with her husband. Her parents had settled in Calcutta and died there, but who they were was never quite clear from her reminiscences which hinted at high connections and lost wealth.

Aunt Majida said in Urdu, "But, mem-sahib, to whom will you return? You said you had no one of your own alive, and when you went there your brother's wife, God forbid, made you pay to stay with her, and for your food."

"Majida dear, our customs are hard for you to understand. I must go back to my own people. I love you all, I love your country, but my bones must rest in my own land. Oh dear! Oh dear! I am talking too much about myself; I'm almost forgetting what I came for. Oh I did come to see you, my dears, and to pay my respects to your dear father, poor dear, I do hope he gets well soon, but, Abida, I came particularly to ask you a favour."

"In this tiny world of mine whatever I can do I shall," Aunt Abida smiled.

"Well, Abida, dear, you know Muharram is not far ahead and my friend, the padre sahib's sister . . . You remember her, don't you, Abida? I brought her here once."

"Yes, I think I do, but it was a long time ago. She was tall like a man and had a very long nose."

She had a nose that looked like an afterthought, not moulded into her face, but stuck on much as a child would model a face; and she was so thin it seemed her zeal for conversion had consumed her flesh.

The padre sahib's sister had a name that was hard to remember, but she did not need a name because it was enough to be her brother's sister. The sanctity attached to his profession—and the fact that the Governor attended his church—made it permissible for the highest born, most secluded Indian ladies to attend her purdah parties where she ardently established good relations between Indians and the English.

So the wives of the Commissioner and District Officers balanced their cups of tea, and teetered on the edges of gulfs of silence, with correct, polite smiles on their lips when language failed them, and the Ranis and Begums smiled back with warm unselfconsciousness.

"You must remember her too, Lily dear?" Mrs Martin persisted. "I took you to one of her parties when I was here about a year ago."

"Yes, Mrs Martin, I remember."

I remembered my discomfort, being the only girl among

many women, and Mrs Martin as proud of me as any animal-trainer, saying brightly, "Now be a good girl, and help to pass the sandwiches and scones." And the padre sahib's sister, reeking with goodness, saying, "What a charming, well-mannered girl!" And Mrs Martin preening, "I brought her up according to the light of my principles and beliefs." And the padre sahib's sister nodding solemnly, "The Light must shine in every home. The Light must reach into the darkest corners of the land."

I remembered standing with the plates of sandwiches and scones in my hands, trying to smile, looking out towards the garden, where silken, jewelled ladies played badminton. Dressed in rainbow saris they flitted like tinted butterflies, and fluttered like moths on the grey lawn, surrounded by flower-beds that spilled colour into the sunlight, and the sound of their voices was like the twittering of birds.

Now at this moment, Mrs Martin's voice was like the buzzing of a bee; she asked questions without really wanting them answered.

"My friend very much wants to see the procession during Muharram. She is very interested in the customs of this country. Of course, I know more than most English people can ever know; I've lived in the best Indian homes, after all. Abida, dear, could you be very sweet and arrange that we should go to see the procession from the house of your relation where I once took Lily and Zara?"

"With pleasure, mem-sahib."

"Thank you, bless you, dear. I'll take my friend to see the illuminations at the Imambaras too. Oh the lovely, lovely lights, like fairyland! I remember that beautiful sweet glow of oil-lamps. My dear, everything is ruined now with electric bulbs, so glaring, so harsh. And in the old days one could avoid the terrible crowds and go on a special day."

"We needed passes that day if we didn't wear European clothes," I said aggressively.

"Really, Lily!" said Mrs Martin, surprised. Then she

laughed her high laugh, but its peaks were frosted. "Don't tell me the child is becoming a revolutionary?"

"A what?" asked Aunt Abida.

"Oh, you know, Abida dear. All these Congress-wallahs who go about making trouble. If I remember correctly the child was friendly with that girl Sita Agarwal whose family was always in and out of prison."

"Sita's uncle went to prison," said Zahra, brightly informative.

I was silent, reminded of that blistering day when waves of heat danced and flickered on the road and the tar reflected the roadside tamarind trees like water, and from the direction of the Council Chamber, where the procession of non-co-operators had been halted, and the police had charged them with heavy wooden *lathis,* the injured were carried back like the dead. Sita and I had watched from the balcony of the house and a hot sickness burned inside us, a fear and an anger; and we had vowed when we were old enough to fight for our country's freedom as the Satyagrahis did, to lie on the spit-stained pavements in front of treacherous shops that sold foreign cloth, to march in peaceful protest, to defy the might of the arrogant whites. From that day we had stopped singing the alien National Anthem at school concerts, and we used to leave the cinema when its first chords were struck. We had felt we were part of a great movement, and the taunts of Anglo-Indian girls at school had lost their power.

"My dear," Mrs Martin's persistent voice went on, "they are all in it for their own good. For every yard of cloth burnt and unsold that girl's father gets a profit, because the cloth from his mill finds a market. It's men like him who benefit from this destructive non-violent nonsense. This man Agarwal's father went about like a hawker supplying cloth to rich households. Would you have believed it possible that one day his grand-daughter would be in the same school as my Lily?"

It seemed hours before Zahid came to say that the car had come for Mrs Martin.

"Ask the boy's nanny to come in for a little while; they can wait in the car," said Mrs Martin to Zahid.

Into the room walked Sylvia Tucker, with Zahid walking behind her like a puppet.

"Hello, Lily." She smiled at me with her ripe lips, her spiced eyes.

"Hullo, Sylvia."

"Isn't this a pleasant surprise?" cooed Mrs Martin. "Doesn't it bring back memories of school?"

It did. Sylvia laughing at my clothes; "Queen Victoria died long ago. Wear a *burqua*, then even your toenails won't show." Sylvia, pointing at the servant sent with me to school, as he waited under a tree in the playground, "A dragon to guard the princess! Can't you be trusted alone?" Sylvia, knowing I was forbidden to talk to boys or dance asking, "Who will be your partner at the school dance? Who is your boy-friend?" Sylvia, saying on Speech Day, "Remember, you are allowed out only to collect your prizes. Don't stay too long, Cinderella, or you'll never be allowed out again." Sylvia, humming 'Rule Britannia' each time she saw us after Sita's uncle had been arrested. Sylvia, scolding her sister Myra, "Can't you keep away from wogs?"

Myra was my friend in spite of her sister. She was plain and timid, and dark-haired, unlike Sylvia. She had sealed our friendship by sharing her greatest secret.

"You know, Laila," she had whispered, tearful and trembling, "Sylvia's a liar. Our mother isn't Italian. Sylvia won't let her come to school, or meet our friends. She's—you know what—she's a dark woman."

"How's Myra?" I asked Sylvia.

"Studying hard to get a scholarship. She wants to be a teacher." Sylvia's accent was the one she had used whenever English visitors came to the school. "Don't you keep in touch?"

"I'm afraid not."

There was a sudden silence.

"Angels passing," giggled Sylvia.

"That reminds me, I mustn't keep my angels waiting in the car." Mrs Martin laughed her high laugh, "Lily dear, I'm sorry I must tear Sylvia away. Good-bye, my dear girls. *Khuda Hafiz*, dear Abida and Majida. See, I haven't forgotten," and she wagged her forefinger coyly.

Zahid followed Sylvia out as if he had no will left.

Chapter Six

MRS MARTIN'S visit was quite an event. No other Englishwoman had visited the house, and certainly not the zenana, since Baba Jan had lived alone in it without his sons.

She had revived memories of happier days, but the mood of reminiscence she had inspired led to thoughts of present anxiety and sadness.

After dinner when I went to my room I was surprised to find Asad waiting for me.

"I have brought the wool Zahra had asked me to buy," he explained.

"She'll be here soon."

He looked paler than usual, his eyes like a lost child's.

"Laila," he suddenly burst out, "is it true that Zahra is to be married soon?"

"They were talking about it."

"The man is rich, I suppose," Asad said, with a bitterness which laid bare his thoughts.

"Better than that," I said. "A worthy member of the Indian Civil Service."

"What is the difference? Money or power, that is all that matters," Asad said.

"Everything else we are taught is lies, Laila. Money is the only truth. I confess to you, Laila, I feel my whole life wasted. Every day at this theological college where I am taught so-called virtues takes me farther away from God. I tried to believe that humility is a virtue, but forced humility is degradation! I must become a part of something greater than myself. I have thought of it for a long time, remembering my father, remembering that day Sita's uncle was beaten and arrested. Do you understand me, Laila?"

"I'm trying."

"But you cannot," he said bitterly again. "Between us there stands a wall of silver rupees."

"It isn't true. It isn't."

"What is true? That Zahra looked at me with tenderness? That her eyes were false and looked at me without seeing me? That Zahra is . . ."

"Were you talking about me, Asad Bhai?" said Zahra, smiling, her head tilted to one side, as she came into the room. "Or reading a poem?"

"Are they always about you?" laughed Zahid who followed her.

"Oh no, Zahid, that is not the way to stop me telling them about you. Do you know, Asad Bhai, your brother is crazy about Laila's friend, the girl who came here today. He can talk of no one else."

"She is not my friend," I burst out.

"I should hope not," said Zahid. "I have seen her with Tommies on the Mall, each time with a new one."

"You are bitter because she didn't look at you," Zahra teased.

"Why should she? What can he give her?" Asad said sharply. "Besides, being dark the price would be doubled and trebled."

Zahra ignored him and went on, "You can feast your eyes on her, Zahid, when she comes to see the procession with Mrs Martin."

"Mrs Martin cannot bring her," I said. "She mentioned only one other person."

Asad cut in, "The more of them the merrier. Let them be amused by their slaves even if the occasion is a religious and sacred one."

"It is not sacred," said Zahid. "It is idolatrous and sinful. Think of it; our religion says the dead should be buried in graves of which no sign remains so that no one will worship at the tombs of those they change into saints. The law of God has been disobeyed enough. Isn't it worse that these *tazias* should be made and considered holy images of the tombs of the Prophet's grandchildren? I tell you the Shias blaspheme and all such processions are sinful; those who take them out are worse than idolaters, and are damned."

"How dare you talk like that, Zahid? *Shias* or *Sunnis*, we are all Muslims," scolded Zahra.

"They curse us *Sunnis*, don't they?" he retorted.

"You haven't a monopoly of hate and self-righteousness, Zahid," I said.

"He has learned the lesson the English teach us," said Asad. "Hate each other—love us."

Zahid looked at his brother in surprise, then said sullenly, "Anyway it will not be safe to go out during Muharram. I have heard boys talking at school that there might be a riot this year."

"Stupid schoolboy talk!" said Zahra. "Why should there be a riot?"

Asad said, "Maybe because there haven't been any for too long, not even Hindu-Muslim ones. Something must be done to prove that the British are here to enforce law and order, and stop us killing each other."

"How serious you always become, Asad Bhai!" Zahra said looking at Asad with melting, teasing eyes. "I want to talk about Zahid's stricken heart."

She began to laugh but stopped short on seeing Hakiman Bua standing at the door.

"Now then, Zahra Bitia, Laila Bitia, it is time to sleep. Asad Bhayya and Zahid, you should not be here so late."

Their presence in our room at any time met with disapproval.

"We were just going," said Asad. "Zahra, here is the wool you wanted. I had forgotten to give it to you at dinner."

"Thank you, Bhai, you are so good and kind," said Zahra demurely.

Hakiman Bua waited until they had gone, then locked the door leading out of the zenana.

"Go to sleep, and no more talking," she scolded as she went out of the room.

But I could not sleep for a long time, thinking of Asad's bitterness and despair.

Chapter Seven

THE days passed, one like another with at first a degree of wonder that the intensity of some moments should be so smoothly absorbed into others, and then even the awareness of wonder was lost.

Baba Jan's condition no longer caused anxiety. Uncle Mohsin came as usual, scented and spruce, no longer urgent about Zahra's engagement. Nandi's name was not mentioned even by her mother. Asad seemed resigned, except that one morning, when I came unexpectedly upon him and Zahra alone, their words sliced into stillness as I opened the door, and her silence spilled anger while his was frozen pain. He did not join us at dinner that night.

The life of the household reverted smoothly to its outward patterns. Once again when relations came to visit us their conversation did not constantly circle round sombre shadows.

Once again we heard the cries of street vendors beyond the high, encircling walls, the rise and fall of chanted couplets. Nathoo, the old man with bandy legs and quivering high voice, who sold golden biscuits and delicately layered, crisp, meat-filled pastries, had never since our childhood forgotten that extra cake as a gift. Shubrati, whose cream-filled gold and silver-covered *Halva* and delicacies had the sweetness of distilled magical honey-dew. Lal Mian from whose great pottery jar emerged gleaming ice-filled cones. With a flick of his penknife across the sealing-ring of flour he squeezed rich creamy ices, and delicately coloured fruit ices. Though he mocked at machines he feared them, because now his rich customers sent for him less often. Kalloo, the fruit and vegetable seller, chanted, "Here are the fingers of Laila, the ribs of Majnu," as he held out the slender, delicate, pale green cucumbers that were his pride.

Once again Kariman, the bangle-seller, found herself welcome. Fat and eternally laughing she rolled along under the weight of the large wicker basket she carried on her head. When she squatted on the floor and pulled away the red cloth from her basket, the light danced and glittered and lay within bangles of every colour, warm and passionate, cool and delicate, silk spun, heavy and fluted, gold-banded, gold-speckled bangles, for tiny wrists and fat wrists. Her fat fingers gently coaxed delicate bangles over the least flexible of hands to fit tightly round the wrist. It took time, but what was time for but to gossip, to joke, to choose circlets of coloured glass for us and then the maid-servants.

She would say: "May the day come soon when I shall put on my Bitias' henna-painted hands red and gold bridal bangles."

And Hakiman Bua would say, "May God so will it, and guard my children from the Evil Eye."

Once again every Thursday Kamli Shah, the holy beggar, would cry out his harsh-voiced prayers that changed to threats if he were kept waiting.

"Mohammed Mian! Daughters of Mohammed Mian! Children of his sons, Kamli Shah is here. Do not forget him. Then Allah will remember you. Bhagwan will remember you."

Cross-legged in the middle of the road, within the gates, he sat, bare-bodied with matted hair and beard and staring eyes. And fear of their mad concentration, their possible power made it impossible to send him away empty-handed. Even now his voice singing over the walls of the zenana brought back shivers of childhood's terror.

Life within the household ordained, enclosed, cushioning the mind and heart against the outside world, indirectly sensed and known, moved back to its patterned smoothness.

Chapter Eight

AUNT Majida sent once again for the family jeweller in preparation for the day Zahra would be married. She sat on one side of a curtain and Ram Das on the other, and I took velvet cases and packets of precious stones from one to the other, while Zahra sat shyly in a corner pretending not to be interested. Even Aunt Abida holding many coloured precious stones in her hands seemed to forget sorrow and weariness.

Ram Das sat cross-legged on the carpet, wizened insignificant and obsequious, but it was said that he was richer than most of the *Taluqdars* who were his customers, and that he possessed priceless pieces of jewellery, precious stones sold to him secretly and cheaply by relatives and courtiers of the last king. They were too proud to sell openly and too desperate to bargain.

Naib Sahib, the manager of the estate, and Lala Ji, the accountant, came to consult Aunt Abida before making decisions for which they were not prepared to take responsibility. They sat behind a screen, and grunted and wheezed over sheets of brown paper that looked as if ink-dipped and intoxicated spiders had danced across them.

Aunt Abida, who had occasionally helped Baba Jan with his estate work, was able to decipher the writing of the professionals by whom tenants had their applications and requests written. It was a source of wonder to me that she sanctioned gifts of wood and loans for weddings and funerals with the same detachment with which she ordered the ejection of those who had not paid their rents, or the digging up of their mud huts if built without permission.

When I passed those sheets of brown paper from Naib Sahib to Aunt Abida and back again, letters and figures and words made up both the problems and their solutions. One's pity floated as lightly as the voices of judgement.

But sometimes those paper sheets were razor-edged when held out by supplicating hands, as on the day Jumman brought his wife's brother's aunt. She was fortunate she had him to help her to the very source of power without costly intermediaries.

He pleaded for her, and she for her son, but no one could plead successfully if her tears could not. They flowed in a gentle stream from her patient eyes, and yet they were sharper than swords. She was as worn and drained of life as the dull, rubbed, silver bangle on her fleshless arm. The lobes of her ears were torn by the earrings she had worn in happier days, and her neck and wrists and ankles were naked of jewellery, witnessing her poverty. She held Aunt Abida's feet with hands that were cracked and blackened with age and work, the nails rubbed back, ridged and horny. When she touched the ground with her forehead, it seemed a bundle of patched rags had been dropped carelessly.

"You are my mother, my goddess. Have mercy!" she cried.

But there could be no mercy, only justice. She was not Jumman's wife's brother's aunt, not an old, broken woman, not a mother pleading for her son, she was a case; she was a letter on a sheet of brown paper.

Naib Sahib's voice recited the facts and suggested the decision. Her son could not pay the rent, had not been able to do so for some time. Concessions had been made, time had been given, because the family had been good tenants for three generations. He pleaded illness, the inability to look after his land, debts, extortion by the village money-lender, the failure of crops. It was an unfortunate case, the dry, factual voice admitted, but one had to be careful. New laws were to be passed which would make the ejection of tenants difficult if not impossible. There were many such cases and it would be ruinous to keep such tenants, specially when there was a demand for the land from others not only able to pay good rent, but a substantial sum beforehand. It was a sad case, but times were hard, rents were harder to collect, land revenue had to be paid. . . .

The voice expressed logic, and the old woman's sobs did not drown it.

"Phuphi Jan," I said as I handed her the paper to sign, "can't you help her? Have pity on her."

She replied, "I do pity her, but what is there for me to do? This is a matter of principle, my child. Life will teach you to subordinate your heart to your mind."

And Jumman led away the old woman because there were many more cases to be decided, and it was getting late.

Chapter Nine

ZAHRA and I seldom had friends visiting us except when relations came to the city; and amongst them I found few like enough or unlike enough to make communication anything but a source of isolation. But a few of the older women who came to see my aunts interested me objectively.

The Hakim's wife, for instance, perpetually, gigantically pregnant, who complained that in restoring the youth of senile Maharajas, Rajas and Nawabs her husband unduly prolonged his own; and the lawyer's wife who made annual pilgrimages to the saint's tomb at Ajmer Sharif because each winter she was possessed by a spirit that recited lewd Persian and Arabic verse and mocked at God; and the painted, powdered, scented young Rani of Bhimnagar with sad, doe-like eyes, whose husband brought home from each annual trip to Europe a new young woman, ostensibly as a companion for his wife; and the Indian Christian lady doctor who wrote a text from the BIBLE on each prescription for non-believers.

There were also the wives of Baba Jan's friends. Thakur Balbir Singh's wife was orthodox and would not eat or drink at our house, but was kind and loving and lavish with gifts. The Rani Sahiba of Amirpur was a large, imperious woman with a dignity which years of unquestioned privilege and authority had given her. Even her formidable husband was said to be frightened of her, since she had whipped a woman in her zenana who had responded to his amorous advances, saying he could possess all the women in the world, but not the women who served her.

But the most interesting of all was Mushtari Bai.

We were about to sit down to dinner one night when Mushtari Bai walked in.

She wore a crumpled *Khaddar* sari and her thin grey hair was pulled back, plaited stiffly and tied with a bit of string.

She was very thin and very dark, with high cheek-bones around which the skin of her face was loose and ill-fitting. Her mouth was large and full-lipped with irregular teeth stained by betel juice. Her eyes were large, ruined, muddied pools of gentle beauty.

When she came in, and bowed in graceful and formal courtly salutation, there was a moment of silence. We said our *Adabs* and my aunts made room for her beside them, asking her to join us at our meal. Ustaniji and Hajjan Bibi, who were waiting to wash their hands, silently left the room.

Their ancient minds were outraged, remembering it was the custom to observe purdah from women such as she had been.

It was eight years ago since I had first seen Mushtari Bai. My father had taken me down the forbidden street whose balconies during the first ten days of Muharram were empty of painted, bejewelled women when visitors climbed the narrow stairs only to hear religious songs of mourning. I remembered the glass *tazia*, the miniature domed tomb, shining, gleaming, reflecting the light of many crystal lamps, the snow-white cloth on the floor; the courtly gentlemen in embroidered caps and *achkans*, and a gracious gentle lady with a deep rich voice, who gave me sweets that were covered with gold and silver so delicately beaten that it clung to my lips and fingers.

I remembered my father asking me to try to copy his courtly salutation, and at the awkward swaying of my hand in the air while I bent nearly double, they laughed but with a kindliness that did not hurt me. My father said to the gracious dark lady in black, "An English governess cannot teach her as you taught us lessons in etiquette and courtesy."

When I saw her again I was old enough to know she was a courtesan. The richest and most cultured of aristocrats had been honoured by her favours; some had squandered their fortunes, until she herself, solicitous for their neglected families, had frowned upon them.

I saw her when she sang and danced at the wedding feast

of the Raja of Amirpur's grandson. Through the thin slits of the bamboo curtains which separated the women from the men, I saw her in rich garments heavy with gold embroidery; and the diamonds she wore shone with a brilliance that brought back to memory the glass *tazia* under the light of crystal chandeliers.

Two other singers had performed before her. They were young and painted and brazen.

The men sat on the white, cloth-covered floor, and crowded round the open space where the singers performed before the red and gold velvet canopy under which sat the brocaded, garlanded bridegroom. The naked eyes of young men and old, in silk and brocaded and embroidered *achkans* and rakish caps, were more aware of the conscious womanhood of the singers than of their artistry. As each singer appeared with her accompanists she met the challenge of many hundreds of eyes and bantering tongues. Servants in scarlet liveries moved round with silver salvers heaped with spiced betel-leaves, covered in gold and silver.

Behind the curtains the women gossiped and giggled, carefully, in whispers.

Then it was Mushtari Bai's turn to sing.

Her *Sarangi* player was a gaunt man who played as if praying, with his eyes shut; and every muscle of the *tabla* player's body twitched in tormented rhythm with the drums.

She sang; and at the first rich, deep notes a hush fell. The perfection of her technique mastered the mind; and the pure tones and depths of emotion humbled the spirit.

The servants stood as still as scarlet exclamation marks.

When she finished singing there was an enraptured release of applause and the men rose up and flung at her feet silver and notes and gold sovereigns. She bowed and humbly acknowledged the tributes to her artistry, and when she left she took with her the dignity of her profession, and the young women brought back its sensuality.

And now she was sitting with us, and her voice when she

spoke was a tortured whisper. After the illness which had robbed her of her voice, she had turned to God to expiate the sins of her life. Her wealth, which she considered tainted, she had given to charities, and she herself became a wandering mendicant. She came sometimes to the homes of those who had once known her greatness; my aunts, who respected her, no longer observed purdah from her. When she came it was a sign of great need, but even now her ragged dignity shunned pity.

Tonight, she said, she had been passing by and had come to inquire about Baba Jan's health. And Aunt Abida exclaimed how fortunate it was because she had not sent the money which was distributed at the Pearl mosque every Thursday, and wouldn't Mushtari Bai please be kind enough to take it and give it to the deserving?

She did not stay long after the meal was finished, and everyone pretended to be unaware that she kept her left hand hidden under the folds of her sari.

I was not the only one who had seen her hiding pieces of bread while we ate.

Chapter Ten

IT was in the first week of Muharram that the doctor advised Aunt Abida to send for my uncle Hamid, and once again a tight heaviness shadowed the house. Our circumscribed sorrow found universal echoes at night spreading and quivering in a circle round the city, and sounding the clear star-crowded sky. In the still chill darkness the rhythmic abstraction of sobbing sound was translated by knowledge into a wailing: "Ya Hasan. Ya Husain. Hasan. Husain, 'Sain—'Sain."

How better could Baba Jan have demonstrated his power than by choosing the very time for moving towards death when the city's black-clad, bare-armed women, and barefooted, bareheaded men sorrowed for the martyred grandchildren of the Prophet?

Aunt Abida and Aunt Majida spent little time outside their father's room; and now, when Zahra and I went in to pay our respects morning and evening, he lay silent with his eyes closed, not showing any signs of knowing we came, stood in silence and went away. His friends came at the appointed hour, but spoke only when outside that room of silence.

In the courtyard of the maid-servants every night after dinner, Ustaniji drew upon the fumbled store of her memories and recited in a quavering, cracked minor key elegiac verses mourning the martyrdom of Husain and his family.

One night she asked Asad if he would read them to her. He put life into every poem he chanted whether it was sad or joyful.

It was the ninth night of Muharram. On the horizon there was a glow as of a forgetful sun rising before moonset. The glow of a million lamps from the illumined Imambaras where *tazias* and banners were laid to rest, lit the sky, and the city was alive with crowds forgetful in that bright beauty of the month of mourning.

Busy sounds made our house into an island.

We went to hear Asad reading, and sat on the string bed beside him. The maid-servants squatted on the floor. Ustaniji and Hajjan Bibi sat on another bed wrapped to their eyes in the light shawls.

Asad began uncertainly, shyly, conscious of Zahra's presence. Then the poetry, the passion possessed him, and there was only the sound of his voice and the deep breathing of the old women.

When he read of the agonies of thirst of the children of the Prophet, cut off from the river by their enemies, the women sobbed softly. Ustaniji began beating her breast, saying "Hasan" "Husain" softly, with a slow rhythm. Ramzano stared at her strangely and joined in. The others still sobbed softly. In Asad's voice was suffering and pain. The beating hands moved faster. The rhythm quickened. "Hasan" "Husain" "Hasan" "Husain" "'San" "'Sain" "'San" "'Sain" "'San" "'Sain". Ramzano's eyes were glassy. The very air in the room was throbbing, taut, tense, Faster, faster, sharper: "Hasan" "Husain"! She shrieked and fell forward.

Asad stopped reading.

"Hush, hush, be quiet." Hakiman Bua scolded abruptly, forgetting her own tears, "Stupid girl, do you want your voice to be heard outside? Stop it now, before Abida Bitia hears you."

Saliman dashed water on Ramzano's twitching face, and quite suddenly we were back in our recognisable world and Ramzano was her tiresome self, too ready to giggle, too ready to wail.

Asad and Zahid went with us to our room; Zahid bursting with comments that set a critical curl on his lips and Asad quiet, his eyes when looking at Zahra defeating his silence.

"Multiply Ramzano a thousand times," said Asghar,

"and you come to the sum total of hypocrisy that is characteristic of the mourning meetings of Muharram."

"It is not hypocrisy," snapped Zahra, "it is genuine grief."

"Can genuine grief be organised? The crowd cries in rhythm, tears flow at the will of the man who chants the dirges, then people cry for crying's sake only. That is why seconds after they have been weeping and beating their breasts they are chewing *pan* and talking casually about their incomes and their indigestion," Zahid went on.

"I think," said Asad thoughtfully, "that it is good to let one's personal grief become part of a general sorrow. It is terrible to weep alone. But it is worse if there is hypocrisy in grief; that is a crime against the only truth I know, which is suffering."

Zahra flushed, and turned away from him.

"But this mourning is hypocrisy," persisted Zahid.

"Oh be quiet!" Zahra shouted.

"Being quiet changes nothing. These people use religion to get rid of their hysteria. They distort historical facts thirteen hundred years old, and divide us when Muslims need to be united against great dangers."

"Will your hatred unite us, Zahid?" I asked. "It makes no distinction between Muslims and non-Muslims."

"I hate those who are enemies of Islam no matter whom they may be, and I am prepared to give my life for it."

"And take the lives of others? Kill in the name of God and it will not be called murder."

"Now where did you read that, Laila?" Zahid mocked.

"I envy you, Zahid," said Asad softly. "I envy your faith and confidence. I am sure of nothing except that hatred breeds hated, and violence and sorrow. Surely it is not good to cause sorrow even if we ourselves suffer?"

"I am bored and tired," interrupted Zahra, her voice jagged with anger. "Settle the problems of right and wrong in your own room where you should have gone a long time ago. Or do you want Hakiman Bua to turn you out again?"

Asad looked at her with a surprised hurt, but Zahid as he left the room, mocked, "Don't use your tongue like the chained knives with which men will flagellate themselves in tomorrow's procession, Cousin Zahra."

When we were lying down, waiting for sleep in the dark room, I said: "I do not understand it. Zahid looks so pale, so small, so weak and yet he has such volumes of hate in him."

Zahra said in a voice of brooding anger, "He does not anger me as much as Asad does; he is like a mongrel dog; kick it and it comes back, its tail between its legs."

And she turned over yawning.

Chapter Eleven

THE next morning we were told we could not go to see the procession in the oldest part of the city, and a message had been sent to Mrs Martin. It was not only because of Baba Jan's worsening condition; but Uncle Mohsin, who skimmed the city of scandal and news, had warned that there were rumours of riots.

Aunt Abida's face held the strain of someone gripping a ledge above a deep drop. Aunt Majida moaned perpetually, "When will Hamid Bhai come? At a time like this it is his duty to be with us. Has the Government bought him? When will he come?"

Zahra and I were restless and quarrelsome, because we could do nothing, because Baba Jan was so old, because his delayed death made us impatient. We had wanted to see the procession, to get away from the house. Now we had to content ourselves watching minor processions on their way to join the main one.

Ramzano and Saliman joined us on the roof of the portico, and we looked out from behind its latticed walls.

Since Nandi had been sent away I talked to them more than I had done.

They were stupid but cheerful, not much older than Zahra and I. Their dark and pockmarked faces were saved from ugliness by the beauty of youth, though its privileges were prohibited, and its spontaneity suppressed.

They had helped their mother work in the house from the moment they had been able to fetch and carry to the time she had died of consumption. She had been sold as a child during a famine, and given to my grandmother who had brought her up, trained her as a maid-servant, then married her to a young man whose family had served our family for generations. He had abandoned her and his daughters for a smart, rustling-skirted, red-coated Ayah, who had found him a job with the English family where she worked.

The sun was high above the church steeple when we heard the distant chanting, "Hasan! Husain! Hasan! Husain! Haider!" It came nearer and the measured sound of bare hands striking bare breasts, the monotonous beat of drums and cymbals made my heart beat with a strange excitement.

Then the barefooted, bareheaded men came in view following the *tazias* carried shoulder-high. There were *tazias* of peacock's feathers, of glass, of sugar, of bright-coloured paper, intricate, beautiful, arched, domed, some as high as telegraph poles, others from poor homes so small that they could be held on one man's head, all hurrying to join the main procession at the allotted time, for burial or consecration.

Zahra sighed, "I would like to have seen the gold and silver *tazias* of Amirpur."

"And the ebony one with its silent followers all in black," I said.

"Bitia, I wish I could have seen the procession of the *Duldul*, the white horse of Hazrat Husain, looking like a bridegroom with its silver and gold saddle and bridle," said Ramzano who longed to be a bride.

"You, Ramzano," teased Saliman, "want to be fed on milk and sweets like the *Duldul*; but remember, soon it will be back between the tonga-shafts, feeling the driver's whip."

"Oh, I am thirsty," said Ramzano. "The sun is worse than whips. I wish I were near the corner where Jumman Dhobi is distributing sherbet today, to all who are thirsty. That wife of his forces him to make all kinds of vows so as to have a son. This Muharrum he is trying to please Allah and the Holy Prophet."

"Last year," interrupted Saliman, "it was his god Hanuman's turn. He made a vow to measure his length from here to the temple across the river. It was when the roads were like the bottoms of frying-pans off a fire."

"It's just as well, Bitia, he is a tall man," Ramzano giggled.

"How much breath have you got in you?" I pretended to scold them, "On and on and on, like crickets by the river."

"Like frogs," laughed Zahra; "come on now, before Hakiman Bua catches you and knocks the breath out of you for idling. There is nothing to wait for up here. Let's go down."

The leaves of the tall trees were heavy in the sun, and in the distance a church spire reached up to the sky, made intensely blue by the budding white clouds drifting somnolently across it. Crows cawed in the eucalyptus trees, a couple of restless sparrows hopped on the wall, grey and white pigeons fluttered across towards the servants' quarters, and a hawk glided high above.

"Zahra Bitia, Laila Bitia," Ramzano broke the moment's long silence, "if Hakiman Bua says anything, tell her you brought us up here with you."

"Otherwise she is sure to find some work undone and scold us," pleaded Saliman.

"A scolding never harmed anyone," teased Zahra.

"I'll tell her not to beat you too hard," I said.

Ramzano and Saliman giggled; they giggled more expressively than they talked, as if they were constantly finding and sharing a secret joke though life was reluctant in its kindness.

As we went down the stairs our laughter left us, and the heavy air closed upon us.

"What shall we do now?" asked Zahra.

"I have a headache," I said, feeling it tightening round my temples.

"Bitia, let me massage your head," said Ramzano.

"Let me press your feet," said Saliman.

"So that Hakiman Bua won't scold you or call you away?" Zahra said.

They burst into giggles and Saliman said, "If we go there

now and look as if we've been laughing Hajjan Bibi and Ustaniji will be angry with us. Let us stay a little while."

I lay on my bed and their gentle hands soothed me, and I sank towards rest.

I did not know when they went away, and was woken by Zahra shaking me, saying, "The food is getting cold. Everyone is waiting for you."

"The sun on the roof must have been stronger than I imagined," I said, reluctantly getting up. "Do you know what that means, Zahra? Summer will be here before we know it. I hate the thought; but at least it will prepare us for hell when we die."

"You will not find me there, but I'll think of you in heaven."

"When you are amusing the old, bearded *moulvis*."

We began to laugh then stopped guiltily.

Chapter Twelve

THE meal was silent as all moments of our being together now seemed to be.

Then Aunt Abida said, "Asad and Zahid are not here. Have you seen them?"

Zahra and I looked up together, and I said, "No. They must have gone to see the procession in the city."

Aunt Majida frowned and complained, "Why did they go today, knowing what Mohsin Bhai had said?"

There was no possible answer, and the silence returned.

We were washing our hands when Hakiman Bua came in, agitated.

"Bitia, the cook's brother has just come from the Central Market. He says terrible things have happened, and many people have been killed."

"Hai!" wailed Aunt Majida. "Allah have mercy!"

"What terrible things? Who has been killed?" asked Aunt Abida, trying to be calm.

"No one is sure. There are police everywhere, and already, miles away from where it happened, they have found people stabbed in the streets." Hakiman Bua's voice held a note of pride, being the first to bring such alarming news.

"Allah! Where are those wretched boys?" Aunt Majida cried.

"Hakiman Bua," said Aunt Abida impatiently, "what exactly happened? Where?"

"The cook says his brother told him it was on the road from Phulganj. It seems some villagers were hurrying to join the big procession in the city, and just outside the big Hanumanji temple the top of their *tazia* stuck in the branch of a *peepul* tree. . . ."

"Why, oh why did they not take care?" Aunt Majida cried. "Everyone knows these *peepul* trees with their evil spirits always bring bad luck."

Hakiman Bua went on: "What was to be done? The branch of their sacred tree could not be cut without getting the Hindus angry. But there are many ways of causing mischief. Someone began to blow a conch in the temple, though it was known there was a holy procession outside. Some hot-blooded persons threw stones at the heathen sounds, and then the fighting began. This kind of mischief spreads like fire in a field of dry grass, Bitia. The cook's brother says the police are on the streets like flies on a summer's day, but they can't be everywhere, not in every little lane. And goodness knows whose death calls him today. Allah have mercy on us!" Hakiman Bua sighed and shook her head.

"Those wretched, wretched boys! Why did they have to go out today?," Aunt Majida kept repeating.

"The man may have been exaggerating," Aunt Abida said wearily, "but not by a word or a sign must Baba Jan be made to feel anything is wrong." Her eyes rested on her sister for a brief moment, then she drew her *dopatta* over her head and went towards Baba Jan's room.

I left Hakiman Bua protesting the man had seen dreadful things with his own eyes, Aunt Majida bemoaning the fate of God's unfortunate creatures, and Zahra palely listening.

I tried to read but could not, thinking of Asad and Zahid lost in the violent core of the teeming city, lost in the maze of its narrow streets, its crowding, smothering houses. It seemed more distant now, as if the wide, tree-lined road that ran to the heart of the city, past this quiet house, through parks, past palaces and gardens, and by the gentle river, led out of one world to another.

About four o'clock when Zahid came, all our anxieties were in the explosion of Aunt Abida's anger. But Zahid, quivering under the fire and ice of her words and looks, could tell her nothing of Asad. They had not gone out together. They were to have met after the procession at a friend's house near the University. At the signs of trouble, sensing the ugly temper of the crowd, and seeing the reinforcements of police arriving, Zahid had immediately gone to his friend's house, and waited for Asad, and then come home. And now he waited with us.

It was two dragging hours later that we heard the sounds for the first time, sharp and crackling like fireworks on a festive night and more ominous because of the similarity. We went out into the courtyard. Once, twice repeated.

"Firing," whispered Zahid.

"It sounds so close," I said, feeling afraid.

"Yes," said Zahid, then cried out, "I can't sit here. I can't. What can I do?"

And Zahra suddenly sobbed. "He said he wanted to die. I didn't believe him. I didn't mean to hurt him. . . ."

Zahid looked at her with a sudden flicker of hatred, and then buried his face in his hands. I was silent with a strange mixture of understanding and anger. All Zahra had felt about Asad and hidden so guilefully was now revealed.

We wanted to be together, but found nothing to say to each other.

Another hour passed. We heard the sound of a car drawing up, but paid little attention, and waited in silence.

Then Ram Singh, the watchman, came hurrying to tell us it was Asad, and the silence splintered into a million shining fragments, and it was easy to breathe.

Zahid burst out of the door, racing down the corridor. Aunt Abida was in Baba Jan's room, but in my excitement I dared to creep in. I whispered, almost soundlessly, "Asad is back."

She started, then inclined her head, and whispered, "I'm coming." All day she had borne a double strain, not letting her father sense her anxiety.

With the help of Ram Singh, Zahid brought Asad in and made him lie down on the *takht* with a pillow under his head. His face was pinched and yellow, his eyelids heavy and his bandaged head drooped. His arm was in a sling.

Zahra had run to call Aunt Majida, who came in crying, "My child! My son! Asad! Allah be praised!"

Asad opened his eyes and they were dull with pain. He tried to turn away his face, and seeing Aunt Abida the tears welled up and he whispered, "I couldn't help it, I couldn't help it."

Zahid said, "There's nothing to worry about. The police inspector who brought him said that they had taken him to the hospital and the doctor said all he needed was rest."

We were able to piece together Asad's story from what Zahid had been told and from his own disjointed description as he gradually recovered.

He had been caught in the panic that turned the watching crowd into a desperate mob whose cruelty was the twisted sum of each individual's fear. "I heard a woman scream as she fell still carrying her child in her arms, and I could not stop, I could not turn around. No one stopped."

He tried to run towards the road leading to the river, but was carried towards a narrow street, and there, lost in a maze of lanes, when he thought himself safe, he saw an old man.

"He was trying to run away from two men with knives. He kept crying for help. I could not run away, though I wanted to. But I could not save him, I could not save him. . . ." Asad's eyes were agonised, and we had to stop him talking.

The men turned on him but, with a desperate strength, he broke away, and seeing an open door he ran into the house, even remembering to lock the door behind him, unconscious in his panic, of the pain in his head and the blood that covered him.

He stumbled up the narrow, steep stairs, and found himself in the house of dancing girls. The women were frightened, but they looked after him, though the men were hostile. He suddenly thought it might help if he mentioned Mushtari Bai, and then they were kinder. They washed him, bandaged him and made him rest; and towards evening one of the men volunteered to take him home. Asad promised he would be rewarded, but the man said he would do it for Mushtari Bai's sake.

With Asad sitting on the bar before him they cycled through streets deserted except by patrolling policemen. Then near the vegetable market they heard the sound of firing. The man refused to go any farther, and Asad, now within three miles of home, refused to go back with him. Alone and frightened of being alone, he ran into the market square. In the far corner by the mosque, a small crowd was scattering, and men still threw stones at the police as they ran. The road across the square was brightly lit, and he saw some policemen on horseback in the distance. He ran towards them and the lights, driven by his fear of the dark and the crowd. Then he recognised Khan Abdul Latif, the Chief of the City Police, and knowing himself safe, collapsed like a puppet with cut strings. Khan Sahib had Asad examined by a doctor, and brought him home. Khan Sahib had been helped when young in his education and career by Baba Jan.

We were conscious of this protective power even without the answer Uncle Mohsin later brought back from Khan Sahib to Aunt Abida's message of gratitude—that to serve Syed Mohammad Hasan and his family was not only his duty but an honour.

When she found that Asad was feverish Aunt Majida had his bed brought into her room. Towards morning we heard her calling, and when I forced myself awake I found Zahra already up; she said she had not been able to sleep.

We found Aunt Majida sitting at the foot of Asad's bed rubbing the soles of his feet. She said in an agitated whisper:

"His fever is very high and he has been very restless. He asked for water a moment ago. Zahra, bring some quickly in that glass. Laila, you rub his feet and I will rub the palms of his hands. That will bring down the fever."

Asad's dry lips moved soundlessly, and he turned his head restlessly from side to side. His feet were burning as I touched them.

Zahra brought the water, and Aunt Majida putting her arm under his shoulders to support him said, "Asad

Mian, here is some water for you. Asad Mian, open your eyes."

Asad's eyelids fluttered as he gulped the water; then as her mother put his head on the pillow and wiped his mouth, and Zahra moved back to put the glass away, his eyes opened wide in a fixed stare, and his groping hand caught her *dopatta* as he cried, "Zahra, darling, Zahra, don't leave me, don't ever leave me. Zahra, Zahra . . ."

His voice dropped into a bottomless well of petrified silence.

That moment seemed endless. Then Aunt Majida said in a cold, hard voice, "Zahra, go to your room. You may go too, Laila."

Zahra was pale with fear and her hands trembled as she pulled her *dopatta* away and ran out of the room.

"Zahra, Zahra," Asad moaned.

I saw the look of anger in Aunt Majida's eyes, tinged with hatred; and my heart ached for Asad whose love was changed into a sin by conventions, and whose secret hopes had been betrayed into a hopelessness now more than ever certain.

She said again, "You may go, Laila," then hesitated and added, "There is no need to remember what he said in his delirium. Allah preserve us from dishonour."

I had not meant to disobey her but now I sensed her weakness, and went nearer Asad, took his hand in mine and said:

"It is Laila, Asad".

"Zahra," he whispered, "Zahra."

"Go to sleep, Asad, go to sleep." I soothed him, stroking his burning forehead.

Slow, heavy tears rolled from under his eyelids; gradually his head became still, and his hold on my hand relaxed.

As I got up, I heard Aunt Majida crying "How could he? How could he be so ungrateful?"

When I opened the door of our room Zahra looked up in fear. "I thought it was Ammi," she said and burst into tears.

"For heaven's sake stop crying. That's one habit of your mother's you don't have to copy."

"How can you be so cruel?" sobbed Zahra. "What can I do now? How will I face her again? How could he do such a terrible thing?"

"He was delirious and didn't know what he was saying. It was wonderful for you until now, wasn't it? You enjoyed having an adoring slave all this time, didn't you? Why did you encourage him? You are a hypocrite like the rest of them," I said angrily.

"It's not true. It isn't, it isn't. Oh, what will happen to me now?"

"Nothing, and you know it. Your mother will take good care no one suspects anything. She is just as concerned about you as you are about yourself. But poor Asad, I wonder what will happen to him."

"You don't seem to understand..." began Zahra.

"No, I don't and I never can, so please let me sleep."

And I lay on the bed with my back to Zahra, struggling with my confused thoughts, pity for Asad, anger at Zahra, impatience with her mother, wonder at the meaning of love and truth and duty.

The next day Aunt Majida moved into our room, while Zahid was asked to stay with Asad whose fever had come down considerably. Nothing was said about what had happened that night, and there was already such a strained atmosphere in the house that an increase in tension was hardly noticeable. But that night had decided that Zahra would be married to the first suitable person, and Asad could no longer live happily in the house.

It was about four days later the doctors advised that Uncle Hamid should be sent for immediately, but before he could arrive Baba Jan died.

Chapter Thirteen

IT was a still afternoon. Since morning my aunts had not left Baba Jan's room except for meals which had become a hurried formality, and Aunt Abida had not spoken except to ask if there was any reply from my uncle to her telegram. Zahra and I stayed in our room.

I was rearranging books to keep myself occupied, and Zahra was sewing when Hakiman Bua came in crying, "Come quickly, children, come quickly, my poor orphans. May Allah protect you and all of us, and comfort those whom He has bereaved. Oh, what will become of us? Allah is merciful. . . ."

We did not wait to listen to her because we understood and were afraid. Death was acceptable only as an abstraction and a speculation, in stories and not in reality, at a distance and not in such cold proximity.

In Aunt Abida's room the maid-servants squatted on the floor with grave faces and sighed and wiped their eyes with their *dopattas* when they saw us. On the *takht* sat Ustaniji and Hajjan Bibi, their faces like crumpled, wet tissue paper and they cried, "Allah, be merciful to us. . . . Allah, be merciful to Majida Bibi and Abida Bibi. . . . Allah, be merciful to the orphaned Zahra and Laila."

I echoed the prayer for my beloved Aunt Abida whose life had no purpose but its dedication to her father; and for a moment the fear of Death left me as I went through the door, wishing to be with her. It was her silence to which I responded and not the mournful murmur of the *Kalmah*, "There is no God but one and Muhammad is His Prophet", rising and falling around the deep voice of Baba Mian reciting from the Quran.

I looked up into her lost eyes as she sat upright on the bed supporting her father. And then inside me was a cold, paralysed horror because his eyes were open and he was looking at me. He was dead; he should have been dead. Yet he was looking at me. I had not covered my head; I had not raised my hand in salutation, and I could not.

In that wondering second I heard a strange noise gurgle in his throat, saw the whiteness of his beard stained with a poisonous black flow, and, screaming, ran from the room. I sobbed in wild terror, and the guilt of that doubting moment, fearing that he had been conscious not of my disrespect but its import; I had pronounced him dead more surely than those who called upon God and the Prophet.

Chapter Fourteen

THE next day, after Uncle Hamid arrived, we were to go, for the last time with Baba Jan, to Hasanpur. For centuries the ancestral village had received back in complete finality the sons it had not been able to hold while they lived.

By nightfall the house was as crowded as for weddings and feasts, except that there was no music and song, and all voices were tuned to death.

The zenana was busy with a life that grew from death. The women from the barbers' families of all the villages belonging to our family whose presence was a sign of celebration and mourning, of joy and sorrow, bustled around seeing to the comfort of the guests. As no food could be cooked in the house of mourning for the next three days, relays of servants brought it from Raja Hasan Ahmad's palace.

Those women who had passed through the stage of tears and sighs and mournful reminiscences sat in groups on *takhts* and beds and gossiped.

In the midst of the bustle there was a point of stillness—Aunt Abida's room. She sat on her bed surrounded by women shrouded in their *dopattas*, her tearless immobility freezing lamentation. As each newcomer entered, embraced my aunts, Zahra and me, there was a resuscitation of sorrow, and again silence and immobility. Aunt Majida's eyes were dry through excess of weeping; Aunt Abida's stony because she had not wept at all.

The Rani of Amirpur's arrival stirred the mourners and the gossipers with a new interest. Even little boys of eleven were sent outside to where the men were gathered.

The Rani Sahiba followed by her daughters-in-law and daughters and retinue of companions and maid-servants moved through the waiting women, acknowledging their salutations with a gracious inclination of her head.

As she stepped over the lintel of the door her maid-servants called out "May Allah protect our lady! May the blessings of the world lie at her feet!"

She embraced my aunts and Zahra and me, saying mournfully, "Allah's will be done. Peace be on the soul of the departed. From Him we come; to Him we return. May He give you strength to bear your sorrows. There is no end to sorrow; sorrow and more sorrow must come to you. This is only the beginning."

All the women sighed deeply. Aunt Majida wailed and Aunt Abida's mouth twitched, but she remained dry-eyed.

"Learn to live with sorrow, my child, for it will be your constant companion."

Angered by this strange consolation, resenting accepted patterns of thought, I felt a strange sense of release. For the first time since Nandi had been sent away I put my arms round Aunt Abida's neck and rested my cheek against hers. She shivered and caught her breath, then holding me tight she burst into tears.

All night a light burned in Baba Jan's room, and Baba Mian kept vigil, reading the Quran. The incense that burned in a corner spread outward through the rooms.

Its smell of death was everywhere. It seeped into the mind, and created memories.

In childhood on warm summer nights Karan Ali, a bearded, ghostly exorcist, walked from room to shadowy room carrying a long-handled iron bowl, and smoked out insects and mosquitoes which hummed around one's ears. The incense smelt sharp and medicinal.

During solemn religious recitals the same incense burned in silver cups. It smelt rich and holy. What quality of mind transformed it now to deathliness?

Gradually the house was dark and asleep, and only the one light burned.

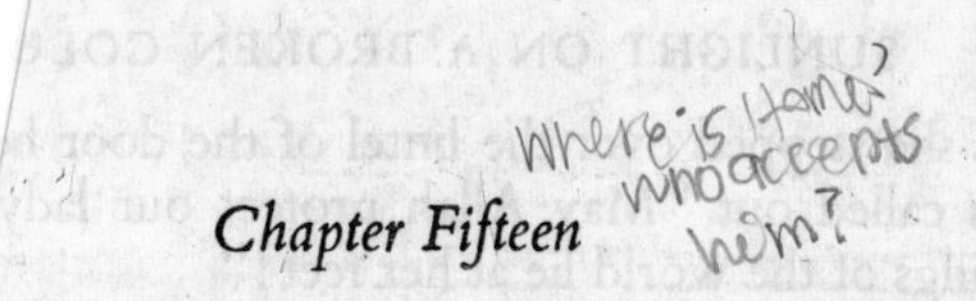

Chapter Fifteen

UNCLE Hamid and his wife Saira arrived next morning. His presence restrained grief. He was undemonstrative both by nature and because he admired Western forms of behaviour. His relations no longer expected him to conform to traditional patterns; and he was too self-sufficient to care for what they thought.

Each time he came home it was like meeting a stranger masquerading as one of the family. In his relationship with his family there was the meticulousness that springs from duty not love.

He looked like Baba Jan must have done at his age; the same obstinate jaw, high cheek-bones, uncompromising mouth and slightly protruding cold eyes. There was a calculated precision in his manner and appearance, his thin grey hair smoothed from the centre parting as if combed a moment before, his thick moustaches neatly clipped. He dressed immaculately in Western clothes, and preferred to speak English.

A similarity of temper had made relations with his father strained. At the end of the last century Baba Jan had been influenced by ideas of reform among Muslims and had sent his sons to English Universities. He had thought the weapons of the foreigners should be used against them to preserve inherited values and culture. To copy their alien ways was abhorrent to him.

He was deeply disappointed when his eldest son chose to join the Indian Civil Service instead of staying at home to look after the estate. To him the estate was the outward symbol of all those values to which the family owed dutiful, sacrificial obedience.

It was too late when Uncle Hamid decided to retire and return home. By then time and sickness had made the communication of motives between father and son impossible.

Baba Jan had never been able to forgive his son for adopting a Western way of living, bringing his wife out of purdah, neglecting the religious education of his sons and doing all this openly and proudly.

Aunt Saira was Uncle Hamid's echo, tall and handsome, dominated by him, aggressive with others. He had her groomed by a succession of English 'lady-companions'. Before she was married, she had lived strictly in purdah, in an orthodox, middle-class household. Sometimes her smart saris, discreet make-up, waved hair, cigarette-holder and high-heeled shoes seemed to me like fancy dress.

Both my cousins Kamal and Saleem were still in England, where they had been sent as young boys.

Because most of her Indian friends considered their education would alienate them from their culture and their people, whenever my aunt talked of her sons she seemed on the defensive. She used to say only a real English education and not its imitation in Indian schools could produce a perfect blending of the best of the East and West. My uncle was above explanations.

After they arrived there seemed to be a new element in the air; an expectancy of unknown yet inevitable changes. In Aunt Abida's eyes was the look of one who has accepted abdication. I felt afraid when away from her.

By late afternoon all arrangements for the funeral had been completed. The men left for the funeral service in the mango grove on the outskirts of the village where the grass grew over the graves of my ancestors.

We started an hour later for Hasanpur. The great house was emptied and desolate.

Chapter Sixteen

THERE was always a sense of excitement at the thought of going to Hasanpur. It was more than the pride of possession seeing the land spread out to the horizon, rich and green; it was the fulfilment of a deep need to belong; it was a feeling of completeness, of a continuity between now and before and after. In the city the past attacked the present, and the future was lost in conflict.

Zahra and I sat near the curtained windows of the car on either side of Hakiman Bua, screened off from the driver. She did not object if we moved the curtains just enough to let us look out.

The car moved swiftly out of the gates, with my grandfather's name and the name of the house, Ashiana, inscribed in black on the marble slabs set into them. The sentry at the gates of our neighbour, the Raja of Bhimnagar's palace clicked his heels as the car drove past.

The towers of the palace were visible through the tall trees that stood sentinel behind forbidding walls.

Bhimnagar Palace fascinated us because it was said to be haunted by the Englishman who had built it in the reign of the last King of Oudh, and strange stories were told of his murder by a jealous Nawab whose beautiful courtesan mistress he had loved.

It was surrounded by lawns and orchards. There was a miniature lake with swans gliding among lotus blooms, and a marble pavilion set in a garden of roses. Here we had played in our childhood and still enjoyed scented, wind-stirred, leaf-shadowed, bird-echoing walks with the young Rani.

The car turned past the ruined, shell-holed walls that had once guarded the private garden of the king's favourite wife. We used to come here from school, a chattering crocodile of girls released from class-rooms, eager to play hide and seek among the spreading roots of banyan trees and the damp gloom of conservatories sheltering strange plants, and palms and ferns.

I forgot why we were in the car in my enjoyment of driving past the places that were dear to me because they were a part of my memories of living and growing up.

We came to a delicate whispering grove of eucalyptus trees and turned into the park of the zoo. A monkey screeched, a high note suddenly dropping low, and children imitated it, screaming with laughter. Birds whistled, animals called, and a lion roared. A jet-black panther paced like a disturbing shadow behind its bars.

"Look," said Zahra in excitement, "the tiger!" It stood and stretched in beautiful self-sufficiency on an elevation before its imitation rocky cave.

"I wish there were bars around the moat," said Zahra. "I always feel frightened thinking it will jump across it one day."

"I am frightened too. I dream about it; I dream it is free and I am trying to lock the doors of the house but always there is one door I cannot lock. . . ."

"How you children chatter!" Hakiman Bua grumbled. "You should be saying prayers for your grandfather's soul."

We became silent. And then the tree-shaded roads, and houses and gardens ended at the heart-shaped cross-roads leading towards the fashionable shopping centre with its clean, wide pavements, its colonnaded, veranda'd shops, offices, restaurants and cinemas.

A bell tinkled in a small roadside temple under a spreading *peepul* tree, and the buildings stopped respectfully on either side of it.

The car moved slowly through the traffic; tongas with bells tinkling and drivers clucking at their horses, cars with horns hooting, British soldiers on bicycles whistling at Anglo-Indian girls who smiled back or tossed their heads with a pretence at indifference.

exciting looking at shop windows, at posters
g films even from a distance. We were seldom
go in, but had to shop from the car, asking for things to be brought out to us. Once an English store had been kept open during a sale so that my aunts and the Rani of Amirpur could shop when no one else was allowed in.

A church spire rose to the right, marking the end of the shops, and the Mall was edged by trees again and gardens and gracious houses, and suddenly against the sky, seeming to block the road, rose the domes and finials of one of a pair of royal tombs.

The car swung to the right, and now the river was not far away, and the first of the bridges was left behind, named after the monkeys that for some strange reason made it their meeting-place, caricaturing human emotions.

"Look," said Zahra, "look at Queen Victoria." A crow balanced on the marble majesty of the imperial head, flapped its wings and flew off cawing.

"Poor Queen Victoria," we laughed.

Mrs Martin used to bring me to this garden every evening. While she sat reading or knitting on a bench I played round the marble pavilion in which sat the throned Empress, orbed and sceptred, elaborately robed in frozen dignity, the white and shining centre of burning green lawns stabbed by beds of flaming flowers.

We drove past palaces that were now clubs and courts, official residences and museums. The sun glittered on the golden umbrella over the dome of the palace that was now an English club.

Zahra said, "Imagine putting real gold on buildings."

"It is gilt," I contradicted.

"When the kings ruled," said Hakiman Bua, "it was pure gold. The *Angréz* took the gold away. There is much treasure hidden in this city, gold and priceless jewels, buried when the nobles fled from the white soldiers. There are tunnels leading from one old palace to another where it is hidden but no one can find it because of the evil spirits that strangle whoever enters." She sighed, "We come into the world with clenched fists but leave it with open empty hands and nothing lasts in this world. May the souls of the dead rest in peace!"

Hakiman Bua was determined not to let us forget the reason of our journey.

The car turned along the road by the river-bank. The slow-moving waters rippled with broken patterns of sunlight. Along the opposite bank washermen had spread out their washing. Gay colours, pastel colours splashed the ground and bodiless shirts and trousers danced on lines stretched above them.

Beyond were the fields, domes and arches of the University.

On the left the time- and shell-ravaged ruins of the Residency rose on their green eminence among creepers and trees and beds of flowers. The Union Jack fluttered on a ruined tower.

Zahra said, "The wind is lazy; it hardly moves the flag."

I said, "They say that flag is the only one in the world that flies night and day, but one day it will not fly there at all."

"I suppose you will take it down," said Zahra and suddenly added, "with Asad's help."

"How can you dare mention Asad?" I flamed.

"Bitia, Bitia! Is this the time to quarrel?" Hakiman Bua scolded.

The car slowed down abruptly as a group of young boys ran shouting in excitement across the road, looking up at the sky. "Catch it! Hold it!" they were shouting.

On a wide sandy space by the river a kite-flying contest was in progress. It was like a small fair with hawkers and vendors calling their wares, and lazy, contented people crowding round the contestants, looking up at the blue sky where coloured kites glided and spun and twisted in skilful manœuvres.

Suddenly, looking at an excited group, I called to Zahra forgetting our quarrel. "Look, Zahra, look! a cock-fight!"

The passionate birds were surrounded by excited people.

"Where? Where?" said Zahra. "Oh, I couldn't see. I wish I could have seen. . . ."

"What is the matter with you children?" Hakiman Bua reproved us. Then because she could never miss an occasion for telling a story she went on: "And what is there to see? Those days are gone when Nawabs lost their fortunes in cock-fights and quail-fights, and flew kites with a hundred- or a thousand-rupee note stuck on them."

The car moved faster and we turned to cross the river.

My favourite bridge was built as if to let one leave the city at a point where the essence of its beauty was captured. The river widened beyond the bridge in a sweeping curve and on its left bank and beyond was a rich skyline; from the mosque of Aurangzeb in the foreground to the Imambaras of the Nawab-Viziers and the distant clock tower piercing through the trees of its surrounding park. Beyond these, invisible, lay the heart of the old city with its crumbling houses of impoverished nobles, its crowded bazaars, its filth, its noise, its beauty, its skill, its craftsmen and artists, its narrow streets and the honey-tongued people who walked them.

We were across the bridge and passing through the outskirts where the straggling town began to wear a rural look. Small bazaars, dusty, fly-infested, unplastered houses, poverty and more dust. Bullock carts lumbered along the road, the tired bullocks and indifferent drivers taking little notice of the car's urgent warning horn. Peasants walked by the sides of the road, carrying their shoes in their hands to save the leather and rest their feet. Women in dusty swirling skirts walked behind them, leading half-naked children with big bellies and merry eyes.

When a car or lorry passed us we had to cover our mouths and noses, and stop our breath in protection against the dense cloud of dust that swept across the road, and filtered in through every crack.

The dust settled on the lower branches of the great

gnarled trees with writhing, petrified roots that lined the road, and on the crops in the fields. In the distance the mango and guava groves were green and the mud-walled villagers were a part of the earth.

Eight miles out of town we passed the white walls surrounding the house and garden Raja Hasan Ahmad of Amirpur had built as a guest house and a retreat. It served as a landmark telling me Hasanpur was near, and the miles from that point seemed shorter.

Soon we were turning in on the Hasanpur road, and the car shook and jumped over ruts. Baba Jan had maintained the road, but repairs were proving increasingly expensive. The dust blown behind us seemed solid. Bullock-carts creaked to a stop to let us pass on the narrow road and villagers crossed over, away from the dust, bowing low in deep obeisance, salaaming.

I felt a sense of contentment. There was a relationship that made these people different from the others we had passed on the highway.

The car crossed a culvert, and as we rocked over it, feeling an emptiness pitching within our stomachs, Hakiman Bua said, "Ya, Allah!" and Zahra and I wanted to laugh, but to the right we could see the path to the mango grove with its graves, and were silenced.

Soon we could see the high, white walls of our house beyond the first huts of Hasanpur. The driver blew the horn and barking pariah-dogs chased the dust through the iron gates. The car stopped before the centuries-old heavy, wooden, copper-studded door of the zenana. We crossed the high, wooden lintel into the dark entrance hall where ancient palanquins once rested, and stepped out into the bright, sun-lit courtyard. The first person to greet us was Sharifan, the *Mirasin*, and the gravity of her manner set the seal of mourning on the day.

Sharifan and her chorus of female relations sang and clowned at every celebration, every feast in the homes of

Hasanpur families and families related to them. They and their *dholak* were a symbol of festivity.

Sharifan was known for her fine voice and her repertoire of folk songs, particularly lewd and suggestive marriage songs, but when she sang the traditional lament of the bride at the moment of leaving her childhood home, no one could remain dry-eyed. She had an uninhibited comic gift of mimicry and her most popular turn was acting a mem-sahib and singing like a mem-sahib, howling like a yodelling cat. In her animated gabble no other words were intelligible beyond "Well—Yes—No".

She always greeted me with a flood of her wordless 'English', affectionately calling me "little mem-sahib". But today she embraced me silently.

Chapter Seventeen

THE house was crowded not only with relatives from Hasanpur itself, but from neighbouring villages. They sourrounded my aunts who sat on the large *takht* in the high-arched, deep veranda. Village women squatted in the courtyard and their children sat by them silently, or stood and stared without playfulness while flies settled round their eyes and mouths. A stale smell of oil came from their bodies. A woman nursed her baby, her coarse shirt pulled away from her heavy breast and the ragged *dopatta* barely covering her.

Again the salutations and embraces, the sighs and the sorrow. My feelings were so dulled by repetition that it did not seem to matter that Baba Jan was dead. It mattered more to be alive myself, and in Hasanpur where life did not seem like a puzzle with its pieces scattered.

Zahra and I were soon surrounded by cousins of varying degrees of relationship. Among them was my favourite cousin Zainab, a plump, shapeless girl of sixteen who accepted her plainness with the good humour that brightened her colourless life. "In the next world I'll be beautiful for ever. If I were pretty now I'd lose my looks by worrying about losing them." She did not hide her interest in marriage. "Now I serve my mother and father and brothers, then I'll serve my husband, my father-in-law and my mother-in-law. But at least I'll be able to wear jewels and nice clothes."

It was Zainab, brought up in a more confined home than me, who told me of sex, ridiculing it because it was frightening, a girl's inevitable martyrdom whose horror could only be lessened through bawdy jokes.

Yet she thought romantically of love, the sad, unfulfilled love of traditional song and story. She had once confessed to me that she was fond of Asad, but she could not think of marrying him because she was not his equal in blood.

Zainab's grandmother had been a dancing girl. Though his first wife had never spoken to her, and they had lived in separate houses, she had been given the respect due to a wife of my grandfather's cousin, and the children and grandchildren of both wives were treated with equal affection. Only in matters concerning marriage and property were distinctions made.

After some time, Zahra and Zainab and I carried out a string bed from the veranda and put it in a quiet corner of the courtyard where we could be undisturbed. Suddenly Zainab said, "Look, there is Nandi", and called out, "*Aré*, Nandi!"

"Nandi," I called happily. "Come here."

She smiled, and moving with swift grace came and sat down on the ground, and held my feet in her hands saying, "Salaam, Bitia. I am happy to see you, Laila Bitia—and you, Zahra Bitia."

"How have you been, Nandi?" I asked.

"I am alive, Bitia." Nandi's eyes were like the dust-covered fields.

"I wish you were back, Nandi."

"I want to go back, Bitia. I don't like living here. My uncle's wife hates me. I do all the work, yet she says I am a burden to her. Even my grandmother beats me."

"Not you," said Zahra smiling, "she beats the devil in you that made you do shameful things."

"You know, Laila Bitia, I did nothing. What happened was not my fault."

"You can't clap with one hand, Nandi," teased Zainab.

"Nothing happens to those who really do wrong because they take care to hide it," Nandi said significantly.

"What have you done, Zainab?" I joked.

"I don't know, beyond telling a few lies about saying my prayers, or how many chapters of the Quran I've finished."

"You know, Zainab Bitia, whom I'm talking about," persisted Nandi.

"Please tell us," pleaded Zahra.

Nandi said, "We poor people get a bad name because we cannot stay locked up. But what of all those uncles and cousins who wander in and out of zenanas? They're men, aren't they? Thieves steal the best guarded of treasure."

"Hold your wicked tongue, Nandi," scolded Zainab. "Don't malign respectable people."

"Respectable people?" mocked Nandi. "Respectability can be preserved like pickle in gold and silver. If this girl—you know the one I mean—had been poor would they have been able to bribe the midwife and get rid of her baby and then buy a husband for her?"

"Nandi, you are shameless and wicked," said Zahra, then turned to Zainab: "Who is she talking about? If you don't tell me I can always find out."

"The *moulvis's* daughter," Zainab said reluctantly. "Nandi, your tongue should be burned."

"You shouldn't be so cruel, Nandi," I said.

Nandi's eyes filled with tears, "I was turned out by my father and mother for less reason. I only said what other people think."

"I must go and sit near Phuphi Jan," I said suddenly. Zahra got up too, "I'll see what Ammi is doing."

"I'll come with you," Zainab said.

Nandi sat quietly on the ground and looked at us with large hurt eyes. I felt sorry for her.

"Nandi, if I send someone with you to say I want you to stay here with me, will your grandmother let you come back?"

"She cannot refuse you, Bitia," Nandi said happily, drying her eyes and smiling.

Chapter Eighteen

AFTER the evening meal was finished Zainab had to go home and see whether her grandmother needed anything. Zahra and I asked for permission to go with her, and pay our respects to the old lady who was not well enough to come to join the mourners. We were oppressed by the atmosphere in the home, and wanted an excuse to get away.

The houses of my great-grandfather's and his brother's descendants were near each other on the edge of the village. It was possible to walk from one to the other through the doors built in the courtyard walls.

Nandi walked ahead of us carrying a lantern and when she saw a man-servant she called out "Purdah! Purdah!" He turned his back and looked away until we were out of sight.

She led us through the yard of the carpenter's shed. I remembered coming here as a little child to watch the men at work, sawing and planing and carving. The head carpenter had once made me a little carved doll's cradle, though I had asked for a bow and arrows.

We passed the sheds where the bulls and bullocks were stabled that drew water from the wells, and pulled the ploughs in the fields, and dragged the heavy carts that carried grain and wood for us to the city. Near them were the cows and buffaloes that provided milk and curds and *ghee*.

I was frightened of those great animals stirring and breathing in the acrid dung-smelling dark, and drew near Zainab. She giggled and pushed me near the stalls. I screamed as I ran after Nandi.

That was the longest part of the short journey; Zainab's home was barely seven minutes' walk away.

I enjoyed visiting it because Zainab's grandmother and

mother wrapped one round with a love that was rich, and uncritical.

They were much poorer than others in the family. Zainab's father was lazy and content with the rent he collected from his small portion of inherited land. He was short with a round paunch and cheeks that seemed like half-filled balloons. His beard was red, his hair white and his voice was like scraping wires.

All day he sat outside the door of his house on a string bed, smoking his *hookah* and gossiping, but was galvanised into action whenever vast quantities of food had to be cooked. He was asked to supervise the cooks and organise the kitchens for every feast in the vast tribal network of the family. The more guests there were the happier he was; counting them in hundreds sent him into a state of ecstasy. He moved among the bubbling cauldrons like a magician.

Zainab's mother had a knowledge of medicinal herbs from which she prepared potions, plasters and purgatives. This irked professionals like the village *hakim* and *vaid*. However she had little time to spare for anything but looking after her own family, and goading her husband to look after their property. She had six children—three sons older than Zainab, and two daughters younger, and had lost two others. Had she had more she would have been as cheerful, because she believed that God looked after them all and they looked after each other.

Her faith in God gave her unlimited courage. Once during an epidemic of cholera in the village, she had stayed to nurse the sick because she believed that there was no escape from what God had ordained, and therefore no point in being afraid.

Zainab was the first to get to the heavy wooden door of the house and it creaked as she pushed it open. Then holding aside the hessian curtain she called out, "Dādi Amma, look who's come to see you, Zahra and Laila."

There was a clatter from the mud-walled veranda on

the left. It was Kalvi, the maid servant's daughter, cleaning pots and pans; and the light from Nandi's lantern fell on her dim figure as she squatted holding a piece of hemp in one hand and an ash-covered copper bowl in the other.

"Salaam," she called out.

"Salaam," we answered.

We passed under the sloping, rough thatch supported on wooden poles that made a shelter against the sun and rain, then crossed the small courtyard into the mud and brick veranda with age-blackened carved wooden pillars. Beyond it lay the long low-roofed room with its small iron-barred windows where Zainab, her sisters and her grandmother lived. At right angles completing the square were two other rooms, used by her parents and brothers.

We followed Zainab into the stuffy room. The lamplight suggested shapes of beds, bundles and boxes crowding the confined space. It fell on the face of old Dādi Amma, deepening her wrinkles, making caverns of the dim eyes lost in the ruins of a once-beautiful face. At the foot of the bed with the bedding pushed away from under her, pressing her mistress's feet sat their servant, the anonymous mother of Kalvi as ugly as poverty, as thin as hunger. Kalvi came and stood near the door with the unselfconscious grace, the intentness, and the intimate yet withdrawn smile of the blind. Her marbled eyes turned towards all sounds.

"Ādāb Dādi Amma," Zahra and I said, raising our hands to our foreheads.

"May you live long, my children," she replied and stretched out her arms on which the ill-fitting skin hung loosely, and embraced us. We said "Salaam" to the maid-servant, and she stretched out her skinny arm in turn and touched our heads. "Live long, children. May you flower and bear fruit."

Dādi Amma felt our faces with her fingers and said, "My

eyes are old, the darkness blinds me, and I cannot see the faces of my daughters as they grow in beauty."

Age had left her more helpless than Kalvi whose blindness had sharpened her senses.

She said briskly, "Zainab Béti, get some sweets for your sisters. Go and get the *halva* made by your mother."

"I'll go, Bibiji," said Kalvi going into the friendly darkness.

Zainab's sisters sat on their beds and stared at us silently, and coyly hid their faces in their *dopattas* when we smiled at them. Dādi Amma spoke of Baba Jan and sighed over old days.

We sat on the beds and ate the *halva* and were content. Then the curtain over the outer door rose and fell and Zainab's eldest brother came in. He was very thin, very pale and had wild curly hair. He had been clever as a boy and his mother had sold some jewellery to send him to Aligarh University. After a year, he returned home a delicate consumptive.

One day he had burnt all the books he had brought back from his college, because his father had wanted to sell them. I had seen them once, on a shelf in his room, Shakespeare, Macaulay, Ruskin, Dumas and Conan Doyle resting against the mud walls under the thatch.

Father and son hardly ever spoke to each other; only his mother gave him unquestioning love, understanding that he felt cheated by life.

He came in and sat down on the edge of his sister's bed.

"Son," said his grandmother, "why are you so silent?"

"I am tired," he answered.

"Go and lie down then."

"I will," but he sat on, then said to me in English, "Now that you have passed your examination, I presume you will not be returning to school?"

"No," I replied.

"Will you study further?"

"I don't know. It depends on Hamid Chacha."

"Everything depends on someone else," he said dryly,

then with a change of tone, "I have been talking to Asad. Do you agree with him?"

"About what?" I asked, and Zahra stirred uneasily.

"About politics."

"Asad is going to drive the English away," he mocked. "Drive them away with Truth and Non-violence. His idealism is really ignorance; he has not studied history. Has it ever happened that anyone has given up power easily? Not even one's parents, who tell one all day how much they sacrifice for one."

He was talking compulsively, as if tired of a long silence, breaking into Urdu every now and again.

"I had a friend at college who used to talk for hours about the Russian revolution. He said we should learn its lessons, and destroy tyranny. So you see he believed in a different method from Asad's. He called himself a rationalist, and said I was doped with religion. He talked to me of Free Will, of the Freedom of the individual, and of plans. Talk! Talk! Talk!" He laughed bitterly and then continued, without caring whether we listened, or understood.

"Make plans! But what if my plans don't fit in with the plans others make? What if my freedom gets tangled with the freedom of others? Life is like knotted skeins of thread, and one gets caught in the tangle not knowing the beginning or the end."

He had to stop speaking because of the fit of coughing that shook him, and I said, trying to hide my discomfort, "Asad is right; we must be free."

"What difference will it make?" he said in a tired voice. "What difference does anything make? Look around this village. The people rotted under the rulers of our own race, as they do under the English and as they will do if we rule ourselves again. Asad has always been a fool, stretching out for things beyond his reach."

Zahra said, "It is getting late, we ought to go."

We said our *adabs* hurriedly and were blessed by the old lady. Zainab saw us to the wooden door.

Her brother disturbed me as if a cripple watched me skipping and dancing by.

Nandi led us with the bobbing, golden light of the lantern into the smoke-smelling mist of the village night.

Chapter Nineteen

AFTER the ritual ceremonies on the third day of Baba Jan's death, when the mourners had been fed and gone, each having read a portion of the Quran and prayed for the dead, and food had been distributed among the poor, we were left to think of the future.

There was a terrace in the oldest part of the house which was almost always deserted. Zahra and Zainab and I used to go there to be on our own.

One day as we sat there, Zainab said, "It won't be long before you are a bride, Zahra. I heard my mother talking about it to my grandmother."

"You have big ears, and a bigger imagination," answered Zahra, smiling with secret pleasure.

I remembered Zainab telling me how the brides of the household had been kept in the rooms behind this terrace, and their bridegrooms crept up the steep stairs at night, and left as stealthily before anyone was awake.

"But why?" I had asked naïvely.

"Why do you think?" she had giggled, "What do you think they went for so secretly? Surely they couldn't flaunt it before their elders."

"Zainab," I asked her now, "do you remember what you once told me about those people stealing up here like thieves to their wives? I was wondering how long they kept it up. It must have been ridiculous after they had children."

For a moment Zainab looked puzzled, then she laughed: "I couldn't understand what you were talking about. My mother doesn't come in front of my father even now, when my grandmother is present."

"And you know Ammi did not speak to me in Baba Jan's presence," added Zahra.

"Well, I think it's nasty."

"It makes no difference what you think about it," said Zainab, shrugging her shoulders.

"I wish someone could explain it to me," I argued. "Hamid Chacha talks to Saira Chachi no matter who is in the room. A thing can't be shameful at one time and not another, for one person and not another. Besides if it is such a shameful business being married and having children, why talk of nothing but marriage from the moment a girl is born?"

Zainab teased, "Perhaps you will go about arm in arm with your husband talking 'git-pit, git-pit' in English. What will you do, Zahra?"

"It depends . . ."

"It depends on whether you marry a 'black sahib' or not," Zainab laughed.

"What will you do?" Zahra asked her.

"Whatever I am told to. Laila, don't look so solemn and I'll tell you a story of a girl who was not like you and believed in old customs. When she was married, and the time came for the ceremony of seeing the face of the bride, she was carried in where the guests were waiting. As you know a bride must not move nor make a sound when the veil of flowers is moved aside each time someone wishes to see her face. After a while the woman who was supporting her felt the girl's body become as heavy as lead. She had fainted. And what do you think they discovered? A centipede had buried itself in her foot and she hadn't even taken an extra breath."

I said, "How stupid and ridiculous! I think it's old-fashioned nonsense. Don't you?"

"I don't think about such things. I try to do as I am told," Zainab said as she got up. "Let us go down now. You are all becoming too serious."

When we were tired of being in the house, we went into the neighbouring orchard. It was surrounded by a high mud wall so that it was possible for purdah women to walk in it.

The breeze rustled through the mango and guava trees, and chameleons slithered through the arching vines. The strong sun made patterns that shifted with the wind in the leaves.

We sat in the shade on the steps of the small, slender-pillared pavilion by the rose-garden and talked of days that had gone and wondered about the days that were to come.

Nandi said, looking at the flowering mango branches, "It should be a good season for mangoes."

"If it doesn't rain at the wrong time," said Zainab, "or too much or too little. One can never be sure of anything."

"If we're here," said Zahra, "I'll pick them and eat them straight from the trees."

"And we'll put up the swing again," I said.

During the rainy season we used to hang a plank on thick ropes, on the thickest branch of the tallest mango tree, and Zainab would sing the songs of the season, as we swung, with our *dopattas* streaming behind, high above the walls, able to look at the green world stretched out under purple clouded skies.

"I think," said Zahra, "that we'll have to stay here in Hasanpur."

"I won't mind," I said, but Zainab was doubtful.

"You would, if it had to be for ever. What about your city friends?"

"I have none. Sita has written she will be going to England to study." And I sighed with self-pity and envy.

"Would you like to go?" Zainab asked.

"I want to go right round the world, don't you?"

"I want to go to the moon," she mocked.

"I just want to go home to my parents," said Nandi.

"You never know where your Kismet might take you," said Zahra wisely.

"Your husband, you mean," teased Zainab, and Zahra giggled, "Don't talk nonsense."

"I'll go one day," I said firmly, "I'll go round the world."

"You don't even know whether you will go to college," Zahra said, "You don't know what is being decided."

There seemed no purpose in dreaming. It was better to gossip until it was time to go home; for between them Nandi and Zainab knew all that happened in the village, and all that should not have happened.

Chapter Twenty

AUNT Abida had become very quiet and spent a longer time sitting on the prayer-mat in deep meditation, after finishing the formal prayers. It seemed as if time meant nothing to her but its divisions into the five hours of prayer sounded by the *muezzin* from the mosque.

Even the old ladies of the village noticed it, and Zainab's grandmother said to Aunt Saira and Aunt Majida, "It is good to pray, but the time has not yet come when she should spend it wholly in the remembrance of God. She should be the mother of sons, and enrich a man's home."

Aunt Majida sighed and cried, and Aunt Saira agreed that something should be done.

One morning Zahra and I were sent for by Uncle Hamid. He was in his sitting-room, and my aunts were already with him. Aunt Saira sat next to him on a sofa and Aunt Majida opposite them. Zahra and I sat stiffly on the straight-backed wooden chairs kept between. Asad and Zahid came in after us and stood by the door until Uncle Hamid motioned them to sit down.

There was silence while Uncle Hamid took his pouch and pipe from his pocket, filled the pipe and lit one match after another to light it.

I looked at the pictures on the wall. Photographs and prints, Rapheal's 'Madonna', 'The Stag at Bay', 'Dante and Beatrice', 'Storm at Sea'.

I looked up at the fan, stretched across the room with its flaps of stiff matting edged with green cotton frills, hanging stiffly from a thick wooden beam.

In summer its slow creaking movement put one to sleep until the coolie sitting outside on the veranda pulling at its rope, fell asleep himself. Then the chorus of curses woke everyone.

Uncle Hamid cleared his throat and all eyes turned towards him.

He put the matches into the ash-tray, leaned back, and after a pause, said, "I've arrived—after careful consideration—at certain decisions regarding your future. You children are now at an age——"

"You had better speak in Urdu," Aunt Saira interrupted; "your sisters will understand you more easily."

He frowned slightly, and continued in Urdu, "You are now at an age when any steps that are taken will decide your future life. I have always believed that elders should not force their decisions on the young. That is why I have asked you to come here to listen to what we think is best for you."

What if we did not agree? What alternative was there for us? I thought. nope

Uncle Hamid went on, "Majida wishes that Zahra should live with her in Hasanpur until—er—until such time as—well—as the situation changes."

Aunt Majida said, "*Bhayya*, I have told you everything depends on you. I told Mohsin Bhai I would do nothing without your advice. If you agree, the marriage can take place at any time you choose. Whom have we got in the world but you to care for us?" And she began to cry softly.

"Majida," he said impatiently, "I have already told you I shall go into the matter carefully. There seems nothing wrong with the young man, but I shall make further inquiries. You must not worry unnecessarily."

Asad's hands were clenched in his lap, and he kept his eyes fixed on them.

I thought of that other 'conference' weeks ago, and was glad Uncle Mohsin was not present at this one.

Aunt Majida sniffed, and wiped her eyes in her shawl.

Uncle Hamid leaned towards me and said, pontifically, "I have always believed in the education of girls; it is the duty of parents and guardians to give them the kind of education that will best fit them for their responsibilities in this changing world." He paused, lit a match and puffed rapidly at his pipe.

Aunt Saira said, "Young men want their wives to be educated enough to meet their friends and to entertain. Nowadays they lay down all sorts of conditions."

"I wish you would stop interrupting with your irrelevant remarks, Saira. I was not even thinking of marriage. It is the principle of the thing that matters." He banged his fist on the table to emphasise each word. Then he searched angrily for his match-box.

Aunt Saira said sulkily, "Zahra, give your uncle the match-box. It is lying near his foot." She was unable to shake off tradition and never addressed him by name.

Aunt Abida suddenly stood up, walked to my chair and stood by me with her hand on my shoulder, and said slowly, "I'm glad it's been decided that Laila can continue her education. It is as her father would have wished."

Uncle Hamid said quietly, "Yes, Abida." Then he cleared his throat, and added, "But there are still some months before schools and colleges re-open. During that time she is free to stay where she chooses—with us, or with you here in Hasanpur. After all, Laila, both places are your home, literally yours, as you have a share in them."

He turned to me, "Laila, what do you wish to do?"

My heart was beating as I said, "I shall stay here."

Aunt Abida's fingers tightened over my shoulders.

"Very well", Uncle Hamid said, "if that is your wish." He pulled at his pipe, looked at Asad and Zahid and said, "As for you, I shall see that your studies will continue as before. Later we must decide what work you are best suited for. Meanwhile I shall arrange for you to stay in a hostel. It is better for you in every way, more conducive to hard work and discipline."

"As you wish, Chacha," said Zahid quietly.

Asad shifted uneasily, then stammered, "I want to leave. I want to go to Delhi."

"What did you say?" said Uncle Hamid, sitting up

erect. Everyone stared at Asad, even Zahra. How had he dared to express an opinion of his own?

"I want to go to study at the Jamia in Delhi," repeated Asad, almost in a whisper, "I believe that is the kind of institution where I can best learn how to serve my country."

"Young man," said Hamid Chacha loudly. "Finish your education and think of politics afterwards, when you are not dependent on others."

Asad flushed, "I shall not be a burden on anyone. I shall work there as well as study. I have thought the matter over."

"You have thought the matter over!" said Uncle Hamid icily, "and you make your own decisions without consulting those who have made you fit to do so!"

It might have been Baba Jan speaking when his wishes were thwarted by those he considered inferior or beholden to him. I was frightened, recognising the voice of authority. Why must power always be used to humiliate?

Asad's hands were trembling and he went on speaking as if he had not heard, "I think—had my father been alive—he would have agreed with me."

He had used the most effective weapon; it had no logical answer and it aimed at both the heart and the conscience.

Uncle Hamid flushed, seemed disconcerted, then said shortly, "I have nothing more to say." He pushed back his chair angrily as he stood up, looked round and repeated, "Nothing more. Everything has been settled."

Through the silence came the *muezzin's* call to midday prayers.

Chapter Twenty One

AFTER Baba Jan's death it was as if tight hands had been loosened which had tied together those who had lived under the power of his will and authority.

Within the year both Aunt Abida and Zahra were married.

Sheikh Ejaz Ali was the man chosen to be Aunt Abida's husband. He was a distant relation whose wife had died of consumption five years before. His son and daughters were married, and he lived in a village, twelve miles from Hasanpur, and looked after his small estate, having retired from the Provincial Civil Service. He had, for a time, served under Uncle Hamid towards whom he still displayed an attitude of deference. He was a tall, thin, negative man who had no other claim to recognition but that he was to be Aunt Abida's husband.

When Hakiman Bua was told of the decision she wept with joy and said, "Allah be praised that the years of my Abida Bitia's life will not be empty. Who can know what is written? This was the man for whom her *Kismet* had kept her waiting all these years."

I envied Hakiman Bua's faith, particularly that last night before Aunt Abida was married. I had not been able to sleep, helpless to convey to her my love and loneliness, and at last had crept into her bed as in frightened moments of childhood. When I put my arms around her she clung to me as if it was she who sought for comfort and assurance. Her tears cramped my heart, misted my mind. Who could answer my questions about fate and duty and suffering?

Later, when Zahra was married, there was little of the ceremonial, spread over many days of feasting, music and dancing, that coloured and brightened the secluded life of the community; yet it was not stripped to the bare bones of its Islamic reality, as a simple contract.

Once again the house at Hasanpur was crowded, but keyed to a brighter note. The zenana stirred and vibrated with movement and noise as guests and maid-servants and children and groups of village women milled around, their voices raised and shrill with excitement. For every woman and girl there was an excuse to wear the richest of clothes and jewels, and the whole house spilled with gem-set colours and throbbed with the rhythm of the *mirasins'* gay marriage songs, and the insistent beat of their drums.

The women congratulated Aunt Majida and wished her joy saying, "Now you are relieved of your burden of responsibility, now you have done your duty. You are free to obey the other commands of Allah and His Prophet. Now you can devote your life to Him and make the holy pilgrimage to Mecca."

The only quiet corner was Zahra's room where she was kept in seclusion. Zainab and I and the ten other girls who were Zahra's nearest cousins, dressed alike in the clothes made for us by Aunt Majida, were the envy of all other girls. All they wanted was to sit and stare at the bride they would be one day.

The elders were more curious about Zahra's dowry. It was displayed in a room guarded by Hakiman Bua who was resplendent in the new clothes and gold jewellery made for her. The women counted the number of clothes, the number and value of the sets of jewellery, pots and pans and household goods. They estimated the cost of the silver bridal bed. This was the information they had to pass on to others who could not be present, and by which the family would be judged.

Then they turned their attention to the clothes and jewels, the scents and oils, the sacks of sugar and nuts and sweets which had been brought by the bridegroom, and judged his family accordingly.

The bridegroom was led into the zenana after the marriage ceremony. It had been impossible up to then, peeping through cracks in doors, and slits in the bamboo curtains, to catch more than a glimpse of his garlanded figure in a gold brocade *achkan* surrounded by his companions, seated under a gold-embroidered relief canopy.

When he came to the door of the zenana, Zainab, being the eldest amongst us, refused to let him enter until his sister had paid us the customary forfeit. We agreed to accept a hundred and one rupees before she let him come in. Excitement rippled around him as everyone tried to push closer, He was like his photograph, curly-haired, full-lipped, with deep-set eyes. He was stocky, a shade darker than Zahra and had a pleasant smile.

I thought as I looked at him, "This is no longer a stranger. This is Naseer Bhai, Zahra's husband."

For Zahra the moment of seeing him was to come much later.

In the morning when Zainab had been applying the paste of henna leaves to her feet and hands she had felt them trembling. During the ceremony itself she had cried bitterly, but was quite calm when the time came to dress her in the bridal clothes and jewels that had been brought by the bridegroom.

Anointed with oil and attar, dressed in scarlet and covered with jewels, her hair gold-dusted, the palms and the soles of her feet henna'd, her face covered with a cascade of flowers and a veil of fine gold threads, Zahra was carried into the room where the women and girls impatiently waited to see the bride.

I felt curiously detached towards that glittering, scented bundle, no longer Zahra but the symbol of others' desires.

The moment came for the bridegroom to be called in. He was led near Zahra, and made to sit down opposite her. A silken *dopatta* was thrown over their heads and the Quran, a mirror, and a burning candle placed between them.

At that moment, in the mirror, Zahra for the first time looked into the eyes of her husband.

Zainab put her arm round my neck, trembling with excitement. I felt withdrawn and alien in my thoughts. That moment would have been the same had it been any other reflection Zahra saw. Did no shadow fall across the mirror? No reflection of pained eyes? Was love so pliable? Was it to be recognised only in poems of unrequited suffering? Why question what others accepted? Why was I allowed to become different?

Around the silent moment the women's voices rose in excitement; jokes mingled with blessings and the *mirasins* sang a song of joy.

Part Two

Chapter One

ALL those people who had so far been a part of life were pushed farther and farther away. After they were married Aunt Abida and Zahra went away to their own homes. Aunt Majida stayed on at Hasanpur with Ustanji and Hajjan Bibi as companions, living in one part of the large house, surrounded by closed, empty rooms with blind-eyed windows, and drifted deeper into the gloom of hypochondriac melancholy.

Asad lived his austere life in Delhi, studying and teaching; while Zahid, though nearer home, was an infrequent visitor. Uncle Mohsin, who reciprocated Uncle Hamid's dislike of him, no longer came to the house.

Old Karam Ali, Baba Jan's servant, died a year after him. Hakiman Bua went away with Aunt Abida, and Ramzano with Zahra. Nandi ran away with a pedlar who used to come to the village from the near-by market town. Only Saliman was left to remind me of past days when it was decided by my elders that she was to be my personal servant.

When, after the death of her brother, Zainab was married there was no one left in Hasanpur for whom I cared deeply. My visits became short and infrequent because Uncle Hamid and his wife spent only such time there as estate affairs made necessary. Not that they ignored Hasanpur and their estate. As *Taluqdar* of Hasanpur my uncle had a crest designed from an old family seal. It was stamped on their stationery and silver, and was worn as a badge on the turbans of their liveried servants.

I went back from Hasanpur to live with my aunt and uncle in the house where I was born and found it changed, and I remembered the past and was sad.

The first night of our return Saliman brought her small string bed, and put it at the foot of mine.

"I thought you might be afraid alone," she said in explanation. I sensed her own fears and loneliness.

The night was warm and heavy with the promise of rain. She had brought the beds into the veranda from the courtyard. The electric fan disturbed the mosquito net and sounded a long hypnotic note. Saliman lay like a cocoon, and I longed to sleep.

Every now and again the circled moon halted in a clear strip of sky on its lunatic chase through monstrous dark shapes of clouds edged with silver. Then in its emerging light the veranda and courtyard and lawn were empty. No other beds, no other cocoons. No water-jars garlanded with jasmine resting on wooden stands. No wooden *takhts*, stripped for the night of their white sheets and carpets and bolsters after Aunt Abida and Aunt Majida and visitors, relatives and maid-servants had gone away to sleep.

The sky was dark, and the first slow drops of rain began to fall. There was no response now from a suddenly disturbed household. No shouts, no bustle, no fumbling with the poles of mosquito nets, no dragging of beds from courtyard and lawn into verandas and rooms. Only the sound of a sudden wind rushing through the trees and then the furious rain.

Saliman moaned, and as the sky split with lightning and thunder, she cried softly: "Bitia, Bitia."

But I buried my head in my pillow and did not answer.

Chapter Two

ON the gates of our house, Ashiana, a new marble tablet proclaimed the new master, but less effectively than the changed character of the house.

It had been repainted a stone colour and the gardens were personally supervised by my aunt, who was not confined to the zenana as her sisters-in-law had been.

New furnishings and decorations altered the rooms, changing them from friends to acquaintances. I missed the ghostliness of the drawing-room. It had had a personality, gloomy and grotesquely rich, reflecting one of Baba Jan's eccentricities.

In their old age Baba Jan and his friends, the Raja of Amirpur and Thakur Balbir Singh, had taken to attending auctions in much the same spirit as had once made them big-game hunters, and they displayed their trophies with a similar sense of triumph. But while they were discriminating about tigers and panthers, and antlered stags, china and crystal, ivory and jade, marble and metal, prints and paintings were crowded together regardless of beauty or genuineness.

Now the room looked naked, its contents distributed between the rubbish-heap, junk-room and Hasanpur. The junk-room was my aunt's delight. She couldn't bear to throw anything away.

"You never know when it will come in useful," she would say of a button or a bedstead, and in the dark godown discarded things decayed, and could not be found when needed.

The furniture, too, was changed. The old-fashioned straight-backed, brocade-upholstered chairs, and the marble and brass-topped tables round which they had been mathematically grouped, were exiled to Hasanpur. The rejuvenated rooms reminded me of English homes I had visited with Mrs Martin, yet they were as different as copies of a painting from the original.

Of the old servants only a few remained. The old cook was replaced by a *khansamah* who was as proud of his testimonials from English employers as of medals won for valour. Instead of Karam Ali with his fund of tales, and his protégé Chuttan who had flirted with Ramzano and Saliman, there were Lal Singh, my uncle's trained valet, and Ghulam Ali who ruled over the dining-room and pantry.

Ghulam Ali was so resplendent in his livery and white gloves that every meal appeared a banquet. Until I got used to him, longing for the informality of past meals served by maid-servants, I fumbled with knives and forks, awed by the array of shining implements playing a part in a ritual, as if the very proper Mrs Martin had never taught me how to use them as a child.

The maid-servants' courtyard was no longer a busy little world on its own with Hajjan Bibi and Ustaniji its pensioners, and Hakiman Bua ruling over it with Ramzano and Saliman as her slaves and the wives of other servants as her courtiers.

I went there only in search of Saliman. She kept her distance from the new maid-servants.

"This Nizaman Bua," she told me, "has a long tongue and when she nags I feel as if I had cleaned my teeth with a *neem* twig dipped in sour lemon juice. Her heart isn't big like Hakiman Bua's: it is like a dried mango seed. As for Begum Sahib's Ayah, I think she's sucked the blood of one of those fine mem-sahibs she worked for, she puts on such airs and graces you'd think she were a white woman come out of a charcoal pit."

"Are they unkind to you?"

"I don't give them a chance, Bitia. I don't go looking for thorns to prick me. But you should see them sometimes—like snakes hissing at each other, and watching which will strike first."

Nizaman was a skinny, sharp-featured woman who considered herself entitled to be respected by the other servants because she was the sister of the woman who had been Aunt Saira's wet nurse. That gave her the rights almost of a relation.

The Ayah was a small, dark woman from the far south. She was at a disadvantage in verbal duels with Nizaman because she could talk neither Urdu nor Hindi well, but she made up for it by the volume of her shrill voice and the expressiveness of her gestures. She had been with my aunt for the last five years and was so well trained as a lady's maid that Nizaman's jealousy could not oust her from favour.

When Nizaman and the Ayah quarrelled Nizaman expected Saliman to side with her, saying, "We are the same, you and I. You are not an outsider. You are like my own daughter."

But Saliman would stay neutral, because she did not care for either.

We heard the calls of the street vendors coming over the high walls but no tradesmen were allowed through the front gates. Even Kamli Shah no longer came to extort charity through our superstitious fears.

No longer did relations, and relations of relations come to stay whenever they wished, and for as long as they pleased. Even Aunt Majida and Aunt Abida came only when there was some special reason and did not stay for long.

Aunt Abida's visits had a curious effect on me, as if I blundered through a forest of light and shadow. It seemed I had to cross an increasing distance, as the feeling grew that my problems had begun to crowd upon those personal ones which were a part of her new life.

My relationship with Uncle Hamid and Aunt Saira was simpler and there was nothing deeper than its outward forms. They looked after me, and I tried not to displease them.

They had little time to spare me from their many interests.

My uncle was on the governing body of many schools, a member of the Executive Council of the University. He represented the *Taluqdars* on the Board of Directors of mills and companies in which their Association had shares, and on civic committees.

However, there seemed to be a SENSE of struggling to retain what had been Baba Jan's accepted heritage. Uncle Hamid seemed to talk of nothing but opposition and obstruction, manœuvring and manipulation, parties and personalities in an increasing struggle for power.

It was part of my uncle's pattern of life that my aunt should be actively concerned with social welfare and various women's organisations.

Apart from their estimable activities in the course of public service, my aunt and uncle were kept busy with social engagements. In winter, during the Season, there were parties at home, parties elsewhere. There were receptions and races, parades and tournaments, culminating in a garden party and ball at Government House. In summer the pattern was repeated in the hill station to which the Government moved.

I was too young to share their social life. We met at meal-times, and on the rare occasions they spent a quiet evening at home. Their conversation was about such matters as float easily on the surface of consciousness. I posed no problems of upbringing. I was outwardly acquiescent.

Chapter Three

I FELT I lived in two worlds; an observer in an outside world, and solitary in my own—except when I was with the friends I had made at College. Then the blurred, confusing double image came near to being one.

Nita Chatterji was the strongest character among my friends. She was short, plump and always in a hurry as if she were tripping on the heels of time. Her large eyes seemed to bulge as if strained, and her mouth closed impatiently over wide, strong teeth. Her hair was thick and waved darkly away from her pale face, to a carelessly looped 'bun'. It was very beautiful, but she deliberately neglected it because of a puritanical obsession against feminine vanity. "When I go to prison I will cut it off," she would say.

"Are you planning to go to prison?"

"Of course not. I'm not a sentimental fool. But if I do all the things I plan to do, the British will have to put me in prison sooner or later. And I'll try to make it later. I'm not like that stupid cousin of mine who tried to shoot some pompous official and was nearly hanged for his pains. Children in politics, that is what terrorists are, heroic but misguided. To fight British imperialism we have to be organised and disciplined, and use the kind of weapons that will not misfire."

She used to say to me when I accused her of being presumptuously self-confident, "The trouble with you is you walk round and round in circles because you have no sense of direction. You sway and bend backwards thinking you are flexible and being fair, but you really are unsure."

Nita and I attended the same English classes and became friends, though we quarrelled constantly.

Shortly after we met she asked me, "What are you going to do after you leave College?"

"I don't really know."

"How typical of your class! You think a degree is a piece of jewellery, an additional ornament to be listed in your dowry."

"Rubbish! I believe my education will make me a better human being."

"I'm afraid I cannot afford such abstract ideals. My education has to help me to earn my living, so I have to make a definite plan. You are all the same, you have money to wrap round you like cotton wool against life. Nadira, with her opium eaters' religion, you with your lotus eaters' humanity. But I like you, because you are fundamentally honest, though everything in your background tends to manufacture hypocrites."

"I wonder why I like you though you talk to me as you do."

"*Because* I talk as I do. I take out the sting from what your conscience whispers to you, by saying it loudly. Then you are so busy defending yourself you need do nothing. Your ancestors probably had court jesters to serve much the same purpose."

When Nadira argued with Nita she defended her religious beliefs with greater conviction than I defended my class because she had no doubts. Her visions of the greatness of the Islamic world in the past was blurred for me by its decadence in the present.

Nadira was the daughter of my aunt's friend Begum Waheed. Like her mother her strongest belief was that Muslims had to defend their heritage.

Nadira's family were comparative newcomers to our city; they had come from the neighbouring province of the Punjab only twenty years ago. Her father was a doctor, known to be clever but said to be so grasping that, before starting his treatment, one had to decide between dying of bankruptcy or the disease.

After he had become successful they moved from their small house in a socially inferior part of the city, to a large house on the Mall. Begum Waheed came out of purdah, began to call herself 'Begum', and sent Nadira to a Convent.

Nadira and I quarrelled frequently about her political beliefs which were tied up with her religious fervour, but we shared other interests—books and music and poetry.

It was our wish to understand Western music that led to our friendship with Joan Davis who led the College orchestra.

Joan's mother was a widow, a matron at the Medical College. Joan had been awarded a scholarship and was very conscientious, simple and generous. She intended being a doctor.

Her home was small and unpretentious. Whenever I visited her and saw her with her mother, I felt a sense of deprivation. Their love and understanding were real, and not only a need and desire; their worlds were not separated by an age of ideas.

When Joan joined our group she had to stand alone in defence of her convictions, because she passionately believed in the rightness and the greatness of the British Empire. When Nita talked of her ambition to join actively in the struggle for freedom Joan said quite sincerely:

"I believe in the English not only because I am an Anglo-Indian but because they have brought peace and justice and unity."

"They have built roads and schools and hospitals," mocked Nita. "They have done good for the sake of doing good and for love of us, and any incidental exploitation is really for our benefit. In any case, how can one be loyal to aliens?"

"The Muslims were aliens," began Joan.

"They settled down here," I reminded her.

"They can go back to where they came from if they think they're aliens," said Nita.

"There speaks the Hindu," Nadira cut in angrily. "Scratch deep, and what is hidden under your progressive ideas? The same communalism of which you accuse me."

When this point was reached in any argument we were all glad to be drawn away from it. God was a safer subject for discussion than His religions.

I said lightly, "It's the P. & O. that is losing you the Empire, Joan. The faster their ships, the easier it is to go back 'Home' and we never get to know our benevolent English patrons."

Joan's weakness in arguments came from the very quality that gave her personal strength. She did not hate as we did. She did not hate Indians as we hated the British; she merely considered them a race apart. Yet she did not identify herself with the English.

"I am an Anglo-Indian and nothing can make it otherwise. My grandfather came here from England; we still talk of England as home, we have more in common with the English than with Indians, but we still remain just Anglo-Indians. It makes one feel like those riders who canter round the ring of a circus, balanced on two horses, except that those horses are trained to keep in step, and their riders are respected."

Joan neutralised in me the remembered venom of Sylvia Tucker. Her friendship blunted the sharp points of prejudice. I could not make Sylvia the excuse for hatred when Joan provided a reason for respect.

Our small group of friends was completed by Romana. She was unlike us in every possible way, uninterested in our arguments and amused by our quarrels because she questioned nothing.

Romana was related to Nadira and that is how we came to know her. Her family had migrated to a small Muslim state where her father was a minor official, but powerful because he had relations and friends in every branch of the State's administration. Also, he had flattered his way into becoming the ruler's favourite.

Romana had many tales to tell. She told us of the treasure-house in the heart of a hill whose secret approach through a maze was known only to its hereditary guardians, giant

Negroes, bearing on their cheeks strange, secret, branded signs. She told us of the necklace that had belonged to a concubine who had been walled alive many centuries ago by a jealous ruler; its giant central ruby was said to drip blood on the anniversary of her death, and the pearls dripped with salty tears. She told of the kidnappings of beautiful women and of the disappearance of inconvenient husbands.

Not even Nita invested her stories with social significance. Romana looked too much part of a fairy tale. She was like an ivory miniature, delicately carved. Her beauty was not disturbing, it gave a sense of diffused pleasure. It was like the warmth of the sun on a winter's day.

The five of us spent as much time together as was possible. When we were not arguing we were dissecting and questioning life, with the fear and the courage, the doubts and the certainty of inexperienced, questioning youth. Our world was bounded by our books, and the voices that spoke to us through them were of great men, profound thinkers, philosophers and poets.

I used to forget that the world was in reality very different, and the voices that controlled it had once been those of Baba Jan, Aunt Abida, Ustaniji, and now belonged to Uncle Hamid, Aunt Saira, and their friends. Always I lived in two worlds, and I grew to resent the 'real' world.

Chapter Four

ONE afternoon when I came home from College, I saw that my aunt had visitors. I recognised Begum Waheed's and Mrs Wadia's chauffeurs, smoking and gossiping on the front steps as if years of relaxation stretched before them.

I did not like Mrs Wadia; she was too haughty and critical.

Mrs Wadia was very rich, the daughter of a Bombay scrap merchant who had been knighted after the 1914–18 war. Her husband was a very senior member of the Indian Civil Service. They were very popular with the English, and referred to all English officials by their Christian names.

At times Mrs Wadia appeared a moulting eagle, at others a well-groomed vulture. Her perfumes, and shoes and lace and linen and silver came from the most expensive shops in Paris and London. She went to Europe every year, was prouder of Western culture than those who were born into it, and more critical of Eastern culture than those outside it.

When my aunt sent for me I had not changed, and the thought of Mrs Wadia's critical eyes deepening every crease on my cotton sari made me resentful in anticipation.

Begum Waheed and Mrs Wadia were in the middle of an argument when I came in. Sitting very stiffly on the sofa next to them was a hawk-like stranger. She had large, staring eyes, under heavy eyebrows. Her greying hair was drawn back tightly from her high, square forehead. Below her aquiline nose, her mouth was thin-lipped and unyielding.

She wore tight pyjamas of green and gold striped brocade, a green silk waistcoat over her shirt and a pale lemon *dopatta* dotted with tiny golden stars, and edged with gold. Her bright clothes and elaborate jewellery were incongruous with her age, but there was a well-bred air of dignity about her.

My aunt smiled and said, "Begum Sahiba, this is my niece, Laila," at the same time looking disapprovingly at my coarse hand-spun sari. "She has just come back from College," she added, explaining my appearance.

The Begum acknowledged my salutation with a nod, and a brief smile that did not reach her eyes. She said nothing.

I sat on the edge of a chair by my aunt and felt the stranger's eyes fixed on me.

"I cannot agree with you, Begum Waheed," said Mrs. Wadia. We must keep out undesirable elements when the Governor's wife visits the park. We must charge an admission fee. I should think four to eight annas will be sufficient for the purpose."

"How can we, Mrs Wadia? It is a *public* park. We had to fight very hard to make the Municipal Board wake up to the fact that there had to be a park for women, and we cannot discriminate now...."

My aunt apologised, "Begum Sahiba, you must forgive us that we are continuing our discussion in your presence."

"Do not shame me with apologies, Begum Sahiba. It is I who must apologise for not ascertaining whether you could spare your valuable time, and for coming with Begum Waheed without asking your permission."

"It has been a pleasure, Begum Sahiba."

Their conversation was stiff with ritual politeness.

"Let us face facts," said Mrs Wadia. "Is it used as much as it should be? Did the women themselves want it? Or did *we* want it for them?"

"They needed it then and need it now," Begum Waheed was saying her voice prepared for attack. "They will learn to want it."

"It will be just like the Club we thought was needed by our ladies"—Mrs Wadia's deep voice curled sharply at the edges. "Who comes there unless forced to do so? I am tired of the tea parties and games that have to be organised every week to collect people."

"You must remember, Mrs Wadia," my aunt said, "that

the idea of a Club is new to our ladies. We have to teach them the new ways of being sociable. We must be patient."

Mrs. Wadia's nose and eyes expressed an amused superiority. "Frankly, I find it increasingly difficult to be patient. One would imagine we were not living in the thirties of the twentieth century but of the eighteenth or nineteenth."

Begum Waheed was not prepared to let the argument drift into irrelevancies. She seemed more than ever like a pouter pigeon with the voice of a belligerent hen. "Purdah women must have a park, whether ladies have clubs or not. Think of the Mughal Emperors and the gardens they"——

"I think of present facts," Mrs Wadia interrupted impatiently. "At the last public meeting the crowd of common women smelt like caged animals. We can't have that. Besides we want the sort of people who will spend money."

My aunt explained to her visitor, her voice oozing with virtue, "It is hard to carry on one's work without money, no matter how noble it may be. However, one has to continue in the service of one's fellow-beings, no matter how hard it may be. I believe our daughters will find it easier, having the benefit of education. That is why I believe in education for women—to prepare them for service."

"If they do not let it go to their heads," the visitor croaked.

"Believe me, Begum Sahiba, that depends on home influence. Now my dear niece Laila is being educated to fit into the new world, but our old traditions and culture are always kept in mind."

The hawk-like eyes looked at me intently.

"Begum Sahiba," Mrs Wadi'a voice was sugar-sweet. "I believe His Highness your brother does not believe in modern education for girls?"

"In Surmai we bring up our girls to be good wives and mothers," the Begum said with formality.

Surmai? I remembered the name. Nadira had told me that a relation of the ruler's was wandering around visiting eligible homes and girls' schools looking for a suitable bride for his second son.

We had joked about it, giving each other marks like cattle at a show. Nadira was sure she had been removed from the list of candidates, because she had argued about politics in the Begum's presence, and declared that marriages had moved away from the Islamic ideal and were like prison sentences without benefit of a trial.

I began to understand why the woman had been staring at me, and was filled with anger against my aunt. She had tricked me into the presence of this hawk-like creature.

I shifted uneasily, my foot tripped the small table by me, and plates of *samosas*, sandwiches and spiced peas spilled in confusion. There were clucking sounds of dismay.

"No damage done," said Mrs Wadia, staring at the Persian carpet critically. She made me feel like an elephant walking over crystal glasses.

"Your niece is being educated at the same college as Nadira?" asked the visitor.

"Yes, Begum Sahiba."

"She does not observe purdah?"

"We observe the spirit of the Quranic injunction by limiting freedom within the bounds of modesty."

Mrs Wadia said with a note of patronage, "We Parsees do not believe in purdah. After all a purdah upbringing is no insurance against immorality. Consider the recent scandal at Laila's college."

I shifted in discomfort. We had been asked not to talk about what had happened, and I had pretended to my aunt that I knew nothing about it.

"What scandal?" the hawk-like Begum asked, lifting her face like a predatory bird.

Begum Waheed and my aunt hesitated, but Mrs Wadia was quick to say, "A Muslim girl, from a strict purdah family, ran away with a Hindu boy from the neighbouring college for boys."

"Why do they have girls' schools near those for boys?"

asked the Begum critically, looking at my aunt as if she were responsible.

But Mrs Wadia had not finished her story. "The boys' parents refused to forgive him. When the foolish boy's money was spent, he yielded to pressure and abandoned the girl. Her parents refused to take her back."

"Quite rightly," croaked the Begum. "She brought dishonour to them."

"She disobeyed the tenets of her religion," said Begum Waheed.

"She betrayed the cause for which we are working," said my aunt.

Mrs Wadia continued, "Because of communal feelings that had been roused by the papers our organisation could not take any steps to help her, as we do other deserted women, and the girl killed herself."

"Wickedness cannot escape punishment," the Begum said piously.

"She was *not* wicked," I blurted out.

"Laila!" said my aunt angrily, and the others stared at me in surprise. They seemed like paper figures, as hollow as their words, blown up with air. There was nothing in them to frighten me.

"Was she by any chance a friend of yours?" the old Begum asked me, her eyebrows lifted. I hated her for looking at me as if examining goods in a shop window.

"No, but I wish she had been. She must have been brave and clever to educate herself in a poor, backward home and get a scholarship. The poor girl must have suffered terribly."

"Suffered? She *caused* suffering," said Begum Waheed.

"What strange ideas the girl has! Dear Saira, do be careful. She may become a Socialist," mocked Mrs Wadia.

My aunt was very distressed. "Laila, you must be joking, defending wickedness."

"I am not defending wickedness. She wasn't a thief or a murderess. After all, there have been heroines like her in

...els and plays, and poems have been written about such ...e."

The word 'love' was like a bomb thrown at them.

"Laila!" my aunt shouted. "Have you taken leave of your senses?" She turned to the Begum whose eyes were now hard with disapproval, her mouth drawn into a line. "I cannot imagine what has come over her. It is so unlike her. She is such a quiet girl." Then she turned to me and said curtly, "I think you may go to your room now."

I was careful to say my *ādābs* very correctly before I left the momentarily silent room.

Chapter Five

I LAY on my bed with every nerve inside me quivering. Yet across the red splashes of my anger the face of the girl came to life in my mind, her face etched by imagined pain. A plain face, with large, wounded eyes. What were the forces within her that gave the strength her frail figure and frightened eyes belied? How had she crossed walls of stone and fences of barbed wire, and the even stronger barriers of tradition and fear? Why in seventeen years had I not learned the answer?

"Laila Bitia! Laila Bitia! Jumman *dhobi* wants to see you. It is very urgent."

Jumman was waiting in the inner courtyard, his eyes strained with anxiety, his hands raised in pleading.

"Bitia, the mother of Nandi is very ill. Bring the Quran Shareef and let its sacred air fan her face. Say a prayer over her. Begum Sahiba is busy and who is there but you to help me now that Abida Bitia is no longer here?"

He took Nandi's name automatically because 'mother of Nandi' was the way he had always addressed his wife. Nandi herself was still dead to him.

"I will come," I said.

It was only a few days ago that his wife had had a still-born baby.

"May you live long," he cried as he turned to go.

I went to fetch my Quran and as I unwrapped the gold cord of its brocaded cover, automatically kissed it and put it to my eyes.

Saliman said, "They say she is possessed by devils. They have twice burnt hot chillies under her nose to smoke them away. They have tried many charms without success. The midwife knows many. Now they want you to pray for her."

I began, "If they had taken her to a hospital . . ."

"Really, Bitia, the things you think of," Saliman said.

"Go to hospital to have a baby with men standing round looking on? Be shameless and be seen by all those doctors and half-doctors? Better to die at home. And who cares for the poor in hospitals anyway? Besides she was well, until the evil spirits found their way."

"Oh, be quiet, Saliman."

The irons were cold in the little room behind the tiny thatched veranda where I had played with Nandi. The room behind it was hot and crowded and dark. A piece of matting covered the one small window. The fire still burned that had been lit before child-birth.

I could hardly see. Jumman stood by the door. Some women grouped round the bed lifted the mother of Nandi towards me, supporting her head and shoulders. I could see the skull of a small animal near the head of the bed. And then I looked at her face, her mouth. It was twisting fiendishly. My paralysed lips scarcely moved. I held the open Quran near her face. and my fingers fumbled as I drew them rapidly through the thin pages.

Nizaman Bua called loudly: "Ya Allah! Ya Rahim!"

Jumman's breath came like a shuddering sob. The woman's face and body twisted. The women around her moaned.

I ran out into the sunshine towards my room.

My hands were trembling as I wrote a letter to Joan's mother.

I called Saliman; "Give this letter to Jumman. Tell him to take his wife to the hospital quickly. Give this money to him. He must get a tonga."

I lay on the bed with my face turned away from the light, and cried.

After her mother died of the 'evil spirit', which was really tetanus, Nandi came home. Jumman had need of her now, and forgiveness was made easy.

She came to my room the night she returned. She clung to my feet, crying: "Bitia, I have lived in hell, and now I am home."

I lifted her up by her hands that were c
with work. She was still graceful and l
mouth and eyes were hard.

I said, "Nandi, I am glad you are back",
stood and sobbed because she was happy that a
girlhood had been restored to us.

Layla wants to humanize them
Just because it's colonial doesn't mean
it should be disregarded.

—Slayered with the
primetive

Chapter Six

FOR some time there was a strangeness between my aunt and me. Her anger was not lessened by the fact that my uncle had disapproved not only of my ill-mannered outburst but of the purpose of the hawk-like Begum's visit, because of the notorious reputation of her brother as a man and a ruler. The hurt to my aunt's pride was softened by time, and she soon became absorbed in the social season which flourished in the rose-pink days of early winter.

Inside me, however, a core of intolerance hardened against the hollowness of the ideas of progress and benevolence preached by my aunt and her companions. Rebellion began to feed upon my thoughts but found no outlet.

Then Zahra came to stay after her return from her European holiday with her husband. When her mother and Aunt Abida came to complete the family circle, bringing with them Ustaniji and Hakiman Bua, it was as if our yesterdays had run into our todays, but like a reflection on wind-whipped waters.

The rooms beyond the inner courtyard were no longer silent. In the main house the routine of life remained unchanged.

Aunt Abida had become thinner and more silent. The finely modelled bones of her face strained against her skin and the calm forehead was now lined. When in repose there was an air of withdrawal about her, but every action was purposeful as if her will dictated a pattern of duty in relation to others.

The two days her husband had stayed she had centered all attention on his care and comfort, as if everyone and everything else was secondary.

I, who used to hurry back home to be with her, was jealous of him, though in their relationship of respect and consideration there was no spontaneity.

The first night she was alone I went to her room when everyone else had gone to bed.

She was reading from her favourite volume of Ghalib's poetry. She was the only one of my aunts whom I had seen with a book in her hand.

"Do you ever read the books I give you?"

"I am sorry, Phuphi Jan, I..."

"I am sorry too. I thought you would learn one cannot live fully out of what is borrowed. You must love your own language and heritage."

"I have so little time. I cannot."

"There is nothing you cannot do if you think it your duty. I tried to teach you that." Then suddenly, in the quiet of the room, she put her hand on my head and said:

"Sometimes I must have seemed very hard. But it had to be so. I had to prepare you for the hardships life brings. We cannot control what happens to us, but we can control our behaviour. One must never blunt one's sense of duty."

I put my head on her lap, and listened to the sound of her voice with a sense of security. I did not know when I fell asleep. When I woke she was sitting very still, her fingers moving in my hair, and it was past midnight.

Zahra had timed her return to coincide with the week of the Viceregal visit.

All the roads and buildings upon which the Viceregal eyes would rest had been decorated for the occasion. Bunting, elaborate arches and gates of painted wood and coloured paper decked the roads, fresh paint rejuvenated buildings. The city was like a woman dressed in festive robes but with dirty, ragged underclothes.

Everybody who was anybody of consequence was involved in the visit—officially or socially. And as the degree of involvement measured personal importance, invitations to the various functions were of vital importance.

A delicate and intricate code, more rigid than any caste

system, determined who would be invited to which function, and only the select few were invited to all. My aunt and uncle, Zahra and her husband were among them.

Zahra had changed very much in her appearance, speech and mannerisms. I knew she had not changed within herself. She was now playing the part of the perfect modern wife as she had once played the part of a dutiful purdah girl. Her present sophistication was as suited to her role as her past modesty had been. Just as she had once said her prayers five times a day, she now attended social functions morning, afternoon and evening.

The six months' trip abroad had served its purpose, and she had acquired that Western gloss which made her fit in perfectly with her new life.

It was a life she enjoyed quite apart from 'doing her duty', though in her mother's presence her words denied it. She had grown prettier and gayer. She was all her husband wished her to be as the wife of an ambitious Indian Civil Service officer.

Naseer's life was shaped by his ambition. Everything about him was precise, weighed and balanced by what he thought was 'correct'. Layer upon layer of good qualities, when unwrapped, revealed nothing but ambition—the core of his being.

Every day he spent a few moments with Aunt Majida, inquired about her health, made brief formal conversation, accepted her blessing, and left her overjoyed at the thought of her daughter's good fortune in having such a husband.

Just as he was more at ease with my uncle, Zahra found more in common with Aunt Saira than with her mother. Not only did they have similar interests and occupations, but Zahra had met my cousins Kemal and Saleem while in England and that made her a tangible link with them.

Chapter Seven

ZAHRA came into my room and, throwing herself across the bed slipped off her shoes, saying, "I'm exhausted. I should never have worn such high heels to the races."

I closed the exercise book into which I had been copying my notes, and put it away.

"Did you win, Zahra? Did you put my two rupees on the horse with the funny name?"

"It came last."

"That will teach me not to gamble," I laughed. "I'd promised to buy Saliman new bangles if I won."

"You'll do better when you start going yourself. That won't be long now. Another year and you will have finished your studies, you will be taken everywhere, you will probably be married. Don't shake your head, you cannot always live an unnatural life." She stretched her arms above her head and her blouse was tight across her breasts. being married = unnatural

No more loose, shapeless clothes, no more stooping and hunching of shoulders to conceal and deny one's body. "Oh," she breathed with relaxed satisfaction. "It was so beautiful! The lovely dresses, the uniforms of the Bodyguard, their lances shining in the sun, their horses, the band, the flowers, everything was so beautiful. You don't know what you have missed." She sat up suddenly. "I've made up my mind. I shall take you to the reception at the Baradari tomorrow."

"I can't go; I haven't been asked. Besides, Hamid Chacha and Saira Chachi would not like to take me. You are different now that you are married."

"I'll talk to them about it and I'm sure they will not object. They are not old-fashioned. If I had had my way I would have taken you everywhere just so that you should learn that there are other things in life than your books teach you."

"Zahra," I laughed. "You talk like a grandmother. Does marriage age one so much? I've told you, I've not been invited."

"Rubbish! What does that matter? It's our reception, given by the *Taluqdars*, isn't it? I won't hear anything more about it. You must come."

"How do you know I want to?"

"You don't know what is good for you."

"Zahra, you said you were tired. Do you really want to argue?"

"I won't be teased, Laila. One day I'll get my revenge when you creep out from between the jacket-covers of your books into the world."

"Which world, Zahra? The world of your past or your present?"

"Wait and see. There is only one—the world one lives in."

"A very wise remark," came a voice from beyond the curtains, and Asad came into the room, but the smile was wiped off his face as he saw Zahra.

"Zahra," he stammered, "your voice sounded like Laila's from a distance."

"Hullo, Asad," said Zahra sitting up stiffly, and her voice had dropped from its confident pitch.

"Asad," I cried happily as I got up to embrace him. "When did you come? Why didn't you tell me you were coming?"

"I decided in rather a hurry. I had some work to do and then there was the temptation to come while Abida Phuphi was here."

He was taller, still thin and pale, but there was a gentleness in his expression that made him appear better-looking than each separate feature warranted.

"I'm so glad I happened to be here too," said Zahra, looking at him with wide, seemingly innocent eyes, her head prettily thrown back. "I haven't seen you for years. You have changed, Asad."

I felt his fingers tighten against mine and then he drew his hand away, and went and stood against the writing desk in the corner by the window.

"I knew you had come home, Zahra," he said simply. "You have changed too."

"Naturally," she laughed. "I'm not a girl any more. I'm a married woman."

"Yes, naturally."

"How is Zahid?" I asked. "He has not been to see me for some time."

"He is well. I think he has been busy studying. He did rather badly last term, and that upset him."

"Has he still got the same funny ideas about dying to restore the glories of Islam?" asked Zahra.

"Yes, but he thinks mine are funnier. In fact he calls me a renegade!" Asad laughed.

"I understand him better than either of you do. It is better to believe in one's religion like he does than not at all. But he should be careful not to get mixed up with politics for the sake of his future," Zahra said with the air of one who was right inside the inner circle of power. "Though he need not worry, really, I am sure Naseer will get him a good job when the time comes."

Before Asad could answer, her husband Naseer came into the room, starched and stiff in his perfectly cut tails.

"Zahra, I've been looking for you. You must start dressing. We must be at Sir John's at least half an hour before Their Excellencies arrive."

"Am I ever late? Why do you worry?" And waving her arm towards Asad, Zahra said, "You remember Asad, don't you?"

"Of course I do," Naseer said. "How do you do?"

"*Salaam Aleikum*," said Asad.

Zahra paused a moment at the door.

"Shall I wear the blue and silver tissue sari with the

silver Benares border, or the red French brocade with the gold embroidery? I've worn most of the others before."

"The gold one will be the most suitable," Naseer said, pursing his lips thoughtfully.

"Very well. I'll see you both soon," Zahra called as she went through the door; and even after she had gone the air was soft with the French perfume she now used, more subtle than her once favourite attar had been.

"You are studying in Delhi, I believe?" asked Naseer very politely.

"Yes. I have been there the last three years trying to——"

"Interesting, very interesting. You must come and see us when we are posted there," Naseer said absently then turned his smile towards me. "I must say good night, Laila. We have to go to a cocktail party."

"Good night, Naseer Bhai."

"Good night, Laila, good night, Asad, I'm glad to have met you."

"*Khuda Hafiz*," said Asad, and taking a deep breath exhaled very slowly.

"Strange how they try to make one feel insignificant by flaunting power and importance. It shouldn't bother me, it's not important, but I was not in the mood to meet Zahra's husband. When I first came into the room and saw Zahra it was as if I had come down in a swing very rapidly. Then suddenly I felt free and wondered why I had ever felt otherwise. But I am talking too much about myself. Tell me how you have been."

"There is nothing to tell. I'm a bit more confused, perhaps." I tried to laugh.

"So am I; so are we all. Yet I feel like that only when I'm doing nothing but just sitting and wondering what to do. When I'm working, not just studying, but teaching the illiterate, going about among the poor, working in villages, organising meetings, then problems do not seem like immovable mountains. One can go on and on arguing about abstract things for ever. It's different when you do something, and see the results. Quite apart from the tangible results, there is such a sense of satisfaction."

Asad's voice had a new note of confidence, though his eyes were still those of a dreamer.

"Do you know, Asad, I can't imagine you in this new role? Will I ever see you as someone other than a shy dreamer? What work have you come to do? Personally I think you wanted an excuse to come."

"Maybe," he laughed. "But it is true I have work to do. There is a great deal of unrest among the students which has been stimulated by this Viceregal circus Zahra is enjoying so much. Some students want to stage a demonstration to show the visit is not as popular as the banquets, bands and bunting suggest. At such a time as this the authorities will be in the kind of mood that might lead to a clash. I am against anything that might lead to violence."

"I would like you to meet my friend Nita. She believes in a qualified kind of violence. Sometimes when she is excited in an argument I imagine her as a fat little figure bristling with armour, swinging a huge broad sword, lopping off the heads of giants. I wonder how the two of you would get on?"

"Badly, I'm sure," laughed Asad. "I'm frightened of fierce females. Which reminds me, Hakiman Bua sent me to tell you dinner is ready."

We walked across the lawn together slowly. Across the courtyard, through the open door we looked into the bright room.

Aunt Majida was bent over a basket cutting betel nuts, Aunt Abida was making pan. Hakiman Bua was sitting on the floor near Aunt Abida waiting for her orders to bring in the trays of food.

We stopped for a moment, very still.

"It looks as if nothing had changed."

"As if our yesterdays had returned."

"When we were impatient for our tomorrows."

a violence that is not spontaneous but organized.

Chapter Eight

ZAHRA could not have chosen a more splendid occasion for my introduction into her social world than the reception given by the *Taluqdars* of Oudh in honour of the Viceroy. The nobility and aristocracy of the Province were hosts to all those of consequence.

Preparations had started months in advance. The *Baradari*, where such receptions were always held, was cleaned and repainted. It looked like a marble casket in the emerald setting of the surrounding lawns.

The terraced houses enclosing the lawns and gardens were freshly painted too, their golden-yellow colour relieved by touches of white on mouldings and pillars. An aura of romance still clung to them though they were now merely the town houses of *Taluqdars* whereas they had once sheltered the beauties of the Royal harem, and the King was said to have walked across their roofs shaded by a flight of pigeons. The two elaborate gates leading into the quadrangle were still decorated with the emblem of the Kings of Oudh—two arched fish in relief.

On the day of the reception it was not only those who were invited to it who felt a sense of anticipation. The whole city looked forward to it as to a fair, attracted by the illumination and the fireworks which were the traditional climax of the evening.

Zahra came to my room in the afternoon, threw herself across the bed and called to Saliman.

"Press my feet, Saliman, I am so tired," she sighed. With her face creamed and without make-up, and her hair pulled carelessly back she looked as she had once been, simple, verging on plainness.

She stretched out her hand and smiled sweetly as I reached for the bottle of scarlet enamel she had put on the table.

"Why are you so quiet, Laila? Why is everyone so quiet? Look at Saliman. She hardly talks now. Her hands are as cold as a corpse, and with as much strength in them. What is the matter, Saliman?"

"Nothing, Bitia," Saliman said listlessly.

"She is probably tired too," I said. "There is much more work than usual."

"Nonsense. I am sure there is more to it than that. You never notice anything, living in your make-believe world."

"I'm in no hurry to leave it."

"Aren't you excited about this evening?"

"No, I'm frightened to go with all of you." I laughed to make it appear a joke. "Zahra, can't I go with Abida Phuphi and watch from the Purdah gallery? You and I were content to do that once."

"Content? I was not content. There was no alternative in those days. You are lucky you do not have to wait until you are married to do all the interesting things I could never do."

"The only interesting thing you have done since you were married is that you have travelled."

"What nonsense you talk! But there is one thing I learned in England which you should remember too—I learned to be proud of my breeding. All those titled people about whom such a fuss is made are no better than we are. The trouble is every woman here calls herself 'Begum' nowadays. Laila, did you know that *Taluqdars* have a right of audience with the King?"

"I wonder if that knowledge would have helped me when the King's groom's grand-daughter called me 'nigger' at school and refused to play with me?"

"The trouble with you is that you are self-willed."

"And the trouble with you is that you have no will. Do you never question your present life in the light of your past? Is it not different from the way you were brought up?"

"I was brought up to do my duty."

"Your duty according to whom? Look at your nails,

smart and long; your mother thinks such talons impure and irreligious. Come on, do your duty," and I reached for the scissors.

Zahra pulled her hand away as if pricked by a thorn, "Laila, don't."

I laughed, "I was teasing you, Zhara."

She smiled ruefully, "Sometimes it is hard to tell when you stop being serious."

She sat up and held her hands away from her as if they did not belong to her, looking at them slender and scarlet-tipped, and laughed.

"Laila, some day I shall put henna on your bridal hands."

"No, Zahra, look in that mirror. See the face of an old maid."

"I can see a face waiting for its bridal veil of flowers. If I say a prayer and blow on the mirror I shall see the face of the Prince who will lift it from your face."

The faces in the unclouded mirror laughed back at us. Then a shadow fell, and Asad's reflection was looking at us with puzzled eyes.

I whipped round stammering "Asad".

Zahra choked with laughter. "I did not expect you of all people Asad."

"I was sent by Abida Phuphi to call Saliman," and he turned to go.

"Won't you stay a while?" asked Zahra, her eyes dancing.

"I'm sorry. I have a lot of work to do. I was just going when Abida Phuphi sent me here. I shall come back, later."

Chapter Nine

THE evening started badly for me. Aunt Saira disapproved of my clothes and said sarcastically:

"There are certain social rules you must learn. You cannot go dressed to a reception as if you were going to tea with your college friends."

I froze with anger, and a sense of helplessness, but Zahra calmed me. She exerted all her charm and tact, nothing could be allowed to spoil her plans for me.

She dressed me in one of her own saris, coral pink, scattered with golden stars. She combed out my plaits and coiled my hair at the nape of my neck, and touched my lips lightly with colour. When she pulled me triumphantly to the mirror I did not recognise the stranger who looked back at me.

My aunts Majida and Abida sent for me to see how I looked in my finery. Even the maid-servants came to look.

It pleased me to see the proud look in Aunt Abida's eyes and the surprised admiration in Asad's first glance.

Hakiman Bua circled a handful of *chillies* and lumps of sugar seven times round my head and cast them in the fire to burn away the Evil Eye.

Nandi called, "Bitia, smile! You look like the moon hidden behind a cloud."

Only Saliman was silent and sad.

Aunt Saira called, "Zahra! Laila! We are waiting for you."

Even before the car turned into the arched gates of the square the sky glowed with reflected light. The *Baradari* shone like a crystal casket of jewels surrounded by palaces etched with lights. In every tree hidden lights bared the delicate tracery of their skeleton branches.

An excited, curious crowd was held back by policemen

from the road circling the *Baradari*. The whole square was alive and full of sound.

Over the white steps and across the marble terrace to the wide-flung glass doors stretched a narrow carpet like a stream of blood.

Inside the large hall there seemed to have been an explosion of light. It blazed from crystal chandeliers and was reflected by the tall mirrors on the walls. It glittered in gems, and from burnished brocades and tissues.

Our seats were well in front, near the central aisle. From this position the two throne-like chairs of embossed gold and silver were clearly visible on the carpeted dais under a canopy of gold-embroidered velvet, supported by slender poles of gold and silver.

Above the hum of voices came the sound of the band playing selections from light opera on the terrace. The hall brimmed with light and colour and movement. Men in *achkans* of brocade and silk, and delicately embroidered finely-woven wool, their heads covered with turbans of tissue and fine silk or coloured caps, men who had stepped out of ancient paintings in their ancestral court dresses carrying swords and daggers with jewelled belts, stood and talked to others in the severe black and white formality of European dress. English women, elaborately gowned and groomed, deeply *décolletée* with bare shoulders and backs, outnumbered the handful of Indian women, wives of officials and *Taluqdars* who were out of purdah. They sat with their heads covered lending deep splashes of colour to scattered points in the room.

Rich and poor, the *Taluqdars* of Oudh had gathered together; from the Maharaja of Bhaktipur whose kitchen budget alone ran into lakhs every year, to Sheikh Qayum Ali who was no richer than some of Bhaktipur's poorer tenants.

From cities, townships and villages they had come to act as hosts on an occasion—becoming increasingly rare—when they could collectively display that traditional splendour and hospitality which was now individually almost impossible.

I sat next to Zahra who pointed out friends and acquaintances, interspersing her comments with nods and smiles.

"That bald-headed man with the red face is the Commissioner of our Division. That straw-haired woman bulging out of her evening dress is his wife. She is carrying on with that man next to her—the Deputy Inspector-General. You wouldn't believe it to look at her, would you? Look at that brooch in Amirpur's cap! That emerald must be the size of a pigeon's egg! There is Mrs Wadia, and Begum Waheed is with her. But she should be sitting farther back. Some people are so pushing they lose all sense of shame. Oh! what lovely pearls the Rani of Shahpur is wearing? They must be part of her dowry. Shahpur married in Nepal and the girls bring fabulous dowries. She is 'C' class, the daughter of a Rana's concubine. So they paid even a bigger price to get a husband of good blood. . . ."

In spite of Zahra's chatter, and my shyness, I looked around and recognised the friends and the sons of friends of my grandfather and uncle. They came to life from pictures and stories. The Kunwar of Deorai and Syed Ali Abbas of Panigarh, inseparable old friends, whose fathers had fought together against the British and had had large areas of their estates confiscated after the Mutiny, talking to the Raja of Bilsa, whose grandfather had been treasurer of Deorai and had helped the British and been rewarded with a gift of his master's confiscated land. Maharajkumar Vijaya Singh descended from the gods, whose ancestors were heroes of myths and legends, who spent his time in Bombay and Calcutta racing horses and chasing Anglo-Indian girls. His younger brother, a nationalist, dressed as always in a white *khaddar achkan* and Gandhi cap, standing with a group of young nationalist *Taluqdars*, talking to the Rajkumar of Harwan who was educated at Harrow and Balliol and was now a prominent Congress Socialist. Rai Bahadur Pushkar Nath of whom it was said that he had not washed his hands for days after shaking hands with the Prince of Wales in the 'twenties, gesticulating in front of Nawab Sibte Hyder whose ancestors had held high office in the courts of the Nawab-Viziers of Oudh, whose grandfather had chosen to share the last King's exile, who was himself a loyalist and a Minister in the Provincial Government. The Rani of Phulgaon, married when a child of nine to a sick man of sixty, grey-haired with the bearing of an Empress, loved by her tenants, surrounded by relatives waiting for the childless widow's death to start litigation, smiling politely at an Englishwoman, tall, fine-boned like a thoroughbred mare in flounces.

If anyone looked at me I felt the lights too bright and myself too conspicuous in my borrowed clothes, with my false face.

There was a sudden silence. The band could be heard playing 'God Save the King' and a glittering procession came through the door. Everyone remained standing until Their Excellencies were seated on their regal chairs.

When the President of the Association began to read the address of welcome. "We, the *Taluqdars* of Oudh are a special class with special privileges. . . ." Begum Waheed, one row in front of us across the aisle, nudged Mrs Wadia and looked round at my aunt, grinning.

My aunt's eyes were fixed on the speaker and she nodded in approval of his words. His speech covered all the problems, aspirations, duties and ideals of the *Taluqdars*. It was a long speech.

The old man next to me began to snore gently and was nudged awake by his neighbours.

"We are aware that the property—er—prosperity of our tenants is our proper—prosperity," the voice of the speaker intoned.

The voice became a drone. The lights in their brilliance induced patches of blankness in the mind between which were spaced applause, the Viceregal reply, more applause, more words, the presentation of a gold and silver casket containing the address, more applause, and Zahra was saying, "Laila! Where are you? Asleep with your eyes open? We

Is Zahra wearing a mask or does she really believe all this? Is she playing a part?

have to go on to the terrace for supper and to watch the fireworks. Naseer has arranged for us to sit not far from where the chief guests will be sitting. It is the best place to watch the fireworks. Keep close to me. There is always a rush."

But I lost sight of Zahra when we had got as far as the space between the dais and the doors. My sari had caught in a nail, and in that moment Zahra and Naseer and my uncle and aunt were lost to me. People were pushing each other to get through the doors. I was pushed towards the open terrace at the back of the *Baradari*.

There was a crowd milling towards long tables set across one end of the terrace. Bearers in white uniforms stood behind them waiting to pour out drinks and to replenish the plates of cakes, sweets, sandwiches, fruit and Indian delicacies.

A tall fat man in a black *achkan* was shouting "I want my champagne in a glass, not in a thimble." There was a sound of splintering glass. The voice boomed "No Glasses? Give me a bottle. How dare you? Bastard! I paid for them. I can drink them all or break them all." There was a crash of breaking bottles.

Two men were forcing the large, struggling man away from the table.

I could see no one I knew. I was so frightened I wanted to cry. I pushed my way back towards the hall. I wanted to get to the Purdah gallery.

A rocket flared up and burst in the sky. Another and another. Coloured stars fell in a curve. They drew a wave of delighted sound from the crowds.

I stepped into the hall now almost empty. The man in the black *achkan* was lurching towards me. A scream died in my throat and I ran blindly towards the farthest door crashing into someone coming through it.

For the briefest of moments his arms were around me.

"I'm sorry."

"Sorry."

We said it together. I looked up at him and away, still trembling.

"You are crying! What is the matter? Can I help you?"

"That man.... There was a drunk man," I had never before seen a man drunk.

"That old windbag," he laughed. "He is really harmless. Just like one of his own elephants."

"I was frightened. I was looking for my cousin." I did not want to be left alone.

"May I help you?"

"Thank you." I felt safe holding his arm, as we went through the crowd. Staring men no longer mattered.

A tree of light flamed with coloured branches and fiery fruit. Stars whirled on giant wheels. Rockets reached the sky and returned in a shower of coloured stars.

"Look how beautiful it is!" He pushed through to the trellised edge of the terrace. "You can see it better from here. Then we will look for your cousin."

"She will be somewhere near where the chief guests are sitting. It will be easy to find her."

Two forts outlined with fire shot coloured stars at each other. Between bursts of light the darkness flickered and smoke filled the lawn where the fireworks danced and crackled.

I felt his warm hand on my arm and we turned towards the narrow portion of the terrace on our right.

A giant rocket flared and lit the whole square with its brilliant light.

"Laila!" I heard Naseer calling, "Laila!"

"That was my cousin's husband," I explained as I looked around.

The light faded, I moved reluctantly towards Naseer's voice. Another rocket blazed upwards.

"Have you seen him?"

"Yes. Thank you for helping me."

"It was a pleasure."

For the first time we looked straight into each other's eyes.

Then the light faded.

"Good night and thank you."

"Good night."

Later, sitting by Zahra, watching the fireworks, I was seeing a young, smiling face with large, widely spaced eyes, and dark hair on which a black cap rested at a gay angle.

The present moments were slipping away as surely as the fires burned out, but the others remained intact, superimposed on all the moments that moved from light into darkness.

Chapter Ten

THE day after the reception the Viceroy was to lay the foundation stone of a new hostel at the University, the last official function before he left for Delhi.

Zahra had been looking forward to this culmination of a week of gaiety before returning to the dull provincial town where her husband was District Magistrate. It was a bitter disappointment to hear there was a possibility of its cancellation.

There had been a considerable amount of public feeling against the Viceregal visit, particularly among the students. There had been no hostile demonstrations—the police had thrown a tight net of security over the whole city—but there had also been no public enthusiasm. On the day of the Viceroy's arrival the colourful procession of military bands and marching soldiers, of the cavalry and mounted police, of magnificently caparisoned horses and elephants, had wound down roads lined with curious but silent onlookers. Only school-children from Anglo-Indian schools cheered and waved the tiny Union Jacks given to them; and groups of paid men planted along the route, shouted slogans of welcome.

Early in the week it had been discovered that a section of the students had made definite plans to demonstrate when the Viceroy came to lay the foundation stone. But the police and university authorities had both been confident they could control the situation, until fresh information was received the night before.

All morning my uncle was kept busy with meetings and discussions. By lunch-time the situation seemed improved. The university authorities were certain they had won over several students' leaders; and security arrangements had been tightened.

Zahra was relieved; she did not have to cancel her appointment with the only European hairdresser in town.

She left the house happily and returned shaken with fright, but only too eager to tell me what had happened.

Everything had gone well. Speeches had been made; the foundation stone had been laid; garlands had been distributed; the time had come for the Viceroy to leave, the band had struck the first chords of 'God Save the King'; people had started to stand up. Suddenly there were shouts from scattered points where the students sat.

"Sit down! Sit down!"

"Sons of 'toadies'. Shame! Shame!"

A crop of black flags sprang up.

There was panic and confusion. Proctors, professors and plain-clothes men turned on the students. The Viceroy, the Governor and their parties were driven rapidly away. The students moved towards the gate still shouting slogans.

As the car passed through the gates Zahra saw students and policemen fighting in a confused mêlée.

Zahra echoed her husband's views that law and order could not be preserved when nationalist leaders preached civil disobedience. My uncle was furious that the delicate balance of university and provincial politics was disturbed. Aunt Abida was concerned to know whether anyone had been injured. Aunt Majida fretted for the safety of Asad and Zahid. I felt curiously detached, as if I were strapped to a chair in an empty auditorium watching a performance.

The next day was a Sunday. Heavily reinforced patrols of foot and mounted police covered every quarter of the city.

On Monday an atmosphere of tension and excitement spread over the wide area of the university and neighbouring schools and colleges. Rumours spread rapidly. It was said many students had been expelled, many arrested, and the police had beaten students within the boundaries of the University, where they had no right to be. It was now known that on the day of the Viceroy's visit plain-clothes men posted at the approaches to the University had kidnapped nationalist and left-wing student leaders, had driven them miles out of the city and had left them stranded on unfrequented country roads.

University students threatened to march in procession to the Council Chamber, and appealed for solidarity and support. They picketed the gates of all schools and colleges.

At a special assembly the Principal of our college reminded us of our sacred duty to preserve the spirit of learning from political passion and partisan politics, and ended by making it clear that anyone who did otherwise would face expulsion. Nita was explosive when we met to discuss the ultimatum.

"We are trained to be cowards and traitors. What is education worth if it does not recognise the freedom of expression?"

"Why should you call anyone a traitor who does not want to risk expulsion?" Nadira asked.

"I am not clear in my mind," I confessed. "Is the cause big enough?"

Nita flared, "It is a simple question of loyalty. We must express our solidarity with our fellow-students. You are the kind of people who weaken all causes; you who are not sure of anything. I would rather you were positively against us."

"Well, I am," said Joan. "I am absolutely against you. To me the whole affair seems childish. This insult to the National Anthem was like children making faces and putting out their tongues at one."

"Whose National Anthem is it?" I asked.

"What other have you in mind?" said Joan sarcastically. "You cannot decide that amongst yourselves. Nadira and Nita quarrel constantly about flags and anthems."

"But we agree about yours," answered Nadira.

Joan persisted, "I've heard you say the British are better rulers than the Hindus would be."

"I did not say that," Nadira burst out. "You are deliberately twisting my words."

"Freedom does not mean a choice between rulers," I interrupted.

"Except to imperialists," added Nita.

Joan flushed and said, "Remember people get the Government they deserve. Why don't you people unite and make yourselves fit for——"

"Oh, stop it!" Romana interrupted. "All you do is talk. If you intend to do nothing and just talk, why not talk of pleasanter things?"

Nita picked up her books and as she walked away said, "I will do something."

Chapter Eleven

I STAYED at home the next day. My uncle sent for me a short time after breakfast. He was sitting in front of his leather-covered office table, alone in his study. Uncle Hamid swivelled round his chair and looked at me with a slight frown, and I felt my limbs disintegrating with fear. His eyes were like frosted steel.

"I was told you had not gone to college today. Has there been any trouble? Have day-scholars been advised to stay away?" he asked.

"No, I was not feeling well," I answered evasively.

"What is the feeling among the students in your college?"

"We were warned against taking part in the movement..."

"Movement!" he interrupted angrily. "What movement? Choose your words more precisely. This is merely a demonstration of irresponsible hooliganism. But I would like to know the feeling of the students," he persisted.

"Most of them have not dared to say anything against what they have been ordered to think," I began stiffly.

"What do you think about it?"

I hesitated, "I'm sorry, I consider the question irrelevant."

"Have you no freedom of thought?" he asked with sarcasm.

"I have no freedom of action."

He drew a deep breath and looked at me searchingly.

"You must know that freedom of action must be controlled until the mind reaches maturity and one's powers of judgement are fully developed."

"Mine are more likely to atrophy," I mumbled, my rebelliousness beginning to outstrip my fear.

He answered sharply, "I respect an independent mind, but

while you are in my charge and until I consider you are fit, you will be guided by me. I will not allow any action of which I disapprove."

"I am well aware of my position, Hamid Chacha. I am well trained."

For a moment his eyes flickered with anger. Then he turned towards the files on his table and without looking round said:

"You may go now."

I found myself walking instinctively towards Aunt Abida's room. Only there I could escape from the questions that seethed inside me. What was one to believe in? Why was I different from Zahra? What was wrong with me?

I spent the day in a withdrawn world enclosed by creeper-covered walls, splashed with orange bougainvilias and scarlet roses. The yellow-green lawn glowed in the winter sunlight which warmed the clear, cold, blue-tinged air.

A white-sheeted *takht* had been taken out on the veranda to catch the sun. Aunt Abida leaned against the large bolster, and I lay with my head on her lap.

Aunt Majida lay with her eyes closed while Hakiman Bua pressed her feet. Saliman sat on the floor resting against a pillar, her sad face held up to the sun.

Suddenly the peaceful, drowsy air was agitated by a distant noise of shouting. There was a wild rhythm in the sound and as it came nearer it was as if one powerful, angry, confident, young voice came from many throats.

I ran from the startled silent group in the veranda towards the stairs leading up to the roof. Saliman followed me.

"What is it, Bitia? What is happening?"

We looked down towards the road as we had always done to watch parades and processions. A flight of disturbed crows cawed and wheeled round the tall *asoka* trees. The bamboo skeleton of a decorative arch partially dismantled, straddled across the road, its torn coloured-paper sign of 'Welcome' flapping in the breeze.

The sound of voices came in chanting unison, the shouted call and the full-throated chorus:

Inquilab..............Zindabad! Long live Revolution!
Inquilab..............Zindabad! Long live Revolution!
British Raj ....Murdabad! Death to British Imperialism.
British Raj............Murdabad! Death to British Imperialism.
Azadi ki..............Jai! Hail Freedom!
Azadi ki..............Jai! Hail Freedom!

Then the road was alive with defiant, determined young people. The sound of their marching feet and angry voices was a surging sea, a roaring tempest. In the forefront was a group of girls. Was Nita among them? They marched across our range of vision and out of it and their voices faded behind them.

Where was Asad? My heart was beating very fast.

"What was happening?" Saliman asked.

"What was happening?" asked Aunt Abida when I returned.

"It was a procession of students going towards the Council Chamber."

"What has happened to young people nowadays? Why must they go looking for trouble?" wailed Aunt Majida.

"They have cats tied to their feet; they cannot sit still," said Hakiman Bua getting up stiffly. "It is time to get tea ready. Come on, Saliman, there is no time for idling."

It became very quiet again. Time dragged. I was restless thinking of what I had seen and heard, and of Nita and Asad and my own inaction. I waited for Asad as once before many years ago when there had been a riot, and he had not come home for many hours. . . .

It did not surprise me when I saw Zahid bringing him into Aunt Abida's room where we had gone after tea.

"Asad!" Aunt Abida's voice was high and sharp.

"Allah have mercy!" cried Aunt Majida.

"Asad Bhayya!" wailed Hakiman Bua. "What has happened?"

"Asad!" I cried and my hands were trembling as I helped him sit down.

Asad's clothes were stained. Blood had oozed through the handkerchief tied round his head.

"I'm sorry. Please forgive me. I always seem to cause trouble," Asad said, smiling ruefully, and looking like a child appealing against punishment.

"Hakiman Bua," Aunt Abida ordered, "bring some hot water and cotton wool. And some cloth for a bandage."

"I knew something like this would happen," said Zahid "So I followed them. . . ."

"Who did this to you, my son?" wailed Aunt Majida.

"My head got in the way of a policeman's *lathi*," Asad smiled.

"Why do you always get into trouble?" she scolded. "Why are you so headstrong?"

"I am obviously not," he teased her.

"He is throwing away his life on wrong causes," burst out Zahid. "Look how effective his non-violence is! It is against human nature. The police were violent, but were they stoned non-violently?"

"There are always those whose faith is not strong enough, whose doubts make them weak," said Asad patiently.

"I saw you grappling with a policeman yourself," persisted Zahid.

"You forget there were girls to be protected. . . ."

"I wonder if Nita was among them?" I cut in anxiously.

"If you described her correctly to me I think it must have been your friend who helped me get this"—he pointed to his head. "A fat girl, full of headstrong enthusiasm. She charged into the police as if possessed. I was hardly the right person to shield her," he smiled.

"Was she hurt . . . like you?"

"I saw no blood, if that is what you mean. But the police were not being exactly gentle and their truncheons and *lathis* are not made of feathers."

I felt sick inside.

"You have talked enough," said Aunt Abida. "Come here, Asad."

She washed and bandaged the cuts on his head and face. They were not as deep as the loss of blood had indicated, but Asad looked very pale and tired.

Aunt Majida and Hakiman Bua called on God to save young people from the sins of disobedience.

"You had better rest, Asad," Aunt Abida said. "I shall have a bed put in my dressing-room." And taking no notice of Asad's protests she added, "I think you had better be left alone."

When Aunt Saira and Zahra came back from tea and bridge at Mrs Wadia's and heard about Asad, Aunt Saira said to Aunt Abida.

"Your brother will be very angry if he gets to know."

"He need not be told," suggested Aunt Abida quietly.

"Asad again!" Zahra said impatiently, then feeling my eyes on her, looked away. "I hope he is not badly hurt."

By nightfall the trouble had spread. It was not only students and their sympathisers who defied the order prohibiting the assembly of more than five persons on the streets, political groups joined them. By ten o'clock there was firing in two different localities, after which a twenty-four-hour curfew was imposed on an area which excluded a part of the Civil Lines and the Cantonments.

The hardships caused by the curfew hardened public opinion against the authorities. If a widespread conflagration was to be avoided it was obvious a compromise had become inevitable. A settlement was reached after a sullen day.

Two students who had led the actual attack on the police on the first day were rusticated; no action was taken against the others; and an inquiry was instituted into the firing in which several innocent onlookers had been injured.

Though Uncle Hamid took a stand against the Government because of the firing, he was uncompromisingly against the actions that had led to the disturbances.

He made Aunt Saira visit the injured in hospital. Coming constitutional changes threw a long shadow before them, and the strategy of elections was a subtle one.

"Why do you not taunt me about inaction as Nita does?" I asked Asad when we talked about what had happened.

"Because the urge for action must come from within you. It cannot be created by taunts."

"Your thoughts seem older than you, Asad."

"Was I ever young?" he laughed.

"I feel happy with you, Asad. I like you."

"I like you too."

He reached out and took my hand in his. I felt secure and peaceful in his friendship. And then Zahid came in breaking the mood in tiny pieces.

"Ameer has come to see you."

"Bring him in," said Asad happily.

I got up to go.

"Why are you going, Laila? You are not in purdah," Asad said.

"Abida Phuphi would mind if I stayed."

I had lifted the curtain of the inner door when I heard the voice, "Hullo, Asad, you giant-killer." I was compelled to turn round. Our eyes met again for a startled moment, and then I almost ran towards the courtyard.

That face, that voice. Rockets bursting through the still night. And now a name I could recognise, and a common bond in Asad.

Yet not even Asad must know, because it had no meaning outside of me, nor any explanation. It was a nakedness to be hidden by each element of my will and feeling.

returning love?

Chapter Twelve

I DID not see Nita before she was sent home. It was arranged very quietly, to avoid any publicity for the college.

Romana and Joan who lived in the same hostel had helped her to pack and said she had appeared cheerful and unrepentant.

She left me a short letter of farewell which ended, "I'll miss you all very much. It could not have been more agreeable to disagree. Tell Nadira I still hope her beliefs will change, or at least her actions will not be based on them. Your actions will, I hope, one day coincide with your beliefs, and Joan's beliefs will change to fit her actions. Romana, I hope, will remain her charming self and bother about neither! I am grateful to all of you for having learned the meaning of friendship."

We missed Nita. In our arguments it was as if we mentally reached out for a step that was not there and stumbled.

Two days after her return home Nita died suddenly as a result of injuries to her brain caused by the blows on her head received during the police *lathi* charge. Her death was to me a martyrdom.

Then Romana left us. What she had long feared happened, and she was called home to be married. The hawk-like Begum who had set out on a search for a bride for her nephew had finally chosen Romana, and her parents did not have the courage to disobey what amounted to an order from their ruler. Romana was sentenced to a life of luxurious incarceration.

Then the time came near for my aunts and Zahra to leave. I tried not to bring the day of parting with Aunt Abida nearer by thinking of it.

Aunt Saira urged them to stay longer but her protesta-

Luxurious incarceration.
Jewellery as chains

tions were formal. Her way of life imposed another pattern in which friends and acquaintances had acquired more importance than relations.

My uncle, unlike her, made no attempt to hide his dislike of the joint family system. Its entanglements, unreasoning restrictions, unreasonable demands and lack of privacy had made him admire and adopt the ordered, individual, Western way of living. Though he had antagonised the vast inter-related clan and lost the leadership and authority of his father, his ambitions for another form of leadership had burst through the narrow confines of a tribe and he was more concerned with the antagonisms he faced outside it.

At this time, when his sisters were leaving, there were more important matters on his mind than thoughts of parting from them. The problems created by the students had not yet been completely solved when he was told of the sale of our neighbour's house.

For two generations it had belonged to friends and its spacious grounds had ensured the privacy of our home, and now the Raja of Bhimnagar had sold it. He had long been in debt, but so had his father before him, and there had been no question of his creditors forcing him to pay them anything beyond large sums as interest, which drained his estate and provided them with a substantial income. Now, he had been forced into selling his house by Harish Prasad Agarwal who had bought out all his other creditors.

Agarwal was my friend Sita's father. He was no longer merely a money-lender like his father had been. He owned a great deal of property, had bought the selling agency of a textile mill, the managing agency of a paper mill, and many brick kilns. The pomp and circumstance of many a *Taluqdar* was subsidised by him, he contributed generously to the funds of the Congress party, but kept on the right side of the Government.

My uncle looked so depressed when he said good-bye to his sisters that Aunt Majida wept to think her brother sorrowed at their departure.

Chapter Thirteen

THE day they left I was told Saliman was going with them. Not all my protests nor Saliman's bitter tears made any difference.

After they had gone I wandered through the empty rooms and across the deserted courtyard as if carrying out a sentence. The silence was not the dead quietness of unoccupied rooms; it was desolate and rich with vibrations of sounds that had recently been stilled.

Nandi was waiting in my room squatting on her haunches.

"They took Saliman away and who or what could stop them? Not all your kind thoughts and good intentions. Better to be my father's mule that sometimes digs in its heels and will not move even when it is beaten, than to be poor and a woman.

"They did not tell me the reason."

"You are not supposed to understand these things. We who are poor need no teaching. There is no one but ourselves to guard us from knowing; and that is no guard to count on, believe me."

"When I used to ask her why she was quiet she would not tell me."

"The stupid fool! She thought that pig would marry her. That fine sahib needed training to juggle dishes at the table, but none to ruin a girl. She is carrying his baby."

"I never imagined. . . . How terrible! Do you mean Ghulam Ali? But nothing has been done to him?"

"Why should it? Who would dare tell Sahib about his favourite? Besides he would have denied it, and would they have taken my word or Saliman's about the kind of man he is?"

"*Your* word?"

"Laila Bitia, you don't know what life can be for us. We are the prey of every man's desires. But if only that fool

Saliman had listened to me. I could have told her no man is worth a woman's loving or trusting. Believe me, I'll marry the first old goat my father finds me if he will keep me in comfort."

"Poor Saliman! I had no idea. . . ."

"Poor fool! But they will arrange something, you can be sure. Some old man will want a young slave to cook his food and press his feet. But she must suffer first. I know, and could have told her. But do you think she would have listened to advice? Did I? Does anyone? No, Bitia, we cannot escape our destiny, or the devils inside us. Oh, Bitia, my heart is so heavy."

"Mine too, Nandi. Stay here with me tonight, and do not cry, because if I start I will not stop a lifetime."

In the darkness of my dreams I walked alone across an unending desert and a cold wind blew the sands on my face, and Aunt Abida's voice called me and Saliman held out her baby to me, but it was a bundle of clothes in Nandi's arms. I was tired and crying, and Asad came towards me holding out his hand but I could not reach it and his face changed and I called out "Ameer" and the sun exploded in the sky.

Nandi was bending over me, "Bitia, do not cry. You are not alone. I am with you."

Part Three

Chapter One

IT was summer when my cousins came back home. Kemal the elder was five years older than me, and Saleem a year younger than he. I was almost nineteen.

Kemal was tall and thin, loose-limbed and lithe. He had his mother's pale skin and large light-brown eyes which he had a habit of blinking nervously during an argument. His manner of talking was gentle and hesitant. He had been very sensitive to manifestations of colour prejudice while in England, and had developed a reserve which changed into a general shyness. Both at school and at Cambridge he had been liked by everyone who met him because of his skill at games, and generous nature. After a period of indecision he gave up the idea of becoming a lawyer and joined the Indian Civil Service, as his father had done.

Saleem was stocky and slow of movement. He had his father's high cheek-bones, and a wide, humourous mouth. He had an inquisitive mind, strong opinions, a hearty manner, laugh and appetite. At Cambridge, to avoid mediocrity because he was no good at games, he became an intellectual. He read and talked Marxism, grew his hair and beard, wore red ties and Russian shirts, decorated his room with Red banners and busts of Marx and Lenin and used the head of Stalin as a paperweight. Then he fell in love with a beautiful Persian. He became an earnest Muslim, arguing that Islam was a spiritually higher form of Communism. The Persian married an American millionaire and Saleem became Nationalist. He had had no doubts about his choice of a profession and became a barrister.

Though the brothers were so different there was a closeness which was born of their isolation from home. Their years in England had taught them to be undemonstrative, and their mother was often distressed by their seemingly inadequate response to her display of long pent-up maternal emotion.

We became friends easily. My life changed. It had been restricted by invisible barriers almost as effectively as the physically restricted lives of my aunts in the zenana. A window had opened here, a door there, a curtain had been drawn aside; but outside lay a world narrowed by one's field of vision. After my grandfather's death more windows had opened, a little wider perhaps, but the world still lay outside while I created my own round myself.

Now I was drawn out, made to join in, and not stand aside as a spectator. Yet the private refuge remained in readiness for withdrawal.

The heat of summer began to weigh every limb, and burn into one's eyes and entrails. The sky changed into a leaden weight. The trees carried their leaves heavily, until the furnace wind tore through them joylessly, covering them with the dust that crept through every crevice and filmed every surface. By day in the darkened rooms the blades of fans swirled fiery air, and unblinking lizards stuck motionless to the walls and disappeared with the suddenness of conspirators.

In the evenings every open space, lanes and streets and lawns became a refuge from oven-hot walls. The hours of relief between sunset and sunrise began to shorten as the heat crept into them.

It was time to go away to the hills.

But before we could leave, Kemal and Saleem had to be introduced to Hasanpur.

I returned with them to find time had changed me towards Hasanpur. As my circumscribed world opened out slowly, books I had read, people I had met affected my feelings towards it, undermining them with a sense of guilt.

I saw poverty and squalor, disease and the waste of human beings whereas before I had looked at them, unseeing, through a screen of emotions.

On the first evening of their arrival when the sun had set

Kemal and Saleem were called out on to the wide front veranda and asked to sit between those who managed the estate. Two elderly *sepahis* stood immediately behind them, while others grouped at the back, all holding long, steel-pointed spears. Paraffin lamps flared and their light fell on the work-worn hands and bodies, the wind-and-sun-worn limbs and faces of waiting tenants. One by one old men and young men walked up, bowed low to salaam and held out in their cupped hands a silver rupee, the token of homage established since the days of my grandfather. Kemal and Saleem touched the money and the *sepahis* took it as their due.

Both outside and inside the zenana were collected men and women and children, relations to the remotest degree of kinship, from Hasanpur and near-by hamlets and villages. Tenants and their wives sat in patient groups. They had come out of duty and curiosity to see and welcome the two young men of Baba Jan's family who had gone away beyond the seas, and had returned at last to their people.

After the *Milad-Sharif* and prayers *mirasins* sang songs of welcome and joy. While food was first served to the men outside Sharifan moaned and mimed her imitation of English songs to amuse the young 'English' masters. Women and children crowded round Kemal and Saleem and smiled and stared and smiled again.

The ten years of estrangement had no significance. Centuries of kinship swallowed them up in a moment.

All day there was nothing to do but eat and sleep. The heat and the sun and burning wind kept us locked in darkened rooms, cooled by screens of water-soaked *khas* roots whose scent was mixed with that of ripe golden mangoes, and pale melons piled near by.

Saleem played his records, and filled the drowsy rooms with the strange sound of jazz.

I wondered about the dead whose graves we had come to visit, whose stream of life flowed in us and through us. They had been kept alive by generations that respected their traditions. Did our alien thoughts and alien way of living push them into oblivion? Or was it final release for them and freedom for the living?

Everything in those days of my years ended with a question mark.

uncertainty!

Chapter Two

THIS summer our home in the hills seemed more beautiful because I saw it through the eyes of Kemal and Saleem who did not yet take it for granted. Their memories gave it a dimension beyond the purely physical enjoyment of beauty. Memories burst around them like crackers, and unfolded like flowers in the sun. They were at moments like two children excited by re-discovering old hide-outs, at others they were young men eager to be part of their heritage again.

Every morning we rode out along the range of surrounding hills. The long hours brimmed with sensory delight in the sky, the sun, the light on the lake and the hills, the shape of the ranges, the wind in the trees and on the water.

The rest of the day belonged to the family. Not that their parents attempted to order their lives; all that the holiday humour of a summer season in the hills required was recognition of a social pattern. Aunt Saira insisted on the observance of social forms and obligations. For Uncle Hamid this season was not only a social holiday; over the parties, the meals, the games of bridge hung the shadow of the coming elections.

As Kemal was on leave only for a month his parents decided to start their season's entertaining earlier than usual with a party for their sons.

Always afterward, I thought of it ironically as a mirror of my environment, while I lived with my uncle and aunt. It did not need bigger issues to reflect conflicting values.

For Aunt Saira the planning of a party was no simpler than for Uncle Hamid to plan a political campaign. Not that it was difficult to feed and entertain over three hundred guests; the problem lay in remembering everyone whom the social code made it obligatory to invite or *not* to invite. It made her lose her appetite and her temper.

Aunt Saira, frowning with concentration, pulling names out of her memory said anxiously, "What does one do about Bhimnagar? Now that he has married some half-caste from Calcutta and insists on taking out both wives together, what does one do? One cannot condone such behaviour."

"Have you written Shekh Waliuddin's name yet? If not, do so," said Uncle Hamid.

Waliuddin was a lawyer who found politics more rewarding than his practice. His political beliefs veered in any direction that promised power. He was as friendly with Congress leaders as Muslim League ones. He won followers by making use of men with influence whom he won over with service and flattery.

"That man," exclaimed Aunt Saira, "that man who instigated Shia Sunni riots for the sake of becoming a leader? Everyone knows he secretly encouraged the rioting, and then came out as the hero who stopped it."

"I am not concerned with his methods. All I am concerned with are the results. Which reminds me, don't forget Agarwal," interrupted Uncle Hamid dryly.

"Agarwal?" Saleem repeated the name as if searching for something.

"His daughter used to be at school with me. Sita Agarwal," I said.

"Sita?" Kemal said sharply.

"Do you know her?"

"Slightly. Met her in London."

"You have never mentioned her."

"There was no occasion to," Kemal said curtly.

"The world is a small place, they say," Saleem smiled. "Even London is microscopic when one Indian wishes to avoid another."

"I must go to Amirpur's for bridge," Uncle Hamid said.

"That reminds me," Aunt Saira said. "What about Dr and Mrs Lal? The way Amirpur dances around that woman is shocking."

"Nonsense! Scandalous nonsense!" said Uncle Hamid

as he was leaving the room. Mrs Lal is a charming woman."

"I can't understand what you men see in her. Bold and pushing," Aunt Saira called after him. "The spectacle men make of themselves! All the ministers spinning round her. . . ."

"Clever woman to achieve what seems to be the general purpose," said Kemal.

"Such dreadful people one has to meet!" she sighed. "Things have changed so much. But you must learn what your position in life is, and where you belong."

"We were left in no doubt about that on quite a few occasions in England—we coloured people," Kemal smiled.

"I like my position in life," laughed Saleem. "It is very comfortable. When I was young I thought otherwise, but that was adolescent masochism which I mistook for Marxism. Mind you, I still appreciate its principles, but I am no Lenin and can establish no Soviets. . . ."

"Linen serviettes?" Aunt Saira frowned. "I do not know what you are talking about."

"How fortunate you are, mother. Oh, brave old world!" Saleem laughed and kissed his mother.

She smiled happily and kissed both her sons. "I am going to rest now. Will you children get the invitations ready? The cards and envelopes are in your father's office downstairs."

"I'll get them," said Saleem and went down the stairs with his mother.

Kemal sat staring out of the window. He never argued with his mother when she talked to him about understanding his heritage and culture; but I knew, because he confided in me, that his readjustment was not as easy as Saleem's.

He said very quietly, as if talking to himself, "When I was a boy I used to sit at this window and look at the hills and the lake. Nothing has changed. I can still see a man's profile in the shape of that peak over there; the same noises come up from the bazaar below; the same human ants move about. The toy yachts becalmed on the lake have not finished the race which started when I was a boy. The house has not changed, the garden hasn't changed, the gardener hasn't changed. These hill people grow no older. They treat me like a little boy. The coolies are the same, in the same rags, with the same smiles and smells. I feel I have never been away. Then I talk to father and mother and their friends and I know I have been away for more than ten years. We talk without knowing what has happened to each other in the course of these years, not even external things. How much greater is the ignorance of the changes within that cannot be described but only felt! At least, when people are near each other they have some slight indication. . . . Yet I am expected to think and behave as if I had never been away, as if the patterns of my thoughts should be familiar to those who have stayed behind. Do you understand me?"

"I do understand. Do you know why? Because without having gone away physically as you did I have never lived completely with the others."

"I recognised that about you quite quickly. That is why I could talk to you and no one else. And now," he smiled, "I can tell you something which proves my point about my mother, about our not understanding each other. I had been back scarcely a week when she asked me whether I would consider marrying you."

"She asked *you* to marry *me*?"

"She said, 'Now that Laila is nineteen it is time to think of her marriage. What could be better than to keep the family undivided? . . .'"

"And the house, and the property," I added.

"You are being unkind, Laila. I think she genuinely meant it . . . not from a material, but a human point of view."

"It is lucky when they coincide. But what did you say?"

"I said, Damn it all, mother, I'm not going to commit

incest. Because that is how I thought of you from the first—as a sister. Not that she understood."

Saleem stamped up the stairs into the room, "What is the matter? Why do you both look so solemn?" he asked.

I smiled. "I have the right to be. Kemal has refused to marry me."

"Kemal has refused to marry you? Add me to the list. I've done the same."

"You have?" Kemal and I said together.

"Well, mother put the proposition to me. . . ."

"To you too? She seems to be very impatient. I had better find someone for myself before she gets quite desperate. And what did you say?"

"I said, 'Mother, I don't love the girl'."

"Thank you for being honest," I laughed.

"I mean not that way," Saleem said quickly. "And she said, 'Love?' in a very superior, shocked manner, eyebrows lifted, nostrils quivering, 'Love? No one in decent families talks of love'."

We burst out laughing together, and I said, "I've been told I'm not loved; I've been rejected twice; and I couldn't be happier. Thank you both with all my heart. I may have hated you as husbands, but I love you as friends."

"A more lasting relationship, I assure you," said Kemal.

"In sickness and in health till death do us part," laughed Saleem. "And now to our task! Let us slay the social dragons."

Chapter Three

THE tiny lawn was as gay as the border of flowers that ran round it on one side touching the fern- and moss-covered slope of the hill, on the other edging the grey tennis court, and in between them spilling over the edge to the terraced vegetable garden and the apple orchard.

Tea-tables sprouted like starched, white mushrooms on the green grass, and grey gravel. The saris of women grouped round them were like colours squeezed on an artist's palette. The suits and *achkans* of the men, and party dresses of the English women provided a dark background with pastel touches.

My uncle and aunt stood by the steps leading down from the gravelled path and welcomed their guests. Akbar and Anwar stood beside them as immaculate as dummies in a shop window, their faces like all the other faces around them stretching into smiles of patterned politeness.

I remained standing a little distance behind, and smiled at everyone too, wondering at the variety of expressions that could be conveyed by facial contortions.

White-uniformed bearers remained poised and alert between groups of tables, under the command of Ghulam Ali, who, in crested uniform and starched turban, treated them as underlings.

Coolies panted up the steep slopes carrying guest-laden *dandys*; teams of uniformed coolies moving like automatons; coolies in dirty, patched clothes moving like ragged scarecrows; all of them smelling of sweat and smoke-filled tenements, their faces strained and streaming, their breath torn from their lungs painfully.

When the scarlet livery of the Raja of Bhimnagar's coolies swept into view, my aunt frowned in disapproval.

The Raja walked in front of his two wives. He was a man of medium height, but his turban lent him stature. His good looks had crumbled with dissipation. A large diamond sparkled on the lobe of each ear, and both his wives were like chandeliers of precious stones. The senior Rani's face was that of a painted pathetic doll. The second Rani—but it couldn't be—it was Sylvia Tucker. Bhimnagar could buy anything; even her colour prejudice. She looked around her with defiant derison, and her eyes wavered a moment seeing me. I looked at her without recognition, and she moved on with a shrug of her shoulders. For quite a while I was disturbed by remembered hate.

There was an extra warmth in my aunt's greeting for Begum Waheed.

There had been an acid period of tension when my aunt had discovered that Begum Waheed had transgressed an unwritten social law and had copied the colour of my aunt's coolies' uniform. It was the sort of thing that inspired my aunt to discourse on the rise of the *nouveau riche*. However, their friendship had survived many such hazards.

Begum Waheed bustled down the steps with Nadira following in her mother's powerful wake.

I noticed Saleem turning to look at her as she walked towards me. We welcomed each other joyfully because together we lost our selfconsciousness in a crowd with which we were both out of key.

Most of the guests had by now arrived and my aunt and uncle moved towards the tea-tables. Aunt Saira's face glowed with satisfaction. It was indeed a most impressive gathering; all those who exercised power in the province, its government, its politics and its society were collected to enjoy my aunt's hospitality.

In accordance with current social customs every conventional English delicacy was supplemented by every conceivable Indian one. Bearers, well trained into respectful anonymity, carried trays heaped with Indian sweets and savouries, while cakes and scones and sandwiches were arranged in tiered stands on the tables. Ghulam Ali hovered over the guests and bearers like a high priest supervising sacred rites.

Guests continued to arrive. Mrs Lal dramatised her entry as usual by arriving late but not last. She paused at the top of the steps, her sari modestly covering her head yet revealing the tight curves and flowing lines of her body, her head tilted, her long neck arched, her lips faintly smiling, her half-closed eyes suggesting a sly eroticism. Her eyes and her voice, which made the offer of a cup of tea seem like the offer of a love potion, stirred every man's heart and every woman's spleen, yet she always kept conversation on the level of naïve innocence, and brandished her virtue like a burnished shield.

Dr Lal was a blurred, smudged person hard to remember in his absence. He was prouder of his wife than any collector of his rarest find. If connoisseurs of beauty were found among the rich and powerful that was further evidence of his taste and good fortune. He was an indifferent physician and fond of drink, but during the season his practice flourished.

Kemal and Saleem hurried to receive them, and as he passed me Saleem grinned and his mouth shaped in a soundless whistle.

The sound of new arrivals came up the drive.

Mrs Agarwal heaved her bulk carefully out of her *dandy* and down the steps, her round peasant face calm and solemn. She looked uncomfortable in silks and shoes and sitting on chairs even after years of prosperity. Imagination clothed her more suitably in cotton, seating her on the ground, barefooted, in a traditional kitchen.

Her husband waved on his coolies impatiently, and waited to help someone out of the third *dandy*.

And there, straightening herself, smiling at him and coming down the steps was Sita.

"Look, Nadira! Sita!"

"Who?"

"The girl who used to be my friend at school."

I did not go to meet her. I wanted to look at her first. The same wide, up-turned mouth, the same dark skin, the same bright eyes. But now the skin glowed, the eyes were exaggerated in length and darkened with *kajal*, the eyebrows arched and lengthened, and the mouth vivid. Her dark shining hair was drawn back, emphasising the oval of her face and long line of her neck, and was piled in a high bun circled with white flowers. Her tight blouse was the scarlet of a parrot's beak, and as green as its feathers was the sari of hand-woven silk. The dot on her forehead, her mobile mouth and long nails picked out the colour of the blouse. Sita's slim body moved like water.

I saw Kemal's jaw tighten and Saleem said something to her which made her laugh nervously.

"She is very attractive and knows it," Nadira commented.

"She used to be quite plain. England has changed her."

"Made her the European's *idea* of a colourful Indian," Nadira said critically.

"She seems to have become . . . alive," I said hesitatingly.

"It's all a question of make-up and clothes and opportunities. She has not been smothered like we are." Nadira's voice was pointed with an envy which stirred within me too.

"Sita!"

"Laila!" we called together. She came towards us and we embraced each other.

"You have changed, Laila. You are much, much prettier but with the same troubled inquiring large eyes." Her laugh matched the drawling languidness of her voice.

"You have changed too," I said awkwardly, very conscious of my English in contrast with hers. "This is my friend Nadira. We were together at College."

Nadira seemed suddenly closer to me. After the first rush of memories, Sita seemed a stranger, and we spoke from across a wide gulf.

"I am so glad to meet you, Nadira. Laila and I used to be together at school."

"A long time ago," I said, wanting to be assured time did not matter.

"A very long time ago," said Sita factually, as she looked around her with curiosity and pleasure.

"There's someone else here who used to be at school with us. Remember Sylvia Tucker? There she is; the Rani of Bhimnagar now."

"Really? How characteristic of her! I would like to go and talk to her. Will you come?"

"I hate her," I said.

"Dear Laila, how little you've changed! Who cares for the rise or fall of Sylvia Tucker?" Sita laughed.

Everyone in the groups around each table was busy eating, talking, smiling, as if there were nothing beyond or beneath the surface of each sociable moment. The Indian women had drawn together apart from the men. Most of the English guests had formed groups of their own.

Nadira, Sita and I smiled at each other to gloss over our growing awkwardness.

"Shall we sit there?" I suggested, pointing towards a table set apart, looking over the terraced garden.

"Yes, of course," said Sita, looking around with an air of cynical amusement.

As we were moving away I saw the Raja of Amirpur hurrying towards Aunt Saira, his manner exuding charm and apologies. His personal servant followed him at a respectful distance, carrying a silver casket containing his special *pān*, and a tiny silver spittoon. And walking rapidly across the lawn to catch up with his father was his eldest son, with someone by his side who was a stranger, yet not a stranger.

I was numbed by the first glance of recognition and then covered my confusion by talking rapidly.

"I like sitting here where I can look across at the hills and turn my back on people. Their hollow voices and hollow words bore me. Look at them! As if they were eternally facing photographers, waiting patiently for the cameras to click, until their faces get set in fossilised grins."

"Laila, do you remember, in all our arguments Nita accused you of being an escapist? Though I did not agree with her that one could not face reality without de-classing one's self, I believe our religion is right in teaching us to live as a human being among human beings. You cannot turn your face away from reality. Sooner or later you will be forced to turn your back on the hills. Why not get used to it?" Nadira preached in a way familiar to me.

Sita leaned back in her chair languidly and drawled, "How interesting to hear you talk in this manner! How delightfully youthful! It is such a long time since abstract problems of right and wrong worried me. Personally I find the experience of living is challenge enough; and human beings are exciting. That is why I lost interest in my studies—not that I was ever as clever as you, Laila. Books are so dead and dull compared to living, warm people. I have disappointed my father by returning after four years with a poor degree, but I have no regrets."

"You are lucky your father could afford his disappointment, and your moments of richness." Nadira's delicate nostrils quivered with hostility.

"I know that," answered Sita coolly. "I'm glad we are rich, I enjoy being rich. It would not make us any less so if I felt guilty about it. I cannot see who would benefit if I were frustrated."

Nadira flushed. Confused by Sita's unexpected aggression when we had still not adjusted ourselves to each other I said hesitantly, "You have changed a lot, Sita. You used to be quite an idealist. Do you remember how we fought at school because one of the Anglo-Indian girls abused Gandhiji? We were such nationalists that we bought hideous saris with the national flag printed around the borders when your uncle went to jail."

"I am still a nationalist, my dear Laila." Sita's voice still had an edge of mockery. "My father's otherwise tight purse strings are always open for the nationalist cause. I wear nothing but Indian silks, and I believe in reviving our ancient art and culture. But I do not find it in myself to give up all I have and go to jail, though I am sure in time a spell in jail will bring its reward. Though my uncle did not think of that." Her voice shook slightly, then renewed its earlier tone. "I remember it upset my father who had just got a contract for cloth from the Inspector General of Police. No, I'm quite sure I can be of less use to the world as a frustrated idealist than a happy realist."

The bearer brought hot tea and I poured it out.

"I take mine without sugar, thank you," said Sita.

"You protest so much," said Nadira acidly, wiping cake-crumbs from her mouth. "It seems as if all your freedom has not helped you to be free of something you are fighting inside yourself."

"A little psychology is a dangerous thing," laughed Sita, her eyes narrowing.

Nothing could have been more welcome than Saleem's breaking in. "May we join you? We are refugees from boredom."

"You are more than welcome," smiled Sita.

"May I introduce Thakur Ranjit Singh, Kunwar Raza Ali of Amirpur and his cousin Ameer Hussain? My brother Akbar, of course, you know, Miss Agarwal. . . ."

"Sita, please," she smiled.

"Sita. My cousin Laila, and . . ." he looked at Nadira questioningly.

"My friend Nadira Waheed."

I thought the beating of my heart would be heard.

"Well, here we are, able to be ourselves at last," said Saleem as they sat down. "I'm fed up with polite talk and I'm starving. Bearer!" he called, and ordered more tea.

"Laila," Kemal asked me, "you must remember Ranjit surely?"

"When I was very young . . ." I began.

"I remember you as a small girl with big eyes and long plaits"—Ranjit laughed—"but I regret we did not meet afterwards. You forget our customs, Kemal. We were not allowed to meet freely when your grandfather was alive, not after the dangerous age of thirteen or fourteen."

"Well now at the lethal age of twenty-five you have my permission to do so," Saleem called out.

"It is a curious thing, meeting in childhood and again after so many years," Kemal said quietly. "When we were talking, Ranjit, about our boyhood together it seemed to me as if there had been no break in our friendship. I felt and feel—closer to you than any of the friends I made in England."

"That is a quality of your Eastern blood," Ranjit said with a smile. "It will take more than ten or twelve years to break the ties of generations of kinship and friendship."

"The trouble with the East is that it does not loosen its hold on anything, and time has really no meaning where the chalcolithic age survives to the twentieth century." Kemal smiled back at him.

There was an obvious warmth and ease between them.

Ranjit was the grandson of my grandfather's friend Thakur Balbir Singh. He had deep-set eyes, thick, untidy hair, a loud, infectious laugh, and an open manner as if nothing were locked inside him.

In complete contrast young Amirpur sat silent beside him, withdrawn, not looking at Sita, and Nadira, and me. Though he had been educated by English tutors he had been brought up with strictly traditional ideas about women. He had been married at sixteen and already at the age of twenty four had five children. It was said he did not know his wife's name because he had never addressed her by it.

Saleem was saying to Sita, fingering his old school tie, "This key to English hearts worked like magic on what's-his-name over there. In the Forest Service, I believe. May be that is why he has that anthropoid look. Quite a zoological couple, don't you think? His wife looks like a honey-bear. He slapped me on the back, talked of the good old school, and made me feel as if I had some special, select quality...."

"A native but one of us, what?" laughed Sita, and then

drew him into gay reminiscences of London in which we had no part. I felt angry and envious.

Kemal's face had a strained look for a moment, and then he started talking to Ranjit and Raza Ali about a tiger shoot they were arranging.

The rest of us were silent. Nadira's face still showed signs of her dislike of Sita.

I was listening to their voices while in a deeper layer of my consciousness, I was still trying to find words, or at least the courage to look up and into his eyes as Ameer stood up.

Young Amirpur was saying gently and patiently, "If you will give me permission. . . ."

"I beg your pardon," said Saleem jumping up, and added, "What about tennis tomorrow? That is fixed, is it not? Both of you will be coming."

"Thank you. I shall be delighted. . . ."

"Thank you very much," said Ameer.

They bowed, and raised their hands towards their foreheads saying, "*Khuda Hafiz.*"

"*Khuda Hafiz,*" Nadira and I said.

"Good-bye until tomorrow," Sita smiled.

For me the animated lawn became crowded with puppets moving in mannered measures, gesticulating and making sounds in accordance with elaborate rules and studied scores. It was suddenly drained of all human interest.

Chapter Four

THE silence and the tension between us ended so easily the next time Ameer and I were together that I wondered at them. For the first time I became aware that barriers built by the mind had no more substance than the fears that raised them; once they were overcome by action, it was hard to believe they had ever existed.

We met two long days after the garden party when Ameer came with Raza Ali and Ranjit to play tennis.

I sat by the side of the court watching them play with a deep sense of contentment. The warmth of the sun touched my skin, tempered by the light wind that sounded deep and orchestral through the needles of the deodar trees. I listened mechanically to Ranjit's laughter and banter as, sitting beside me, he commented on the play, and I watched with sensuous pleasure the sculptured strength and grace of young bodies in movement.

Ameer came and sat beside me while Ranjit joined the players.

He stretched his legs lazily, tilting the cane chair backwards, his body relaxed and supple.

"That was a good game," he said politely, looking at the handle of his racket.

"Yes, it was," I answered shyly.

"Kemal plays well, and Saleem could be quite good if he ran a bit more."

"He is not exactly built for speed."

He laughed with me, and the awkwardness dissolved. He looked at me, and I did not look away.

Gradually, while talking of my cousins, of the party, of Asad and Zahid, of impersonal things, it seemed as if the inculcated restrictions that had made communication difficult with any one outside my small circle had become as tenuous as webs; and it seemed we were continuing a conversation started a long time ago.

It became possible to talk of our first meeting.

"It was strange the way it happened . . ." he began.

"It was stupid to get frightened of a man who could not possibly harm me.

"I am glad you were or I would not have met you. I had never expected to . . ."

"Expected? How could you have? I mean strangers don't expect . . ." and I hesitated, stammering.

"I had heard about you from Asad," he explained. "And I used to see you drive past the University every morning. It had become a kind of habitual routine until I began to wait for you and used to get anxious if you were delayed or did not come." Then he added lightly, "I must confess it was a pastime with most boys to hang about the gates waiting to see the girls go by."

"That was one of the reasons why my aunt and Begum Waheed used to say young men were not ready for co-education, because they were not taught in their homes to meet girls in the proper way."

"I can assure you," Amer smiled, "there was nothing improper about my——"

"I didn't mean to be personal," I interrupted, feeling my cheeks warm with embarrassment.

"Anyway," he said with a deliberate lightness of tone, "you were quite unaware of my existence. You belonged to another world, guarded by a thousand taboos fiercer than the most fiery dragons."

"Until one day I ventured out into another world. . . ."

"And Destiny literally threw you into my arms."

"Then came a day when you got past the dragons and stepped right into the castle."

"Because Asad cracked his skull. But I could not wish for Destiny to continue using such drastic methods."

"You did not have to. Destiny brought you peacefully

here to this small world in which people cannot avoid each other even if they loathe each other."

"Destiny had little to do with it. I had to scheme like a conspirator. Destiny's job was done. I think Destiny's purpose is merely to shock us at moments into a state of awareness; those moments are milestones in between which we have to find our own way. I found mine into this world by the poor relation's entrance. True I had to swallow my pride, but it was obviously not too big a mouthful. Here I am, alive, and well, and not choked to death!"

"And I am not an unconscious murderess."

"But beware, people can be murdered and still move about in a semblance of living."

We laughed together and I was oblivious of all else but the banter and the laughter, until I saw the coolies who picked up stray balls stiffen into obsequious attention. I saw my uncle walking across the lawn and my laughter and sense of freedom were congealed within me.

As he came up to us and answered Ameer's salutation with an inclination of his head, he motioned to us to sit down and lowered himself into an armchair. His face was set in its usual stern lines, and there was a preoccupied expression in his eyes.

There was silence for a while. Then as he sat in the gentle sunshine watching his sons playing, the lines on his face relaxed. He began to take an interest in the game, and to talk to Ameer of his student days when he had been a sportsman.

I felt a kind of wonder, as if layers of a mask were flaking off and I was seeing my uncle more clearly as a human being than a symbol of authority. Ever since his sons had returned home I had caught fleeting glimpses of a human side of him I had not known before.

When the game was over and the players joined us Uncle Hamid seemed completely relaxed and happy to be with his sons, and the sons of his friends.

He said, "Laila Béti, will you ask Ghulam Ali to have tea

brought out here? It will be much pleasanter than in the house. As your aunt has gone out you will have to act as hostess."

It seemed to me there was a new note of gentleness in his voice. Or perhaps I imagined it, and the change was in myself. Everything seemed so much more beautiful, and everyone so much nicer.

Tea had hardly finished when the pleasant atmosphere was disturbed by the discordant announcement of the arrival of Mr Agarwal and Sheikh Waliuddin. They came and settled like ravens in the midst of the happy group.

When the ceremonious greetings and polite preliminaries were over they turned the conversation towards the purpose of their visit. They had some matters of political importance to discuss.

I thought it best to leave them, and reluctantly walked towards the house. I had noticed how quickly my uncle's face had changed and hardened into lines of anxiety and aggression.

For some time Uncle Hamid had been absorbed in problems and controversies relating to the elections that were to be held under the new Government of India Act. There was hardly another topic of conversation at parties and card-tables. Constituencies and ministries were distributed among gentlemen like cakes, and ladies were offered seats in both houses like bouquets.

Most of Uncle Hamid's friends were confident of success. To them party affiliations were mere labels; a concession to democratic forms. They believed they would succeed as in the past, because of the pressure their power and influence could put on voters.

Uncle Hamid was among the few who recognised the challenge of the Congress and the reorganised Muslim League now that millions of ordinary men and women were being given the right to vote by the new constitution. He pointed out to his friends that the Congress had the strength of long years of dedicated struggle and sacrifice for freedom, and the Muslim League was gaining strength from its appeal to the political and economic fears of the Muslims as the largest minority in the country, and to their religious emotions and pride.

The struggle for political power had to be more intense than ever before because greater power would lie in the hands of those who would form the new Government.

It was Uncle Hamid's first attempt to enter national politics. At first he had thought it best to represent the *Taluqdars* from their own constituency. They had four reserved seats in the Provincial legislature, the election to be held by the *Taluqdars* from amongst themselves. But the Raja of Amirpur preferred one of his protégés, and persuaded Uncle Hamid to stand for a 'safe' constituency which covered his and the Raja of Bhimnagar's estates.

Through the windows I could see the shadows sloping across the lawn, and moving from the valley to the opposite peaks. Soon it would be twilight, Ameer would have to go, and I was missing so much time with him. I turned over the pages of a magazine, my grasshopper mind unable to concentrate.

I heard the voices of my uncle and his unwelcome guest, moving towards the house, and, dropping the magazines hurried out towards the porch. As I passed them on the front steps Agarwal smiled his ingratiating smile and said, "Sita is sorry she has not been able to come and see you, but she has had a bad cold."

"I am terribly sorry. I hope she gets well soon." I answered, and felt a twinge of conscience because I did not really care.

When I got back I found Saleem sitting watching the others play. I was not surprised knowing he must have stayed to listen to the older men's conversation. He lost no opportunity of joining—even instigating—interminable political discussions. He considered he had already mastered Indian political problems.

Ameer, waiting at the net for his partner to serve, threw

a welcoming smile at me. I felt my cheeks and ears burning, and turned towards Saleem saying, "I am glad those men have gone. I do not like them. Even when they are being charming it seems as if a smooth silk cover were stretched over something hard and scaly."

"It is your instinct, my dear Laila, which makes you uneasy. Those gentlemen are the instruments by which the historical process is going to destroy your class, though both of them hang on to the fringes of feudalism."

Saleem was in his element being able to expound his views.

I tried to look attentive as he went on. "I found them most instructive this afternoon. They brought home to me why our Province is known for its culture, and our home-town for its nuances of courtesy and grace. Nowhere else could the impossible, acrobatic feat have been performed of stabbing one in the back right under one's nose! And with such charm, humility and poetry that the stabber and the stabbed both appeared to be accepting a gracious favour from each other. I had a lesson in practical politics, which makes all one's theoretical studies seem like the pipe-dreams of opium eaters."

"Hamid Chacha was looking very disturbed when I saw him just now walking back with those two. . . ."

"Waliuddin had come with the news that he has joined the Muslim League, and—very reluctantly, of course—had been chosen to contest father's seat."

"That is significant. Waliuddin backs only the side he thinks will win. Why did he bring Agarwal with him?"

"The Congress and the League have agreed to sink their differences when it comes to fighting the British and the parties they support. Agarwal expressed his profound regrets, and hinted he would be obliged to use pressure on Bhimnagar, who is deeply in debt to him, to withdraw his support for father. Both of them vowed it was a proof of friendship and regard that they had come to warn him. They suggested he should go back to his original plan, and get nominated by the *Taluqdars* to represent them from their special constituency."

"It sounds like a game of musical chairs," I said. "It seems immoral turned into a political game by adults. Strange how different politics appeared when Asad talked about his beliefs, or when Nita and I used to argue."

"The Asads and Nitas of this world serve a useful purpose even for the Waliuddins and Agarwals. 'The devil can cite scripture for his purpose.' They must be given a scripture to cite by your friends," Saleem said derisively.

There was a brief silence, and then Saleem said, "I forgot to tell you Begum Waheed is also standing as a Muslim League candidate."

"Really? I suppose it is only logical. Now she can carry on her Islamic crusade on a really big scale. Nadira must be delighted."

"She is a nice girl. I quite like her."

"That was fairly obvious," I teased him.

"Why don't you ask her over? She was too shy to accept my invitation to ride, even with a whole troop to act as chaperones."

"The trouble is I must ask Sita too and Nadira does not like Sita. By the way, you to whom all mysteries are clear, tell me why Kemal dislikes Sita?"

"It's no mystery and he does not dislike her. On the contrary, he was very much in love with her and probably still is. It happened shortly after they met in London. She seemed to welcome his attentions until matters became too serious."

"Do you mean Kemal wanted to marry her?"

"He did. But for all her sophistication, scratch her and you'll find an orthodox Hindu full of prejudices against Muslims."

"That is not fair, Saleem. Could a Muslim girl marry a Hindu boy? Our religion forbids it."

"Under certain circumstances of self-preservation that was a necessary prohibition."

"Some people would say you blaspheme against the final and eternal expression of the Divine Will," I teased him.

"I am not interested in theological arguments. But Sita's attitude opened my eyes to the realities of the communal problem, What can you expect from a religion which forbids people to eat and drink together? When even a man's shadow can defile another? How is real friendship or understanding possible?

"Ranjit is your friend, isn't he?"

"He has no such stupid prejudices."

"His grandfather did not eat with Baba Jan, but was his greatest friend."

"You cannot reduce a whole political and social problem to an individual one," Saleem said impatiently.

"And you cannot generalise," I retorted.

Any further argument was prevented by the others joining us.

As we moved towards the house, Saleem said, "You must all stay for dinner. We'll play bridge afterwards."

"Good idea," said Ranjit.

"I'm sorry, I must go," said Raza Ali. "In the evenings my mother expects me to eat in the zenana with her."

"What about you, Ameer?"

"Well . . . I . . ." he stammered and I willed him silently to stay. Then to Raza Ali he asked, "May I, Bhai Sahib?"

"As you wish," Raza Ali answered.

"Thank you," Ameer said to Saleem, "I shall be very happy to stay."

As we were walking into the house he said to me very softly, "At this rate of swallowing it I'll have no pride left."

Chapter Five

THE atmosphere at dinner was affected by my uncle's mood. It was quite a relief when he asked for coffee to be sent to his study saying he had to finish reading some important papers.

We moved into the sitting-room. When Ranjit remarked that he thought Uncle Hamid was not looking well, Saleem found a welcome opportunity to reiterate his theories about the political situation. Very soon an argument had whipped everyone out of their earlier lassitude and anyone listening to the raised voices would have imagined there was a quarrel in progress.

I found I had mislaid my handkerchief and as I moved to the door Ameer sprang up to open it for me. The others were too engrossed to look round.

He said anxiously, "Are you leaving? Do you find this conversation boring?"

"You can hardly call it a conversation," I laughed. "No, I am not bored, I am just going to look for a handkerchief. But I confess I am tired of talk and more talk without anyone doing anything about it. I would welcome silence."

"Sometimes one cannot act as one wishes to, and yet silence is impossible."

"Then I'll have to learn the language others speak."

"Maybe we could find one in common?" Ameer said lightly.

I smiled to hide my confusion, and went quickly out of the room.

When I returned Kemal had assumed the tone and pose of a public speaker. "Gentlemen, there is only one party we can possibly join, the party that binds landlords and tenants in ties of mutal love. If you do not make the Party's cause your own you thrust a dagger into the body politic of the great order to which we have the proud privilege to belong."

Above our laughter and mock-applause we heard Uncle Hamid's icy voice. "It is a privilege of which I am proud, and of which none of you are worthy."

He was standing at the door pale and tight-lipped, and in the sudden silence Kemal said nervously, "It was meant to be a joke, father. . . ."

"A joke!" my uncle's voice exploded harshly. "Our existence is threatened and you think it a joke! Our fathers and forefathers handed us down rights and privileges which it is our duty to preserve. I have no use for ingrates who enjoy privileges without accepting responsibilities."

He turned and walked out of the room and the discomfited silence lasted for a few moments. Then Ranjit said, "It is late and time to go."

Kemal and Saleem walked down the drive with Ranjit and Ameer. I stood alone at the window and watched them until they were lost in the shadows.

The stars were dimmed by the light of the waxing moon and the range of hills was etched against the luminous sky like stage props without depth. A necklace and crown and clusters of light were repeated in the waters of the still lake. The silence and clarity of the crisp night and the memories of the evening disturbed my whole being.

The sounds of Aunt Saira's *dandy* approaching were magnified in the stillness. Her sons came in with her.

"Who was the young man walking down with Ranjit?" she asked.

"Raza Ali's cousin, Ameer," Kemal answered.

"Ameer? Raza Ali's cousin? Which cousin could that be? I have no recollection of that name? And I know the family well enough. He must belong to the other branch," she said disparagingly.

"What do you mean by 'other branch'?" asked Saleem.

"The old Raja's second wife's family. They were very ordinary people; no breeding. What does he do?"

"Teaches history I believe, at Aligarh University. A Junior Lecturer, I think."

"I suppose Raja Sahib supports him?"

"Does it make any difference, mother? Ameer seems a nice boy, more interesting than Raza Ali any way," protested Kemal.

"Certainly it makes a difference." Aunt Saira raised her voice. "All the difference that good breeding makes. You really must try and understand these things."

"Please, mother," Saleem interrupted. "We have had enough arguments for today. I think we should call it a day."

"Call it a day or night," Aunt Saira grumbled in English. "The truth remains the truth."

Kemal burst out laughing and hugged his mother saying, "You are priceless, mother, and that means you are worth more than anything on earth."

I tried to smile, but a day that had been bright had ended with a depressing sense of foreboding.

Chapter Six

I WAS permitted to go out with my cousins because they insisted I should be allowed to do so. However, my aunt was firm in her belief that an unmarried girl's freedom should be restricted, and there were many formal parties to which I was not invited or taken. I did not mind. Parties were an excuse, unimportant in themselves. Only Ameer's presence mattered. The conflicting values of the world that I lived in with my aunts Abida and Majida and the one I lived in now made me so full of doubts and questions, I retreated more and more within myself.

My problems were a submerged part of the general pattern of ease and enjoyment. Life was regulated by the invitations that poured in by post and messenger. Oblong bits of gilt-edged cardboard, and crested bits of paper measured one's importance, their selectiveness determined one's position within the geometrical design of circles that constituted Society. Though the patterns within the one were copied from the other, Indian and English circles moved exclusively most of the time, but occasionally crossed and touched at tangents.

Though many more English guests came to the house than in my grandfather's lifetime there was not one in whose friendship there was the quality which had existed in the relationship between Mr Freemantle and my grandfather. Mr Freemantle, who had lived only a year longer than Baba Jan had requested in his will that he should be buried near his friend, and only a simple marble cross distinguished his grave from the others in the family graveyard in the mango grove at Hasanpur.

While the season lasted, the same people shuffled into different combinations day in and day out, in the same homes, at the same kind of lunches and teas and dinners, at which the number of courses determined standards of hospitality and the number of titled and officially important guests determined social prestige. Men and women, automatically splitting into separate groups, handled the proprieties and rites of 'mixed' society as gingerly as most of them handled unfamiliar Western food, crystal and cutlery. Those women who were at ease with men were regarded by the others with suspicion and hostility—much as domesticated animals in fenced-off fields might re-act to one of their species who dared to wonder into unguarded spaces and yet keep within reach of safety.

The only person who rarely entertained in his home was the Raja of Amirpur, because purdah was very strictly observed in his household, and he did not think it seemly to invite men and women there together. His lavish feasts were given in the banqueting hall and on the garden terraces of the Ritz Hotel which had been bought by his father in a moment of pique after he had been refused accommodation in it.

This season the Raja of Amirpur had started a new fashion in entertainment. He would take his guests to the cinema after every party, and all the balcony seats of the solitary cinema would be reserved.

The reactions of our elders to a form of entertainment to which they had been introduced late in life was a source of amusement to us. During every love scene and at each kiss their embarrassment became palpable even in the dark. My aunt usually reacted with a spell of coughing and buried her face in her handkerchief. The Raja of Amirpur once walked out for the duration of a particularly passionate love scene because he could not witness such a display of shamelessness in the company of respectable ladies.

I, who had once been solitary, began to be happy. For the first time, I was a part of a group which had a life of its own outside the larger circle.

Our controlled freedom made both Nadira and me secretly envious of Sita who, ostensibly, cared for no conventions but those she herself wished to accept. In the company of men, while we were selfconscious, she asserted her femininity—though she did not exploit it like Mrs Lal. She expected and accepted attention while we were embarrassed by it.

Raza Ali of Amirpur had fallen completely under Sita's spell, humble as a bond-slave, his will submerged. Others flitted in and out of her orbit depending on how long they were on holiday. They varied in type from the bearded English poet searching for the 'Soul of the East'—who antagonised the English community by wearing Indian clothes and eating with his fingers—to the young subaltern with fierce moustaches, cultivated English drawl, hearty phrases and Cavalry stance who was as near a copy of his senior Sandhurst-trained officers as they were of their English prototypes.

The only man who was studiously indifferent to Sita was Kemal. My heightened perception made me understand why she was more than ever gay and flirtatious in his presence, and he so attentive to Mrs Lal in hers. I felt angry with her and sorry for him when I could spare them a thought.

The only woman who was a rival to Sita was Mrs Lal. Mrs Lal and Sita gushed over each other with a sweetness that only dislike could engender.

But over all the tension stretched the silken happiness of being young and alive.

Chapter Seven

THREE letters pulled me back to a world to which I had become oblivious. The first was an almost indecipherable postcard from Nandi, which she must have had written for her, praying for my health, long life and happiness, conveying her respects and salaams to every member of the family and each servant individually, and telling me with deep sorrow of God's kindness and goodness in taking Saliman away from this world of grief and cruelty.

My aunt who must have read it before handing it to me, commented on the inevitable fruits of evil. I did not let her see the tears that smarted in my eyes as I turned away from her.

I remembered Saliman in the aloneness of my room, because there was no one who could share her loss with me except Nandi who was beyond reach.

The second letter was from Aunt Abida's husband to my uncle. He had written that she was in hospital after a miscarriage, out of danger but still seriously ill. He asked for permission to move her to Ashiana as soon as the doctors thought it advisable.

Zahra's letter to me gave more details. After writing at length about her busy life in Simla—with passing reference to the Viceroy and Members of his Executive Council and other important people she had met—she ended with a paragraph from her mother's letter about Aunt Abida.

It appeared that when Aunt Abida had been taken ill the local midwife had been called, because the only woman doctor in the near-by township was away and her mother-in-law refused to allow a man to attend to her. It was only after her condition had become dangerous that her husband insisted on calling in the Civil Surgeon who had taken her immediately to the Medical College Hospital in Lucknow.

I was filled with anger against the murderous hypocrisy

and bigotry that had let Saliman die and nearly killed Aunt Abida. I had not written to her for a long time; I had not even thought of her lately. When I had heard, four months earlier, that she was to have a baby at last, I had been happy for her, not thinking that any risk might be involved at her age and in her delicate state of health.

And now I was frightened of death, overcome by the fear that she might have died without knowing how much she meant to me. I wanted to be near her. A sense of guilt grew in me, and a fear as formless as the shimmer of heat on the lake enveloped me.

I went to Aunt Saira to ask her if I could go to Aunt Abida while other impulses, willing me to stay, were still weak within me.

Aunt Saira was in her room dressing to go to a party. The hours of her days seemed marked by appropriate changes of costume—morning, afternoon and evening.

She was sitting at her dressing-table carefully powdering her face and the Ayah was combing her hair.

I said compulsively, "I want to go down to Lucknow. I want to be with Abida Phuphi."

Aunt Saira's hands dropped to her knees in surprise.

"What a strange idea!" she said, her eyebrows knotted. "What use would that be? What could you do? She is being well looked after. Besides, how can you travel alone? And Kemal is leaving soon. You are overwrought. You must not worry too much. Everything will be all right."

"I would like to be with her."

"That is understandable; but one must keep one's sense of proportion. Anyway, we'll talk about it later when your uncle comes home." Her tone dismissed me.

I turned away with a sense of relief that the decision had been taken away from me, and yet hated myself.

Later in the evening when I said to Ameer, "I want to go home to be with Abida Phuphi", and he looked at me with shocked and pained eyes, I felt curiously happy.

"Must you go?" he asked anxiously. "We have all to go very soon. Holidays do not last for ever."

"I should be with her," I said, trying to convince myself.

"Should be? Or want to be?"

"I am so unsure; I feel I am being selfish, that I have a duty. . . ."

"You have a duty to yourself; your own life to live. Others cannot live it for you; they can be selfish too. One has to make a choice, even if it is difficult." He looked at me with eyes that asked more of me than words.

The sound of my heart beating filled my ears, and in the crowded room we were alone. We were sitting without touching each other, and he was not looking at me any more, appearing casual except that his hand shook as he put out his cigarette, but we were nearer than we ever had been.

"I'll stay," I whispered, looking at the others who were unaware and laughing and talking.

"Thank you," he said softly. "One never knows how much time is lent us."

But Time had no meaning because I could not imagine it having a beginning or end at this complete moment.

Chapter Eight

I WAS glad I had not insisted on going away. The swift passage of days that brought our inevitable separation nearer made Ameer and me more conscious of each moment together, though we were unable to be alone and our deepest feelings remained unexpressed.

Each morning the moment of waking was a joyful welcome to a new day. When my eyes opened to the first sight of the towering peak framed in my bedroom window it was no longer ominous and brooding with the forces that had once gashed its wooded slopes and thundered down to destroy the unsuspecting settlement by the lake. It was withdrawn yet protective with a powerful divine serenity.

In this luminous world prayers could not but be answered and Aunt Abida could not but be well again.

It was a world in which Uncle Hamid's politically fused outbursts were festival-time crackers, Aunt Saira's sermons were school-room lessons mechanically repeated and gossip was the buzzing and biting of harmless mosquitoes.

When Kemal's name began to be linked with Mrs Lal's my aunt was deeply disturbed. My cousins did not take her worries seriously. They told her it was unintelligent to pay attention to the gossip of women whose minds remained smothered in the *burqas* they had outwardly discarded, and men who met women socially but mentally relegated them all to harems and zenanas.

The realisation that happy days had slipped by with a stealthy swiftness came when Ranjit invited us to a farewell party for Kemal. It had not seemed possible that Akbar had to go, and others would soon have to follow.

Yet no shadows could settle for long over resilient young minds and we looked forward to the party as if it were our first and not the last together. When the day came we did not care to look beyond it.

The sun was setting as we walked down towards the lake. It had exploded golden and flaming clouds that fanned above the western peaks and were scattered in delicately tinged puffs across the high blue sky and the rose-pink and grey eastern horizon. A soft grey-bellied indeterminate animal-shaped cloud with a golden-pink back sprawled high over the lake. It grew in coloured luminosity until the waters below it glowed in harmony, but were sombre in the distance with the reflection of the darkening hills.

Purple and blue mists crept upon the ranges of hills discovering new hollows and spaces among the ridges that were tinted by the deepening, changing colours ricochetting off the clouds from the invisible sun.

Gradually the greyness spread upwards. When we reached the willow-edged road that circled the lake the stars were becoming visible in the darknening sky, and the lights on the hills and roads were brightening in the growing obscurity and dancing in the dark waters.

Only Sita was with Ranjit when Nadira and I walked into the main room of the Boathouse followed by Kemal and Saleem. I felt a pang of disappointment not finding Ameer and Raza Ali with them. We had all been asked to come early. I felt he should have been waiting for me.

Sita was as vivid as a scarlet flame in the dimly lit room. I wished for Kemal's sake too that the others had arrived.

Ranjit greeted us as happily as a child displaying its handiwork. "Look's different, doesn't it?" he said with a gesture that encompassed the room.

Its character had been transformed; it was no longer the staid Victorian room where the Raja of Amirpur gave sedate parties. It's ornate furniture had been taken away, and the lights dimmed with paper shades. The carpet had been removed and the wooden floor polished for dancing. Candles in beer bottles flickered on an improvised bar in the corner.

Dressed in a green *achkan* and orange turban Ranjit's personal servant stood behind the bar, incongruous with his long, white, combed beard and bearing of a Rajput warrior.

"Raza Ali will get a bit of a shock," Akbar said. "It will be hard for him to recognise the place."

"Raza Ali needs to be given a few shocks," Sita said with a grimace. "He is so good he makes me want to scream."

"You must have had considerable practice in suppressing your screams," Saleem said.

Sita did not answer.

Ranjit called from the bar, "What about a drink?"

"A small whisky for me, please," Saleem answered.

"Same here," said Kemal.

They seemed like truants from school. They had learned not to drink in the presence of their elders.

"Mine's a gimlet," Sita said. "Gin has the virtue of looking like water. The one thing my mother will not allow me to do is drink. She hates it, I think, because my brother cannot hold his liquor. She says the most dangerous words in the English language are: 'What will you have?'"

"What will you have, Nadira and Laila?" Ranjit laughed.

"Nothing, thank you," we said together.

"Good girls," purred Sita.

Nadira flushed and I said, "Come on, Nadira, let us put away our coats."

We went through the glazed veranda and into the dressing-room.

"I don't like her," said Nadira suddenly as we changed our shoes. "I don't like her superior airs. I don't like the way she treats Raza Ali like a dog to be petted and shooed away according to her moods. I don't like him for letting her do it. I wish I hadn't come. It is so artificial. I feel so out of place. I don't dance, and I'll be a bore."

"It will be all right, Nadira," I soothed her, because she had echoed my own depression. "We will have fun watching people and talking. And why do you let Sita upset you? She is not as hard as she pretends to be. There must be some reason for this veneer. Besides," I teased her, "you do not have to worry. At least one person I know would have hated being here if you had not come."

Nadira's shy, embarrassed smile contradicted her protests. "Nonsense, Laila, you imagine too much."

I was sure then of her love for Saleem, but in my heart was the certainty that no one else could feel as deeply and purely as I did about Ameer.

When we rejoined the others Ranjit, Kemal and Saleem were standing near the bar absorbed in an argument. Sita, sitting to one side, was watching them silently. I saw the unguarded expression on her face as she looked at Kemal, thinking herself unobserved. Then she became aware of my presence and it was as if a light had been switched off.

Ranjit was saying, "It is easier for you. Your parents do try and travel a part of the way with you, but mine cannot. Our worlds are so different."

"Unfortunately our generation is caught in the stresses of a period of transition——" Saleem began a trifle pompously.

"Oh I know all that," Ranjit interrupted impatiently, "but it does not help me if I think of myself as part of a social problem. I am human. I want to enjoy myself. The trouble is the old people want it all their own way. Suppose I wanted to enjoy myself like my father and grandfather did and spent my evenings with the ladies who live above the shops in the Chowk? I'd be called a waster. And if I join my friends and dance and drink a bit, I'll be called a loafer. I've had to plan this party as if it were a conspiracy, send away Raza Ali's servants, bring Hari Singh who would see me commit a murder and not give me away, and invite guests as carefully as if they were accomplices. It takes the fun out of everything." He added ruefully, "You, at least, have had your fun in Europe."

"It does not last for ever. You have to come back," said Sita.

Kemal said, "Cheer up, Ranjit. Think what an edge furtive enjoyment gives to harmless pleasures."

"Harmless pleasures!" Ranjit said. "Our elders and

betters think there is no difference between dancing and going to bed publicly with a woman."

Nadira said primly, "I think it is quite understandable. Saleem was right, we are paying for being the product of two cultures. . . ."

"Abortions, you mean," Ranjit laughed. Then looking at his watch he said, "I wonder what has happened to Raza Ali and the Lals. They had said they would come early. Not that anyone misses a bore like Lal, but a beautiful wife is the best of passports to anywhere."

Kemal, looking at his watch, said, "I wonder why Raza Ali has not come."

"He is probably saying his prayers," scoffed Sita.

"Why shouldn't he? What is wrong with that?" Nadira asked resentfully.

"We will all feel better listening to something other than the sound of our own voices," Ranjit said and began walking towards the gramophone. Sita joined him saying, "I'll help you choose a record."

When the music started I wished Sita had chosen something gayer and had not underlined my mood with her choice.

As the first few chords were struck Kemal jerked up from his chair and held out his glass to Hari Singh.

"Small whisky, and lots of soda."

A strange note in his voice made me look up and I saw a fleeting look of distress on his face before he turned away, and started to cross the room towards the glazed veranda.

Sita was humming softly, and turning slowly and gracefully in time to the music, her eyes almost closed, her head to one side and a faint smile on her lips. Then, suddenly, as Kemal passed by her she put her hand on his arm and said, "Dance with me, Kemal, I remember you waltzed beautifully." But her carefully gay voice had a tremulous edge.

For a brief moment Kemal stood very still; she took the glass from his hand and put it on the arm of a chair, and turned towards him slowly and without a smile in her eyes, stretching out her arms.

Saleem, who had been talking to Nadira with his back towards them, turned round and, seeing them, froze into a moment's stillness, then turned back and began talking again very rapidly.

I felt I ought to be angry with Sita; instead I wished to cry.

There was something strange about that silent dance. And then the spell was broken by a faintly mocking laugh. Mrs Lal stood at the door clapping her hands. In unrelieved black she was as rich and warm as soft, bursting purple grapes on a copper bowl.

"No, no, don't stop! Go on!" she purred; but the dance had ended and only the record played on.

"Do forgive me for being late, Ranjit," she said, sliding towards him, holding out her slender hands, looking at him as if she were late for an assignation. "I was waiting for my husband. He was called away suddenly to Amirpur House—something the matter with Raja Sahib. Oh what it is to be a doctor's wife! In the end I came along after leaving a message that he should follow as soon as possible."

"I suppose Raza Ali and Ameer will not be able to come," Ranjit said. "Pity! God knows when we will all be together again."

"They may come later," she said casually.

"I hope so," Ranjit said.

The hope and wish were irritant splinters in my mind. Time moved in jerks thereafter.

The room became crowded. There was a sparkle of music and laughter and dancing. It was around me, but I was alone in my silent world.

Nadira and I sat most of the time by the long windows overlooking the lake. The stars crowded upon each other in the moonless sky and around the milky way their whiteness was like powder between the brighter constellations. Silhouetted against the lights of the English Club, on the curve of the bay, skeletal yachts rode at anchor. Sounds from the distant bazaar came across the water, and dark shapes of boats splashed across it.

Inside the room the dancers moved across the open doors and a corner of the busy bar was framed in the low, dividing window.

With unusual detachment I noticed how much Kemal and Sita were together.

Mrs Lal was more than ever gay, surrounded by bemused men, but her eyes watched Kemal and Sita stealthily yet constantly.

Dinner was almost over when Dr Lal arrived. He was alone. In his opinion the Raja had appendicitis but there seemed no urgency to operate. A specialist had been sent for from Calcutta. He seemed piqued about that.

No one asked about Raza Ali or Ameer. It was taken for granted they would not come. Yet I could not reconcile myself to it.

Another hour passed by very slowly. Nadira did not notice my long silences; she was happy because Saleem so obviously preferred being with her to joining the others, and kept returning to sit near her. He had just gone to dance. She interrupted my thoughts with a laugh.

"You are staring into the room without seeing anything."

"I was watching the dancing," I protested.

"It looks odd if you shut your ears, and do not hear the music. People pushing each other around in the strangest way. It looks almost indecent. I do not wonder our elders get shocked."

I said shortly, "Some of the people who criticise would get excited seeing a woman in a *burqa*."

The music stopped. Mrs Lal appeared framed in the door, laughing back at her partner. She walked languidly towards us, her eyes sweeping the length of the veranda swiftly.

"What are you girls doing here in the dark? What secrets are you disclosing?" She leaned out of the window, her body curved like a cat's. "How fresh and sweet the air is! So different from that smoke-filled room! I do not blame you for sitting here." Then with sweetness coating her voice she said, "I thought Sita had joined you."

"She has not been here for hours," Nadira said. "She has been too busy dancing."

"Not dancing—not for a long time," said Mrs Lal with an edge of malice, as she stared down to where the water lapped against the wooden piles. Then she turned to the man waiting patiently behind her and said gaily, "There are so many boats lying useless in that mysterious place down below. Let us go boating; it will be fun. It will clear our heads. . . ."

Saleem who had come in while she was speaking caught her by the hand and said, "After this dance, Sona, you haven't danced with me for ages. I insist."

Though he spoke lightly I caught the anxiety in his eyes as they searched for Kemal and did not find him.

"I said, "I'll be back in a few minutes, Nadira."

I knew the Boathouse well. There was a wooden staircase from the bathroom into the small garden.

The bathroom door was unlatched. I hurried down the worn steps. It was dark, and the light from the street lamps filtered through the branches of trees on the gabled red roof, and the green wooden walls. At the foot of the stairs I stopped and called softly, "Sita, Sita." There was no answer. I called again "Sita", and there was only the sound of the water lapping against the wooden piles. I was frightened and ran back to the dressing-room and lay on the couch. My head was really aching now, and the sound of the music from the other room throbbed in it.

The door leading in from the bathroom opened stealthily, and seeing me Sita drew back sharply, then came in defiantly her eyes red, her face drawn.

"Someone might have locked the door," I said, controlling myself as best I could.

She shrugged her shoulders, and sitting down at the dressing-table began to comb her disarranged hair. Then she said to my reflection in the mirror, "Don't look at me like that."

"Why can't you leave him alone?" I said bitterly. Her eyes filled with tears, and her defiance collapsed.

"You would not understand, you cannot. You do not know what it means to be in love."

I thought with a secret joy, "You can never know it as I do", but said, "You had a strange way of showing it all this time."

"There was no other way. I thought I ought to stay away from him because it was so hopeless, because we could not be together."

"He asked you to marry him. You chose to refuse."

"Could I do otherwise? I, Sita, loved him, Kemal, and still do. Two individual human beings. But it would have been the daughter of my father and mother marrying the son of his parents, with different backgrounds and different religions, two small cogs in a huge social machine."

"How could you think like that if you loved him?"

"I could because I loved him. Our love is our own, inside us, but our marriage would have been outside ourselves, everyone else's. I thought about it until it seemed easier to die."

"You thought about it too much. If you had loved him with your heart instead of your mind——"

"How would you know how I loved him?" she interrupted fiercely. "How can you know what I have been through? I loved him enough to let him go."

"Then why didn't you do that completely? Why couldn't you do it a little longer?" I accused her. "He is going away."

She began to cry again. "That is why," she cried. "Because I will never again be able to see him like this, never feel free to think of him as I did even when I was not with him."

She controlled herself and said flatly, "I am going to get married."

"You are going to get married?" I repeated mechanically.

"At least my parents will be happy. They have found me a suitable husband and I have consented."

I did not feel any curiosity, I was too shocked. "Sita, you cannot mean it, you cannot possibly do it without knowing...." I left the sentence unfinished seeing the look in her eyes.

"I met him once. I could meet him or anyone else a thousand times and it would make no difference. Do not think I am submitting to an arranged marriage; this is my own choice. I cannot ever marry for love and I do not want a masquerade. If it has to be this way, then my parents are the best judges of the man with the best qualifications for being a husband. They have a wider choice; it is only love that narrows it down to a pin-point. If I did not love Kemal, I could not think of all men as potential husbands."

"What you are saying is wrong and perverse. You cannot do it, Sita." It was as if I were pleading for myself. "It would be better never to marry. You can work...."

"I cannot face it. I must end it. Can't you see I must not be free to hope?"

"Marry Kemal, Sita, marry him without thinking about it so much that you cannot see anything ahead but doubts. If you believe in it enough it will be all right. It must be."

"I'm not a saint, Laila. I'm not a martyr. I react to criticism and hatred even if I do not show it. Let me keep my love intact. I cannot expose it to the judgement of others like a criminal waiting for their verdict. You know your uncle and aunt would hate me. Would it be right to drag Kemal between my love and their hatred?"

"You do not love him enough," I accused her, suddenly sure of my own capacity to love.

"How can you know? How can you judge?" she blazed and we glared at each other as if we had been fighting over a lover.

"Oh, here you are!" Sona Lal's honey and acid voice came from the door. With a smile that had not reached her heavy eyes she looked mockingly at Sita. "You have been missed by everyone."

I was taken aback by Sita's sudden transformation. She was once again what she had appeared to be, self-assured, bright and brittle, so that I wondered if I had imagined all that had just happened. I covered my face with my hands, pretending I was soothing away my headache.

"I am flattered," Sita said, "I did not think anyone would be so concerned about my movements."

"One never really knows what others are thinking about one." Mrs Lal came towards the mirror, adjusting the folds of her sari, and as Sita moved towards the door she said casually, "Raza Ali's wife was talking to me about you only this morning."

"How interesting! I did not think she was interested in me."

"Oh, not in you, but in Raza Ali."

Their voices were like stilettos, but they were smiling at each other.

Mrs Lal said blandly, "A woman hates it to be known that she is losing what is hers."

"What is she losing that is hers? Suppose Raza Ali does like me—even loves me, he takes nothing from her that she ever had. She hasn't lost the things she married him for—his name, his wealth, his children."

"Jealousy, dear Sita, is not logical."

Sita smiled at her, very sweetly and walked towards the door saying, "I hate to cut short an interesting conversation with an expert, but I must go and put everyone's mind at rest."

Mrs Lal sat in front of the dressing-table, her shoulders hunched, fumbling nervously in her bag. I saw her face in the mirror and felt as distressed as if I had stumbled on a naked secret. It was the face of a middle-aged woman with slack lines of defeat, the once-inviting eyes dull with despair, the once-passionate mouth dragging with bitterness. Another mask removed; first Sita and now this seemingly invulnerable woman!

I dragged myself up, but had not taken more than a couple of steps when she called out sharply "Laila!" Then in almost her normal voice said, "I'm sorry, but could you help me with the clasp of my necklace. It seems to have caught in the border of my sari."

I bent to release it, and knew she had been drinking more than usual.

"It is all right now," I said, as I straightened up and prepared to go.

She did not seem to want to be left alone. "Do you think I look all right? I have forgotten my lipstick. Pity you do not use any." She grimaced at her reflection in the mirror and sighed. "Youth is beautiful. But how foolishly innocent and trusting it can be! Take my advice. You cannot store innocence and trust beyond their season, they rot."

She took a cigarette out of her case, and lit it with difficulty using match after shaking match. Then with determined casualness she asked my reflection.

"You are very fond of Kemal, aren't you?"

"Yes, of course."

"Do you think he is in love with Sita?"

"How should I know?" I stammered.

"I was just curious," she said shrugging her shoulders. "After all she is a friend of yours."

From beyond the door came the sound of her husband's voice, thick with drink, calling, "Sona! Sona!"

A spasm of hatred hardened her face. She got up without replying, her silent dismissal of him more shocking to me than any expression of contempt. Before leaving the room she said, "Someone ought to warn Sita it is dangerous to be too sure of one's self."

I felt the pain had seeped from my head into every muscle of my body.

I walked quickly through to the veranda.

There was someone sitting in the corner of the alcove looking out of the window. At first the dimness of the light made him a silhouette, then my eyes picked out the familiar lines.

"Ameer!" I was on the point of tears.

"Laila!" He sprang up, and took my outstretched hands in his, and I was safe and secure and smiling.

We went and sat by the window together, and around us was the loveliness of the night on the water and the surrounding hills, and the sound of voices and music came from some distant, unimportant world.

"I had to come, if only for a minute. I could not leave until the others had gone to sleep, and I was frightened you would go away."

"I knew you would come. Yet I was afraid, because it is time Nadira and I went home, and I could not have waited longer. . . ."

"I did not know until tonight how many seconds there are in an hour and how many hours in each second," he said ruefully, trying to smile. "And how one begins to hate people. I must see you tomorrow, alone."

"How can I get away?"

"You must. Please try."

"I will. About ten? At the corner bookshop?"

"Thank you. I'll be waiting."

Chapter Nine

I DID not find it as difficult as my fears had imagined to get away alone in the morning. All that was necessary was to discipline myself to patience and silence until everyone had gone out.

I ran most of the way down the hill, through the smell, flies, filth, spit, open gutters and ragged crowds in the lanes between the smoke-grimed, rusty-roofed, precarious, pigeon-trap houses of the bazaar and into its wide main street.

I saw Ameer standing at the slope where the bazaar ended and opened towards the clean, fashionable world.

It seemed the sky was blue from the palette of angels, and the light was reflected from their burnished wings.

Yet all I could say in wonderment was a breathless "You are here!" and he answered smiling, "Of course I am. Didn't you think I would be?"

"Yes. . . . Oh yes."

"I came early because I did not want you to wait. Besides I could not trust my watch; it seemed so slow. Was it difficult getting away?"

"No. Nobody asked me anything."

"I am glad. I was angry with myself for asking you to take this risk. . . ."

"All one has to do to avoid trouble," I said, "is not to draw attention to one's self."

"Well, then, we had better get away from here."

I looked about me instinctively to see if anyone who knew us were in sight. The outside world came into focus again.

A rabble of coolies ran forward with their *dandy*, calling "Dandy *huzoor*. Dandy *huzoor*." pushing each other.

"No. No. No." They were as embarrassing in their rage as beggars.

One of the men moved to the side of the road and leaned

against the railings, racked by a fit of coughing, his cadaverous, exhausted face distorted.

I said, turning away, "Imagine making him carry one up a steep hill. It would be murder."

"And yet," Ameer said, "how would he live if everyone thought that? These people are too proud to beg, and too poor to live on their land. There are no simple answers. . . . But cheer up! You must not look as if you were responsible for his troubles." And walking up to the man he slipped a coin in his hand saying, "Run along and get two horses for me."

We rode in silence up the short cut to the ridge. The track was narrow and rocky and climbed steeply, sometimes skirting precipitous drops, sometimes easing through undisturbed oaks and deodars. Through the vibrant stillness of the moss and fern and tree-covered slopes, over the fallen leaves, there was the sound of distant water flowing down rocky channels, and the pervading sigh of the wind. Roads and houses and playgrounds were lost from vision and thought.

A sense of peace flowed into the veins of my body.

We crossed the hump of the ridge and guided the horses carefully down the other side. Few people came here but for wood-gatherers, or enthusiastic hikers, or riders exploring the beauty and solitude. Certainly none of those who went round and round the social mulberry bush.

In a clearing among the pines we dismounted. Ameer led away the patient horses, used to carrying unknown riders all summer and loads of grain and merchandise all winter, and looped their reins securely round a branch.

I waited among the cathedral columns of the tall trunks, aware of a sanctified beauty in their strength and the delicacy of the tufted needles, and prayed wordlessly to guard my happiness against a formless fear that wept deep within me.

We walked to where a spur of rock jutted out forming a wide ledge with an unobstructed sweep of vision. In silence we looked across the sweep of the ranges like petrified waves stretching towards the distant snows. Above a haze of heat their visionary summits reached to the skies, ineffably serene, withdrawn yet beckoning, the culmination of dreams and desires, a release from struggle and pain, the cool, clear touch of divinity.

The moment when Ameer kissed me had no beginning; it was as pure and eternal as the snows we had been watching in deep communicative silence. It was a part of every moment before it, the moment for which I had been born to become a part of existence before and after it, to know its meaning and fulfil its purpose. I knew a sense of such completeness and harmony that it seemed I was the earth, the sky, the light and the snow.

A horse neighed, and a wood-cutter crashed across the twigs and leaves of the path behind us, and we returned from a great spaceless, timeless distance.

"I love you very much," he said and I was shy of him and the word: "I had to tell you before going away."

"Going away?" The world fell into separate little pieces.

"I have to go back. My father had written some days ago asking me to return but I kept putting off replying to him. Then last night when Raja Chacha got ill Raza Ali said we would have to return to Lucknow. We are leaving tomorrow."

His father . . . his obligations. I thought with wonder that he had had a separate life of his own, as unknown to me as mine to him, and with greater wonder that we should have travelled across the years to this point together when there was no separateness and my life was his life. He was going away because of last night . . . of another man's illness.

"Tomorrow? So soon?" I said in despair.

Of course nothing could stop it. All the machinery of power would plan the journey, the reservations, the bookings even if others had to vacate their seats on the train, change their plans. Trains had been delayed even for us, I thought bitterly, and this was the Raja of Amirpur.

He was saying, "I had to ask you to come today because God knows when we shall be together again."

He kissed my eyes that were straining against tears, and my hands that held his desperately.

"There are so many things I have thought of since I knew I loved you; and that must have been from the moment you fell into my arms."

I smiled in response to his teasing. "But, Laila, I have nothing to offer you, nothing but my love."

"What more do I want?"

"I am poor. I am nobody, nothing. Your people would never approve of me. Oh I know Kemal and Saleem like me, but even they would think of practical things, and why shouldn't they?"

"Why do you keep talking of others? What about me? It is my life."

"I have thought of that more than anything else. I love you, and think of you and what is best for you."

"Then why did you bring me here? Why did you tell me you loved me?" I said bitterly. "I am sorry. Forgive me. But I love you, and you seem to forget that."

"Do you know, Laila, that is the first time you've said it? And now I wonder at it. Why me? Why? And yet it is because I know you do that I can say what I must."

Sita. I heard her voice again and felt her sorrow and cried out against it. "It cannot be that love must always, always be denied. What are we to do?"

"Will you wait for me, Laila? I'll work hard. May be I shall be able to find something better. Do you know, I have often wished I had learned to swallow my pride earlier and asked Raja Chacha to help me get a job in some Government Service. But in the days when we were students Asad and I used to scorn all that."

"Ameer, you are wronging me by thinking nothing matters but money and position. You are bringing me down to the same level as—as everyone else."

I thought of Zahra, of my aunts.

"I want to share your life whatever it may be."

"That is what gives me courage, Laila. That is why I have asked you to wait. Then if you are still sure, if you still feel as you do now, we will fight the whole world."

All of them, I thought, the living and the dead, and I said, "I can never be more sure."

He went on as if saying something he had said to himself many times before. "You can go on with your studies. That would mean another two, even three years. By then something might turn up for me. If we believe in each other it will not be long to wait."

"I love you, Ameer. I cannot do anything but wait."

It was easy to say it then, because when we were together time had no quality but of timelessness and fears no meaning.

Chapter Ten

I JOINED the University for post-graduate studies with my uncle's indifferent consent and my aunt's passive disapproval.

My uncle became involved in the intensification of political manœuvres as the elections drew nearer. He had accepted the position that he could not successfully oppose Waliuddin, and had decided to stand as a representative of the *Taluqdars*.

It was as if he had become involved in a gigantic game of chess, or some mathematical problem of permutations and combinations. There was no political passion, only an implacable wish for power.

My aunt's life was a reflection of her husband's as she struggled to secure her position of leadership among women. A new class of rivals was emerging in the women's organisations she and her friends had so far dominated.

Saleem began to attend the courts but in a desultory manner because his heart was in politics. His growing friendship with Raza Ali and his attachment for Nadira, influenced the direction of his beliefs.

Raza Ali had thrown himself into the work of the Muslim League with a fierce determination. He who had been shy and speechless in Sita's presence now thundered against those who were the enemies of resurgent Muslims. In his quasi-military uniform, completely out of character with his gentle face and delicate figure, he exhorted young men to join the National Guard which he commanded.

The effect on Nadira of her work for her mother's election was dynamic.

She used to accompany her mother into narrow lanes and small houses of whose existence she had not been aware, to address meetings and win over a class of people she had known only in theory.

Progressives accused her mother of being a capitalist and a communal reactionary, and religious fanatics attacked her for being out of purdah and addicted to immoral Western ways.

The closer Nadira and Saleem were drawn together, the farther apart she and I were forced by our irreconcilable views. In our college days when arguments were an end in themselves she had been more liberal.

I still found Saleem, when he was not crusading, a pleasant companion. But he was not as close to me as Kemal had been. Saleem's opinions and relationships were formed in terms of himself, therefore he could not respond to another's needs. His feelings for Nadira were genuine, but his self was not subordinated. His unhappiness would always be a shadow reflected on hurt self-esteem, whereas with Kemal it would always be the substance.

I knew that Kemal accepted pain to overcome it. I knew it from his letters to me. But he seemed to be happy with his work and the opportunity it gave him to get to know his country and people.

On his short and infrequent visits home during these months Kemal took no part in the arguments which had become so frequent. Yet he never gave the impression of being without convictions or one who took life lightly. His silences were not empty, but had the strength of an unspoken personal faith. While he was with us there was a sense of respite, voices lost their asperity, there was time for laughter and the house changed from a political headquarters into a home.

Chapter Eleven

I BEGAN to live on two different planes of thought and speech and action. Often, when imagination slipped its guard, the outward life in which Ameer played no part became blurred by the inner one in which only he and I existed. I would sometimes find myself slipping from one into the other. My sudden withdrawals and absences were irritants to those around me, and they accused me of indifference or absent-mindedness or selfishness, depending on their mood.

Strangely it was Nandi who came nearest the truth because she was genuine to herself and me. In the middle of her stories and her gossip she would stop and say, "You are lost again, Laila Bitia. Who has taken you away? Where are you? Come back, Bitia."

Not that Nandi would have approved of being in love. Her bitterness was as intense as her capacity to love had once been. "A man's love is no different from an animal's. He takes what he can get, because he is not the one who has to bear the consequences. It is the injustice of the gods that a woman alone must be fearful."

For all that I was relaxed with her I could not talk to Nandi as freely as she did to me. There was always the distance of a servant between us.

Without being asked to do so Nandi had begun to do my work as Saliman had once done, finding the time from busy days helping her father and looking after her motherless family.

Nandi was not liked by the other women servants. She was too unlike them. Her body wore the coarsest cloth like sculptured drapery revealing the firm, fluid lines of some ancient bronze. She mocked them with her friendly smile and hard eyes.

She seldom spoke of Saliman, but one day she came to me

heavy-eyed. "I dreamt of Saliman last night. She was struggling to lift a heavy stone from her head, but when I went to help her she turned away from me. She was angry with me, Bitia, because I did not help her when she needed me."

I said to soothe her, "You cannot blame yourself. What could you have done?"

"She shook her head stubbornly. She needed help and did not get it. And is there justice if the man who murdered her lives and prospers? A snake should be killed. Do you know, Bitia, what was wrong with Saliman?" She was talking so rapidly she brooked no interruption. "She was full of fears and she showed it. That is what one must never do. One goes through life with jackals stalking behind. They look like lions and tigers when you are frightened, and if you show them your fear they eat you, bone and marrow. But if you turn on them and threaten them, just snap your fingers at them, they turn into jackals again and run away."

Nandi remained moody for some days. In one respect I noticed a change in her behaviour. ·She had avoided Ghulam Ali. Now she was polite to him and would take the laundry to Ghulam Ali herself.

When Nandi walked with a bundle of clothes balanced on her head, her breasts taut, hips slightly swaying, her body moved like sensuous music. Ghulam Ali became her slave. She tormented and tantalised him with the consciousness of her beauty, and the absolute rectitude of her conduct.

Ghulam Ali had always treated all the other servants with contempt. But something began to go wrong. Nobody could have blamed Nandi for starting it, but a hint dropped here, a small complaint there was enough to goad the latent hostility of the sevants.

I gathered all this from Nizaman's and the Ayah's complaints to my aunt. My aunt was not prepared to disturb the efficient running of the household because of gossiping maidservants.

But Nandi had the patience of calculated hatred. One

night Nandi's frenzied cries for help roused the sleepers in the long silent row of the servants' quarters. They knew that Nandi was alone that night, her father having gone to consign the ashes of a relative to the sacred waters of the Ganges. She wailed hysterically and told them she had woken about midnight by Ghulam Ali trying to assault her. When she screamed he had run away.

With the fervour of defenders of virtue the servants fell upon Ghulam Ali who had lorded it over them for too many proud years, and beat him more when he called Nandi a liar.

My uncle could do nothing to protect Ghulam Ali nor to punish Nandi, though he believed she had lied, for Nandi had become a heroine. After Ghulam Ali's dismissal she went about her work singing.

Chapter Twelve

NO one seemed to talk any more; everyone argued, and not in the graceful tradition of our city where conversation was treated as a fine art, words were loved as mediums of artistic expression, and verbal battles were enjoyed as much as any delicate, scintillating, sparkling display of pyrotechnic skill. It was as if someone had sneaked in live ammunition among the fireworks. In the thrust and parry there was a desire to inflict wounds.

Even visitors argued. A new type of person now frequented the house. Fanatic, bearded men and young zealots would come to see Saleem; rough country-dwelling landlords and their 'courtiers' would visit my uncle. Saleem had, metaphorically, discarded his old school tie and my uncle his spats and gloves. Suave, sophisticated tea and dinner parties had become infrequent, and Government House receptions an interlude.

Every meal at home had become an ordeal as peaceful as a volcanic eruption.

Had both father and son not been so strong-willed, their conflicting ideas would not have led to so many wordy quarrels. Uncle Hamid felt that Saleem should be forced to see where his real duty lay, and he was also distressed at seeing how much Saleem neglected his professional work.

My uncle had been away on a canvassing tour, and it was our first meal together after four days.

I could hear Saleem's voice as I came into the drawing-room. He was standing by the fireplace, his hands in his trouser-pockets rocking gently on his heels as he spoke.

Uncle Hamid sat in his favourite chair, his head resting on its high back, and the lines of his face deepened by tiredness. Aunt Saira was sitting by the tall brass-columned lamp, knitting. I sat down at the other end of the sofa beyond the circle of light.

Saleem was saying, "In the final analysis, what facing is the struggle for power by the bourgeoisie. really a peasant's movement, but when it come division of spoils even class interests are forgotten. For example the four hundred or so *Taluqdars* insisted the British should give them higher representation than the thousands of other landlords."

"It is not a question of numbers alone," protested Uncle Hamid, sitting up and waving his pipe in negation. "We *Taluqdars* have ancient rights and privileges, given by a special charter, which we have to safeguard."

"What do those privileges amount to today?" Saleem said with a touch of derision. "They were given by the British as the price of loyalty, and as people become more politically educated they must question such rights. They must fight them."

"Our rights do not conflict with the rights of the people; traditionally we have been guardians of their rights"—Uncle Hamid jabbed his pipe accusingly at Saleem. "You talk of education. This city's educational institutions owe their existence to our donations. We contribute lakhs a year to them and to charities. One day, I hope, you and your brother will do as much for this city and its people as your forefathers have done."

Aunt Saira nodded in approbation and smiled as if conscious of her own share in the good work.

Did their vision wander over the gardens, the grassy slopes, the arches and the domes, the river, the bridges, the verdant banks, the graciousness and the poetry, of the lovely, loved, lotus-eaters' city?

"Yes, yes, of course. One respects tradition. One fights for one's self, one's interests. But you cannot expect the tenants to love you for it."

"That is because so-called reforms are destroying the personal ties between landlord and peasant. Surely a Government and its changing officers cannot have personal relations or traditional ties with the tenants? With whom are the people in constant touch? Their landlords or local political leaders?"

This was no argument; Uncle Hamid was justifying a way of life Saleem took for granted.

"Who are these leaders, in fact? People with nothing to lose and much to gain. Men without responsibility who can make wild promises. I tell you, not only the landlord but the State is endangered by them." Uncle Hamid banged the arm of his chair at every word of his statement. "Do not think in terms of England where people have learned to respect their rights through the centuries."

"A beginning has to be made some time."

Uncle Hamid ignored the interruption. "How can landlords but be uneasy at the thought of such reserves of power being vested in officials at a time when it is uncertain what class of persons will obtain political power?" He pointed his pipe at Anwar like a schoolmaster's ruler, and said prophetically, stressing each word, "It will be open to any future Government to abolish the landlord system altogether, in spite of statutory safeguards."

"They cannot take what belongs to us. The land is ours," protested Aunt Saira. It was as simple as that to her.

The dinner-gong incongruously sounded an echoing interruption.

"Dinner is ready," said Aunt Saira, getting up with a sigh of relief.

"It can wait," said Uncle Hamid impatiently.

"No," protested Aunt Saira. "Your argument can wait, but dinner cannot."

"Argument," Uncle Hamid burst out. "Argument! It is a question of our existence."

"The food will get cold," Aunt Saira persisted, moving towards the door and Saleem turned to follow her. I waited for Uncle Hamid. He got up wearily, looking at Saleem with a strange, brooding look. To him it was a desperate attempt to make his son believe in what was his testament.

We took our places silently at the table. On the starched

white tablecloth, red roses in a silver bowl splashed their violent beauty. Light from the delicate chandelier was warm on rosewood, glittered on silver and copper, glimmered on crystal and glass, lay softly on china plates and the paintings on the ivory walls, and deepened the folds of lime-green damask curtains. Uncle Hamid's 'question of existence' was very unreal.

Thoughts of beauty were real; thoughts of Ameer were real.

Saleem could not let an argument die an unnatural death. He began, "What you said, father, about the landlords' fear of abolition is the crux of the matter. This fear for their existence is the basis for the formation of a new party which is interested in keeping the *status quo* intact, that is favoured by the British and is fundamentally opposed to progressive, national movements."

Saleem was relaxed, enjoying his food and the sound of his voice.

Uncle Hamid said with heavy sarcasm, "This Muslim League in which you are so interested, I have heard it called communal and reactionary by nationalist Muslims. Certainly most of its leaders—and many are my friends—are of the kind you would call 'reactionary', according to your political theories."

Saleem flushed, "I believe the Congress has a strong anti-Muslim element in it against which the Muslims must organise. The danger is great because it is hidden, like an iceberg. When it was just a question of fighting the British the progressive forces were uppermost; but now that power is to be acquired, now the submerged reactionary elements will surface. Muslims must unite against them."

"Muslims of the world unite!" I whispered, partly to tease Saleem who was becoming pompous, and partly through boredom. All this had been said so often, so endlessly repeated.

Saleem frowned and turned slightly away from me, ignoring me.

"The majority of Hindus have not forgotten or forgiven the Muslims for having ruled over them for hundreds of years. Now they can democratically take revenge. The British have ruled about two hundred years, and see how much they are hated."

Aunt Saira said suddenly, "Oh dear, there is no question, it would be better to have the British stay on than the Hindus ruling."

Uncle Hamid said with a touch of asperity, his temper on edge, "You have learned a lot of lessons very quickly, Saleem. I always found it was possible for Hindus and Muslims to work together on a political level and live together in personal friendship."

"You misunderstand me, father. My best friends are Hindus. But there was not the same sharp clash of interests as there is now. Times have changed. Your political experience is of a time that is running out. Yours is a feudal attitude."

"Words? Theories! Irresponsible talk!" Uncle Hamid burst out. "I am a part of feudalism, and proud to be. I shall fight for it. It is my heritage—and yours. Let me remind you of that. And that you enjoy its 'reactionary' advantages. You talk very glibly of its destruction, but you live by its existence. It is, in fact, your only livelihood."

"That is not fair," Saleem protested hotly. "It is not fair bringing an argument down to a personal level."

"Argument!! I told you I do not believe in arguments for arguments' sake. I believe in what I was saying."

"So do I, father."

"Then act according to your beliefs. Be prepared for sacrifices. Have the courage of your convictions and stop living on reaction." Uncle Hamid's face was distorted by anger.

Always, every day there was an explosion of anger at some point. But this was different, near the bone. I felt my stomach tighten with a hatred of words.

Aunt Saira looked at her husband and son with distressed

eyes, as if mentally wringing her hands before a conflagration.

The servants moved about, changing plates, pouring water, serving food, expressionless automatons.

Saleem stammered trying to control his anger and hide his hurt. "I do not understand, father. There is no question of living on anything. . . . This is my home. I live with my parents. If you feel like this . . . I never thought . . . but I am ready to leave and find a job."

Aunt Saira looked at Uncle Hamid in mute appeal, but his anger was being aggravated by its own unreason.

"You have already got a job. If only you would attend to it."

Saleem's eyes were very dark and fixed, and his hand shook as he pushed away his plate. He spoke with a deliberate slowness unlike the assured, enthusiasm with which he had started the evening.

"I had no intention of giving up my work. After all both interests can be combined. I felt the issues on which these elections are to be fought to be vital to our future. I wanted to do as much as I could. The pressure will not last long."

"You have no intention of giving up your career? When did you start it? Did you qualify to be a lawyer or an election agent?"

I felt like crying out against the ugliness of it all. Aunt Saira made small sounds of distress.

Saleem's self-control was near breaking-point under the double-attack of his father's taunts and anger.

"Begum Waheed needed helpers."

"So did I."

"You did not ask me, father."

"Ask you? I have never made demands on my sons. I did my duty. I educated them. After that it was for them to recognise their duties and responsibilities. And I certainly would not have let you neglect your work for mine. But why should Begum Waheed do that? Your career is not her concern. She does not have to support you."

Saleem's anger burst its barriers. "Neither do you. I want nothing but my rights as your son. My career may not be Begum Waheed's concern yet, but it will be. I intend marrying her daughter."

Aunt Saira cried out "Saleem!"

I felt the tension of shame relax. This was something real and not mean and petty.

Uncle Hamid was silent for a surprised moment, then he banged his fist on the table.

"You can marry anyone you like. You can do what you like. But independently of me. As long as I am master of this house, I decide who lives in it."

And pushing his chair so that it crashed backwards, he walked out of the room as Saleem began bitterly, "I do not question your right. I shall not outstay my 'welcome'."

The expressionless servant put the chair back in its place. I kept my eyes lowered.

Aunt Saira moaned, "Saleem, you must not say irresponsible things in anger."

"I did not say anything irresponsible. But what father said—"

"Your father was hurt. He did not mean what he said."

"I meant what I said."

"But about—Begum Waheed—about—Nadira?" my aunt stammered with embarrassment.

"About Nadira more than anything else."

"This is not the way——"

"What is the way then? A lot of pretence and hocus pocus? Should I have sent coy messages through Laila?"

"Do they—do they know? Have you told Begum Waheed—and Nadira"—her voice trailed off. It was all so much against her conventions.

"Of course not. I said it now because I had to. Nadira's mother is no different from you. She would be shocked to the core if one were as straight-forward as that. You have to go through all the motions. Pretend it's all your idea and your children would never dream of anything as shameless as deciding for themselves. But after what has happened today it will be different. As soon as I can get a job, I shall marry Nadira—if she consents—without any fuss and bother."

"Oh no, Saleem. Oh no! You must not do anything hasty. Everything will be as you wish. Just be patient. Nadira is a nice girl. Her family may not be all one hoped... Nadira is a sweet girl. Everything will be done in the proper way."

"That is all that bothers you," Saleem blazed. "All that has been said means nothing more to you. I have been called a parasite and told I live in this house on sufferance and all you can think of is what is 'proper'."

Aunt Saira cried, "You must not talk like this, Saleem. Many things are said in anger and not meant. Your father loves you." The tears trickled slowly down her cheeks as she searched for her handkerchief. Saleem wiped them with his and said gently.

"Don't cry, mother. I hate to see you cry." She kissed his hand and put it to her eyes.

"You were away from us too long."

Saleem cleared his throat.

Aunt Saira held his hand and pleaded, "Please go to your father. Say you are sorry."

"Say I am sorry? But——"

"He is your father. You have a duty to your elders."

"But he started——"

"He was hurt."

"If you wish it, mother."

"And you will never again talk of leaving home?"

"I did not start it."

"Let us finish it then," said Aunt Saira, smiling through her tears as she got up and put her arms round Saleem.

Chapter Thirteen

I HAD planned to pay Aunt Abida a visit during the December holidays. Then Ameer wrote that he would be coming to stay with Raza Ali for about a week, but was not certain of the exact dates. I could not risk being away when he came, and wrote to Aunt Abida that I had too much work to make up, and would not be able to get away.

Her affectionate, understanding reply added to my sense of guilt towards her, but I was helpless in the consciousness of a stronger pull.

Until Ameer came the days were tense waiting for him and after he came they were strained with pretence. Each word and look and action had to be watched in case it betrayed how we felt for each other. Through every stretched-out hour of the day I waited for those moments when my thoughts would assume shape, sound, and touch.

The whole city was richer because he was in it, and every street, and turn of a road held the possibility of his appearance.

We were hardly ever alone. We stole moments of truth, but each one was edged with the expectancy that others would come in and we would have to switch back into their reality.

When Aunt Saira was present I felt her watching, as if waiting for a slip in a game of blind-man's-buff. She was excessively polite to Ameer, to hide her actual disapproval of him.

We thought of hopeless, wild plans to be together. The longest time we could sit together was when we went with Nadira and Saleem to the pictures; and held hands furtively like children.

Then the day came for him to return, and it was impossible for us to face the renewed separation with so much left unsaid, with nothing stored up and complete, to make it bearable.

His train was leaving late at night, and I was determined to find a way of seeing him alone. I had to find a way.

I told him I was going to visit a friend at the students' hostel and wanted him to pick me up at the gate at six exactly. It would be dark then. It was strange, once the decision was made, how easily one's mind schemed each consequent lie. I told Aunt Saira an old college friend had come for the day, and had asked me to meet her at the hostel in the evening. As it was the only chance I had of meeting her could I please go? The car could drop me, and I would be seen home. I waited for her to question me because my lies made a circle of suspicion round themselves, but Aunt Saira was preoccupied with her own affairs and said nothing beyond saying 'Yes, of course' very shortly as if it were silly of me to bother her with small matters.

All day my nerves shivered. I waited for a thousand accidents vividly enacted in my mind.

It was five minutes after six when the driver dropped me at the tall gates. There was no other car on that dark, deserted side road. I could not stand there waiting and walked towards the porch. The watchman was a man I did not know and felt relieved. I explained I had come to see a professor whom I knew had left on leave months earlier.

Then I walked back to the gate, pretending to be disappointed. Still emptiness. The old man came up to me, curious and solicitous, shoulders hunched against the cold.

"The car has gone?" he said. "Come and wait inside."

"It will be coming back," I assured him.

"It is cold here," he insisted. I thought he looked at me suspiciously. My heart was beating very loudly.

And then I saw the lights of the car slowly approaching. An eternity of anxiety was over and I was out of the unfriendly darkness and in the warmth of the car beside Ameer, and the old man stood curiously by the gate watching us speed away.

Ameer's arm was round me, protective and tender and he said anxiously, "You are trembling."

I said, more sharply than I wished, "You are late."

"Five minutes at the most. I was held up at the railway crossing."

We were on the main road now and I ducked from the light of approaching cars, twisting down in the cramped space.

"Where shall we go?"

"I don't know. Where is there to go?"

I burst out crying.

"Please, Laila, please don't cry. We are together . . ."

"It is so horrible, so horrible. Sneaking and lying, as if I were doing something wrong."

"I am sorry, Laila. I am sorry. I should not have——"

"Can't you see, it has nothing to do with you or me. It is just that everything is made so sordid."

He was silent and I forced myself to be quiet.

The car shook and bumped. I could see fewer street lights from where I crouched, and the lighted tops of trees moving past. The car stopped and Ameer said gently, "It is all right now. Get up."

We were on a track on the undeveloped side of the river. There was a vibrant unbroken sound of crickets and frogs that was a part of the river's silence. Distant lights accentuated the darkness.

Ameer held my face between his hands and I blinked back my tears and smiled at him.

"I love you very much, Laila."

"I love you too, Ameer."

His arms were a circle of safety, and his mouth a seal of tenderness, and in being together there was such purity of completeness that the world dissolved from perception.

The dark stillness was torn apart. A car's lights blazed towards us and I ducked low down and Ameer sharply started the engine. The car passed with a derisive blowing of the horn and a smothering wake of dust.

I began to cry again.

Ameer switched off the engine, stroking my hair. "No, please don't——"

"What shall we do? Why should it be like this? For how long? Why?" Hysteria welled up in me.

"Let me tell them——" he began.

"Tell them what? What is there to tell?"

"That I want to marry you. We have nothing to be ashamed of. We have done nothing wrong."

"What would be the use? You cannot marry me yet. You said so. And until then, if they knew, it would be impossible to live with them, with their disapproval. I know them."

"We will get married. We will manage somehow."

And now that he had said it, I became calm. It was unreasonable of me and I was ashamed.

"Forgive me, Ameer. I'll wait. Just as we had planned. It will not be long. You will find another job."

"Yes," he said miserably, "I will find another job."

"It is just that I hate these lies. Everything becomes sordid. Like filth splashed on something clean."

Ameer kissed my moist eyes, "You are so pure to me, so beautiful. I wonder at it that you should love me. I feel so humble."

"Oh no—not you. I feel like that."

Suddenly, looking at each other's rueful faces, we laughed.

And then he said softly and sadly, "I must take you back."

"So soon?" I cried. "It cannot be even an hour."

"It is," he said gently. "I cannot risk keeping you away longer. I am grateful for even this."

"I am too, deeply and truly."

"When I leave you at the gate, don't look back or I may follow you in," he teased, to ward off the despair that was creeping over our mock-courage.

"Or I may run back to you."

"We will pretend I am just going home for a while."

Suddenly his voice was husky and he put his arms round me as if afraid, "Don't let them take you away, Laila. Don't leave me."

"I am always with you," I said softly, feeling my strength when he needed it.

He kissed me on my forehead and my eyes. "Smile, Laila. I love to see you smile."

But I cried all the way home.

Chapter Fourteen

A WEEK before Begum Waheed's election, Asad came to Lucknow to work for her opponent.

I was sitting in the veranda of my room drying my hair with my back to the sun. Winter was slipping gently towards summer and the air was losing its invigorating crispness. The flowers in the garden were beginning to look weary.

Asad came up so softly behind me that I cried out in fright as at the sound of a phantom voice when he called my name. Then in relief and joy I hugged him tightly, repeating "Asad! Asad! How wonderful, how wonderful to see you!"

There was about him still the air of a young ascetic, heightened by the thinness of his body in its coarse, hand-spun clothes and the fine bones of his sensitive face and the depth of his dreaming eyes. He had become better-looking than in the earlier, gauche days of his adolescence.

Asad seemed embarrassed by my exuberance and flushed slightly. "I am always happy to see you, Laila, wherever and whenever it may be."

"It is not often enough, Asad. I wish you had never gone away. I wish you were back." I stretched out my hand to him in spontaneous affection.

"That is one wish that can never be granted," he laughed, then with a change of mood he said wistfully, "Strange—how strange it is. After all this house was my home for many many years. The house has not changed, yet everything has, and it cannot mean 'home' to me ever again. How many years since the day I left—surely not as long ago as it seems?"

"Five years, I think. I was fifteen when Baba Jan died."

"And I—eighteen."

"And now I am twenty and you are twenty-three. How old, how old we are!"

"But 1937 is young, and exciting, with everything changing and moving forward." Then he checked himself and said with a teasing smile. "Age suits you. You are prettier than ever."

"It suits you too, Asad. You still look like a monk, but an attractive monk."

He laughed with me, then leaned forward in his chair saying, "I am not a monk. I am very human. Why do you always treat me as if I were not? You used to talk of me and my poetry as if I were not the poet but one of my own poems. And now when you write to me—or talk to me—about my work I have the same feeling, as if you thought of me not as a worker but the work itself. It is most disconcerting."

There was an unusual warmth in his eyes, and his fingers tightened over mine. I felt a sudden panic, and drawing away my hand began to rub my hair with the towel so that it covered my face.

"Nonsense, Asad. It is just that I admire what you do." I began.

"What I *do*," he repeated softly, and leaned back with a faint sigh.

I changed the subject quickly. "Why did you creep up like a conspirator without any warning?"

"I wanted to avoid the others so I came by the back door. I wanted to see you before the family circle closed in upon us like a clamp," he smiled.

"You need not have bothered. The 'others' are all out busy convincing people they are dying to serve them. Asad, I am so glad to see you. You are like a breath of fresh air, and I feel I've been locked up for ages in a dark room full of stale air. You don't huff and puff and blow yourself out into a big balloon full of hot air like the others do."

"Prick the balloons," Asad laughed.

"They are self-sealing," I said. "It is strange, I am laughing now but it is not funny at other times. I feel just angry—and frightened too sometimes. Such hatreds are being stirred up. How can we live together as a nation if all the time only the differences between the different communities are being preached? I cannot understand why Saleem can't see the danger."

"Why Saleem in particular? He is honest in what he believes in. I may not agree, but my own brother does."

"But Saleem was influenced by the same political theories as I. He lived for so many years where democracy and tolerance—I don't know how to express it."

"You get confused when you get emotional. I know because I have to fight with myself to keep my emotions in control. Why should Europe make any difference? After all, quite a few young men there believe in Fascism, not that I mean Saleem is a Fascist."

"Fascism! This 'ism, that 'ism—all theories one learns about or just talks about! I believed in studying political science, but what does it, in fact, amount to? When I hear people talking who are in power—or hope to be in power—then I feel I might as well never have learned anything. Have Begum Waheed or Waliuddin or Agarwal ever read a book on political or economic theory, or for that matter any book?" I burst out.

"But at least they have to talk in democratic terms. They have to go to the people for their votes, and talk to them more than Hamid Chacha and his friends ever had to do. That in itself is an improvement."

"Nonsense! They merely use slogans and appeal to the lowest instincts—to fear and fanaticism."

Asad smiled patiently saying, "You must not let your own vision become narrow. So much is happening in our country that is new and exciting."

"I want to get away from it all."

"But you cannot run away from your thoughts, being what you are."

"What can I do?" I asked impatiently.

"Do something, anything. Otherwise you will always be restless and confused."

"It is easy for you to say 'do something'. What can I do?" I said angrily. "What can I do in my circumstances?"

"Forgive me, Laila. I did not mean to preach. I merely said what I believed."

"I am sorry, Asad." I stretched out and caught his hand in mine. "I suppose I project the anger I feel against myself, and take advantage of your patience."

"Remember I am human and not an abstraction." He smiled affectionately.

I flushed and said, "Some day, when I am independent, I shall learn to live as I want to."

There was silence as both of us withdrew into our separate worlds of desires and regrets. Then Asad said hesitantly, "I spent a few days with Ameer before coming here."

I became tense, and the desire to tell Asad about Ameer overpowered me. I looked up towards him compulsively, and his eyes told me he already knew.

"Did he—did Ameer—say anything?" I stammered.

"No," Asad said quietly. "No. Nothing beyond what one says about mutual friends. But—will you believe me, it sounds strange, but I feel and know things about you without anything being said."

I felt disturbed, trying not to recognise Asad's real feelings towards me, and was resentful of the danger to the relationship I wanted to maintain.

"I wanted to talk to you, Asad. I wanted to tell you all that is locked up inside me. There is no one else I can talk to. You have always been such a dear friend."

A shadow flickered across Asad's eyes. He said hesitantly, "Are you quite sure about it? About Ameer?"

"Yes, of course. Why do you ask?"

"I do not want you to be hurt. You are so easily hurt."

"Why should I be? How could I be unless Ameer——"

"I did not mean that," he said quickly. "I meant—I meant the difficulties, the others."

"Others do not matter."

"If you are clear about that. . . ." His voice trailed into silence.

'The others' began to take shape in my mind. A horde of people who dictated the terms of one's living, symbolised by Uncle Hamid and Aunt Saira. Cold, disapproving eyes. Sharp tongues. I could fight them all when the time came. When would the time come? How long the days of waiting!

Chapter Fifteen

IT was a very slow train that stopped at the tiny station five miles from Aunt Abida's village. It stopped at small stations all the way and took over an hour and a half to cover the twenty miles. At every station it spilled out gesticulating, clamouring, anxious peasants and their families and bundles. At every station it swallowed more anxious, clamouring, gesticulating peasants and bundles and women and children. Like frightened cattle driven by the sound of the clanging station bell, the guard's impatient whistle and the urgent hooting of the engine, they rushed from one packed compartment to another searching for enough space to squeeze in.

At every station, on every dusty, windswept platform men, women and children sat and sprawled by bundles and belongings, and slept and ate and watched the train coming in and pulling out as if suspended in an eternity of waiting for trains that would never arrive, on a journey that had no beginning.

At every station the servant who had been sent with me stepped out and stood by my compartment and, with the authority of his livery and crested turban, drove away the rustic rabble that rushed towards the compartment reserved for servants of first- and second-class passengers.

No one got in to spoil my solitude as I sat and watched the fields and trees and hamlets swing past in a slowly circling arc while my dreams kept rhythm with the wheels on the rails.

Aunt Abida's husband was waiting for me at the station. He had grown a pointed beard and its trim, clipped whiteness lent his negative features dignity. He welcomed me with measured words of greeting, inquired about Uncle Hamid and the family with polite formality, and was silent for the rest of the journey as we rattled in the vintage car over the rutty, dusty road.

There was something incongruous about this venerable man with his old-fashioned manner and appearance as he sat behind the wheel of the machine and handled its gears. He should have been driving a carriage, or sitting astride a jog-trotting country horse, and I should not have been sitting beside him in an open car, but been bundled into the sheeted palanquin in which most of the other women still travelled between station and village.

My mind travelled across the scrambled centuries of our lives. There was a wave of nostalgia for Hasanpur, that rose out of the fields and the groves, the dung and the dirt, the poverty and peace, the eternal sameness of the village patterns; and it grew and merged into a longing to be with Aunt Abida until I found myself at last in her welcoming arms.

Hakiman Bua was waiting behind Aunt Abida and embraced me with tears of happiness in her old eyes, and a shower of blessings as she drew her hands over my head and face and cracked her knuckles against her forehead.

I followed Aunt Abida up steep and narrow stairs to that part of the house in which she lived and where I was to stay. Her rooms were austere and neat. The only ornaments on the cream-washed walls were Quranic texts in beautiful calligraphy. A photograph of her father, my Baba Jan, hung above a cabinet filled with books.

The iron-barred windows looked over fields and groves stretching to the downward curve of the sky.

Aunt Abida and I settled down on the *takht* in her room and Hakiman Bua squatted on the floor with her gaze fixed on me as if all the treasures of her world had been set before her eyes.

We talked as if all lost time were spilled out before us. We talked of the family, of those in Lucknow, of those away, of every single one connected to the household that had once been ruled by Baba Jan. It did not strike me until later that we had not talked of Aunt Abida herself. I had caught a glimpse of a withdrawn, settled sadness behind the love and joy that brightened her thin, pale face; but at the time I was too selfishly absorbed. To love and be loved was the answer to every question.

The time for the midday meal came all too soon. We went downstairs and stepped out of our private world.

The house was a simple one built around a square courtyard.

Aunt Abida's husband and the other members of his family were already collected round the long *takht* in the veranda on which the food had been laid. He had come to eat with the women as a concession to me for my first meal in his house. Thereafter, as was his custom, he had most of his meals in the outer part of the house with his friends and kinsmen.

As I watched Aunt Abida and her husband, sitting at far ends of the *takht* from each other, silent in the presence of his mother, separate entities whom my imagination could not bring together, I wondered if my aunt had ever dreamed about marriage as I did.

I felt the eyes of the women and the girls fixed on me, even when I was not looking at them. They looked at me as if I were someone from another world. No subtleties intervened between them and their curiosity. I had met them all at some time or another at family gatherings; Uncle Ejaz's mother, wrinkled, near-blind and partially deaf, and her widowed sister corpulent and asthmatic; his own widowed eldest daughter, sour and sharp-tongued, and her daughter, dominated by an embittered mother, younger than me in years but older in looks and resignation.

Desiccated and colourless women wrapped in shapeless clothes and flowing *dopattas*, mourners at the obsequies of life.

After washing my hands as I moved towards the *takht* on which the others sat cross-legged Uncle Ejaz's daughter said in her acid voice, "Will you manage? You must be used to tables and chairs."

Aunt Abida said to me gently as if she had not heard, "Come and sit by me, Laila, as you always used to."

I began to sense conflicts lurking behind outward forms of dutiful relationships.

Uncle Ejaz began to ask me about the preparations for Uncle Hamid's election.

The old mother hearing Uncle Hamid's name, said in her loud voice, "This child, Laila, must be of marriageable age. No doubt she will marry one of Hamid Mian's sons, and Zahra will marry the other."

Her daughter began to tell her that Zahra was already married, and she cackled, "Imagine! Married to a stranger while there are suitable boys in the family!"

Uncle Ejaz said impatiently, "The boys in the family are sometimes unsuitable."

His daughter interrupted, "One can never be sure about outsiders," and looked at Aunt Abida with eyes spiked with spite.

There was a short, sharp argument ending with Uncle Ejaz angrily leaving his daughter in tears, his mother wailing about her helplessness, and Aunt Abida trying patiently to calm everyone.

I gathered later that the young girl's proposed marriage to the son of her father's brother was being opposed by Uncle Ejaz because the boy was uneducated. The women of the household blamed Aunt Abida, hinting that she alienated him from his family.

In the days that followed I grew to sense the extent of their antagonism against Aunt Abida. They resented the sensitiveness of a character beyond their reach and understanding. They attacked what was bigger than their comprehension with petty thrusts.

The jealousies and frustrations in that household of women were intangible like invisible webs spun by monstrous, unseen spiders.

And yet without each other they had no existence. Physically and mentally their lives crushed each other.

I was disillusioned in my hopes of an escape into peace,

I suffered more because of Aunt Abida's acceptance of life—and her silence.

Yet when we were together there was peace enough, specially when she would read to me in her clear, calm voice the poetry that she had taught me to love. When she was with me I felt her quiet strength and her faith in God that was its source. But I always wished her eyes did not seem to be looking at some distant sorrow.

Only when it came near the time for me to go did she break down and, holding me close, weep uncontrollably. Then she was so near to me I felt I could tell her of my dreams and my fears and of Ameer, but even at the closest moment the distance of tradition remained.

When I said I was unhappy to go back to the others she said, "Do not disappoint me. I would have you strong and dutiful."

"Dutiful to whom? To what? To what I believe is true? Or those I am asked to obey?" I wanted to say.

"Your elders are your well-wishers and guides. You must honour and obey them," she continued.

"But there is so much they cannot understand. Things change, they are not the same for Hamid Chacha as they were for Baba Jan and now they are different for my generation."

"Some things never change. Obey your elders and do not hurt them."

"But why should they hurt me?"

"You must learn that your 'self' is of little importance. It is only through service to others that you can fulfil your duty."

"But why always through unhappiness, Abida Phuphi?"

"Happiness and unhappiness are within you. You cannot demand happiness and you must learn to accept unhappiness."

When she came with me to the wooden door that led outside, and other women were present, her eyes were dry and her voice calm as she said, "God be with you."

Hakiman Bua and I cried without restraint.

Chapter Sixteen

A FEW days after my return Nandi was the focus of trouble again. Her father and her husband said that Ghulam Ali was constantly hanging around the gates of the house threatening to cut off Nandi's nose in revenge for the dishonour she had brought him.

No one took them seriously. The smooth-spoken, superior Ghulam Ali could not be associated with such crudity. The servants were obviously indulging their innate love of the dramatic.

Nandi herself seemed the least frightened, though she never went anywhere alone.

She said to me snapping her fingers, "I think that much of that jackal. If only I had had a strong, young husband I would have had him make a eunuch of Ghulam Ali for threatening me. Sometimes I wish I hadn't accepted a doddering old man."

There was a coarsening of Nandi's speech and beauty that saddened me. She should have been tended carefully.

"Why, Nandi, you are not thinking of running away again?" I teased her.

"There is no one worth the trouble, Bitia," she grinned, "Except that I would have liked a child of my own. When I die there will be nothing to remember me by. I'll be gone just like this——" She blew into the air.

"But you'll be born again. Don't you believe that?"

"Of course. But what then? Suppose I die today, and tomorrow I come back to you as a sparrow like the silly creature that pecks at itself in your looking-glass every day, would you know me? I wouldn't be Nandi any more, Nandi would be dead. When I married the old man I was angry with the world, and I did not want to be like Saliman."

Then she remembered Ghulam Ali and mocked him and cursed him.

But Ghulam Ali did take his revenge after all—not when Nandi was alone, but right in the middle of a crowd.

Nandi had gone to watch a gay procession marching down the street. A circus had come to town and its brass band heralded its presence with a raucous blowing of horns and trumpets and the beating of cymbals and drums. Clowns tumbled and grimaced in front of *tongas* and *ekkas* that carried bright posters with large garish paintings and drawings of the performers. A sleepy, moth-eaten elephant brought up the rear, and on its back sat a man shouting through a megaphone, his bloated voice calling everyone to 'the most daring show in town'.

There were no other shows, anywhere, except the cinemas.

Urchins ran along with the procession snatching at the leaflets the elephant driver threw at them. Pariah-dogs chased around with excited barks.

People were drawn out of their houses by the colour and the noise.

And Ghulam Ali attacked Nandi as she stood laughing in front of the gate. The knife glanced off her face cutting her outflung arm, but it scarred her bright beauty for ever, flaming across from cheek to chin.

It was hard to see in that desperate, dishevelled man, who was overpowered by angry men, the self-possessed white-gloved bearer who had waited so correctly at our silver- and crystal-decked table.

Chapter Seventeen

THE day of Uncle Hamid's election came at last. It was a glaring and windy day. Warm surly gusts of wind shook the leaves off trees and whirled them with the dust it swept off the streets in rushes and eddies. The wind blew summer across the threshold.

Only Kemal's presence made it bearable. He had turned up unexpectedly the evening before—'to give the old man moral support' he had joked. But to me he had said, "I felt the need to be near him at this time. We have grown apart so much; I imagine he is happy to have me near."

There was so much I wanted to say to Kemal but everything was reduced to commonplaces by the constant intrusion of others.

Saleem was in his element. He had plenty of opportunity for acting his favourite role of master-political-strategist ever ready with political analyses.

He told Kemal triumphantly of Begum Waheed's election as if it were his personal success rather than hers.

"That we won by a few votes, after a recount, is no indication of our real strength. It merely shows how politically ignorant the masses are, how unprepared for democracy," Saleem said.

Kemal replied quietly, "They have not been given much of a chance, have they? I mean, democracy is not merely an abstract thought, is it? Not just planted from above."

"Exactly," I added, gaining strength from Kemal, "without being matured, and given roots it cannot be judged."

Saleem went on, "Muslims who are in the Congress are being used as dupes to give it a secular appearance."

"How you've changed!" Kemal said. "You used to say the British encouraged Hindu-Muslim quarrels and drove them apart in order to divide and rule."

"And now I wonder how far apart we will drive each other ourselves," I said.

Kemal forestalled Saleem's reply by saying lightly, "I am a government servant, and shall do whatever I'm ordered to do by whoever is in power. So let us go and see how father is doing in the most ideal of elections, with no parties, no political alignments, just a back-stabbing contest among friends."

A couple of hours later Kemal came and drew me out of the refuge of my room and books.

Kemal explained, "A few purdah women are being rounded up who are *Taluqdars* in their own right—and father wants you to help them if necessary. Some of them have no notion what it's all about."

As we drove along he said, "It's an experience I would not have missed for anything. I would not have believed it possible. The flower of our aristocracy behaving like horse-traders, bargaining for the price of their votes."

"Yet I wonder whether it will be better when the Agarwals of the world take over with their merchant minds."

I was sorry the moment I had taken Sita's father's name. Kemal's face clouded and his mouth tightened.

He drove silently through a crowd of cars and tongas and curious onlookers to the steps leading to a side-terrace of the white and shining *Baraderi*.

As I climbed up the stairs a rush of memories assaulted me. This was where I had first met Ameer.

There was a thin girl in white sitting in the ante-room to which Kemal had directed me. We knew each other by sight and smiled with the embarrassment of knowing we were on opposite sides.

I got up nervously and walked towards a door to the left through which I could see some paintings, but turned back from the threshold seeing a fat, red-faced man in a dark suit dozing on an armchair by a long table.

"That must be the Deputy Commissioner Sahib waiting in there to record the votes." The girl volunteered information.

Because of his wife I knew Mr Cowley better than other officials. She was a gentle, soft-spoken woman, an artist who genuinely loved India. I liked the peace of her home where there was gentle cultivated talk of books and music, and one felt one could live without arguing about how to live.

The girl said, "I think I'll go home. Nothing is happening and it doesn't matter anyway. Everything will be decided by the men. I came only because I was asked to."

"So was I," I said.

We smiled at each other politely, and fell back into silence.

Of the dozen who came to vote I knew only two—the Rani of Phulgaon, compact of charm and dignity, the consolation of youth that age held a promise of beauty; and the Begum Qamar Zamani, decendant of the kings of Oudh. Her words were poetry and her gestures of regal grace. That she had consented to emerge from her crumbling old palace was a tribute to the ties of friendship.

The girl said, "I am going now, Good-bye."

A little later a curtained car drew up and a fat man with enormous moustaches helped out a fatter woman who walked heavily up the steps, her feet bare, her head and face covered. She was as loaded with jewellery as a peasant woman attending a wedding, and gold anklets clanked around her columned ankles.

The man, ignoring protests, saying he was the Rani Sahiba's manager and could not leave her alone, walked into the inner room with her.

A few moments later, I heard an angry roar, and the man rushed out mouthing incoherent apologies followed by a red-faced Mr Cowley who said to me, "Could you please come in and help? The Rani Sahiba does not seem to understand that fellow cannot tell me for whom she wants to vote."

The Rani was heaped on a sofa, looking like a frightened animal in unfamiliar surroundings.

I said slowly, "You have to vote for four out of the eight whose names are on that paper."

"Vote? I do not understand. And I cannot read. Manager Sahib knows."

"Tell her," he said with a forced desperate patience, "I shall read out the names and she should nod at the ones she wants to select."

Mr Cowley marked the list with crosses while she nodded. Then she signed her name as if newly taught to do so.

"Phew!" he breathed. "That's that, and I hope it's the end. Now the Rani Sahib can go back to her village having exercised her democratic rights. . . . Thank you, my dear, thank you."

I smiled mechanically as I led the simple Rani outside, but I felt anger building up inside me against Mr Cowley because of the patronage that had crept into his voice. Who was he to expect her to understand what it had taken his people centuries to learn? But for the grace of circumstances and education there go I, I thought, looking at her ugly shape heaving into the curtained car. Yet she is more true to herself than all the simpering, sophisticated ladies with their modern small-talk oozing out of their closed minds. She is closer to the people than us, sitting, standing, eating, thinking and speaking like them, while we with our Bach and Beethoven, our Shakespeare and Eliot put 'people' into inverted commas.

I wandered miserably across the terrace longing for Kemal to come and take me home; but there was only the coming and going of cars and tongas, the sound of car-horns and tonga-bells and the hum of men's voices.

Racing pigeons from one of the golden houses wheeled across the pale, heated sky. A crow cawed on the white roof above me, then flapped in uncertain flight and came to rest on the uplifted hat of the portly, benign man on horseback immobilised in bronze in the centre of the emerald lawn. Bird droppings whitened his gubernatorial head and shoulders. That benign face had stared at me since childhood from the walls of my grandfather's room. This had been a man who had entered into the hearts of the people he met, not aloof and wrapped in authority. He and Mr Freemantle had made one forget the English were aliens and rulers. Yet how could one forget? There was that moment when seeing a film about Clive, and hearing their applause, I had been stung by the thought, "These ordinary British soldiers sitting around are my rulers."

I walked round to where the terrace widened. Here was the door I had run through into Ameer's arms.

"Laila!"

I turned incredulously towards the ghost voice.

"Laila!" It called from near the steps.

"Ameer," I said faintly, walking towards it, and seeing him running up the steps said, "It can't be, it can't be you."

"It is. Flesh and blood. Look, pinch me," he laughed, but stood away from me because of the people on the road.

"It can't be," I repeated stupidly, feeling my face flushed and burning. "And yet," I said half in jest, "it must be. I haven't reached that exalted spiritual state yet where I can clothe my thoughts with flesh."

"I'm no mystic manifestation," he said lightly. "Very mundane reasons have brought me. I've come about a job."

"But you didn't tell me."

"I had no time. I came by the midday train. I'll tell you more about it this evening. Kemal has asked me to dinner. I swallowed another mouthful of pride to ask Raza Ali to ask his father to use his influence to get me a job that was going in the University here. I wanted to be near you," he ended simply.

"Near me." I repeated and my joy was clouded by the thought of evasions and lies and the constant need to be on guard.

"Why, Laila," he said anxiously, "don't you want me to?"

"How can you say that?" I said quickly, ashamed of my fears.

"Do you know you haven't said one word of welcome?"

"There is nothing I can remember to say."

"I love you, Laila. Why do you look so sad?"

"I'm stupid. I want to cry when I'm so happy."

He looked around him at the hateful crowd below.

"I must go now. Raza Ali will be waiting. I'll see you later." Half-way down the steps he turned.

"I forgot to tell you. Kemal will be coming round with the car. He sent me to tell you."

Dear, understanding Kemal, and then Ameer was gone but I felt his presence more close and real than the whole bright world around me.

Chapter Eighteen

THERE was a constant stream of visitors all evening to congratulate Uncle Hamid on his success. They covered him with garlands until only his face and arms and legs were visible behind the glittering, fragrant mass.

Uncle Hamid was so moved by happiness he lost his emotional restraint and embraced us. Aunt Saira was radiant, beaming with pride as if she had contributed to the victory.

Everyone drank sherbet, ate silver-covered *pān* and sweets, and talked of all Uncle Hamid had achieved and would achieve.

When darkness fell the house shone with light and hummed with voices. The telephone rang constantly, and cars and carriages came and went.

The servants celebrated too. Nizaman sent for sweets, had prayers said over them, sent some to the mosque, and distributed the rest among the other servants after keeping aside a share for each member of the family. Nandi's father, the gardeners, and the coolies drank their country wine, danced and sang songs, and their drums throbbed in the night air, and Uncle Hamid did not mind the noise.

Tenants from the estate came and settled down for the night on the veranda, and in the servants' quarters.

Aunt Majida and Aunt Abida sent word they would be arriving the next morning.

When the Raja of Amirpur came and was welcomed with elaborate courtesy, only I was conscious that the celebration was not complete because Ameer was not with him.

The Raja sat in a circle of deference. He had been the real force behind Uncle Hamid's success.

He said to Aunt Saira, with his eyes lowered, "*Masha-Allah*, Bhai Sahib won magnificently."

"With God's grace and your kind help," Aunt Saira said with formal humility.

He said in the same tone as hers, "I did my humble best. Victory is in God's hands. May He give us strength. We need good soldiers to fight for our cause."

Uncle Hamid said gravely, "It is alarming how many of our friends were defeated in the general constituencies."

Amirpur shook his head portentously. "It is a revolution. Congress commands a majority, and will be asked to form a government. It is nothing short of a revolution."

"A revolution," echoed Uncle Hamid gravely. "They will press for further land reforms——"

"With disruptive effects on the whole social structure," added Amirpur. "We must continue to fight for what we have."

Aunt Saira said indignantly, "They cannot take away what belongs to us. No Government can behave like thieves and robbers."

Saleem interrupted, "What about Russia? The Russian Revolution has had a more far-reaching effect on the minds of men than any religion."

"He's off again," Kemal whispered to me, grinning.

"Let's go," I whispered back.

"It will seem rude," he answered.

Aunt Saira said in a pontifical tone:

"Do not talk of those godless people in the same breath as you talk of religion."

"I'm afraid, mother, what those godless people say to the hungry and homeless carries more weight than the talk of the holiest men."

Amirpur said as if talking to a naughty but favourite child, "My dear son, Begum Sahiba is correct. We do not need to concern ourselves with atheists. Our religion has pointed the way to man's material betterment while still following the path ordained by God."

"I'm going," I whispered to Kemal. "This is worse than politics."

Their indiscriminate use of God's name embarrassed me. Besides they who condemned idolaters for making gods to serve their spiritual needs themselves turned God into many shapes with each twist of their minds.

I slipped away quietly towards the door, but there was Ranjit blowing in like a hurricane of goodwill and cheerfulness.

"*Ādāb* Chacha. *Ādāb* Chachi. *Ādāb* Raja Chacha," he said, bowing in salutation. "When is the feast? When is the real celebration?"

"You are always welcome, son," smiled Aunt Saira. "Come and join us tonight."

"No, no, Chachi. You cannot put me off so lightly. I can eat here any time. It is my home. I want a proper feast. What is your opinion, Raja Chacha? Are we young people not entitled to a feast with music and singing, nothing but the best?"

"Certainly, certainly," said Amirpur benevolently. "And let us hope one day you will invite us to celebrate your own success for I believe you are quite a rising political star. And now I must leave you to bully your Chachi."

There was an elaborate exchange of courtesies as the Raja Sahib was escorted to his car.

Ranjit made sure Uncle Hamid and Aunt Saira were out of earshot and said, "I say, Kemal, what about a party? I'll collect a few friends. There will be a beautiful moon later. We'll go and wake up the ghosts in the old palace. That old ruin looks too lovely to have been just a hunting lodge; we might attract the ghosts of lovely maidens. What about it?"

Kemal said dubiously, "May be father wouldn't like us to leave them tonight."

"They are in a good mood. They will not mind, I'm sure," Ranjit said persuasively.

"If we go," I said, "may we go to the river instead, Ranjit? By the weir?"

That was where I wanted to be tonight with Ameer, where the silence and the peace of the river above and below the weir was stronger than the rush and turbulence of its waters through the gates. Across the waters, at this point, the trees and fields stretched into silent, uninterrupted space.

"All right then. After dinner?" Ranjit was irresistible, living always on the sunlit surface of life.

"After dinner," said Kemal.

Ranjit roared away in his impudent little car.

Ameer came after an eternity.

All through dinner I sensed Aunt Saira's hostility to him in a glance, a turn of phrase, an expressive shadow flickering over her face. My nerves which quivered always to emanations of dislike or disapproval, making me raw to any hurt, were doubly sensitive.

Why, I thought, should she feel as she did? Was it a reflection of her feelings for me? Because of the antagonism neither of us dared express but hid behind a careful, formal politeness? Why did it exist between us? Did she resent it that I could not give her the love and affection I gave so spontaneously to Aunt Abida? Did she think my withdrawal was stubbornness? Did she feel there was no submission though I was obedient? Was my obedience itself a challenge? Or was it more simple than that? Did she think it was Ameer who stood in the way of her wish that I should marry her son and tidily settle both the problem of my future and my share in the family property? Or was it merely that Ameer did not measure up to her conventional ideas of wealth, security and breeding?

I was absent from the cheerful flow of conversation. It was unusually free of arguments.

Saleem succeeded in casually mentioning our plans for a picnic at the right moment, and we were given permission to go.

After a short while we went to Kemal's room. Saleem said he had promised Ranjit that he would pick up some friends, so he left in his own car.

The moon had risen and the garden, the trees, the house were clear in its light, with a softness the sun could not give them.

When Kemal had gone to bring his father's car Ameer and I were at last alone.

"You looked unhappy all through dinner," he said. "What was worrying you?"

"There is nothing I can hide from you, can I?" I said smiling.

"I feel with you, and through you," he said.

"I had a feeling Saira Chachi was watching us, even when she was not looking at us. Like being frightened of a presence in the dark that is not really there."

"I felt it too." He hesitated then said, "She doesn't like me, and your uncle would not approve of me as a husband for you. I don't qualify—not by their standards."

"Please don't say that. I have told you it does not matter. I am not a child. I'm twenty."

"It is not easy to fight conventions, to defy one's people——"

I interrupted him, "I have no courage, Ameer. I have never done anything I really believed in. Perhaps I believed in nothing enough. I have never been allowed to make decisions; they are always made for me. In the end not only one's actions but one's mind is crippled. Sometimes I want to cry out, 'You are crushing me, destroying my individuality.' If I did that they would think me stubborn and rude, or say I imagined things. Do you understand? Or do I really create problems?"

"Of course, I understand. But what we have to face is very real, all kinds of prejudices made real. It needs courage."

"When I think of you, I have all the courage in the world, because about you there are no doubts. That is the only thing I really believe in. Take it away and nothing, nothing is left."

"I am frightened, Laila, not of them but of myself, because I feel unworthy. All I know is that I love you."

It was as he kissed me that the curtain was lifted, and there was Aunt Saira standing at the door with Kemal behind her.

She could not have been there more than a few moments before Kemal led her away. But in that silent, unending time, I saw a naked anger and hatred in her eyes that paralysed me, and I began to shiver uncontrollably.

"Laila, please . . . please, Laila," Ameer cried, "look at me."

I said with an edge of hysteria, "Oh well, that's that. The moment of decision taken out of our hands."

He held my shaking body in his arms. "I'm glad," he said fiercely. "I'm glad."

"I am not frightened of them," I said. "I'm frightened of all the ugliness."

I clung to him and sobbed.

He said gently, "It is natural to be frightened. I feel as you do. But nothing can harm us if we are together."

Kemal came into the room with an exaggerated air of cheerfulness.

"A bit of a mess, that was. You might have been more careful of course," he grinned. "You might have warned me."

"I'm sorry, Kemal," Ameer said quietly. "I love Laila."

"Good lord, why must you tell me? I'm not blind. Anyway, what about setting out? The others will be waiting."

"But, Kemal," I cried, "how can we——how can I——What about——?"

"What about what? Pull yourself together. Nothing terrible has happened, has it? And don't worry about mother. I know how to handle her. She is so scared of scandal one has only to frighten her with it, and a neat little facade of respectability is built up." He kissed me lightly on my cheek. "Come on now, cheer up. You have something to celebrate after all, so shall we enjoy ourselves tonight?"

"But tomorrow . . ." I stammered.

"Tomorrow will soon be another yesterday." He laughed.

As we drove through the gates I looked back. In the morning the sun would come and waken me in this house as it had done since I became a conscious being. Yet I had already left this home for ever.

Ameer's hand held mine tightly.

Part Four

Chapter One

THE sun was breaking through scattered clouds, and its warmth flickered over goose-fleshed skin as I drove towards Ashiana, the home of my childhood and adolescence.

The mists of a winter morning still rested on village ponds, among the fields and groves and on the river when I crossed it into the city.

Tattered settlements for refugees had erupted on once open spaces. Ugly buildings had sprung up, conceived by ill-digested modernity and the hasty needs of a growing city.

My eyes saw with the complex vision of my nostalgia and sadness the loved arches and domes and finials, the curve of the river, the branching of the roads, the unfamiliar names and changed lettering of the road signs, the ruined Residency on its green elevation without its flag, the proud Club that had been a palace and was now a Research Institute, the pedestal without its marble Empress and with a vagrant lying across it in deep sleep, the faded feudal mansions, the Mall with new shops and restaurants and cinemas, pavement booths as in a bazaar cluttered with tawdry signs, old buildings with neglected frontages, the church with a new annexe to its school where children no longer sang 'God Save the King', the Government House flagstaff carrying the tricolor, the quiet, deep-shadowed trees lining the road.

The first of the three-storeyed cement blocks of cheap flats, built by Agarwal where the Raja of Bhimnagar's palace and garden had once been, came into view with washing hung across the balconies, and shrill voices called for the start of another day.

I was nearly home.

Cotton-wool clouds were being pulled apart into wispy

flakes that formed and disappeared into a growing blue clarity. The sun's increasing warmth began to suck up the last dew from shining leaves and silvered blades of grass, and sink into the flesh. Yet I shivered as I drove through the gates of Ashiana.

The marble slab, on which the neat black letters of my uncle's name were fading, was half-hidden by a wooden board that swung away from careless nails. On both gate-posts hung other boards on which large black letters called attention to the qualifications of a doctor, a dentist, a lawyer with names that originated from the far north that was no longer their homeland.

I turned into the drive, and the car jolted over its uneven surface. The bordering hedges were as unkempt as the matted hair of a wandering mendicant. What had once been smooth, green lawns were brown, uneven spaces bordered with plots of tangled plants and a few forgotten flowers growing like weeds.

Patches of damp and peeling plaster disfigured the house like the skin of a once beautiful woman struck by leprosy. Over the porch creepers of bougainvilia flamed orange and red and purple against the blue sky.

I stopped the car outside it, and sat for some moments holding within me the rush of emotions like a spasm of nausea.

A low fence of crude wooden poles and straggling wire cut off the main house from the garden in front of the rooms where my aunts and the women servants had once lived.

A child's toy cart was lying on its side by the rose-bushes on the divided patch of grass. A bicycle stood in the veranda, and towels hung on the railings of the upstairs balcony.

I got out of the car and went through the porch into the wide veranda. The main doors were locked, their wire gauze encrusted with dust. A panel of the glass doors behind it was cracked. The brass fittings were black.

When I had consented to look round the house for the

last time I had thought I would break down. So I had come alone, wanting no witnesses. My most private emotions were contained by this house, as much a part of its structure as its every brick and beam. Its memories condensed my life as in a summary.

Yet, now, standing before its disintegrating reality I was as still as a stone in unstirred waters.

There were strangers living in the rooms where I had once searched for my lost father and mother, where I had found refuge in the love of my aunt Abida and Hakiman Bua, where I had developed through conflict with Zahra and Aunt Saira, where I had learned comradeship through Asad and Kemal and tested my beliefs in arguments with Saleem and Zahid, where my will had been disciplined by my grandfather and Uncle Hamid, and been freed by my dreams and love for Ameer.

There were strangers living in the rooms once so private and guarded, strangers who were names in Government files balancing Saleem's name against theirs—he labelled 'evacuee', they 'refugees'. Their presence here, and Saleem's in their erstwhile homeland, was part of a statistical calculation in the bargaining of bureaucrats and politicians, in which millions of uprooted human beings became just numerical figures. The official words describing them had no meaning in terms of human heartache.

I stood in the sunlight, and looked into the cold shadows of the sightless house with its locked doors.

I heard the sudden clear gurgle of a child's laughter. An ayah with a fat child straddled across her hip had come to pick up the toy cart. She stared at me curiously, and the child fixed its suddenly serious unblinking gaze upon me.

I walked away towards the back of the house where the servants had lived.

The conservatory behind the overgrown tennis courts was like a rubbish dump with broken flower-pots lying outside, palms with split, brown leaves, discoloured barrel-shaped pots, and plants that grew wild.

The garages and stables were empty, but some of the servants' quarters were not. The strangers' servants looked at me curiously. One of them must have hurried to tell the watchman, because when I turned into the kitchen garden, I saw him coming towards me from the far end of the grass-grown path.

He stopped and stared incredulously, then stumbled on his hurrying old legs and cried out "Laila Bitia" with joy and welcome in his quavering voice, and toothless grin.

"Laila Bitia, salaam! Why did you not tell me you were coming? I would have been at the door to welcome you."

"I did not know I was coming, Ram Singh. How are you? How is the family?"

"The old woman came to the end of her days. I am alone, Bitia. My son works as a peon in the Collector Sahib's office. The gods have been good to him. But I am alone. I would have opened the house for you if I had known."

Then the tears welled up in his sunken eyes.

"The house, Bitia, this is not how you should have come to the house. I saw you grow up in it, and I should have seen your children, and the children of Kemal Mian and Saleem Mian grow up in it. Bhagwan should have taken me from this earth before I saw this happen."

I consoled him but his tears and his words had opened my closed heart. I turned with him towards the house with every nerve alive and quivering.

And now the house was a living symbol. In its decay I saw all the years of our lives as a family; the slow years that had evolved a way of life, the swift short years that had ended it.

It was fourteen years ago since I had left this home to make another home with Ameer. The second half of a century was now two years old. My daughter was nearly as old as I had been when my grandfather had died, and the house had buried one way of life and accepted another which, in turn, had finished with Uncle Hamid's death five years ago.

Fourteen years were as fourteen moments, but the years that had gone before were as many centuries. Like the suddenness and fierceness of birth and death, and the gentleness of growth.

Mind and memory reacted as to a sudden touch of molten fire.

I said, at the open door, "Ram Singh, leave me alone."

He sighed and left me to wander through the house, and across the fourteen years.

Chapter Two

THE silence in the house was more disturbing than the signs and smell of being uninhabited through the long summer and the season of the rains. It was not the peaceful silence of emptiness, but as if sounds lurked everywhere, waiting for the physical presence of those who had made them audible. There was a sense of arrested movement in the few pieces of furniture that had not been removed to Hasanpur.

When I had started out from Hasanpur in the morning to see the house for the last time before it was sold Aunt Saira had wept without restraint. Her tears had washed away the constant aggression between us. I had listened with pity to her vain 'ifs' and 'buts' and 'might-have-beens' which sought to evade unchangeable realities.

A few months after the partition of the country Saleem had left for Pakistan, and it was left to Kemal to help her live according to the standards she had been used to before his father died.

She could not face the fact that Kemal had no alternative but to sell Ashiana. It was part of her refusal to accept the fact that her world had gone for ever. She had clothed herself in remembered assurances of power and privilege just as the story-book Emperor had donned his non-existent clothes, but there was no one to make her see the nakedness of her illusions. Traditional courtesies had restrained everyone. She only knew that power and privilege still existed, that position still counted; except that others, whom she had once patronised, possessed them.

The fabric of her illusions had begun to wear thin, but it wrapped her in simulated warmth. Her eyes refused to see dust and decay; they created a twilight that did not pick out cobwebs.

She had continued to live in Ashiana though an ever-decreasing number of servants made it more and more difficult to keep the house in good order. It began to mock its erstwhile grandeur. And events beyond her control became increasingly pitiless.

When Kemal married and was posted to Delhi his expenses increased while the income from the estate steadily decreased. There was no one now to supervise its management—Aunt Saira had known only the fruits of possession, not the mechanics. Her son's suggestion that she should cut down expenses by living in a smaller house seemed outrageous, and obviously inspired by his wife—whom she had resented from the start. For Kemal's marriage had been against her every principle and dream. He had committed an even greater crime than I had; he had married a non-Muslim, Mrs Wadia's daughter.

When Perin Wadia had returned from her expensive school in Switzerland her conscious cosmopolitanism had blossomed into the even more conscious nationalism which was fashionable towards the end of the war.

European and American aesthetes and intellectuals and the 'smart set' of Bombay and Delhi had discovered the art and culture of ancient India simultaneously.

It appeared at times that neo-Indians wore their nationalism like a mask, and their Indianness like fancy dress.

Perin Wadia, like others of her group, had transposed the Ajanta look into the twentieth century in the manner of her dress and coiffeur, though she spoke of ancient culture in European idioms. She had even tried to learn the Bharata Natyam style of dancing, and gone to an *ashram* in the south for a period of meditation.

Mrs Wadia had hidden her vain disapproval under a show of affectionate raillery at her daughter's 'youthful eccentricities', especially as two of Perin's wealthy American school-friends had gone with her to the south to 'search for Truth'.

But then Perin and Kemal had met in Delhi and married.

My Aunt had had hysterics; Mrs Wadia had emigrated with her husband to England.

I had been a little surprised when Kemal had told me he was going to marry Perin; she was so unlike Sita. Maybe that was why he had married her. She had been so ready to defy everyone to marry him; and he had never ceased being lonely.

It was less surprising that Perin loved Kemal. He was genuinely all she wished to be; he believed in all those values her cosmopolitan intellectualism sought for. They complemented each other.

Two years after her son's marriage Aunt Saira had to face other and graver shocks.

At the end of a long, legal struggle landowners had to accept the fact that their feudal existence had been abolished constitutionally as swiftly as by the revolution they had always feared.

Hundreds of thousands of families were faced with the necessity of changing habits of mind and living conditioned by centuries, hundreds of thousands of landowners and the hangers-on who had lived on their largesse, their weaknesses and their follies. Faced by prospects of poverty, by the actual loss of privilege, there were many who lost their balance of mind when their world cracked apart. Others retired to anonymity in their villages.

Palaces and great houses wore the signs of neglect. Shops and surgeries, brothels, and law-courts lost their best customers. The expanding city with its rash of new buildings, its new citizens had new scars added to those left when the royal era was destroyed.

This was the end my uncle had prohesied. This was the end our theories and enthusiasms had supported. Like Death and all dissolution it was an end easier to accept with the mind than as a fact.

When Asad once said to me, "The ugliness is inevitable. When palaces are pulled down and mud huts are exposed to view it is not a pleasant sight. There is rubble and dust in any demolition. But from this debris we shall build again", I had answered impatiently, "Asad, stop talking like a text-book. The trouble with all of you who go about changing the world is that you become petrified. All this is so easy to say, but when I think of the worries and despair, the material problems of my family and friends I cannot look objectively beyond them."

"You will," he said, "if you think of those who always knew that despair."

"It is harder to begin to learn."

He looked at me, surprised. "Surely, Laila, you don't mean what you are saying. You are talking against all you believed in, just like those you once called reactionaries."

Was it that I resented and envied his cohesion of thought and action, and therefore could not love him as he wished, seeing him still as an abstraction, not a man?

Even while we had argued I had recognised how my emotions gnawed at my logic. I recognised my dreams had always been of change without chaos, of birth without pain.

Aunt Saira had had no such mental conflict. She had railed against the 'robber' Government, railed against the nobodies who had destroyed a class through jealousy, railed against us who told her it was useless to rail against the inevitable.

And then a new law had come like a death blow. All those Muslims who had left for Pakistan were declared 'evacuees' and their property declared 'evacuee property' to be taken over by a Custodian.

As Saleem had gone to Pakistan his share in all the property was taken away. With scrupulous honesty Kemal declared his share, to the last pot and pan and stool and chair. He was grateful he had not been harassed as so many others had been by petty officials who ordered humiliating searches of houses and lengthy cross-examinations.

Part of Ashiana was taken over by the Custodian, and later the Hasanpur house was threatened with similar dismemberment. Kemal asked his mother to let him sell Ashiana and buy up Saleem's share in Hasanpur with the money so as to save the ancestral house.

At first she refused to listen to him. She made herself ill with anger against the way of the world, the Government, her son and his wife. "What right have they to steal what is ours? Will they never be content with how much they rob? Is there no justice? Is this a war with Custodians for enemy property? Did they not consent to the partition themselves? Why treat those people like enemies who went over? Were they not given a free choice? Were they warned they would lose their property, and have their families harassed? If they want to drive out Muslims why not say it like honest men? Sheltering behind the false slogans of a secular state! Hypocrites! Cowards! It is good Saleem has gone away. They will destroy you and all fools like you who have trusted them. The Banias!"

Kemal tried patiently to explain as if to a child the inevitability of such unpleasant laws and regulations because Government policies could not but reflect the violent aftermath of the Partition. He pointed out how much more property had been left behind by Hindus in Pakistan. But she turned on him in the bitterness of impotent rage and said he did not care for his traditions or for her; he had sold himself to a Muslim-hating Government and married a 'Kafir', a non-Muslim. He retaliated as bitterly by asking her why she did not go to live with Saleem in the Muslim neo-Paradise across the border.

Then she had cried with the pathetic tears of an old, lonely woman.

It had been as painful as love turned cancerous. Kemal had understood and forgiven, because a real core of suffering was hidden beneath the mass of her prejudices and absurdities.

As I stood inside the quiet house, so soon to become merely a piece of property, I felt their remembered pain as my own.

Chapter Three

I OPENED the door of Uncle Hamid's office. The high bookshelves lining the walls were empty. The long, heavy, leather-covered table and chair, and an old swivelling bookcase were the only pieces of furniture left in the room.

In that chair Uncle Hamid had sat when he exercised authority. He had been sitting in it when our wills clashed for the last time.

I remembered how frightened I had been, how determined not to show my fear, how I had prayed to still the beating of my heart, and fixed my mind on Ameer to help me through the ordeal.

"You are quite clear in your mind about the decision you have made about marrying this—this young man?" he asked.

"Yes."

"You understand, I do not have the same old-fashioned objections as your aunts."

How much easier, I thought, it was to face positive, prejudiced, emotional cruelty than this farce of broad-minded reasonableness.

"I merely wish to point out the possible consequences of your decision. This young man——"

Why did he not use his name?

"—has no means to support you as you have been used to living."

"I don't care to put a price on myself."

He shrugged his shoulders, ignoring my outburst in that familiar way which crushed me more than any reproofs.

"Material facts cannot be altered by not caring about them. I would advise a mature, and not adolescent, approach to your future. The step you intend to take is a final one. Of course, you yourself have a considerable amount of property."

"If you are implying that Ameer thought——"

"—including a share in this house."

"I do not want to live in this house."

"I have no desire to force you to do so. Your financial affairs will be settled justly, and you will be independent of us as soon as you have finished your studies."

"I cannot stay here any longer."

"I am afraid I cannot allow you to live anywhere else while I am responsible for you. You must surely share my desire to keep our family differences from being made public."

"I can go somewhere else, to some other university."

"As the young man is, I believe, going to live and work here perhaps that would be advisable, but it may not be possible."

"You could make it so."

"I am glad you consider my help to be of some value. Anyway, the position is clear now. You may go."

Had he said I was being disinherited I could not have been more effectively cast out.

My marriage was arranged at the same time as Saleem's so that the happy celebration of one could disguise disapproval of the other.

Later, when the years had chastened his pride and taken away the external props on which his relationships had depended, and he needed the human affection which alone offered respite from loneliness, Uncle Hamid had made hesitant gestures of conciliation, mostly through my child. He showed her affection which he had not expressed even to his own children, particularly after Ameer's death.

But I did not want to think of that.

I turned the bookcase round and round as I had done when a child.

This room had been the centre of activity during the election fifteen years ago, and crowded with well-wishers that bright day of my uncle's success in his first election. Nine years later he had had his first heart attack sitting at this desk. In those nine years he had seen the gradual crumbling of all his dreams and ambitions.

Politically he had fought a losing battle against new forces that were slowly and inexorably detroying the rights and privileges in which he had believed.

Socially he had seen that way of life going to pieces which he had cultivated so carefully; the new ruling class either derided it as a slavish copy of the British, or simply were ignorant of its conventions and had no wish to learn.

Emotionally his family had grown away from him. Kemal's success in the Civil Service pleased him, but he could not approve of his sympathetic even enthusiastic attitude to the changing pattern. Saleem had left home to join a British firm, lived in Calcutta, got on splendidly with his British colleagues, swaddled his mind in his old school tie, and agreed with his wife, Nadira, that partition of the country was the only solution of all its problems. Aunt Saira had never been a mental companion to him, and her unsubtle reactions to all that perplexed him made him irritable. While he sickened within him with the perplexities of the inward stresses that were undermining his world she passed facile judgement. "What can you expect," she would gibe "when a Government is run by people who wear *dhoties* to parties and put their dirty feet up on sofas?"

Uncle Hamid took to gardening, and playing bridge, and reading numerous newspapers. Occasionally arguments would flare up as a matter of habit, but they had become a form of intellectual exercise when even the pretence of shaping events was not possible for him, and action outstripped theory in the world outside.

Action, in fact, became violent in the closing years of his life, and peace an inward, personal achievement. There came the war, the Japanese threat to the country, the news that thousands of captured soldiers—and officers—had joined the Indian National Army as their allies, then the violent eruption of extremist nationalism when Congress leaders were imprisoned in 1942, then the riots that spiralled across the country from the East to the West to the North gaining murderous momentum towards their bloody climax in 1946. And in 1947 came the partition of the country, and the people of India and Pakistan celebrated Independence in the midst of bloody migrations from one to another.

During the war Uncle Hamid had begun to listen to every news bulletin, read every paper he possibly could. The habit persisted. Through the years he passively allowed himself to be battered by the speeches and statements that poured from the legion of leaders and propagandists of every party as they bargained with the British and each other, incited emotions and pleaded for peace, spoke for and to the people, unscathed while blood flowed and hatred spawned.

Death spared him the putrescent culmination, the violent orgasm of hate that followed the independence he had worked for in his own fashion. He was buried with traditional religious ceremony in the village graveyard by his father's side.

It was easy to be detached as I looked back; easier than when every thought and action had waited for the morrow.

Chapter Four

IN the sitting-room, once so formally furnished, a few discarded dusty chairs and tables emphasised its size, and shadows flickered over its emptiness while my footsteps echoed from its marble floor to the high, carved ceiling. There were marks on the walls left by paintings and mirrors that had been removed to Hasanpur. The tall naked doors leading to the veranda and garden were bolted.

This was the room that had frightened me as a child with strange noises, and sudden shadows, but now there were many living ghosts to drive away imagined ones.

I hurried through to the dining-room. The dining-table had been too large for the room in Hasanpur and looked abandoned without its attendant chairs. Around it had been enacted the ceremonial ritual of meals, and the passionate clashing of wills and theories and beliefs. When those countless words had been spoken who had known what they presaged?

At this table the family had gathered and had the final argument by which it was ultimately scattered.

Zahra was the only one absent because her husband had to be in Delhi for one of many conferences to discuss administrative and practical details of the coming partition of the country. She herself was busy with the background of parties and receptions.

I had come from my home in the hills at Kemal's request, because he wanted the family to be together to discuss the future before making any final decisions. He had written to Saleem that he intended staying in India when the Government offered the right of opting for service in either country. Most of his Muslim colleagues had decided to go to Pakistan, and Saleem had questioned the wisdom of his choice.

That last meal together in Ashiana was like many other argument-punctuated ones in the past, yet unlike them because this argument permitted no evasions; it was conclusive. I imagined each one of us missed Uncle Hamid as I did, feeling he might have held us together, ordering us with illogical, yet now welcome, authority.

Saleem talked with his usual didactic self-assurance. I found his verbosity soothing—it covered up the silence which I had learned to use as the only safeguard of vulnerability. Yet it provoked irony.

"My dear Kemal," Saleem said, "I appreciate your idealism but aren't you being somewhat romantic, even quixotic? Let us examine the facts. In a month's time the British will have gone; their rule will be over."

"And they will have reverted to their original role of traders," I said.

Even Kemal frowned at me, but before Saleem could say anything his mother moaned, raising her eyes to heaven, "Oh the things I've seen come to pass and the things I have yet to see! It is written that when the end of the world is near the lowest will become the highest."

Saleem went on as if he had not been interrupted, in the manner of a patient parent ignoring a backward child.

"Independence will have been attained, not only for one country, but two. There will be a new Muslim country born—Pakistan. We must think not in terms of India now, but India and Pakistan."

Nadira drew a sharp breath, and her eyes shone. I envied the joy of her triumphant vision.

"The important question is—what will be the relationship between these—er—separated Siamese twins?"

As no one applauded his joke, Saleem went on, "Let us imagine the worst that could happen. Suppose the sporadic violence that has preceded partition continues after it—though when one considers that the leaders on both sides have accepted the decision, there is really no reason why it should——"

"Except the logic of inculcated hate," I said. "Remember your classics and the tale of the Dragon's Teeth."

"If, God forbid, our young Cassandra's forebodings are correct," Saleem continued, "then it will be worse than a civil war. The British will have pulled out their forces in good time; mixed forces of Hindus and Muslims, in the army and police, will have to stop Hindus and Muslims killing each other."

"God forbid. Is there no end to it?" cried Aunt Saira. "Why must you talk of killing and death? It is unlucky."

She went on softly muttering prayers to herself. More and more each day she was withdrawing from the Western attitudes she had sought to cultivate just for her husband's and her sons' sakes.

"On the other hand," Saleem expounded, stabbing the air with his forefinger, "everything might settle down peacefully. That is where leadership counts. Even so, I maintain, there will still be discrimination against those Muslims who stay in India."

I said, "Saleem, you do go on and on expounding the obvious. It makes one impatient. All you want really to say is that you think Kemal should not have decided to stay on here."

Saleem protested. "It's not as simple as that. One must explain one's position. It is important for us as individuals and as a family to understand each other."

"That is it," Kemal said. "As a family more than as individuals it is important. I don't want the family to split up. There is too much of that in the air nowadays. I want us to remain united. As it is we get together so seldom. Imagine it if you went to Karachi——"

Aunt Saira interrupted, "I do not understand, son. Saleem is in Calcutta; he will go to Karachi. What is the difference? This will still be his home."

"Mother, I wish it were as simple as that. He will, in fact, be going to another country! Don't you see, we will belong to different countries, have different nationalities?

Can you imagine every time we want to see each other we'll have to cross national frontiers? Maybe even have to get visas," he added wryly.

"Oh, come on, Kemal," Saleem laughed, "there is no need to be as dramatic as all that. Visas indeed!"

"Saleem," asked Kemal earnestly. "Have you decided to go?"

Saleem looked somewhat discomfited. He said with less assurance. "It is not the same for me as for you, Kemal. I have to go where my company sends me."

"Is it *sending* you? Has it given you an ultimatum of sorts?"

"Well, it's like this. It has been suggested that I should take charge of the branch in Pakistan. That is, you understand, a promotion. On the other hand, if I stay, I have been warned that prospects are not so bright here. I will not have to *leave* the firm, but cannot hope to get as far as I certainly can—and will—well, I mean to say, in business one has to face facts. These firms must think of the general atmosphere—you know what I mean—Muslims will not be as welcome from the sales point of view. Let's face it, Kemal, these firms are not here for our well-being or their health. I must consider my future prospects. I have a family to think of. You Government servants have been given an option, with safeguards. You can choose either country——"

"Not really. A choice presupposes both sides mean the same to me. They don't. This is my country. I belong to it. I love it. That is all. One does not bargain——"

He stopped and flushed, as if embarrassed by any suspicion of sentimentality. Saleem, also, had lost some of his self-assurance.

He said, "You will have to face suspicion, prejudice, even hatred."

"Perhaps I have already done that. Maybe I know better than you what I have to face or have faced. But I believe in my country. I have to fight for what I believe in. You forget I never shared your views. I cannot condone something I believe is wrong."

"There is no point in talking of rights and wrongs now, Kemal. I believe I was right, and am still right. What has happened had to happen. Be a realist. Think of the future. Naseer has opted for Pakistan. He has it on good authority he will become a Secretary the moment he goes there. Have you thought of what will happen to you?"

"What I have not thought of is promotion or to save my skin. I have thought of loyalty."

"That is not fair," Nadira burst out. "You have no right to question others' loyalties. There is such a thing as the loyalty to one's own faith. Pakistan needs us to build it up as a refuge where all Muslims can be safe and free."

"Safe from what, Nadira?" Kemal said, his eyes burning. "Oppression? By whom? According to you that danger exists here—there will still be millions of Muslims here. Who is to look after them? Those whom you warned them against? Or those who prophesied doom? Are they going to stay and share it? Are you?"

I felt the sickness inside me that always came with tangled, unexpressed emotions. My heart was with Kemal, but there seemed no way of helping him. I had learned too well the futility of arguments which involved beliefs.

Saleem tried to calm him. "Kemal, let's not become emotional about this. You wanted us to speak frankly. I admit Nadira has gone off rather at a tangent, but I am facing this quite objectively. I think we have no future here, and our children have even less."

Kemal's voice quivered with suppressed emotion. "I see my future in the past. I was born here, and generations of my ancestors before me. I am content to die here and be buried with them."

"God forbid," cried Aunt Saira, "that you should use such words. Let them be said in the same breath as the names of your enemies."

Nadira said sullenly, "One's ancestors left their homes when they first came here. People do migrate from one country to another."

"That gives one the freedom of the world," I said.

"For most Muslims of this sub-continent Pakistan connotes something different from other countries of the world," Nadira replied sharply. "Let us be logical."

"Then let us return to our ancestors' homeland. Let us return to Arabia, Turkestan, Persia."

"You are not funny, Laila. I have a right to express my opinions just as much as any of you," Nadira flared. "I wish to go to Pakistan, and Saleem is happy to do so."

"Your ideals and Saleem's prospects harmonise perfectly, thank the Lord."

"What right have you to make fun of me? You believe in nothing. All you can do is to be sarcastic and destructive," Nadira stormed.

From the edge of unhappiness and uncertainty on which we had all been balancing we were searching blindly for props—ugly or otherwise.

Kemal's face paled, and he said in a gentle but defeated voice, "Please let us not quarrel amongst ourselves. That is so important now. God knows what we will have to face later."

All that followed was of no importance. Our future had been decided.

Less than two months later Saleem and Nadira left for Pakistan and it was easier for them thereafter to visit the whole wide world than the home which had once been theirs.

Chapter Five

FROM the dining-room I went into the gloomy pantry. Its window-panes were opaque with dust, and cobwebs clung to the wire-mesh that had kept out flies and winged monsoon-bred insects. The china of the deep sink was chipped and yellow where persistent drops of water had dripped through the unheeding months. Empty shelves and cupboards lined the stained walls.

This had been Ghulam Ali's domain until his embittered, lusting love of Nandi had driven him to violence and prison.

Where was he now, I wondered? Had he exploited the exodus into the new land, or taken advantage of the pitiful flight of refugees to escape as others had done from the consequences of misdeeds?

I opened the door leading out into the courtyard, and the sunlight burst upon me, dancing from the clear, blue sky.

Nandi was, at this moment, in my home looking after my daughter. She was no longer the girl who had tantalised men and antagonised women because she was so completely, naturally and fearlessly feminine. Ghulam Ali had scarred her face, the years had added unsightly layers over the lines of her nubile body, and respectibility had smothered her mind and spirit since she had stopped being a washer-woman and become an ayah.

Nandi had remained unquestioningly loyal throughout the period of my struggle against my family. The other women servants had subserviently reflected their mistress's moods by working for me as for a stranger. Nandi had gone to the other extreme, neglecting all work for mine.

She had wanted to leave with me saying, "I cannot be faithful to the salt of those who are unkind to you," but it was not until my child was born that I had let her leave her doting old husband and father.

I could not have done otherwise. She came to me one

day, carrying a tin trunk and a roll of bedding and said, "I have come home, Bitia. I have come to look after my little one. I heard you were looking for an ayah. How could I allow a strange woman to look after my baby?"

Nandi was the smartest ayah in the neighbourhood.

A few months after her arrival, when she could no longer conceal it, she confessed she was expecting a child.

She said quite simply, "It is not my husband's, of course. How could that old dotard give me one? If I had stayed at home, even if *he* had not dared, my father would have thrown me out. Or the old fool might have fancied his youth had returned and claimed the child, and I would have been tied to him for ever. I could not endure him any longer, and I wanted the child. So I came to you, knowing I would be safe here. But, believe me, Bitia," she added quickly, "I would have come to you and my little one anyway."

And she stood proudly, holding my baby above her ripe belly, crooning to it, "My little jewel, my star child, my moon-flower."

Whose child she bore would have remained a mystery to me had Nandi not told me herself. In a circuitous way Nandi's fate was linked up with my friend Sita's amours, and her father's fortunes.

Agarwal's business prospered with the war. His water-diviner's keen sense for potential wealth became sharper; and he missed no opportunity of making more and more money.

The orchards and gardens of the Raja of Bhimnagar's house, which he had bought, much to my uncle Hamid's regret, were merely so much valuable space. He cut down trees, dug up lawns, filled up ponds and built sheds and godowns for a small factory producing tents, ropes, buckets and pails for the army. The scent of flowers and fruit blossoms and the song of birds that used to come across the walls to 'Ashiana' were replaced by the clang of metal, the hiss of furnaces and the shouts of workmen. Instead of a dozen gardeners hundreds of men found employment, and a small settlement of huts grew round what had been the servants' quarters.

The palace itself could not longer be lived in, and lay abandoned while Agarwal speculated how to use it profitably.

Then one of Sita's conquests—an architect she took under her wing in her role of patron of the arts—was given a chance to express himself through a block of flats that would introduce the city to modern architecture, and her father to a new source of income. In the gracious, old-fashioned, sleepy city where living in flats was unknown, the many-storeyed building with its garages and shops was a startling innovation. Rich families from Calcutta, fleeing from the threat of Japanese bombs, and officials of war-created departments moved in almost before it was finished.

Nandi's father and husband prospered with the increasing demand for washermen, sweepers and bearers. They had to employ men to take the piles of dirty linen down to the river to be washed. Then even better fortune came their way.

The Americans came to town. Restaurants and dance halls mushroomed among the staid, colonnaded shops in the Mall. Tonga-drivers put up their fares, and servants their wages. Anglo-Indian girls found the newcomers irresistible, imagined themselves on the road to Hollywood.

Naked little beggar-girls and boys learned to wiggle their hips to the mutilated words and rhythm of 'Pistol packing Mamma', and to wink as they stretched out their hands saying, "C'mon, babe". The rest of the town went its way with its customary politeness, and its private sense of shock.

It was a brief interlude, like a sudden gust of wind across the fields rippling the waters of the river, and it left no trace.

Except that Nandi found she was going to have a baby.

"Oh no," protested Nandi, greatly shocked. "Of course it was not an 'Umreecum'. How could you think I could do such a thing? Am I that kind of a girl? Did I ever go near those monkey-faced *Angréz* soldiers? I'd rather have died than let the white men touch me."

Her lover was the bearer of an American soldier on leave, a light-eyed, swaggering man from the Northern Frontier.

From childhood Nandi had been fascinated and frightened by the tall, turbaned, fierce-looking men with long locks and bold eyes, who came from their wild mountains as money-lenders and intimidated meek southerners into paying extortionate rates of interest. And now she had met one of their kind without this frightening occupation. Only the fascination remained.

Had he not been staying just a fortnight Nandi might have resisted temptation, but time made lust urgent. Had he not been a wanderer, here today with one master, and gone tomorrow with another, she would have run away with him.

As it was she was left with his child; and no regrets.

She said, "I will not let my son become like my people, washing the dirty clothes of others, standing in the waters of ponds and rivers, winter and summer. I shall send him to school, and one day, who knows, he may become a *babu* in a big office."

So I sent the little boy to a school run by Jesuit Fathers. Maybe one day he would become more than the clerk Nandi dreamed he would be. Maybe he would be a Civil Servant, an officer in the Army or Police, a Member of Parliament. After all others from his school were that today.

I smiled, thinking of Nandi as I walked towards the un-kept garden where she and I had played as children.

Chapter Six

THERE was a fountain at one end of the garden which had been our delight when, as children, we had flirted with the spray from the jets of water that spurted from the mouths of two marble fish coiled round each other. It was not aesthetically pleasing, but my grandfather had bought it because fish were the emblem of the Province.

There were decayed leaves and caked mud in the dry fountain. I sat on the edge, and looked around me. A scarlet rose climbed up the garden wall, a vibrant patch in the neglected garden.

Across the wall and through the sunlit, animated leaves of the tall trees beyond it, I could see the double-storeyed tenement-like buildings that had replaced the workers' huts in the adjoining compound. Behind the block of flats, and where the small factory had once been, Sita's father had built rows of cheap houses, cashing in on the needs of the refugees who had swarmed into the city after the partition.

Agarwal was not only a rich business man now but had achieved his politcal ambition and was a minister. His octopus grip was tight on the political centres of power in the city at every level.

I remembered him when he had schemed with Waliuddin against Uncle Hamid. Though they were so unlike they could not be separated in one's thoughts, like the tall, fat clown and the thin little one who had rocked us with laughter in the circus that came to town every year when we were children. These were no comedians; they gorged themselves on human weakness, though they were both model fathers and husbands.

Waliuddin had not been successful like his friend. He had tried to straddle one fence too many, and had fallen into obscurity as a lawyer in a small town in Pakistan.

After the Partition he had stayed long enough to arrange

for the secret sale of whatever little property he pos
He had dramatically sworn loyalty to an independent
in the market square where he had once swayed his listeners
to support whichever cause he currently supported. He had exhorted the Muslims, demoralised by the bloody events near the border, to be loyal to their Indian homeland. And then one day he and his family had stealthily crossed the Eastern border. But his delusions of political grandeur had come to nothing. Others were already entrenched in positions of power; his genius for political scheming proved unsuccessful among those born and bred in the regions where he tried to become a leader. He was not even made an ambassador like most of his erstwhile colleagues. He had to content himself with living on the profits of the vast property he had claimed as compensation for the alleged wealth he had left behind.

Though I thought of Agarwal with distaste it was otherwise with his daughter, Sita. Memories of childhood's friendship burnished all thoughts of her, and all our scattered meetings through the years.

Sita was a leader in the new social world. She won people with her charm, intrigued them with her calculated attack on conventions, titillated them with her cynical coquetry, impressed them with her hospitality and her wealth. She had become a patroness of the arts, a benefactress of impecunious writers and artists, a collector of ancient works of art and young lovers.

She had little time for her husband, but he was ambitious, fond of drinking and gambling, and glad of the progress he made because of her. He had been made a director of Agarwal's concerns.

They built a beautiful house in New Delhi, very modern and Western in appearance and conveniences, very Indian and ancient in its decoration. It reflected Sita's character.

The last time Sita and I had been together here in Ashania was a few days before I married, when the atmosphere of the house was charged with my family's disapproval. We had sat in this garden, out of reach of the fountain's spray, and she had said, cynically:

"You make me feel so much older than you though we are the same age. You are a child dreaming romantic dreams of love. What has love to do with marriage? It is like mixing oil and water. Love is anti-social, while matrimony preserves the world and its respectability. Follow my example. I married with my mind unblurred by sentiment, and everybody is happy."

I said with the priggishness of an innocent in love, "I feel sorry for you, Sita."

She threw back her head and laughed, and the diamond she had taken to wearing in her nose glittered like a splinter of glass.

It was the Sita she had not been able to destroy who had travelled a day and a night to come to me after she learned of Ameer's death.

In those days of my silence she used to talk to me of herself as she had never done. She sensed that I needed to be distracted from the unending, inaudible self-communication that made it impossible for me to talk to others. She knew that nothing false could come through to me, and she talked to me of Kemal.

"After he got engaged he told me we had to stop seeing each other. Oh yes, we used to meet, whenever we could, wherever we could, even after I was married. Being away from him was like stopping to breathe. I am not ashamed to tell you. I was not ashamed then; I was just careful. I had to be, or I could not have been with him. He hated—and resented—the deception more than I did. I think it is the sense of possession in a man that is hurt, not his sense of morality."

She was sitting by the window, in relief against the distant sky. She had no touch of make-up, and her hair was loose round her shoulders. Was her pain drawn out as an echo of mine?

"Forgive me, Laila, if I talk in clichés. I have nothing

new to say. It makes one sound like a commonplace character out of a commonplace book."

She got up to put out her cigarette, and went back to stand at the window with her back towards me.

"I had children by my husband though my body revolted against the touch of any man I did not love. But it was bearable if I had a hope of being with Kemal, as if that cleansed me. After he stopped seeing me it did not matter what happened. If my body could accept one man without love it could accept others. One discovers so many reasons for sleeping with a man once love is put out of the way. I think hate is as good as any. Certainly it is the only feeling that remains in memory."

Suddenly she started crying, silently, with no distortion of her face, just an endless stream of tears, and she turned to me, and said fiercely:

"Don't pity me. I live as I must. I can no other way." Then she restrained herself and said softly, "I'm sorry, Laila. But I want you to turn your mind away from pity—for me or yourself. You will never lose what you have had, and what you had was the fulfilment of your dreams. I made fun of you once, because I knew you were right and I did not have your courage."

The sound of a long-shut door being pushed open brought me back to the garden and the sunshine.

The old watchman came slowly towards me. He had put on the brown woollen coat that had been part of his winter uniform.

"Ah, Bitia. I wondered where you had been all this time. I thought I would open the doors and let some air into the rooms."

"You have done well. I would have had to go right round the house to get into my old room."

He sighed deeply, "No, Bitia, you should not be wandering alone in an empty house. But at least my old eyes have rested on you once again. Kemal Mian used to come sometimes, and I could pay my respects. But Saleem Mian and

Zahra Bitia came only once since they went away, and stayed only a few days. Tell me why do they not come to stay with Begum Sahib? It is not right that children should leave their mothers alone in their old age. That is the time for which they gave them birth and brought them up."

I said, "It is not easy for them to come."

"Not easy? But why, Bitia? They tell me that one can fly through the skies as they did in old tales of the gods. They can come here in a few hours," the old man persisted.

How could one explain that Time and Space were not the only obstacles?

"They will come when their work permits," I said. "Zahra Bitia's husband is very hard-worked. He is in a high position in the Government."

"That is good," he said. "Like Kemal Mian, and Asad Mian are over here."

He had to point out that no 'outsider'—not even one related by marriage—could be superior to his own masters.

Then he started again. "Bitia, you should not wander in the empty house. . . ."

I said, "I shall sit here a little longer. I am waiting for Asad Mian. I had written that I would come at twelve o'clock, but I started from Hasanpur early. Wait outside for him, and when he comes, tell him I am here."

He looked distressed by my dismissal of him, and then, folding his hands before his face, said, "As you say, Bitia", and shuffled away.

Chapter Seven

SALEEM had come on leave after two years. He was now one of the senior executives in the new branch of his firm, and his success had put a gloss on his self-assurance and self-esteem. He was still as ready as he had ever been with his theories, prophecies and analyses of every possible problem. But in talking of the relationship between the two countries after partition he was cautious, and detached. It was as if, being a representative of one of their concerns, he had identified himself with the British attitude of disengagement.

So much had happened since the family had been separated that was hurtful to the human spirit, that the reunion was doubly joyful. Saleem was touched to find old friends unchanged in spite of the backwash of revengeful hate and suspicion that had spattered the humane, poetic soul of the city. He was glad of the feeling of recognised identity in Hasanpur after having lived among strangers who knew him as an individual without a background.

All of us shared that sensation of 'feeling' our roots—whether severed or not—like the pain felt in the extremities of amputated limbs.

After many years we had visited Hasanpur together to pay our respects to the dead and to the few still living.

The trees and the fields were unchanging, but the house and the gardens reflected the declining fortunes of the family. The shadow of litigation to abolish landlordism hung over the estate, yet there were still villagers collected to welcome us and it seemed time had not really moved towards the inevitable end.

Nadira had mellowed, but in a different way from her husband Saleem. Her youthful enthusiasm, for an Islamic Renaissance was no longer aggressive; it had been canalised into devotion to her new country which was now a symbol of her ideals. She had become a selfless social worker among the pitiable refugees who had swarmed across the border in their millions, and had devoted herself to the service of unhappy victims of rape and assault and abduction.

She had seen too much of the reality of suffering to trust demagogic slogans, and had learned the pity that drove out bitterness.

There was a mutual desire to avoid arguments between those amongst us who had gone away, and those who had stayed. Arguments were no longer intellectual exercises when we were exposed to the reality of our separate predicaments.

I remembered a day this reality had been brought home.

We had gone with Ranjit to his club.

Ranjit was unchanged, overflowing with goodfellowship and a zest for life, though his personal life had not been happy. He had been married to an attractive girl from a princely family, smart but uneducated. She proved to have a physical defect which made it impossible for her to carry a child. For five years he resisted his mother's pressure to marry again in order to have a son to carry on the family's ancient name. As her insecurity increased, his wife's barrenness created monsters of jealousy. Ultimately her scenes and insults to his friends led him to act as she had feared, and he sent her back to her parents and married a village girl his mother chose for him, and she bore him five daughters in a row.

There were not many people at the Club that evening. Ranjit explained that it was usually crowded on dance nights, and Bingo-playing mornings. And we laughed as he mimicked, "Shades of all the spurred gentlemen, the cock-eyed colonels, and stuttering subalterns that looked down their noses at us in the good old days! Bingo—by Gad! Have we strayed into the Sergeants' Mess by mistake?"

Old hunting prints and cretonne curtains hung in the hall, neglected reminders of a British past.

The neighbouring card-room was crowded, but only half a dozen people were in the bar. There were no familiar faces.

We sat at a table by the fire, and warmed ourselves with talk of the days that had gone.

There were four men perched on the high stools by the bar. One of them—wearing a pale blue turban, his beard emphasising his youth—sat apart from the others, drinking silently. Occasionally he would swivel on the stool and look at us. It made me uneasy.

I said to Ranjit, "Do you know that man with the blue turban?"

"He is a refugee; lost his family in the riots. I'm afraid I know very few people here. Once upon a time, there was hardly a soul one did *not* know. Saleem, you went away, and these others have replaced you. Fair exchange is no robbery they say—but you took our language and our manners, and we were brought a cacophony of sounds that grate the ears, and manners that sear the soul. Nevertheless, we hope our city will breathe its ancient spell, and the fierce men from the North will be lured into lotus eating."

The blue turban turned round and away, and the attentive back twitched.

Kemal smiled and said, "Let us drink to the city of our birth, where men do not fight because it is too much effort when the sky is blue, the sun is warm and the game of chess has to be finished. Let us toast the spirit men sneer at as 'effete', but which will last for ever because it is civilised."

I said, "He is listening to us."

"And why not?" laughed Ranjit. "Where else would he hear such wit and wisdom? Shall I ask him to join us? After all it is our city's hospitable tradition that all strangers are acquaintances, and all acquaintances friends."

"I drink to you, Ranjit, as exemplar of that tradition," Saleem joked. "I am glad you are effete enough to forget your political affiliations, to say, 'Welcome, friend' and not 'Go back, traitor!"

A serious note broke into Ranjit's voice. "I would say that to a traitor even if he were my best friend."

The blue turban twisted right round, and a voice thick with hate and anger said, "They're all bloody traitors—every bloody Muslim—deep in their bloody hearts."

There was a terrible moment of silence enclosing the man's torrent of abuse.

Then Kemal, livid-faced, was moving towards him, "I'll tear your tongue out of your lying throat."

And Ranjit was beside him, pale and menacing. "Leave him to me, Kemal. He has insulted me, not you."

There were suddenly many people in the room, a confusion of movement, and the white-clad bearers were immobilised pale ghosts, the man in the blue turban had disappeared, and shamefaced strangers were moving away apologetically.

Saleem and Nadira were stunned by a sudden sense of being alien and vulnerable, but for Kemal and me, such incidents held a challenge. They tested the mettle of our loyalties and faith at a time when all values were on the boil and spewed the scum of opportunism and falsehood.

Zahra, when she had come in her turn, was less sensitive than Nadira had been. She had always lived in a protected world, flexible in accepting the conventions of whichever society she was in, and inflexible in supporting them.

She climbed the ladder of her husband's success with as much complacency and expediency in one capital as another. She was still gracious, charming and ready to 'do good', a member of every government-approved committee for social service and women's welfare.

She and Aunt Saira were happy in each other's company. For Aunt Saira it was like looking into a mirror and seeing her reflection untouched by age.

Zahra had been sent for when Aunt Majida was thought to be dying. But there was a tenacity in the frail woman's hold on life that made her continue to cheat death as though she had learned it's every trick through the long, sick years of her life.

She was in no condition to leave familiar surroundings and go to live with Zahra, and Zahra could not visit her often enough. Apart from restrictions of movement between the two countries, Zahra was apprehensive of the possible effect on her husband's career of too many visits to India.

In any case, but for her mother, she had no great desire to be there. She denied the country of her birth with the zeal of a convert.

So it was that though I had come to Hasanpur to meet her, after the first spontaneous joy of reunion, our differences came to the surface. But our disagreements were no longer youthful differences of points of view; they shaped our lives, and echoed bigger divisions.

In the end, inevitably, we quarrelled, and though we made up before we parted I realised that the ties which had kept families together for centuries had been loosened beyond repair.

It had started one day when she had been complaining of the humiliation of having to report her movements to the police ('one would think I were a criminal or a spy' she said), and I had teased her that she behaved as if she were in hostile territory, looking over her shoulder for secret agents.

She said sarcastically, "My dear Laila, you sit in the safety of your retreat in the hills and make fun of us who face reality. I have never been very clever, but at least I have worked among the poor and the refugees. I have seen things for myself, and heard the truth from those who actually suffered. Wait till your child grows up. You refuse to see the injustice and prejudice that are destroying your Muslim culture and your language. It is your duty to see your child does not grow up without a knowledge of its heritage."

I do not know what angered me more then, the remark about my responsibilities to my child coming from one who had never known what it was to be alone, and fend for herself, or the sarcasm about my 'retreat' from reality.

I had known the fear of violence, murder, rape and mutilation, as hate-blinded revengeful men had streamed over the border closer and closer to that retreat in the hills. Had the silent hills turned suddenly into flaming volcanoes, and the primeval forests released their wild beasts, the terror would not have been greater than waiting with my child for the beasts that had been men.

I had shared the fear of those others who had fled from the valleys to safety on the higher slopes, the fear behind the the special prayers for God's protection, the fear of the fiery markings that branded Muslim homes.

My anger drove me to personal thrusts and gibes.

"Where were you, Zahra, when I sat up through the nights, watching village after village set on fire, each day nearer and nearer? Sleeping in a comfortable house, guarded by policemen, and sentries? Do you know who saved me and my child? Sita, who took us to her house, in spite of putting her own life in danger with ours. And Ranjit, who came from his village, because he had heard of what was happening in the foothills and was afraid for us. He drove us back, pretending we were his family, risking discovery and death. What were you doing then? Getting your picture in the papers, distributing sweets to orphans whose fathers had been murdered and mothers raped."

I did not stop to listen to her cries of protest.

"Do you know who saved all the others who had no Sitas and Ranjits? Where were all their leaders? Safely across the border. The only people left to save them were those very Hindus against whom they had ranted. Do you know what 'responsibility' and 'duty' meant? To stop the murderous mob at any cost, even if it meant shooting people of their own religion."

Zahra replied with equal anger, "What is so extraordinary about that? Do you think we did not have the same sense of duty on our side? Do you think the same things did not happen there? You are so prejudiced."

Her words defeated me. They showed me that all avenues of understanding between us were closed. I had appeared to her prejudiced, taking sides, when I so passionately believed in friendship and tolerance.

But we made up, Zahra and I, as we had always done; there was so much we had in common, so much to remember.

We walked in the walled garden where we had played, and by the tree on which we had hung the ropes of our swing. We talked of those who had gone away.

Chapter Eight

ZAINAB and her family had gone to start a new life in the young country which offered work and hope to those who had courage and endurance. They were happy, occasionally homesick, but grateful for a secure future.

The mud walls of their home in Hasanpur had begun to crumble with the wind and rain, and two old cronies who had once worked for them, lived in the ruins where the weathered wood still survived.

With Zainab had gone Sharifan, the singer who had entertained me with her mimicry and jests, and her golden-voiced daughter. Sharifan was now a woman of property. Her daughter's voice had given them an entry to the houses of the new-rich, the newly-powerful; it had been used by film stars with pleasing looks and sour voices. It had made them as rich as those whose feudal patronage had once been an honour, and certainly richer than we were now.

Zainab, whose peasant common sense and good humour had made her accept the drabness of her life when a girl, had grown into a contented woman. Her husband was a senior clerk in a Ministry, and looked upon with favour by the Minister. Her eldest son had become an army cadet, and would one day be an officer. They had built a small house in a Co-operative Housing Society, and were paying off the loan by renting the first floor.

Suddenly Zahra laughed. "I forgot to tell you. Zainab's husband is being sent as a clerk to the Embassy in Washington. Can you imagine Zainab in America?"

"Zainab in America?" I repeated. "Zainab in the moon! Do you remember how she laughed when I said I wanted to go round the world? 'I would like to go to the moon,' she mocked, because she believed she would never leave Hasanpur. It seems I will be the only one never to go far from home."

Perhaps because her life was so different from what we had imagined I thought of Romana.

She had been the beautiful, fairy-tale Cinderella who had married a Prince, lived in marble palaces, worn pearls the size of pigeon's eggs and travelled from one capital of the world to another.

I met Romana during the war when she and her husband had come one summer to the hill-station where I had made my home.

I discovered then that there was nothing real about Romana but her beauty, and she was its prisoner. She lived for it, and pampered it, because she was dependent on it for all she could possess. She encouraged admirers, not because she was a flirt, but because they gave her a sense of security.

In later years I saw her pictures in glossy magazines. Once upon a time they were of 'Their Highnesses' with other Highnesses and their hangers-on. Then they changed to 'Their Highnesses' with other Highnesses and those they hung-on to. For times had changed sadly since the integration of the Princely States, and Their Highnesses were left with titles, no states, reduced incomes and unchanged habits and tastes. To play polo, entertain, race, drink, flirt or fornicate with the proper air of aristocratic nonchalance needed co-operation between those who had the means and those who had the titles.

So Romana continued to be her husband's most valuable companion, especially in Europe and America where the mixture proved irresistible of Romana's exotic, Eastern beauty and her husband's centuries-old title.

She and Joan had been the least complicated of our group. Joan had remained unchanged, earnestly devoted to her work, not allowing herself any emotional entanglement or self-dramatisation.

We corresponded with each other, not frequently, but with constant affection. She had not wanted to leave, but her parents had insisted on going 'home' to England after independence, and she had too strong a sense of duty to leave them alone in their old age.

She had written once, "It is not possible—at any time, at any age, to forget the place and the atmosphere where one was born and brought up. I find myself comparing, and contrasting everything with India; and—would you believe it?—when my parents now talk of 'home' they do not mean England!"

Mrs Martin kept in touch also. Every New Year she sent a card, writing a short letter at the back. She still made tender inquiries about her 'young charges', her 'dear, dear Ranis and Begums' as if she were still a Governess on holiday from some Maharaja's palace, and not ending her days in a House for Retired Gentlewomen with Spiritualism as her sole interest. The nostalgic dreams of an old woman over seventy remembered comfortable, far-off days and had forgotten the changes between.

During the war she had been put in charge of a Holiday Home for officers. "One must do one's little bit for one's country," she said. After the war the Raja of Amirpur helped her to be employed as housekeeper at Government House.

There I met her, and on Independence Day in 1947, she who had so carefully taught me 'God Save the King' when I was four, stood by me and my little girl and heard her join the other children in singing their country's anthem. Many of the children were fairer-skinned than Sylvia Tucker who had called me 'nigger'. (How the memory persisted!) Sylvia had gone for ever, having left the bankrupt Raja of Bhimnagar for an American Air Force Sergeant.

Mrs Martin had been too ladylike to say what she thought of Independence, though she applied to the British Government for an assisted passage home within a few months, but she said with ponderous solemnity, "My dear, we have done our best, and now it is for you to carry on. What is so comforting is that the man at the helm of affairs is so much like a British gentleman".

She wrote once that she had spoken to the Raja of Amirpur at a séance, but, in fact the Raja outlived her.

He lived in retirement at Amirpur, dignified and aloof, bearing the landslide of adversities with courage. His palace in the city had been requisitioned as a Government hostel for legislators, and the huge, rambling house on the outskirts, with its ornamental gardens divided into building plots, was the centre of a new colony for refugees.

The last official occasion on which he appeared in public was four years after Independence, when he welcomed the President of the Republic to a reception given in his honour by the *Taluqdars*.

There were no illuminations, no fireworks, no champagne, no glitter of precious gems, orders, silks, brocades and ceremonial uniforms. This last reception of the *Taluqdars* was a staid tea-party given by hosts who were soon to have their 'special class' and 'special privileges' abolished.

Dusty portraits and marble statues of stately ex-Presidents of their Association, and of Imperial representatives, looked down with anachronistic grandeur on tea-tables bearing tea becoming tepid, cakes tasting stale, and Indian savouries growing cold. Guests in *Khaddar* outnumbered those in more formal attire. The handful of Englishmen present—businessmen, educationists, technical experts—were no longer treated with awe or deference, but with regard and affection as friends and equals.

With grace and courtesy Amirpur presided over this swan-song of his order, while those who had habitually bowed before authority hovered round their gentle, dignified guest still hoping for manna from Heaven.

Outside the police band played English and Indian tunes, and the disturbed pigeons flew round the marble pavilions on the green lawns.

Raza Ali and his family had gone to Pakistan where he lived quietly and looked after the property he had bought just before partition, which had multiplied in value after it.

He had never been very happy in strange surroundings, and had been pushed over the border by the momentum of his speeches and theories rather than by action. So he was now content with charity, prayers and pilgrimages.

But those days of youthful and ardent campaigning had ended very differently for Zahid, his most zealous lieutenant.

Full of bright hope and triumph Zahid had boarded the train on that thirteenth day of August which was to take him to the realisation of his dreams, on the eve of the birth of the country for which he had lived and worked. When it had reached its destination not a man, woman or child was found alive.

I shivered in the sun, as I sat by the waterless fountain. There were ghosts that could not be laid by the passing of the years.

I pulled myself together, and walked towards the room that had been mine, that I would always think of as mine no matter who lived in it, I looked across the neglected lawn towards the blank, boarded windows and bricked-up arches of that part of the house where strangers lived.

There my aunts Abida and Majida, their companions and maid-servants, had lived a more leisurely life, closer to our inherited culture than we had here across the dividing courtyard and garden. I had often sought refuge there when the conflict of cultural values had been confusing.

The thought of Aunt Abida brought a painful sense of her actual presence. The conflict between us had never been resolved, and it was as if I were constantly striving to reach out to her to do so. I wanted to believe in communication after death so that I could tell her what there had been no time to say. But I loved her and Ameer too much to be content with anything but absolute truth in relation to them, and could not accept consolation while even a shadow of doubt separated reason and faith.

Aunt Abida was dead by the time I arrived in response to her husband's telegram. There was some consolation in knowing she had died in Hakiman Bua's arms.

Hakiman Bua was the only one in that alien household to understand what Aunt Abida and I had meant to each other. She tried to comfort me by saying Aunt Abida had smiled through her pain when they had told her I was coming. It was as if my message had released her, for she died within the hour.

As I looked at her peaceful face it seemed as if she were happy to have slipped away to rest. In death as in life there was something for me to learn from her. I had come too late to tell her of my love; I could only pray for her forgiveness with silent tears. I learned then that humility, love and grace could not bargain with Time. And looking at the peace of her face I felt spiritually cleansed.

When she had written to me repeatedly over the past six months to come to her in my sorrow, not being well enough to come to me herself, I had been too bitter to respond. I knew now that bitterness corroded one's own being. At the time of my loss I had lost the power of understanding and reasoning. I only knew that Aunt Abida had been tender when Ameer was dead, but had been harsh when he was alive; as if his death and my pain were the price of her forgiveness.

I had felt bitter towards all those in my family who had turned against me when I was a bride, yet tried to comfort me in my widowhood.

But in that moment of revelation by Aunt Abida's dead body I learned that happiness had its own strength and was its own protection; sorrow needed to be shared.

I had been deeply hurt by Aunt Abida's attitude to my marriage. Aunt Saira's active hostility, and Uncle Hamid's cold disapproval did not really matter. I imagined myself a poetic rebel against false values. Besides I did not love them.

But that Aunt Abida should treat me as if I had committed some unpardonable crime bewildered me. From whom else could I expect understanding? However wrong and rebellious my outward actions might seem surely she knew me enough to see the innermost springs and motives, and know they admitted no falsehood?

She refused to see me or reply to my letters once I had told her I could not obey her, nor my family, and deny Ameer.

I wept that last time I was with her.

"Phuphi Jan, I have done nothing wrong."

She was cold and unyielding and drew away from me.

"You have been defiant and disobedient. You have put yourself above your duty to your family."

She had seemed cruel to me beyond reason if her own life were witness. Austere and without happiness she lived and looked after her husband and his family.

"Phuphi Jan, you are looking at me as if I had committed a sin."

"You have let your family's name be bandied about by scandal-mongers and gossips. You have soiled its honour on their vulgar tongues."

I knew then that understanding was impossible between us. She was part of a way of thinking I had rejected. I had been guilty of admitting I loved, and love between man and woman was associated with sex, and sex was sin. My innocence was insulted, my own inhibitions outraged. No one could stop me marrying Ameer if only to prove the purity of love.

Aunt Abida and I were never to meet again.

In this room into which I was now walking the witnesses of the simple ceremony of marriage came to ask me if I would take Ameer to be my husband, and I left it as his bride with the blessings of not one of my elders.

Chapter Nine

AFTER the sunlit garden the room was chill and shadowed, and its air was stale. My eyes had not adjusted themselves to the change of light when I saw a reflected shadow moving in the mirror and shivered at the intrusion. I walked up to it, and in the dim light which erased the lines of age and experience saw the girl who haunted me and made me a stranger to those who did not see her through the mask of time.

There was a dusty stool among the derelict pieces of furniture. I brought it to the mirror and sitting on it, exhausted, stared at my other self, longing for release from the ghosts that kept me from acceptance of the present.

I had been that other when I had last stayed in this room, and Ameer had been with me.

In the morning, when we were getting ready to leave, he had looked around with distaste.

"Thank God it is over," he said. "I am glad to go. This room is haunted. It is part of a house that does not welcome me. It is full of all those things in your life that are unknown to me—and hostile."

I laughed as I kissed him. "Why are you being so morbidly imaginative? Try and look at it my way. My past was time spent in preparation for my future with you."

He recovered his good humour and laughed too saying, "Actually the explanation of my mood is quite simple. I resented being asked to stay here last night merely because your family made us come back after the wedding for a ritual ceremony to keep up appearances."

I said, "Should I have felt the same because your relations, the Amirpurs, took me to their home with traditional ceremonial as a bride?"

He answered quickly, "Not at all. After all motives

matter more than actions. They brought me up, and they are genuinely fond of you. They welcomed you not only as a daughter-in-law but as a daughter. Your family, on the other hand, look down on me. They have not forgiven me, and probably never will, because their prejudices are part of their way of life."

"What do they matter?" I said. "What does anyone matter now? We are starting life on our own, in our own home."

"It is hardly bigger than this room, almost bare . . ." he began, but I covered his mouth with my hand. Then bowing low before him, copying the affected manner of film heroines, I said, "Lord of my life, a hut would be a palace with you, and the whole world too small for our happiness."

We were happy. Our happiness was all that my imagination had created, but with an added dimension of which I could not have been aware without experience of it. Through the body's worship, the consummation of passion, and the desire of each sense I was filled with a profound sense of mystic fulfilment. Through physical union came the knowledge of the oneness of separate beings. We, being part of each other were part of the whole creation, knowing no beginning nor end, only the consciousness of being.

This inner completeness could not be communicated by words to others outside the circle of its experience; it was visible in the contentment with which I accepted the ordinary elements of everyday life.

I was happy to have a home of my very own, to live in it as I pleased without dictation, though it was small and simple, and without scores of servants as in Hasanpur and Ashiana.

Most of Ameer's friends became mine too, though I had not known young men like them before. When Uncle Hamid became head of the family I met only the sons and daughters of the rich and privileged who wore the trappings of modernity.

Ameer's friends were mostly poor, often slovenly, always

rebels. They had no external props to shore up their personalities; they could not buy or bully their way to power or recognition; their minds were their only weapons. They were never dull, those earnest young poets and writers and political theorists who made the cause of every underdog their own, who hailed every Revolution as their holy war.

Often I caught a hollow note in the protestations of some, especially those who were as dogmatic as the most fanatic *moulvis* and priests, and as ruthless as Inquisitors in their determination to force their ideas on others.

There were some who used 'intellectualism' as forgers use counterfeit coins.

We were often short of money, and Ameer was hurt if I suggested I should use mine, or if I did so, trying to hide it from him.

Had we lived somewhere far from my family it might have been different. But their presence pervaded everything, like an aroma distilled through the years from the privileges they had enjoyed, which was fading but not obliterated. He imagined that even his successes were attributed to his relationship with those who were influential.

It had seemed too unimportant at the time to be taken seriously, especially as we professed to have values that were different from those of the society in which we had been nurtured.

In the beginning I blamed my elders because it was their world and its values that had broken into ours. I was not ready to accept that vulnerability was self-created.

Now, in this room, I remembered what Ameer had said so many years ago. His resentment had had a core which had accumulated irritable matter around it with the passing of time.

The shadows began to take shape a year after we were married when I told Ameer I was to have a child. I was too sure of myself in my contentment. I felt as if no one before had known this miracle, a new life within one's body, living by one's flesh, blood and breath, created by love, the manifestation of our coming together, inseparable for ever in a separate being.

I used to pity the children of lust and duty and boredom, and even more those who bore them, giving their bodies without love, with shame or even repulsion. I remembered what we used to be told about the relationship between men and women, the whispering, the insinuations.

Ameer seemed to become moody and quiet; it distressed me, but he would reassure me always. It was sad to realise later that love could create its own need for secrecy, because Ameer kept his plans a secret from me until all the formalities had been completed.

Early in 1942 he joined the Public Relations branch of the Army, and by the end of the year he was sent to the Middle East.

He was cynical about what he had done, comparing himself with the 'rice soldiers'—those who had joined the Army without convictions, or even against them, because it was hard to get a good job, or as well paid a one. What was it worth being a lecturer teaching young men to live as compared to an officer teaching young men to die?

Many of his friends had already joined the Army, most of them had not found suitable work elsewhere.

After Ameer had gone I left the house we had rented, and bought a small cottage for myself in the hills we had loved. It was a refuge for my loneliness. I was glad I was able to break from traditional customs, and did not have to return to live with my family.

Asad, who had been our closest friend, was arrested in the August of the same year as Ameer left. His letters had always been a source of comfort and they came regularly even from prison.

The greater part of my life became an infinity of waiting. There was the child to provide a purpose for living, filling the days with her need for love and care.

Ameer had joked when he was leaving, "At least I have

the assurance that you will be safe when I'm away. Shahla will look after you." (He had chosen her name.) He was right.

Sometimes, during the season, I would accept Sita's or Romana's invitations to parties down by the lake, in one or the other of the restaurants that had come into existence during the war. War-enriched people, war-stranded princes, unable to visit Europe for their junketings, women with as easy virtue as men, had discovered a new pleasure resort. There was something macabre in their desperate, frenzied gaiety in contrast with news of the war and political violence.

Where I lived there was peace; only hill-men and their women came along the steep paths carrying heavy bundles of wood and charcoal. There was no sound but of the wind in the pine trees.

Some part of me—primevally superstitious—was suspicious of happiness, and prepared for its end. Through the months that followed the news that Ameer had been taken prisoner I had never given up hope—consciously—that he would return. But it seemed I had never known the meaning of the word when I was told he was killed, trying to escape.

The war ended that year.

My sorrow spewed out bitterness and despair. I lived and moved through an endless tunnel with no exit. Each cell in my body was hollow, yet a shapeless weight dragged me into darkness. I neglected even my child, and it was Nandi who looked after her—and me.

But the child brought me back from the mere motions of living to life; she and Asad. He was still in prison, but his letters conveyed his faith in living without being didactic. They led me out of self-pity, through the negation of despair, into a recognition of struggle and positive acceptance.

He did not say I was selfish to withdraw into solitude, but I knew he wished it otherwise. He did not preach that my inaction was wrong, but his own life taught otherwise. He wrote to me "Each one of us has to find our own way when we seek to come to terms with life. Maybe it is expediency that makes me act as I do, because it is the only way I feel reassured. As an individual, alone, I am vulnerable. When I am part of a cause I am as indestructible as the cause. When I live for myself I am weak and afraid, when I work with others I have their strength."

After his release Asad went back to Delhi and resumed his educational work among the poor, but after the riots in the autumn of 1946 he left to work in the Eastern riot-stricken areas, and by that winter, after the Congress had accepted office in the Interim Government, he was drawn into political work in Delhi.

In my seclusion the urgency of the years of change and turmoil was made real through Asad. We had dreamed when we were young of Independence; he was now part of it with all its undreamt-of reality—its triumphs and defeats, its violent aftermath, the breaking-up of our social order, and the slow emergence of another.

Asad's name had begun to appear in the papers as one of the promising young men in the Congress. It was no surprise to me therefore when he was sent as a delegate to the United Nations.

He reminded me of the days when we had talked of seeing the world—as remote a possibility then as of reaching the moon. He wrote nostalgically of the days when we had all been young and so full of arguments and untested ideals. Of those who were nearest to him I was the only one left, since Zahid's death.

The manner of Zahid's death had been a terrible test for Asad's faith in non-violence. He had accepted it as such, believing that bitterness and retaliation could only breed violence and start a never-ending cycle which was a negation of life; but he was human and it needed a conscious effort of will to restrain his bitterness.

Whenever we were together, in spite of our mutual

affection, there was a consciousness of embarrassment because our feelings had not changed.

Once he put it into words. "What can I do to make you remember I am human? It is not easy for me to remain fettered by your ideas of me. I am no saint, and never have been. There have been women who have seen me and known me as a man, and all the time I have wished it were you. But you think of me always as if I were your idea of me and not myself."

I could not tell him then that I did not wish to deceive him with my mind's acquiescence while each cell of my body remembered Ameer.

But now I wondered how much my mind had been deceiving me, how much falsehood there was in my excessive truth.

I looked more closely at the face that stared back at me from the dusty mirror. That was how she and Ameer would be for ever while I grew old.

She was so different from me, that girl whose yesterdays and todays looked always towards her tomorrow, while my tomorrows were always yesterdays.

I began to cry without volition and seeing myself crying in this room to which I would never return, knew I was my own prisoner and could release myself.

There was a sound of footsteps outside and the old watchman was saying, "I left Laila Bitia here an hour ago. She must be inside."

Asad's voice called, "Laila, where are you?"

I got up quickly, wiping my eyes as his tall, thin figure was silhouetted at the door.

"Laila," he said, blinking at the shadows, "what have you been doing so long in this empty house?"

"I have been waiting for you, Asad. I am ready to leave now."

READ MORE IN PENGUIN

In every corner of the world, on every subject under the sun, Penguin represents quality and variety—the very best in publishing today.

For complete information about books available from Penguin—including Puffins, Penguin Classics and Arkana—and how to order them, write to us at the appropriate address below. Please note that for copyright reasons the selection of books varies from country to country.

In India: Please write to *Penguin Books India Pvt. Ltd. 11 Community Centre, Panchsheel Park, New Delhi 110017*

In the United Kingdom: Please write to *Dept JC, Penguin Books Ltd. Bath Road, Harmondsworth, West Drayton, Middlesex, UB7 ODA. UK*

In the United States: Please write to *Penguin USA Inc., 375 Hudson Street, New York, NY 10014*

In Canada: Please write to *Penguin Books Canada Ltd. 10 Alcorn Avenue, Suite 300, Toronto, Ontario M4V 3B2*

In Australia: Please write to *Penguin Books Australia Ltd. 487, Maroondah Highway, Ring Wood, Victoria 3134*

In New Zealand: Please write to *Penguin Books (NZ) Ltd. Private Bag, Takapuna, Auckland 9*

In the Netherlands: Please write to *Penguin Books Netherlands B.V., Keizersgracht 231 NL-1016 DV Amsterdom*

In Germany : Please write to *Penguin Books Deutschland GmbH, Metzlerstrasse 26, 60595 Frankfurt am Main, Germany*

In Spain: Please write to *Penguin Books S.A., Bravo Murillo, 19-1'B, E-28015 Madrid, Spain*

In Italy: Please write to *Penguin Italia s.r.l., Via Felice Casati 20, I-20104 Milano*

In France: Please write to *Penguin France S.A., 17 rue Lejeune, F-31000 Toulouse*

In Japan: Please write to *Penguin Books Japan. Ishikiribashi Building, 2-5-4, Suido, Tokyo 112*

In Greece: Please write to *Penguin Hellas Ltd, dimocritou 3, GR-106 71 Athens*

In South Africa: Please write to *Longman Penguin Books Southern Africa (Pty) Ltd, Private Bag X08, Bertsham 2013*

READ MORE IN PENGUIN

THE DARK HOLDS NO TERRORS

Shashi Deshpande

Sarita returns to the family home, ostensibly to take care of her father, but in reality to escape the nightmarish brutality her husband inflicts on her every night. In the quiet of her old father's company Sarita reflects on the events of her life: her stultifying small town childhood, her domineering mother, her marriage to the charismatic young poet Manohar (who turns vicious when he realizes his career is going nowhere and that his wife has overtaken him professionally), her children...As she struggles with her emotions and anxieties, Sarita gradually realizes that there is more to life than dependency on marriage, parents and other such institutions—and she resolves to use her new found truths to make a better life for herself. *The Dark Holds No Terrors* is a tremendously powerful portrayal of one woman's fight to survive in a world that offers no easy outs.

THAT LONG SILENCE

Shashi Deshpande

That Long Silence is the story of Jaya, wife, mother of teenage children, and failed writer, whose familiar existence is disrupted when her husband is suspected of business malpractice. The family's future threatened, Jaya is confronted with difficult truths about her past. A skilful, haunting novel, *That Long Silence* is a vivid portrayal of a woman trying to erase a 'long silence' begun in childhood, rooted in herself and in the constraints of her adult life.

'A book that will change lives. Unforgettable.' —*The Evening Post*